SEEDS OF MEMORY AND MYTH

Myths are the backbone of a culture. They are the common property of every human being, deeply imbedded in our behavior, perhaps even in our racial memory. Here in one volume are the first refrains of songs begun centuries ago.

Beowulf, composed about A.D. 725, is one of the earliest extant poems in a modern European language. This myth, like other great medieval myths, is a saga of rousing, barbaric paganism, tempered throughout by a newly acquired Christian spirit . . . . Beowulf's submission to Wyrd (goddess of death) remains side by side with the sacrifice of Christ and spiritual salvation.

In her presentation of *Beowulf, The Song of Roland, Sifrit, The Cid,* and others, the author sets these myths in historical and literary context. She traces their development from tales told by the light of ancient campfires to masterpieces of world literature that have deep and intense meaning for people today.

Norma Lorre Goodrich is Professor Emeritus of French and Comparative Literature, and former Dean of Faculty, at Scripps College of the University of Southern California. She studied at the University of Vermont, which has since awarded her a D. Litt. degree; the University of Grenoble, France; and Columbia University, where she received her Ph.D. and was the George W. Ellis Fellow "for outstanding academic achievement." Her other books include *Heroines, The Holy Grail, Guinevere, Priestesses, King Arthur,* and *Ancient Myths* (Meridian).

MEDIEVAL MYTHS

Norma Lorre Goodrich

A MERIDIAN BOOK

MERIDIAN
Published by the Penguin Group
Penguin Books USA Inc., 375 Hudson Street, New York, New York 10014, U.S.A.
Penguin Books Ltd, 27 Wrights Lane, London W8 5TZ, England
Penguin Books Australia Ltd, Ringwood, Victoria, Australia
Penguin Books Canada Ltd, 10 Alcorn Avenue, Toronto, Ontario, Canada M4V 3B2
Penguin Books (N.Z.) Ltd, 182–190 Wairau Road, Auckland 10, New Zealand

Penguin Books Ltd, Registered Offices: Harmondsworth, Middlesex, England

Published by Meridian, an imprint of Dutton Signet, a division of Penguin Books
USA Inc. Previously published in a Mentor edition.

First Meridian Printing, June, 1994
10 9 8 7 6 5 4 3 2

REGISTERED TRADEMARK—MARCA REGISTRADA

LIBRARY OF CONGRESS CATALOGING-IN-PUBLICATION DATA
Goodrich, Norma Lorre.
  Medieval myths / Norma Lorre Goodrich.
    p.   cm.
  ISBN 0-452-01128-0
  1. Literature, Medieval.   2. Heldensage.   I. Title.
PN667.G55   1994
809'.02—dc20   93–47080
                                          CIP

Printed in the United States of America

To my son, Jean Joseph Lorre, with my love.

———————

Contents

Preface

THE FOLLOWING NINE hero stories come originally from handwritten, parchment manuscripts which are among the treasures of the Western world. Many of these manuscripts are close to the oldest documents we possess in the following modern languages: Welsh, English, French, Spanish, German, Gaelic, and Russian. With two exceptions these stories date from the early Middle Ages.

The term "Middle Ages," as opposed to "Ancient World," and the word "modern" (*modus*=manner; *hodiernus*=of today) dates, according to Professors Kukenheim and Roussel, from 1469 (*media tempestas*=middle of the storm), 1518 (*media aetas*=middle age), and 1604 (*medium aevum*= middle period).

The sources for this book are as follows:

CHAPTER 1: *Beowulf* Only one manuscript exists. It was discovered in England in the seventeenth century by Sir Robert Cotton among nine other parchments which together form the Codex Vitellius Axv in the British Museum. Sir Robert Cotton had spent many years acquiring manuscripts that had been dispersed throughout England after the seizure and destruction of the monasteries. After his collection was sold in 1700, the manuscripts were lodged in Ashburnham House. In 1731 the *Beowulf* manuscript was damaged by fire, as the charred corners one sees in photographs of it attest. In 1753 it was placed in the British Museum.

The first two copies were made in 1786 by the Danish scholar G. J. Thorkelin, one by Thorkelin himself and one by a copyist. These two handwritten copies are in a Copenhagen museum today. Aside from early printings referred to in the introduction to Chapter 1 of this book, one could list many others and many translators of this work into poetry and into prose. These are four unabridged translations to which the interested reader should refer, since each one of them is in itself a masterpiece: Francis B. Gummere (Harvard), Charles W. Kennedy (Princeton), Edwin Morgan (Glasgow University), and William Ellery Leonard (Wisconsin). The *Beowulf* of this book is an original version, made without reference to the preceding, and done despite their superb scholarship in order to establish the literary themes which are the subject of this book, and retain the Anglo-Saxon of the original.

CHAPTER 2: *Peredur, Son of York*   The manuscripts of the *Mabinogion* are in Peniarth Castle in Wales. They were published and translated, for the first time, by Lady Charlotte Guest from 1838 to 1849, and subsequently in Paris by H. de Villemarqué (1842) and J. Loth (1899, 1913). The diplomatic text was established for *The Red Book of Hergest* by the Welsh scholars J. Rhys and John Gwenogvryn Evans in 1887 and for *The White Book of Rhydderch* by John Gwenogvryn Evans in 1907. Both of these definitive texts include the Peredur story. The abridged translation presented in this volume is taken principally from a text of the manuscript called Peniarth 4, which forms a part of the White Book *Mabinogion*. Scholars have believed that it was written before, or contained parts of earlier material than that in the *Red Book of Hergest*, which appears from the character of its script to date from *c.* 1375 to 1425. Both Padraic Colum and Sidney Lanier have written about Peredur. There is a modern translation (1948), by Gwyn and Thomas Jones, entitled *Mabinogion*.

CHAPTER 3: *The Story of Roland*   This present translation follows the manuscript called Digby 23, from the Library of Oxford University, the handwriting of which is believed to be that of an Anglo-Norman scribe. The only other principal manuscript, dating from the fourteenth century, is in Venice. An early Latin adaptation is called *Carmen de prodicione Guenonis*. The Roland story was translated during the Middle Ages into Welsh, German, English, and Dutch. With so many "Franks," as the Crusaders were called, around Constantinople, Syria, Palestine, and Egypt during the Crusades, one could easily believe that the *Roland* served as a prototype for all medieval epics.

The Oxford manuscript was printed in France by Francisque Michel (1837, 1869), by Clédat (1870, 1887), by Léon Gautier (1872). Mrs. A. C. Marsh made an English translation in 1854. The best-known edition and translation is that of Professor Joseph Bédier. Variants of 484 verses from five manuscripts (another from Venice, Paris, and Châteauroux) are given in the *Chrestomathie* of Karl Bartsch, Edition XII (New York, 1958). There is a modern translation by Merriam Sherwood (New York, 1938).

One approaches this poem with a very real reverence, for it is, in its way, as beautiful and as unique a work of art as the *Beowulf*.

CHAPTER 4: *Berta of Hungary* The story which the present author calls *Berta of Hungary* exists, in the version written by the Belgian minstrel Adenes li Rois, in six manuscripts. There is also another version of the same story, *Berta de li gran pie*, in manuscript from: MS. fr. XIII, Library of Saint Mark, Venice. Four of the manuscripts of Adenes are in the National Library of Paris (MSS. 778, 1447, 12467, 22404), and another is in Rouen (Belles Lettres 175). The story was first published in Paris in 1832 by Paulin Paris, the father of the brilliant medievalist Gaston Paris.

The text followed in this book is the manuscript called Belles Lettres 175, in the Library of the Arsénal, Paris. It was collated and printed in Brussels in 1874 by August Scheler. The reader will note that most of the other material in this book dates from the early Middle Ages, the period Professor Gustave Cohen called the "Age of Genesis." The *Berta* story falls into the so-called Classical or Great Century of the Middle Ages, the thirteenth. This might explain why there are so many manuscripts, aside from the fact that our author served Guy de Dampierre, Count of Flanders, as well as Marie de Brabant, Queen of France. He was also a protégé of the Princess Blanche, daughter of Saint Louis.

The *Berta* story was written in modern French by Louis Brandin (Paris, 1924); in his version, according to information given in the preface, the Adenes manuscript was supplemented by other incidents from the Venice manuscript. Dean Arthur Sideleau in his excellent book *Chansons de Geste* (Montreal, 1945) has translated into modern French a part of the *Berta* story. I know of no translation into English.

CHAPTER 5: *Sifrit* There are altogether twenty-eight manuscripts of *The Nibelungenlied*, but three are considered the best: the Munich manuscript, the parchment manuscript in the monastery of St. Gall, and the third in the "ducal library of Donaueschingen." The scholar Karl Lachmann announced its first publication at the University of Berlin in

1816, and it has been printed many times, especially the three best manuscripts. This volume follows a text of the St. Gall manuscript and is particularly indebted to its earliest translation into French, as the introduction to Chapter 5 will explain. This earliest French translator spent ten years on her work, basing it upon the St. Gall text, comparing it with editions published by Hagen, Lachmann, Karl Simrock, M. Schoenhüth, and then referring it painstakingly to the St. Gall manuscript itself. The English reader may remember William Morris' *Sigurd the Volsung*. There are many translations, among them one by Professor Daniel B. Shumway (1909), one in rhyming couplets by Dr. Arthur S. Way (1911), and ones by S. H. Hamer and Gertrude Henderson.

CHAPTER 6: *Tannhäuser* The Tannhäuser legend translated here comes from an anthology of short pieces, entitled *Salade* (mixed greens), by the French author Antoine de La Sale. The book, written between 1420 and 1440, was dedicated to Duchess Agnès de Bourbon, sister of Duke Philip the Good of Burgundy; the original French presents no difficulties for the translator. La Sale, who died in 1464, some ten years before the printing press began to be used, was well known in his time. His work, of which the original is now in the Bibliothèque Nationale in Paris, has been reprinted many times. The title *Salade*, which is probably an anagram of the author's name, is a word of Provençal origin. The legends of medieval Provence, where La Sale was born around 1388, reflect close connections with German literature, both countries having once been part of the Holy Roman Empire.

CHAPTER 7: *Cuchulain* Cuchulain is the principal hero of the second group of Irish legends, those of the demigods. The first group of legends deals with the various invasions of Ireland, and with the ancient gods of the land. The story of Cuchulain is told in greatest detail in two manuscripts: (1) *Leabhar na hUidre*, or Book of the Dun (cowhide cover), and (2) *Leabhar Laighneach*, which means Book of Leinster, but which is also called Book of Glendalough. Although the manuscript called the Yellow Book of Lecan adds other material concerning Cuchulain, the best and most coherent account comes from the *Leabhar na hUidre*. Irish scholars date the manuscript by its handwriting, saying that it was probably written around the year 1106. As to when the story took place, if indeed it ever happened in actual life, scholars tend to prefer the eighth century.

The manuscript chiefly followed here is the *Leabhar na hUidre*. The original manuscript is preserved in the Trinity College Library, Dublin. The text was published by Ernst Windisch under its Gaelic title transliterated as *Táin Bó Cúalnge* (Leipzig, 1905). Thus, the story of Cuchulain is often referred to as the *Táin*, or as the Cattle Raid of Cooley. Scholars estimate that if published consecutively, the legends of old Ireland would run to several hundred large volumes.

CHAPTER 8: *Prince Igor* In a manuscript entitled *Sbornik*, Count Pushkin discovered the Prince Igor story-poem, which he printed for the first time in Russia in 1800. He had bought the manuscript from a monk. Since the original burned during Napoleon's invasion of Moscow (1812), the *Igor* was reprinted in 1864 by Pokarsky from a copy found in the archives of Catherine the Great. A polyglot edition, Russian, Polish, and Czech, was printed in Lwow, Poland, in 1886, by Soltykov-Romanski. It was also published in Berlin by Boltz and by Eichoff in Paris (1839)—neither of which revision the present author has found. The Rambaud partial translation used in this volume is from 1876. Subsequent scholarly studies have been made by two modern authorities, Professors Henri Grégoire and Roman Jakobson.

CHAPTER 9: *Cid* There is only one manuscript of the *Poem of Mío Cid*. The noted Spanish scholar Ramón Menéndez Pidal says that this precious document was preserved in the Convent of Franciscan Nuns at Vivar, the town where El Cid was supposedly born. I believe that the manuscript has been privately owned since 1775. It was first published in 1779 by C. Tomas Antonio Sánchez in Volume I of his anthology, *Coleccion de poesías castellanas anteriores al siglo XV*. The second publication was in Paris in 1858, and the third was in Spain in 1864. The first English version may have been that of Robert Southey, *Chronicle of the Cid*, London, 1808. This epic was the subject of Victor Hugo's magnificent poem *Le Cid Exilé* and also of the Massenet opera *Le Cid*.

In his dedication to his edition and translation published in 1942 by the Hispanic Society of America, Mr. Archer M. Huntington tells us that the manuscript was privately owned at that time by Don A. Pidal y Mon of Madrid. Mr. Huntington was fortunate to have made his edition and his verse translation from the manuscript itself. This present abridged translation follows the original Sánchez text. The reader should be alerted to the fact that there had apparently been some tampering with the manuscript through the ages, and that the date given in its last lines should not be taken too seriously, as it appears to have the number *C* (100) missing from it, owing to erasure.

—NORMA LORRE GOODRICH

Claremont, California
November, 1976
November, 1993

1

Scandinavia: Beowulf

INTRODUCTION

THE EARLY HISTORY of Britain from 55 B.C. to A.D. 1016 may be divided into four periods corresponding to four groups of Indo-European peoples, each of which left its mark upon English culture, and each of which contributed to that composite language which is our own.

The first group were the Celts, whom Julius Caesar described in his *Gallic War*. This book is a most valuable historical document, giving us our first direct account of the peoples living (55 B.C.) in northern Europe. According to Caesar the Celts were a warlike people whose priests were called Druids. The Arch-Druid lived in Britain and from there controlled and incited the Celtic tribes on the continent. These priests were well educated, Caesar assures us, and they kept their archives in Greek. Caesar himself wrote Greek fluently and had studied as a young man in Rhodes. Celtic languages are still spoken today—in Wales, Ireland, and Brittany (France), for example. Subsequent Roman legions remained in Britain until about 410, when they began to be recalled. A "barbarian" emperor replaced a Roman one in the city of Rome in 476.

Both Celtic and Latin, however, failed to prevail linguistically in Britain. Soon after the recall of the Roman legions, tribes from Scandinavia and Germany—the Angles, Saxons, and Jutes— settled in Britain. Unlike the tribes who were at the same time invading Gaul and Italy, the Anglo-Saxons did not adopt the language of their subjects. They continued to speak their own Germanic tongues, which became in time the basis of the English language.

Their chieftains such as Hengist and Horsa (c. 449) acquired land by circling it with oxhide strips much in the same manner that Vergil describes the Tyrian Queen Dido as doing in Carthage.[1] At approximately the same time (c. 445—453) Attila the Hun was ravaging Gaul and Italy. The Anglo-Saxon poem *Widsith,* from which you will read material in the following pages, dates presumably from this period. Scholars have said it could be the oldest poem in any modern language!

There were no major invasions in England from 445 to about 800, except for the Anglo-Saxons. During these years the Merovingian Dynasty was ruling in France (486—751). One Germanic people, the Angles in Northumbria, were creating a literature. St. Augustine had begun their conversion in 597, one result of which was the introduction of the Latin alphabet. By adding to it their own runic characters to represent the sounds (such as "th") that did not exist in Latin, the Angles had a convenient tool.

Poetry and learning flourished in monasteries, such as the one of the Abbess Hilda (658—680) where the poets Caedmon and Cynewulf may have lived. Around the year 500 lived in Wales and Scotland the great Celtic hero King Arthur, whose life became later an inexhaustible inspiration for poets and chroniclers.

Before 750 the greatest literary work of the Anglo-Saxon culture was composed, probably also in Northumbria. The following pages will retell its story. It is the epic *Beowulf,* a work so beautiful that students continue to learn Anglo-Saxon in order to read it.

Beowulf has 6,359 verses or half-lines. Each verse may have two accented syllables, a pause, and then the second hemistitch of two accented syllables. Instead of rhyme there is an interesting alliterative device, often consisting of a repeated consonant in the first verse that is echoed again in the second half.

God mid Geatum	[*God amidst the Geats*
Grendles daeda	*Grendel's deeds*]
wlanc Wedera leod	[*The proud Weder lord*
word aefter spraec	*Words after spoke*]

It is a type of trochaic meter, a rhythm that has survived

[1] See Norma Lorre Goodrich, *Ancient Myths,* New York, Meridian, 1994, pp. 205-206.

in one form or another in English poetry. Alliteration is
also a prime asset to English poets.

Another feature of the poem that has attracted the reader
is the great number of kennings, or compound words that
evoke vivid pictures. A woman is called a *freodwebbe* or
"peace-weaver." The poet says his hero went *ofer swan-
rade*—"over the swan-road" in his "foamy-throated" ship.
This Germanic propensity to form compounds has also persisted. The reader will note that in the following adaptation some attempt has been made to exclude words of French-
Latin origin except the few words such as "name," "gem,"
"dragon," "north," "south," "female," etc., which are in the
original text, either because they represent a common Indo-
European origin or because they were words (such as
"candle") learned from the Romans. A few Celtic words were
used because they are historically justifiable. The principal
anachronism is the use of many Danish words ("sky,"
"anger"), which only came into English after 800. They
were too evocative of the mood of the poem to be banned.

The vocabulary of Anglo-Saxon was not extensive. English,
which takes its name from the literary Angles, therefore set
out upon a long career of appropriating words from scores
of other languages, a process that still continues. Because of
this propensity to explore other literatures and other lands,
English has one of the largest, if not the largest, vocabularies
of any modern language.

During the ninth century England underwent its next invasion, this time that of the Danes, who finally had their
King Canute crowned there in 1016. There had been a great
interest in learning and culture during the reign of Alfred
the Great, who was born about 843 and became king in 871.
He was a learned scholar himself. He had lived and studied
in Rome. King Alfred attracted scholars to his court, founded
schools, and himself translated from the Latin into Anglo-
Saxon Boethius' *Consolation of Philosophy*.

Alfred's predecessor and example was Charlemagne, during whose reign in France scholars from many lands were
persuaded to come and produce works of history and literature that have, in very fact, made this king immortal. One
of the prelates and poets whom Charlemagne attracted was
an Anglian named Alcuin. In 782 this distinguished scholar
left the city of York in Northumbria to become the Bishop
of Tours.

There were two results of the Danish invasion: (1) the
fusion of Danish and Anglo-Saxon which resulted in the
simplification of the resultant language, and (2) the destruc-

tion of the monasteries in Anglia, the previous center of
literary life. There are other reasons for interest in the
Beowulf epic aside from its age and linguistic value. One
is its story. Another is the unique insight it gives us into the
heroic age of the earliest literate Germanic people. Tacitus,
who completed his *Germania* in A.D. 97—98, has given us
after Caesar almost the only document of value concerning the
barbarians, who even in his time were already on the move,
in vast migrations that at the end of a few centuries produced not only the modern languages of western Europe,
but also its modern cultures and states. Between Tacitus
and *Beowulf* there is a long silence of more than 600 years
while these peoples and cultures were becoming stable. It
would be a mistake to call them "Dark Ages," as the great
poet who wrote *Beowulf* has little difficulty proving.

Our poet confirms much of what Tacitus has said. He tells
how these peoples lived, and where. He describes their lives
and customs. He makes us understand their thoughts, their
aspirations, and their notion of life. More than that, he
shows us in *Beowulf* their idea of what a man should be.
Many of their ideas survive in the modern world.

Without this poem the modern world would be at a loss
to explain the institution of feudalism that suddenly con-
fronted classical tradition and Roman law with a way of life
often in complete variance with such Roman ideas as the
divine right of kings. The historical period that ended about
1500, and which is known as the Middle Ages, was in a
way one long struggle between two very different cultures.
Beowulf shows us in formation many of the feudal ideas that
were to flow so gloriously in knighthood and the code of
chivalry. It also demonstrates how the old Scandinavian gods
were supplanted, with extreme difficulty, by Christian
theology.

The reader will find a strange mixture of paganism, nature
worship, the conflict between good and evil so reminiscent
of Zoroastrianism, Hebrew traditions, Christian teachings,
Oriental dragons, and funeral pyres like those of India,
Greece, and other Teutonic myths. Scholars believe that
the Asiatic traits go back to the common Indo-European
heritage.

Some inconsistencies in the text may be due to interpola-
tions made in the original poem by the two scribes who
copied the manuscript. They must, indeed, have been
shocked by it! If, on the other hand, they were Anglians,
they must have been thrilled. The love of the sea and ships
runs all through Anglian literature, and it would seem that

the strain of sadness in this great poem also runs through
English literature.

Only one copy of *Beowulf* in its original form has ever
been found. It was discovered by Sir Robert Cotton in the
seventeenth century. Two copies were made of it in 1786
by the Danish scholar G. J. Thorkelin. It has been published and translated frequently since 1833, when Mr. John
M. Kemble of Trinity College, Cambridge, prepared the
text a retelling of which follows.

Beowulf is prefaced by a part of the *Widsith*, or *Wanderer*, which may be of interest because of its antiquity and
secondly because it should refute any preconception about
the Anglo-Saxons as having lived in anything resembling a
"Dark Age."

BEOWULF AND THE FIEND GRENDEL

"I SHALL UNLOCK my hoard of words at your will. I shall
unfold before you, O King, the story of my wanderings, for
truly I have roamed long years over this wonderful world."

The fire burned brightly in the castle hearth. On his high
seat the king of Anglia, well wrapped in furs, lounged carelessly while his earls took places below him preparing to hear
a renowned bard who was raising his harp and clearing his
throat. Gusts of wind blew fragrant wind smoke out the
open doors or curled it about the heavy oak rafters. The
night had fallen early, but the hall door stood wide open
at either end of the rectangular room. . . . No enemies would
enter, for the land was at peace. The Angles had long before
stopped their restless wanderings over the North Sea. They
had cut Northumbria into marches, and the marches into
shires. The once fierce Vikings had long since become peaceful farmers; their leaders were called earls. Over them all
ruled a fair king, noteworthy because he upheld the freedom
of his people, earls and carls [2] alike.

[2] Common people.

These Angles, lovers of poetry, had ages before skimmed over the North Sea, westward from Sweden and Denmark, until they founded their new kingdoms in Britain: Mercia, Northumberland, and East Anglia. In the south of their new homeland their brothers, the Saxon kings, ruled Sussex, Wessex, and Essex. The Roman legions, who for four hundred years had kept order in Britain, were only a distant memory. Their missionaries had returned, however, to convince these settlers from over the seas to put away their worship of their pagan gods—Freya, Woden, Thor, Eostre, and the awesome Wyrd,[3] goddess of death.

"O King," sang the bard, "I have tramped the whole world over in the course of a lifetime. Every mighty king have I seen with these eyes. Every land have I understood, each with its own customs and habits, each with its own law. One truth have I learned above all others! A king who seeks to rule his people and his lands without warfare must take this as his plan: he must work first and foremost for his people's good!

"Therefore since the world began, this wandering star upon whose breast we live, one king has shone more brightly than all others. He was Alexander of Macedon.

"In the far-flung realms of Rome have I wandered, as a guest made welcome for his songs. In imperial Rome have I seen great Caesar ruling in all pomp and majesty. Through the lands of Greece have I also roamed, and farther eastward even than that. I have seen the splendor of Persian kings. I have glimpsed the sands of Africa and watched the foreign folk who dwell in Egypt's land. I have looked eagerly upon the wealthy men of the East and gaped at their trading vessels proudly riding the waves of Italy's harbors. Men have I seen who dwell by the Ganges' waters, whose flood waves ride down into an unknown sea near Eostre's far home. Lombardy have I seen also, and Franconia.

"In the halls of great kings the mead has always flowed freely; there gold armlets were the reward of my songs. . . . I have sung before the chiefs of the Angles here in Britain, and before the Jutes on the Island of Wight, and in the cold lands of the northernmost Picts and Scots. I have sung before the Saxons and the Swedes and the Danes, and wayworn fared to where the Elbe River joins our northern sea. I have willingly sought the hordes of fierce Huns over whom Attila holds sway, and stopped on my way home at the mead halls of the Franks across the sea. Pirates of the northern

---

[3] Or "Weird."

coasts have I recalled in my songs, and fought my way into the eastern land of the Finns. Six hundred shillings of pure gold has been my fee, and acres of land as a gift from the Queen of Mercia. Born was I in the Anglian land of Britain, and there shall I die, a faithful son of song.

"One truth would I set high above all others," repeated the gleeman. "Only the king who loves his people is beloved in turn of them. That king alone shall never be forgotten. Bards even now unborn shall sing of his feats, his strength, his faithfulness, and his openhandedness. Let the bards be ever entrusted to write the songs of a hero, and his people will have them to sing always."[4]

The last sound of the harp drifted across the hall. Slowly the king roused himself. Pulling one of the massive gold armlets from his own arm, he sent it to the bard. The world was, indeed, very wide; and he for one had too much to do at home in Anglia ever to fare so far. What was the life of a man? What, indeed, was the life of a king unless he worked hard for his people who had raised him to the throne? What more than the flight of a gull through the mead hall, a sudden bright sweep of white wings against the smoke-blackened rafters? Only the unselfish, only the great in heart were worthy of being sung by the bards.

"Sing us the song of the Angles," ordered the king. "Tell us again our own story that we may steep ourselves in kingship. Sing of *The Hero*."

Like a distant foreword to the swelling song the heavy rumble of the waves, driven by the evening tide, moaned and tore at the shore. They were the same waters that washed the headlands of Denmark, the olden home of the Angles. . . . The great hall was still. The song they would hear was such an old one, sung down the ages, recalling a time so long ago that only the great in heart had been remembered from it. . . . Gently the gleeman stroked his harp, in long, lonesome chords like the mournful sound of a wild wind shrieking through darkness. Shivers pierced the bones of the listeners as the old, homely words rang again in their ears:

Sing of the Danes in the days gone by, deeds of our kings who were scatheless in war! Tell about Scyld, the son of Scef, how he stole the mead from the foemen's halls, how he ripped their thrones from under their feet, how he drove his prow through the ways of the whale, how he gulped down tribute from all of the tribes that clung to their cliffs by the chilly sea.

[4] From *Widsith*.

Shout about Scyld with his strength and his might, building wide mead halls ribbed with gold. That was an earl—that Scyld, son of Scef! Ah, what a king we had! In the distant days of the Danes!

The great king called Scyld ruled for many years over the seafaring peoples of the north, and God gave him a fair, strong son to rule after him. According to the old king's will, his body was borne down the sea cliffs and placed on the earlmen's ship. Bronze shields bright with gold flashed along her gunwales, and from her masthead flew the shining flag of Scyld. The dead king, dressed in full mail and wearing his gem-studded crown, was laid on the open deck. On his chest lay heaped the wealth he had gathered during his long rule over the sea realms. Battle-axes and swords lay flashing in the winter sunlight about his body. Sadly the earls pushed the shining ship away from the jetty and watched the first deep swells of the sea catch her and sweep her along over the deep. To this day no man can say what became of King Scyld or his seaworthy ship! The waves hold him in trust—the wild, western sea.

The Scylding kings, descended from Scyld, reigned in Denmark for countless ages until the people became a whole, one in heart and mind. Then ruled an unselfish king named Hrothgar, who dreamed of a deed that would awe the bards so deeply that his name would be recalled among the Vikings forever more. Hrothgar unfolded his plan. He would have built in Denmark a great hall, so lofty, so heavy with gold, so braced with iron bands, that its like the northern folks had never thought to witness! There on a lofty seat Hrothgar would sit in state, night after night, giving rings to his earls, granting wealth to young and old alike, sharing even before his death all the gold of Denmark.

In this way and to this end was built Heorot Hall, the house of the deer, a wonder so famous that gleemen from all over the sea-swept lands came to gasp at its rows of stag's antlers, its bronze-bound doors, its lofty ceiling, and the lavishness of King Hrothgar. There every evening sat the Danish earl with his Queen Wealhtheow beside him, the handsome two, givers of gifts. From the lands around earls came to swear fealty to Hrothgar.

Night after night, however, the fiends of evil, those who live in the underworld, writhed and curled with hatred as the sweet sound of the harp rose from the hearthside. Jealous and full of anger, they leered as the soft song of the scop [5]

[5] Bard

praised the All-Powerful. He who had fashioned the earth, with its level fields and shimmering pools, with its girdle of sparkling green sea, He it was who had thrust the sun and moon up into the blue skies where they could stand as torches, as beacons for all homecomers over the seas. He it was who had bespangled the soils with russet leaves and reeds and who had breathed the breath of life into beings.

Hrothgar and his eldermen lived happily in Heorot Hall until the day that Grendel, a living fiend out of hell, a Satan who ruled over the swamps and marshes, came stalking toward them. Grendel and his folk had been banished to the fens eras before because of their slaying of Cain. To Grendel's accursed folk belonged the ghouls, the dragons, the lemurs, the elves, and all evil curs. The giants [6] also had been outlawed along with Satan because they had fought against God. Therefore God was giving them a fitting reward through everlasting ages.

So in the dark night, gliding among the shadows, Grendel crept steathily toward Heorot. Drooling with spit, stinking and hairy, he leaped the outside walls, and stopped to listen. . . . No one had heard him. Only the leaves rustled overhead. . . . Then with a bloodcurdling scream he rushed headlong into the hall where the Danish warriors were sleeping. Careless and carefree they slumbered on the benches, heedless of woe, until Grendel's scream tore them from their sleep. Before they could think, he had crashed through their midst, his claws sunk deep in two warriers. Hurriedly he snatched up others, one or two at a time, until he had slaughtered thirty of Hrothgar's doughtiest earls. After the whole company had awakened, he lurched from the hall and took flight, leaving the partially eaten bodies strewn and mangled, among the rushes of the floor.

The deaths were not discovered until dawn. King Hrothgar was appalled. He gathered at once that his strength or that of his earls together could do nothing against the evildoer. The struggle was too uneven. Within a few days Grendel crept back, and again the king awoke to find his fair hall in a shambles, the boards all overturned, and his warriors, torn by the monster's claws, spread about the floor.

Whoever had escaped the ogre's greediness fled for his life across the land of Denmark. In time the great hall was empty. No suppers were held. No scops or gleemen came to Heorot any more. Nor was there any more giving of

[6] From Scandanavian mythology, as from Greek.

rings. For twelve long years Grendel haunted the realm of Hrothgar.

No treaty, no peace, no ransom, no fee—nothing could allay the wrath of Grendel against the kingdom of Denmark! Night after night the accursed Shadow of Death crept through the woods, prowled about chieftains' dwellings, snatched his prey at random without thought for rank, youth, or years. Stealthily he lay in wait, caught men in his traps, and flung them headlong into an endless darkness.

Men looked for him, straining their eyes fearfully to peer through the rolling fogs of the moors, dreaded the thump of his heavy paw on their shoulders as they hauled in their nets. They scanned the beaches for him at twilight. They saw him behind every bush and stone of the path, or stood stock-still listening for the crunch of his bare pads on the pebbles. So many bloody deaths! So many screeching loved ones! How could a man know where the fiend would turn up next? What does a man know anyway of the fiends that crawl through the black night?

In the dark of evening Grendel lumbered into the empty hall, hunting for food. One thing alone he could not touch— the throne of Denmark! Only that had God forbidden him to soil.

There was wretchedness in the land, sorrow, wretchedness, and cold fear! Hrothgar and his few trusty earls held meetings and tried to find an answer. They prayed to their idols. They cooked up new magic broths. They called upon their pagan gods to thwart all dragons, all fiends, all evil, all nightmares. . . . In their hearts they thought only of hell, not knowing, not having yet heard of the Lord God. . . . Cursed is he who slips from the true path and hands his soul back to the hell-fires! Blessed is he who on the day of his death finds peace in the breast of his Maker!

Hrothgar lived on, his days flowing from a cup of sorrow, powerless in the grip of the ogre, beaten and heartsick.

Those were black days shadowed by the awesome blackness of night. . . .

Meanwhile in the land of the Geats across the sea the bitter news had come. The sorrows of Denmark reached in time the ears of the Geats. King Hygelac heard it and mourned! His earls heard it and shuddered!

Beowulf heard the news.

Of the race of men he was the strongest. Boldest among the bold was this vassal of Hygelac! Greatest in heart among all great hearts was this chief of the Geats, this Beowulf!

"Come! Let us haul down the ship!" cried Beowulf. "Over the path of the sea bird, through the wake of the swan, let us fly to Denmark," he said. "This king of the Danes needs men!"

At first the wise eldermen nearest King Hygelac's throne worried and fretted, for the sea was wide, and Beowulf dear to them all. Finally they yielded, however, and helped him choose fifteen strong warriors. Then they studied their hidden lore and found that their gods were willing. One of their number was called who knew the paths of the sea and who spoke to Beowulf of the tides and the landmarks. He warned him of black rocks and swirling shoals.

Under the sea-girt cliffs the shining ship was readied, laden with coats of mail, swords, and gleaming war harness. Bidding farewell to their king, the sturdy warriors embarked. Last of them all strode their mighty leader, his feet strong and steady on the bobbing craft. Turning their backs on Sweden, the fearless warriors cast off and leaned to the oars.

Like a bird, like a swallow, like a slender gull the glistening ship sped forward. She cut a path through the clear, green sea, her prow wreathed in bubbles and foam. The winds caught her like a bird and blew her swiftly southward. Across unknown waters the light floater lunged and ploughed into the swells. The salt spray blew strong on the warriors' foreheads.

By the first hour of the second day the dark fjords of Denmark rose on the skyline, reaching up toward the clouds from their tide-beaten sands. Sounding cautiously and tacking, the pilot brought the swift craft unharmed to the shore. The sea lanes had been followed aright. The coast had been won.

From his lighthouse on the cliff, the coast guard of Hrothgar saw the Geats disembarking. Spurring his horse, he galloped down to the shore and bespoke them.

"Who are you, warriors in war dress who clamber from your seagoing ship? I am an earl of Hrothgar, king of the Danes. Never have shield-bearers so grim of face ever landed before on our shores! Do you at least know the password?"

Then as he spoke, the Danish earl suddenly saw the leader Beowulf. In fright and amazement he stepped backward. His hand shook on his horse's reins. "Never in my life," stammered the Dane, "have I seen a man like this one! Who in the world is this warrior?" he asked, still staring at Beowulf. "Surely this is a hero, one we must know for his deeds of strength. Please, may I know your kindred and the aim of your trip to this coast."

Beowulf unlocked his word hoard. "We come, indeed, from across the sea. We are folk and vassals of Hygelac, king of the Geats. Perhaps you have heard of my father. His name was Ecgtheow." The Dane gasped. His guess had been right. This was, in truth, a hero and the son of a hero.

"My warriors and I have come to your lands as friends," Beowulf went on. "Have no fear of us! We have heard of some fiend of darkness who is foully mistreating your king. Perhaps we can help him."

"Then hasten back to your ships," bade the coast guard. "Dress yourselves in your coats of mail. Grasp your shields and your axes. Hurry! I will lead you to Heorot Hall. Take no thought for your ship. I shall see that she is well guarded and circled about with hawsers. Her mighty heart shall find rest in our waters."

Setting their boar helmets [7] well over their ears, the fierce warriors from Geatland strode up the sea cliffs after their leader. Shortly the lofty gables and gleaming roof of Heorot Hall came into sight. They stopped and wondered at its cunning workmanship, for truly there was not a building like it in all the world. The coast guard left them. Still gazing up at the high turrets, the warriors drew near the hall over a street of stones. Their swords clanged against mail. On an outer gate to the castle they rested their shields and then climbed the stairs to the door.

They were met by the herald Wulfgar. He curtly craved to know their names, and their will in striding so roughly over the roadway. In one glance he noted their arms and their bearing.

"We are vassals of King Hygelac," answered Beowulf. "We will speak of our errand to your king, that most worthy of men."

Leaving them standing at the door, Wulfgar stepped into the hall and drew near his king. This herald was himself an earl from the highborn kindred of Wendel. He knew how to speak to a king, how to stand behind his chief's shoulder.

"We have here, newly sprung from the sea, a band of Geatish warriors. Their leader is a man named Beowulf. They beg leave to tell you their errand, O king. Do not forbid them entry. They have the mien of earls, and their chieftain is a mighty warrior. Greet them as earls, O Hrothgar!"

---

[7] The boar was sacred to the goddess Freya.

King Hrothgar answered his herald at once. "Surely I
know this leader, or knew him when he was a child. He
is the son of Ecgtheow. Hrethel the Geat gave that leader
his only daughter in wedlock. This is their child Beowulf!
Now, indeed, has he come over the sea to me in my sorrow.
I heard that this youngster had the strength of thirty men
in his handgrip! Call for gifts to be brought at once! Round
up our warriors! All you can hail are to come here at once!
Go quickly first to the door and make them welcome."

Wulfgar escorted Beowulf and his men into the hall, allowing them to keep on their coats of mail and their helmets,
only begging them to leave their swords, axes, and javelins
outside the building. With fitting words he led Beowulf to
a dais.

In this way Beowulf and King Hrothgar faced each other,
each one from his dais on the opposite side of the hall. The
younger man spoke first. "Hail to thee, Hrothgar, king of the
Danes. You know my kindred, my name, and my rank. In
my youth, it is true, I have done some deeds that have
been held worthy of my father. We of the Geats have sor-
rowed to learn how you are beset in Denmark by a bloody
fiend named Grendel. My own king and earl has sent us to
offer whatever strength we have against fiends. My own kinfolk have watched me, drenched to the skin with foul-
smelling blood, struggle to the death with a lemur. I am the
one who crushed the wicked Elves. Swimming far under the
waves I have oftentimes wrestled with the whales in the deep.
In war I overcame the Westerners, who were riding ahead
of their own downfall anyway! I crushed those bold warriors out of their lives!

"Today I am ready for Grendel. Grant me this trial, O
King! You see that I have come from far over the sea to
try it. I would do battle with your Grendel! I would seize
your monster barehanded. Without sword or shield I would
grapple this fiend as a token of my fealty to King Hygelac.
Here in your hall shall sleep whichever one of us our Lord
may will. If this beast of yours worsts me, then only send
to my uncle and king the gems that are set on my shield.
It is the work of Weland the smith; it is thus a priceless
heirloom that should be shipped home to my kinfolk."

"This I thought was your errand, dear Beowulf," answered
King Hrothgar. "This I thought was the aim of your wandering over the deep. I knew your father back in the days
when I was a young man, newly throned. Now I am old and
heartsick. My head bows. My eyes weep with shame to have
to acknowledge my weakness. My throne, as you see, is

almost a barren spot. My lands are becoming a wilderness. What has Grendel wrought in this kingdom! Often at night, swollen with beer, have my warriors sworn to topple this fiend. Then when the bleak, white light of dawn has crept over the misty fields, we have strode through this very hall strewn with their bloodstained bodies!

"Let me speak no more of my woes, great hero. Take your seat at my board, and let me drink to your health. Eat and be merry, my friend, who have sailed over deep water so boldly to save us all."

Straightforth a bench was drawn out from the wall and a meal set before the warriors from Geatland. Highborn vassals waited on them at the board, poured the sparkling mead into their cups from carved beakers with scrollwork handles. As they ate and drank, Hrothgar's gleemen sang them songs of the bygone works of the Danes.

Then one of Hrothgar's earls, a warrior named Unferth, who sat legs-sprawled at his king's feet, began to bait the guests. He was a spiteful man who could not stand hearing about the wonderful trip over the sea from Sweden. He could not let anyone best him in war-work!

"Say! Are you that Beowulf who swam a race with Breca when both of you, swollen with pride, wanted to fathom the depths of the fiords and risk your lives in deep water? Why, there isn't any man, friend or foe, who wouldn't blame such a shameful feat! Under the wintry waves you swam for a week, sliding the slopes of the sea, learning its hidden kingdoms while the waters boiled and hissed in the storm above you? Breca beat you, though. He was stronger by far than you, Beowulf! So the morning tide swept him to his home shore, where he lived to carve out a realm all by himself. He was a good man, that Breca! He kept his word at least.

"What, you Beowulf," Unferth continued. "I look for a far worse fate for you if you think you dare spend a night in this hall with Grendel!"

"Now listen, friend Unferth," snapped Beowulf. "I have kept still while you, drunk as an earl, have poured forth your flood of words about Breca. Now I'll tell you the truth. So hearken! I happen to have more strength in the sea, more breath for the dive, than any other man.

"If you truly care to hear that tale, I'll be glad to tell you myself how it was. I speak the truth. When Breca and I were boys, in the first hot glow of our manhood, we swore an oath that we would pit our strength against the sea. And so we did. We bore our naked swords in our hands, thinking to use them against whales as we struggled up through the tideraces of the coves. In deep water Breca could neither outswim me nor lose me among the peaks of the swells. Nor did I try to outstrip him. Thus we were together for five days and nights upon the sea until a huge flood swept us asunder. That happened during the height of a storm, through a night so black we couldn't see where we were heading. A wind so fierce, as wild as a battle, shrieked down from the north. It drove tons of gray water into the fiords. The waves were unleashed.

"Then all the daring of the big fishes was awakened. The winds had stirred up their cold blood. Well, against such foes my hand-knotted mail stood me in good stead. My gold-heavy harness buffered my chest, just as in battle. A thousand-hued beast pulled and dragged at my limbs, striving to suck me down to the depths with him. He held me close in a death grip. However, I was happy enough to stab him in the belly with the point of my blade. I gave him the taste of death with this hand of mine that you see.

"Those aren't the only foemen, Unferth, who have threatened me with their snarls. I have known for some years how to wield a weapon. No loathsome fishes, not even all of them together, have yet been able to drag me down against my will.

"Well, dawn broke. The eastern light flooded the sea, and I finally caught glimpses of land. I finally saw bleak crags and the headlands buffeted by the gale. There in shallow beach water rolled my foes of the night, put to sleep as it were, by my sword. True it is, indeed, that they ceased henceforth to prey upon war ships on the shores of my native land.

"Wyrd often saves the earl who is not yet marked for death—when he still helps himself in the fighting. I also had the good luck to kill nine sea prowlers, or nicors. Under heaven I have never heard tell of a mighty battle so hardly waged. Have you, Unferth? . . . Still I kept up my even stroke. The waves bore me ashore amidst the jagged crags of Finland. It was there on a sandy strip that I waded ashore.

"Neither Breca," said Beowulf, "nor any one of you in the flashing of swords has ever done deeds of worth so dearly won. I do not boast before you—even though I know that you, Unferth, have murdered your own brethren. You shall be doomed for it too, to hell, in spite of your cleverness. Let me tell you one more thing. Grendel would never have dared such outrage here in this hall if your might in war were as great as you say it is! Grendel found out long ago that he had nothing to dread. So has he lusted after this hall, and

wanted to suck your blood. He knows he can kill more of
the Spear-Danes! He knows he can tumble you all down
to death!

"But I, a Geat, have brought a gift for your Grendel.
Without his foreknowledge I have here to give him three
things: a fighting heart, my dauntless will, and my great
strength. After this night whoever may wish to sing in your
mead hall may do so. After tomorrow's sun rises in the
east upon the sons of men, each one of you may enter this
house in freedom. I, Beowulf, swear it."

King Hrothgar heard Beowulf and believed him. He, the
aged, baldheaded king of the Danes, felt a hush steal into his
heart. So among his heroes there were songs of happiness,
and jokes, and toasts drunk to the Geats.

Then through the great hall Queen Wealhtheow walked.
She, from whose garments gold dropped, greeted the men in
the hall. First she bore a cup of mead to her beloved husband, the king. She begged him to take it from her own
hand, and to drink. Hrothgar thanked her and took the
goblet. Then the queen passed from earl to earl, young and
old alike, bearing to each one a golden gift. She was a
queen and the daughter of a queen. Then the highborn lady
held out her hand, heavy with rings, to Beowulf. Wise in
her words, she thanked him first and then thanked God that
her prayers had been answered. She said that she had faith
in Beowulf, that she trusted his earlship, and that she was
deeply beholden. The freeborn queen held out a cup to
the hero.

Beowulf answered the queen, "I wished when I let float
my sea-wood on the whale's way, when I set sail with my
war-band, to answer with my life the challenge of Grendel. I
shall live out my years, as befits an earl, or I shall end my
days right here in your lofty hall."

Queen Wealhtheow was gladdened by his words. Then
she took a seat beside the king. After that there were boast-
ings in Heorot! Then did the warriors brag before their
stainless queen. Then were they light of heart! Their oaths
grew bigger and bigger!

At last King Hrothgar arose. He knew what a fray was
shaping up for the small hours of the night. He felt the cold
of the evening shrinking his limbs. He felt in his bones that
the fiend was even then prowling outside in the misty half-
light, searching for men's blood. All the warriors stood as
the king bade farewell to Beowulf.

"Never before in my years as a king have I given my realm
to another, as I give it now to you, Beowulf, son of Ecgtheow.

This night, stand in my stead. Uphold my name with all your might. I give you my hall, this proudest of buildings. Be wakeful, Beowulf, against our foe. He is coming tonight. I feel it . . . . If you fulfill this deed, know that no wish of yours during all your lifetime shall go unfulfilled by me."

Then King Hrothgar left the hall with his earls. He wanted to go to bed with his queen.

Carls stood ready to take from Beowulf his coat of mail, his helmet, and his heavy sword. Then the Geat lay down on the pile of furs that had been set for him, laid his cheek against the bolster, and waited. His men also lay down to sleep, tired from their long sail and the frightening tales of the day and evening. They could not know whether they would ever see another sunrise, or if they would live through the night to follow the sea tracks home to Sweden. The night was cold and very still. The fire in the central hearth had burned low. Soon all but Beowulf slept . . . .

Then through the black moors wreathed in fog, Grendel came creeping, God's ire upon him. Out of the swirling mists he stalked with outstretched claws, hunting toward the dimly lighted hall. To his wonderment the door was barred. Grendel had not foreseen that! With a snarl the fiend stepped backward, stiffened his muscles, and lunged at it. Iron bars sprung loose. Wood splintered. The door burst from its hinges.

Grendel was inside the great hall. All about him the Geatish warriors lay stretched out on their fur beds, sunk in sleep, heedless, unhearing. For a second Grendel stopped to scan them. Darts of red fire shot from his deep-set eyes. Rolling his huge head from side to side, Grendel glared about him. Then he laughed.

From his end of the hall Beowulf watched the ogre, weighed his endowment, and waited to see how Grendel would strike. Quick as a wink the fiend pulled at the warrior nearest him, cracked his bones with one twist, ripped at the body with his talons, split open the jugular and drank the hot blood as it gushed from the torn throat. Then he ravenously broke apart the hands and the feet, and swallowed them.

Without warning, Grendel suddenly dropped the mangled body and sprang straight across the hall at Beowulf. The hero had raised himself on his left elbow. Beowulf had just time to stretch forth his right arm as the ogre rushed upon him. He caught Grendel's right hand, and still without rising from his bed, stopped the monster's onrush. For an instant

the two stood stock-still. The shepherd of evil then looked
down into the icy-cold eyes of the hero. Grendel was chilled.
The cold shiver of death ran through his spine as the fingers
of Beowulf tightened like steel over his bones.

Wild waves of fear ran over the ogre. His only thought
was flight! Without even gathering his strength, he lurched
backward, away from the vise, away from the eyes that were
working foreign magic on him. As Grendel began to pull,
Beowulf sprang to his feet. He did not let go Grendel's
hand. On the contrary, he began slowly but surely to push
it backward — despite all the strength of Grendel. Of the
two Beowulf was the stronger. Grendel felt his hand, his
arm, being slowly pushed backward. Great shudders rolled
over him. Then Beowulf began to twist the ogre's arm.

With a howl of pain Grendel leaped wildly backward,
Beowulf still gripping his hand, into the benches and boards.
Back and forth across the hall the two fought, the hunted
and the grim hunter. Boards crashed to the floor. The
beakers of mead spilled in huge puddles. Against the walls
the Geatish warriors huddled in knots or scrambled to safety
as the two threw each other against the oak timbers. The
wood cracked from the blows as if the iron bands about the
outside of Heorot would be burst, as if the roof would cave
in at any moment over the din of the struggle. Grendel
lurched madly toward the door, hoping to pull Beowulf outside into the black night. Back and forth the two giants
wrestled.

Then Grendel began to scream. Mouth open, eyes shooting red fire, he howled in mournful, quivering bursts of
pain. Again and again he howled his death shriek until all
the ruffians in hell stopped to listen. Beowulf would not
let go the hand. His heart was bent on the ogre's death.

As the twain stood locked together, Beowulf's squire roused
himself from his fear and strode forth behind the fiend. Lift-
ing his sharp-biting sword, he tried to rescue his master.
Then did the Geatish earls see before them another wonder.
Blow after blow of the sword fell upon Grendel's shoulders
without even leaving a scratch. Then did the earls know the
matchless wisdom of their leader! Beowulf had somehow
known to doff his coat of mail and to lay down his weapons.
No tool made by man had any strength against Grendel.
Daunted and shivering, the squire stole back to his corner.
Breathless, blanched with fear, the warriors awaited the
outcome.

Beowulf to their amazement had not yet squeezed out the
last of his strength. Before their wondering eyes they saw

him suddenly wrench the ogre's arm backward and snap the armbone from the shoulder. A gaping wound spurted blood from Grendel's armpit. Beowulf's face, white with anger, flashed back cold fire into the red eyes of the fiend. Eye to eye they glared in unspeakable hatred for one last moment. . . . Then the arm gave way utterly. The bones parted, the muscles burst, the flesh tore, and the fiend — at last free from the grip of Beowulf — fled full-tongued into the darkness.

Grendel knew that his days upon earth were numbered.

In the hall Beowulf the Geat stood alone. He had done what he swore to do. He had rid the house of evil. He had saved the kingdom of Denmark. Gladly Beowulf fastened the token of battle, the bloody arm of Grendel, in the rafters of Heorot.

The next morning the Danish warriors began to creep back to their king. As soon as they heard the bright tidings, even the earls from their far-off homes and byres set out bearing gifts for the hero. All day long they crowded into the hall and stood speechless. Awkwardly and gladly they nudged each other and gawked at the hero. There in the roof above their heads hung the arm of Grendel!

No one spoke of where he had gone, or of how he had ended his days. Wyrd had doomed him to die. No one stopped to think that he must have fled to the boiling pool of the nicors. There Grendel was watching his blood flow out into the seething tarn. Warriors and eldermen never went near that poisoned pool. As they rode through the woods, they always swerved their horses' heads away from those paths.

In the hall of the kind King Hrothgar the scops were already at work shaping with beat and flashing words the story of the black night's struggle between Beowulf the Geat and Grendel. In their song they did not forget about Sigmund and how his name was still renowned long after the day of his death.

They said again how Sigmund had dealt with a dragon, a fierce, writhing, wealth-hoarder hid in white rocks. They told how the many-hued worm had burnt up in his own fire, and how Sigmund had outfitted a ship all loaded down with his heirlooms. Sigmund was the greatest of wanderers since ever the world began, they said. The tales of his might were a refreshment and a challenge to warriors. They also sang of Sigmund and his many fights with the Jutes. His very name was a beacon, for men throughout the earth had faith in that hero. They thought of him as always behind their shoulders. They said he was a faithful friend in evil days.

Now here was Beowulf a like hero, he too standing alone and beloved in full daylight, before the eyes of men!

Hrothgar, the keeper of golden rings, walked forth from his wedding bed, his queen beside him. Together they climbed the steps to their hall and gazed in wonder and speechlessness at the arm of Grendel.

"May God be thanked," sighed the king. "I have withstood so long the wrath and wolfishness of this ogre. This Beowulf has the strength of a god. Whatever woman bore the body of this child in her womb, whether or not she still lives I cannot say, may well enough know that she was blessed in her childbirth. My dear Beowulf," cried the king, "now shall I love you like a son." With tears running down his cheeks the king clasped the hero. "Inasmuch as I can reward your work, ask me for any boon. Ask only, and it shall be awarded. Beowulf, you have won already by this deed a deathless tomorrow. May God uphold you!"

"It was the deed of gladness," answered the hero. "Still I could wish that you had seen the bloodshedding yourself. I am sorry that I could not keep more of Grendel to show you than just his hand, his arm, and his shoulder. I guess by now, however, that his life's blood has flowed out of his body."

Of all the warriors in Heorot only Unferth was closemouthed that day. Hour after hour crowds gathered, and people talked about the arm of Grendel — how its claws were stronger than metal which no metal could cut. Then carls were bade to bedeck the House of the Hart. The wine house and the guest house were hung with curtains shining bright against the wooden walls. Gold cups and dishes were set on the boards. Despite their best efforts, however, the women could not hide all the cracks in the walls.

The iron bands had been sprung during the struggle of Beowulf. The wood was weakened and splintered. Only the rafters were unharmed. Lucky it was for the hall that Grendel fled when he did! He could not escape Wyrd. He could not fly his tomorrow! That's very hard to do. Let him who wishes only try it! Every man in this life will go lay him down on the bed where Wyrd has decided to nail him, after life's meal.

I have never heard tell of so many tribes as came to the winehall that night! I never saw so many great chieftains surrounded by so many brave warriors!

Then Hrothgar gave to Beowulf a golden flag, a chest for heirlooms with handles of wrought iron, a helmet, a coat

of chain mail, and a sword of great worth which had been
borne once before by an older hero. Hrothgar held the cup
to Beowulf's lips. Before so many great warriors Beowulf
blushed.

That was not all either. Then Hrothgar called for eight
war horses to be driven to the steps of the hall. Each one
bore a saddle as finely wrought as a throne. Nor was that
all. The king gave a fine, worthy gift to each of the warriors
from Geatland and handed out a sum in gold for the one
that Grendel had eaten.

After the giving of gifts the gleemen brought forth their
joywoods, tightened the strings, and began to sing the "Finns-
burgh Lay." During the evening Queen Wealhtheow also
thanked Beowulf, gave him an heirloom ring, and asked him
to watch over her children in the case that her husband died
before they had reached manhood.

It was with a hush in their hearts and smiles on their
lips that the weary Danes dropped on their beds of furs.
Henchmen had placed, as was their habit, each warrior's
gear and trappings above his pile of skins. Thus you could
see the burnished helmet of each warrior set in readiness
above his head. It was the Viking habit. Even as a man
plowed his fields or chopped trees in the woods, his byrnie[a]
and his sword were always at hand.

The northmen were a dauntless people.

They were to pay dearly those few winks of sleep in the
hall, the Danish warriors. Down in her lair the mother of
Grendel seethed with ire at the death of her only son. This
ogress too was begotten of the blood of Cain, whose brood
had been doomed forever to the icy floods and freezing
waters of the earth.

When night had fallen, the she-demon stole forth toward
the hall, which she entered unheard and unseen. In her un-
holy hatred she grasped the first warrior she found and killed
him as he lay slumbering. Then there was an uproar in the
hall. Midnight terror seized the Danes, the same cold ache
of fear that chills a virgin so that she stands helpless in her
tracks, or the pangs that make women wince when they stand
beside the battle and watch their men.

Among the furs and the cots the Danes, without stopping
for helmets or byrnies, wielded their swords at the ogress.
Some had time to grasp their shields. The ogress, however,
did not linger. She had made her kill and wanted no more of

[a] Body armor.

a fight. The frightened warriors watched her dart out the door and head for the moor. As soon as King Hrothgar heard what had happened — learned also that the slain warrior was his boon companion and dearest friend — he sent for Beowulf. That hero had been lodged in a neighborhood guest house.

"Did you spend a dreamless night?" asked the hero.

"Do not ask after me," cried King Hrothgar. "My beloved friend has been slain right in my own hall, he who stood nearest me year after year in my wars, he who was my trusted friend and elderman. Look! Grendel's arm, which you so proudly hung up in my rafters, is gone. His fond mother came in the dark of night and carried it back to her den! Ah, woe is me! Alas, for my kingdom and my kinfolk!

"It is true," added the king, "that the husbandmen for years have glimpsed these twain, the he- and the she-fiend, tramping the moors at night. Folks believed that one was the dam of the other. Who the father could have been, they never knew. These ogres dwelled in the forsaken and untilled meadows, in the secret haunts of the wolves, on barren headlands storm-beaten and wild, in the doubtful paths of the swamps, or under the swift-rushing waterfalls as they thunder into a glen and sink to an underground stream.

"A mile from here is a tarn with rocky caverns and gulches. Around its edge the tree roots are entwined so high and so thick that they cast black shadows out over the water. It is a dreadful sight after dark.⁹ There are shooting fires on these waters. Not one of the sons of Denmark knows the hidden lore of this spot.

"If you hunt a stag through the woods and drive him across the heather right to this tarn, he will halt and let the hounds tear at his hide and his throat rather than jump into its blackness.¹⁰ Whenever the thunder grumbles, huge billows will rise from the depths and slap at the sky.

"I leave it to you, Beowulf. You should make up your own mind even though you cannot foresee the traps that will entangle you. If you will do this for us, and if you live, you know what wealth will be yours, for you and your men."

Then Beowulf, son of Ecgtheow, pondered awhile and spoke. "Do not let yourself fall into glum grief, O King. Is it not better for a man or a king to avenge his friend rather

⁹ Tacitus says, in his *Germania*, that the ancient Germans often drowned their cowards and their lazy men in such swamps.
¹⁰ Passages such as this one have made some scholars believe that either the poet or the scribes who copied the manuscript were familiar with Vergil's *Aeneid*.

than to let an old misgiving rankle in his heart? We all of
us know the end of our days; therefore let him who can
make the reckoning with wrongdoers. After his death men
will say that was his greatest deed.

"Lift up your head and your heart, O King. We must
follow after this dreadnought, hard on her tracks. I swear to
you she shall not slip away from us. She shall not dodge
me though she hide in unfathomed waters, or in the earth's
bosom, or in lonely woods, or on crags! Let her try it
and see!"

Shaking with happiness, the king called for horses, and the
band of warriors set out from the hall behind footmen who
bore their shields and carefully followed the tracks of the
ogress. Their path led them past sharp cliffs, along narrow
trails unknown and untrodden, past headlong boulders strewn
across barren, treeless, wind-haunted heights. Underneath a
black cliff where the incoming tide smashed on the shingle,
they stumbled upon the mail hood of Hrothgar's murdered
vassal.

Looking down, they saw that the water bubbled with blood
or burning venom. From time to time the warriors blew
their war horns. They sat on the beach and watched the
hissing wavelets. Strange things swam just under the surface.
Ever and anon a huge, scaly back of some sea snake would
ripple darkly on the oily waves. From the crags over their
heads, cumbersome dragons leaned over the water. They
stretched out full length to catch in their claws any ship
that heedless of jeopardy might round the point. When they
heard the sharp sound of the horn, they withdrew, bitten
with anger. Beowulf cut one of the sea snakes off from its
life. His lance stuck quivering in its still living flesh. Other
warriors harpooned it and hauled it on the shingle for all
to see.

Meanwhile Beowulf made himself ready for war. He
donned a garment of hand-linked mail of many hues. It was
strong enough to safeguard the trunk of his body from neck
to groin. On his head he fitted his white helmet, heavy
enough to protect his skull from the weight of deep water,
sharp enough to cleave a path as he swam, and shaped like
the lovely body of a white swan. Beowulf bore in his hand
a sword lent by Unferth, who now that he was sober had
forgotten the bitter jealousy he had shown when drunk.
This weapon, named Hrunting, was made of brass, dyed
with drops of poison, and dipped in blood. Hrunting had
never failed its wielder, yet Unferth did not have the courage
to wield it himself, but gave it to Beowulf.

When he was ready to dive, Beowulf spoke a few last words to the king. "First, O King of the Danes, remember that whatever happens, I hold you as my father. It was you who so swore. Then I ask you to send my wealth to my king, Hygelac of the Geats. My sword I bequeath to Unferth. I hold you to your word as regards the safety of my followers. With Hrunting I shall live or shall die." Without waiting for an answer, Beowulf leaped into the oily tarn.

Down and down he swam for the better part of a day before he came to the bottom. Soon the ogress, fierce and bloodthirsty, she who for more than a hundred years had queened it in the depths, saw that a man — a queer being of the upperworld — had sunk to her realm. Quick as a wink she grabbed the hero and hugged him tight around his middle. Her long claws fumbled to tear his flesh from his bones. His byrnie, however, was so skillfully woven that she could not pierce it.

Seeing this, the ogress began to swim, still holding the hero tight in her grip, farther and farther, deeper and deeper into the holes of the sea floor. No matter how fiercely he squirmed, Beowulf could not get his sword arm free. Goggling fishes swam up against him, cutting his thighs with their sharp horns, jostling and bunting the unlucky Geat.

Then Beowulf saw that they had at length reached the entrance to a cave, the upper part of which was above water. He was able to suck huge mouthfuls of air into his lungs. He shook his head and began to peer about him. Huge, overhanging vaults rose high above his head. From somewhere shone a queer, pale fire, a blinding light that hurt his eyes.

Despite the glare he made out the ogress all right. There she loomed, the huge giantess of the sea. At once he lunged for her with his sword. It was no use. At the first blow the fabled sword Hrunting bent and chipped on her hide. This was the first time that the wonderful weapon had ever betrayed a hero! Since the sword was useless, Beowulf would have to rely on his strength. So must every man, in the last face-to-face.

Therefore the peerless warrior grasped the ogress by her shoulder, with no thought for the blows she was raining on him. Before she slipped from his grip, he had bent her back to the ground. However, she wormed out of his hands, backed away for a bit, and then rushed him. Wearied and short of breath, Beowulf lost his footing, rolled over on the ground, and sprawled there helpless at her feet. Then it was that she thought to pierce his chest. Her blow was well-aimed and thrust with a mighty will, but the breastplate of Beowulf stopped the blade. Before she knew what had happened, he was up on his feet again.

Now there has existed in the world, time out of mind, a truly unbeatable weapon. It is an old-time sword, crudely fashioned, and so clumsy that humans cannot wield it. This sword had been smithied long ago by the giants. It was their own personal blade. Beowulf could hardly believe his eyes! There it hung, on the wall of the cavern, just above his hand. He knew it at once from the songs of the bards that he had heard in his childhood. Without thinking twice he reached up his hand and pulled it toward him. Without it he was lost and beaten. Swinging it high above his head, he brought it down on the ogress. It was not too heavy for him. It was indeed a wonderful weapon; it did its work well. The sword severed the little ring-bones in the ogress's throat, and sundered her body.

Before his amazed eyes the ogress staggered and sank to the rocks. Great drops of black blood dropped from the sword blade. In his turn Beowulf slumped against the stones. He could hardly believe it! The blade had obeyed him! The awesome deed was done!

As Beowulf leaned thankfully against the rocks of the cavern wall, panting and shaken to the marrow of his bones, a golden light fell about him in the den, as if some heavenly candle had been lit. By its friendly glow the hero made out the lifeless body of Grendel sprawled on the slippery shale. With one blow he cut off the head, in earnest of the ogre's murdering trips to Heorot, in full reward for his foul deeds.

Above, in the world of men, the warriors who had sat all these hours, their eyes fixed on the hissing caldron, saw streaks of blood on the waves. "The she-wolf of the deep has killed Beowulf," they whispered. By that time it was high noon. Sad and disheartened, King Hrothgar and his Danes left the shore and tramped back to the hall. Only the Geatish men stayed by the tarn, hoping against hope that their leader would return, or that they could recover his body.

Although Beowulf looked long at the wealth amassed in this underworld realm, he took nothing but the sword hilt which he still held in his hand. Even the blade of the often-sung sword had melted in the seething blood of the ogress. It had thawed just as ice does in spring at the word of the Lord, and sets free the tumbling waves from their jail.

Trailing the head of Grendel, Beowulf swam upward through the cloudy water until he at last set foot gratefully on the shore. There his thanes awaited him, overjoyed to see their earl safe and sound. They helped him off with his war gear, and then setting the ogre's head on a pikestaff, they set out on their homeward trip. Four of his Geats staggered under the weight of the fiend's dripping head! How the Danes gasped when they saw Beowulf and the Geats bring that ugly sight into the hall! The women were close to swooning!

"Now your warriors and thanes may sleep without dreams in your hall," Beowulf told the king.

Hrothgar answered, "Let every king and earl acknowledge henceforth that you are a well-born hero! Your rewards shall be great. I foretell that you will long be the delight of your people, for your strength is as great as your coolness and you are a beacon for all our offspring. Is it not wonderful how Almighty God in the breadth of His thought has spread out wisdom, lands, daring, and might among menfolk over the earth, all under His kingly sway?

"Ponder this," continued King Hrothgar. "Think how sometimes God grants to one man, to some gifted son of one tribe, lands, towns, hamlets, and wealth! This man begins to live without weighing the warnings of illness, or old age, or the whispered curses of his foes. Then one day when his guardian angel is asleep, death strikes him down with a well-shot arrow. Such a man had scorned Death because of the gifts God had bestowed on him. His mind had become mean and selfish. He had not thought to lavish gold rings upon his trusted friends. The reckoning comes, and another — perhaps even a foreigner — reaps all his lands and wealth!

"Therefore, good Beowulf, trust not the promptings of pride! The bloom of your youth is upon you. Someday you too shall fall, to the biting dart, or to the sea's unleashed fury, or to the cold bite of iron. I too ruled as a proud king here in Denmark, until the coming of Grendel."

With such words and more Hrothgar thanked Beowulf and stood as a father to him. Because of the deeds of the hero, the land of Denmark slept soundly. The hero's work was done.

As soon as the morning fowl had announced the sunrise, Beowulf and his men bade farewell. Loading their fees and newly won wealth on their ship, they pushed out into the sea. King Hrothgar wept to see their ship grow small in the distance. He feared that he would never clasp Beowulf in his arms again.

BEOWULF'S BARROW
ON THE HEADLANDS OF HRONESNESSE

UPON HIS RETURN to Geatland, Beowulf gave over to his own King Hygelac all the gifts, the horses, and all the wealth he had won by his hardihood. Every good vassal should do likewise. It is shameful to keep wealth for oneself, or to stir up one clan against another.

Hygelac was also the uncle of Beowulf, the brother of Beowulf's mother. By this tie the hero belonged to the kingly house of the Waegmundings, rulers of old in Sweden. Beowulf the Geat behaved fittingly, bestowing his heirlooms on his friends at home. Men spoke well of him from golden tongues — that he was plucky, that he was law-abiding, that he was a lion in battle — and the strongest warrior alive. They also added that he was manly, that he had never struck a carl or a woman in his own house, even when he was roaring drunk. It was a shocking thing that the Geats did not choose him for their chief earl and king, a man of such golden mettle.

Some evil fellows said behind his back that Beowulf was white-livered and a slacker. This kind of talk was a great sorrow for the hero to bear. Hygelac, however, rewarded Beowulf. He gave his nephew lands, a throne, and a hall of his own. After Hygelac's death there was a war in Geatland until finally Beowulf came to the throne and ruled the whole land for fifty years. He was a wise king, careful and safe. Then after fifty years a foul worm, a dragon, took it upon itself to hold sway through the heavens at night.

I don't know how all this wrack came about.[11] It seems there was a worm that slept upon a pile of treasure, which it had zealously heaped up under a stone bluff. Leading to this hoard was an underground way cut through the rock.

[11] The manuscript is incomplete around verses 4426-4455.

Anyway, a man, a culprit, some craven fellow, some outcast from the tribes of men, either stumbled upon or wandered into the dragon's lair. However it came about, some fellow spied the treasure.

In the olden days earls often amassed great wealth which they added to their tribe's heirlooms. Some bygone race of men had all died leaving their hoard under the sea cliffs at the very edge of the waves. They had carried it there, this heavy gold hardened in fire, saying, "O Earth, take back your wealth. Now there are no more heroes to gloat over it from their hollow eyesockets. Those who earned this wealth were undoubtedly men of backbone. In their youth they wrestled and wrested it from you, O Earth. After their years of feasts and mead halls, bold death has borne them away out yonder. No Jute is left to wield a sword to save this hoard. No one is left to swing the battle-ax skyward. No man will ever again drink from this golden goblet! Even those who burnished it have stolen away, beyond the beaches. All, all are dead.

"Let it sleep in the earth. Let the helmet molder along with the coats of mail, along with the shields that stood up well in war against the bite of the foeman's blade. Since he who wore them so pluckily is dead, let his wealth and trappings rust also. In our halls the joywood is silent, no longer stroked by the gleeman's swift fingers. The hawk no longer darts forth from the gauntlet to soar through the air for his prey. No prancing steed champs at the bit and neighs before our hamlets. Such a plague has wasted our tribesmen!" Then the one last singer faded away, too. His flesh wasted from his bones. He too died. Death rotted the skin from his body.

Then the old scourge of dusk swooped down upon the warderless hoard. It is he who burns up the sky at night in long trails of yellow flame, who flies above houses in a whirlwind of shrieking wings and gagging smoke. He it was who wanted the hoard for himself, and who crouched over it in the heart of the headland, gloating and rubbing his scaly loops round it and over it. For three hundred years it had been his, not that it brought him any true warmth or gladness.

At last a man robbed the worm of a goblet, took the golden gift to an earl and tried to win his freedom with it so that forgiven he could belong to some tribe of the Geats again. The earl granted his plea and stared in amazement at the well-wrought gold.

The worm awoke. At once he sniffed the smell of a man. At once he feared his hidden lair had been looted while he slept. How had a man dared to come so close? He must

have trod next to the dragon's head so as not to be spell-
bound. Quickly the worm sniffed around the rocks, and
coiled his bulk through the boulders. If only he was not too
late! If only he could catch the thief, he would blow fire
over every inch of his body. He would singe off his hair
and melt the fat from his bones! When he had made sure
that the man was no longer lurking about, the worm hunted
through his hoard. Yes, one goblet was missing, indeed!
Then in his baleful heart he waited for night to fall so that
he could make his reckoning. His throat burned, for the
stolen goblet was the one from which he used to drink.

Then as soon as the cloak of darkness had shrouded the
lands and the restless sea, the worm took to the air, burning
the houses of men, belching red fire in his anger and sorrow.
Neither chick nor child was left living the length of the
seacoast. The roar of the fires and the thunder rolled inland
to warn the Geats. It was already too late. Before daylight,
when the dragon flew home to sleep, he had burned up the
hall and even the throne of the Geatish king.

The black news was brought to Beowulf. The white-haired
king took the tidings with calm, believing that he must have
in some fashion broken a law without knowing. Then was
Beowulf heavy of heart as he saw the woe of the Geats.
Then did his kingship weigh mightily on his shoulders. His
will, however, did not falter. He never once thought to ask
of another that which he feared in his bones to undertake
himself.

Beowulf called for his blacksmiths and said what he would
be needing — a buckler of steel — for wood or hides would
be burned by the dragon. It was in his mind to fight to the
death with the worm. Beowulf never once thought to summon his warriors from their far-flung houses and byres. He
alone would wrestle since he alone was king. Nor would he
listen to tales of the dragon's havoc. It was better to rehearse
the thoughts of his past deeds.

It was Beowulf who had cleansed the mead hall of Hrothgar! He it was who alone and unweaponed had struggled
with Grendel, and he who heedless had swam to the depths
of the tarn to kill the she-ogre. He was also there at that
fight when Hygelac folded under his deathblow.

King Hygelac of the Geats had been struck down by one
mighty swipe of the foemen, the Frisians. From that dreadful fight Beowulf had survived, only because of the un-
daunted will in his body. He had leaped into the sea, bearing the weight of thirty war harnesses, and swam for his life.
Only a handful of Frisians lived after to tell the tale. Alone

and wretched, Beowulf fought the cold and the tons of sea
water. He followed the sea tracks all the way from Friesland
across the North Sea to the shores of his homeland.[12] There
Beowulf swore fealty to the son of Hygelac and kept his word
until that earl's death.

No man could shake a finger at Beowulf. All the days of
his life he had sought the path of right, escaped traps, killed
foes, and ruled fairly. Now it was time for him to stand up
to the fire-breathing worm. Taking thirteen earls with him,
he set out from his mead hall, angered in heart and mind,
against the peace-breaker. He had already found out the
cliff where the dragon slumbered during the daylight. Beowulf had also seen the goblet; it had been given into his
hand by the thirteenth man, the one who had started the
broil. Sorry and frightened, this man was their pathfinder
across the fields. Half against his will, the thirteenth man
led them to the dark cliff and showed them the cavern, its
mouth toward the sea. Cold waves broke against it.

From their high place on the cliff Beowulf and his band
could look down and see the yawning opening of the cavern,
where the worm hid watching his wealth. Threads of gold
hung in long festoons from the rock walls. Thousands of
costly stones flashed brightly upon their pile of gold. They
threw beams of light far over the foamy waves.

After he had planned for the struggle, Beowulf sat down
on the rocks and bade farewell to his warriors:

"How well it all comes back to me now, the length of my
days! I was seven years old when King Hrethel took me
away from my father to bring me up by his throne. He fed
me, taught me, and gave me gifts in token of our kinship.
I was as dear to King Hrethel as any one of his own stalwart
sons — as Herebeald, or Haethcyn, or my beloved Hygelac.

"Those were bleak days when Haethcyn drew his bow
taut, standing afar off, let fly the straight-aimed arrow, and
so killed the heir to the throne. What a bloody deed it is for
a boy to kill his own brother because he stands in line first
for the throne! Hrethel was brought low by his grief. How
sad it would have been for a king to see his second son
dangle from the hangman's gibbet! What sleepless nights
for King Hrethel! His flesh crawled and tingled with sweat,
for he could not bring himself to avenge the murder of one
son by that of another. He could not stand the thought of
black, raucous crows picking at Haethcyn's flesh as his body

---

[12] The story is corroborated by Gregory, Bishop of Tours (538–594), in
his *History of the Franks*. He was the "historian of the barbarians."

dangled from a gibbet. The breaking of each new day only
made more bitter his sorrow.

"Wild-eyed and disheveled, King Hrethel roamed every
night through his throne room, which was empty and still.
Only the face of his dead son peered at the king from the
dark corners. How much death must an old king have seen
on the field of war, in the play of swords, without its grin-
ning jaw coming over his own hearthside.

"To drown the soughing of the wind through the treetops
old King Hrethel tried to sing to himself. Old sad songs
came out of his throat one after the other. Grief for his
oldest boy, lying streaked with his own red blood, rose in
sobs to his throat. There was no way to cast off this sorrow,
since no deed of his could wipe out the misdeed. Therefore
Hrethel turned from the gladness of earth to the gladness of
God. He kept on walking until he had passed out of the
world, leaving his lands and his wealth to others.

"After the leave-taking of the king, war broke out between
us and the Swedes. It was in this fight that the second son,
Haethcyn, tasted red death in his mouth. I earned my fees
that day. In that loud battle I strode forward alone, cutting
a swath with my sword, as I swore I should do as long as
breath stayed in my lungs. That was the day I killed the
dreaded crow, the warrior Hugh. I marked him out in the
fray, for he carried the banner of Sweden. My sword, it is
true, could not break a hole in his harness, so I grabbed him
in my arms. I gripped Hugh so hard that I squeezed his
heart out of his bone-box."

The warriors heard him carefully. Then Beowulf stood
up and looked down at them threateningly. "You know I
have wagered my life time and again in my youth. Now that
I am old, I still will not shirk the hardships of kingship. If
I can in some way lure this snake from his hole or cut my
path even into his very den, you know that I am ready to
do it.

"You are my witness," he added, "that I take neither sword
nor ax nor any weapon at all to this struggle. I am hoping to
hug this worm, as I did years ago with Grendel. I am planning to crush his shiny body in my grip and grapple this
vermin against me. But since I foresee that the heat from
his fiery breath would kindle and burn me, I shall hold this
iron shield as a curtain.

"I swear to you now, as I've sworn before, that I never
shall yield one foot's length before him. May God hear my
words and see that I keep my oath! I here swear it before
you and Him. The winged worm and I are about to do battle.

Keep yourselves here on the cliffside. You will be out of harm's way and far enough from the fire's tongues. From here you will see which one of us two stands up . . . when the fiery vomit is quenched."

Then Beowulf fixed tightly his helmet and coat of mail. Holding his new shield before him, he picked his way down the turf of the cliff and strode proud and alone up to the cavern's mouth. Such a fight is not for cowards! Let only the bold fight dragons! . . . He had come to a cleft in the rocks through which poured a red-hot torrent. There was no way at all to go further.

Beowulf stood and taunted the dragon. His words were rough and his curses resounding. "Come out of your hole, filthy, murdering fiend," shouted the hero. The hollow echo bounced on the rocky cliffs and awoke the dragon. He knew it was the hated words of a man. His answer was a roar and a belching of fire that swept around Beowulf, licking his legs and his feet, which the shield did not cover. Beowulf crouched low so as not to fall, for the very ground shook underneath him.

Then the huge worm uncoiled his length and rolled forward to do battle. For an instant he and the hero stood ready. Fear gripped them both. The snake wavered back and forth, and then darted forward. He breathed out long curls of reddish fire. Beowulf, behind his shield, thrust forth only his right arm. In it he had picked up the sword of Ing, well known in olden lore. To his grief the blade bent and burnt up as it flashed on the hide of the worm.

This showed that Wyrd had already written — and none could change it — that this was the day of death. In this battle would Beowulf die. None could gainsay it.

The sword of Ing betrayed its earl. This should not have happened, for it was old and tried, well-smithied and strong, the sword of Ing. Beowulf could only hammer away at the dragon, who burned him up with his breath. That day Beowulf would yield. He would step back, give ground to the snake. That very day would Beowulf step backward, out of his life. His body was charred in the fire. His breath was halting and sore.

From the top of the cliff the warriors never uplifted their shields. Their swords lay ungrasped and idle. Instead, they looked down on their dying earl; their mouths fell open with fear, and they fled away into the bushes. Only one of them stayed. He was a real earl whom even the sight of death could not turn from the bonds of friendship.

This one earl who did not flee was named Wiglaf. When

he saw his king bent low in fire but still fighting, Wiglaff recalled the pledges of a vassal. He thought of the oaths he had made as an earl. Frightened though he was, the young Wiglaf could not run away. With tear-stained eyes, he watched his king still struggling like an earl with the worm. In the boy's ears sounded the old high deeds of the Waegmunding line, his kinfolk and Beowulf's also. Wiglaf recalled the high seat of the king before which he had stood to be dressed in the tokens of manhood, the heirloom sword, the shield, and the mail of his father. Up till this day he had done no feat of arms. This would be his first battle.

Turning in wrath to the earls who cowered behind trees, Wiglaff called, "I remember our oaths. Have you all forgotten? Don't you recall in the house of our king we swore great words? When the king bestowed rings, we bragged very loudly how in the day of death we would pay him back — and many times over — with the weight of our deeds! Why do you think he picked us from among all the warriors? He only a few minutes ago reminded us all of our duty and said that he held us faithful. He only just warned us to be worthy of sword and helmet.

"Well, the day when he needs us is almost spent! Are you going to fail him now, when he has never failed you? Let's go! Let's hurry to him in his sorrow! Pick up your swords! Follow me! God knows I would rather die licked in the fire by the side of my king than to live out my days twitted and scorned as a craven. How could I carry my sword across fields to the mead hall of Beowulf if everyone knew it was only a pretty toy in my hands?"

Without waiting for their answer, Wiglaf brandished his sword, scrambled headlong down the steep path until he stood shoulder to shoulder with Beowulf. Amidst the heat and the choking smoke he tried to shout to his earl, "Dear Beowulf, carry on the deeds as you did in your youth. You said you would never stand evil. You swore you would fight all the foes of mankind!"

Beowulf did not hear him. "Now I bid you, dear Earl," Wiglaf continued to shout through the clouds of black smoke, "to save your own life in this struggle. You are not alone any more. Take new heart. I am here beside you. Can you hear me?"

Now the dragon became all the more swollen with anger, red with hate, to see his two foemen still standing. With evil guile he swirled his tail around their limbs and blew billows of flame at their bucklers. In a twinkling the wooden shield of Wiglaf was in ashes. Nor did his coat of mail save his skin or his flesh. Wiglaf did not turn tail, however. Instead, he hid behind the left arm and strong shield of his earl.

Then Beowulf felt his young kinsman's shoulder against his. Beowulf's heart rose. He gained new strength for another last rush at the worm. With a mighty blow he thrust his own beloved sword Naegling into the head of the dragon. What had Wyrd fore-ordained? Naegling blunted and this time broke into kindling. Naegling, spotted with rust of the years, lacked in strength. The fine sword betrayed its wielder. Beowulf's arm was too strong. It was not given to him to win his fights with man-smithed weapons. The sword bent in his hand, splintered, twisted, and broke.

Then the scourge of the earth, the fire-belcher,[13] rushed for the third bout with the heroes. This blow cost Beowulf dear. The burning jaw and red-hot fangs of the dragon came within inches of his face. Then the worm sank his claws deep into Beowulf's neck, buried them deep below each ear.

The bards through the ages have said how the young Earl Wiglaf stood daring and strong by the side of his king. In this he only fulfilled his sworn oaths. He took no thought then of saving his skin. He did not flinch or cower, even when his hand was burned by the foe. Without a yellow streak in his body, Wiglaf kept hitting the worm from under the shield, aiming low at his guts. Again and again he thrust at the soft white belly of the snake, until little by little the fire began to lessen. Then Beowulf too rallied. With his whetted dagger he slit a gash in the serpent's middle. Thus did Beowulf bring him low! Thus did he shorten his days of harm and evil. Thus the two earls brought the snake down from his lofty sway over the world.

Beowulf lived still, long enough to have his heart gladdened once more. Once more was his life made worthy of praise, even as his eyes grew dim. The gaping tears in his throat burned and stung, for the poison from the worm was slowly seeping through his body. Shortly he felt that it had reached his chest. Still clear-headed, however, Beowulf sank down on a rock near the wall of the dragon's cave. From there he could look inside. He sat and wondered at the hoard of gold and winking stones. They reached almost to the roof. Beowulf marveled to see how the walls were up-

[13] In ancient India the god of thunder, Indra, pierced a cloud with his thunderbolt, causing the cloud to split and flood the dry earth with rain. The hot breath of the dragon, which is the symbol of the cloud, represents the hot winds of drought.

held by huge trunks of rock that the waves had cut from the headland.

As the king fought Death, his earl brought him water in his cupped hands. Wiglaf washed out the gaping tears in his earl's throat. He smoothed the torn flesh and cooled it with more water. Then he carefully slid off Beowulf's helmet. Both knew that the king's days were running out quickly. They both saw how Death waited at his elbow.

"Now would I send my battle gear to my son, if only I had one," whispered Beowulf more to himself than to Wiglaf. "For fifty winters no neighboring king has dared to set foot on my soil. I have bent my head to the will of Wyrd. I have kept what was entrusted to me. I have never sought an unrighteous broil. I have never broken my word. Therefore I leave this life with a light heart.

"Would you go into the dragon's lair, my peerless Wiglaf? Fetch me out some of his hoard. It will brighten my eyes as I take leave of my lands and my kinfolk. The world grows dim already."

Wiglaf had never thought to see on earth such wonders as the hoard of the dragon. Weapons of bygone ages, their hilts encrusted with sparkling gems, tall goblets, chain mail, gold armlets lay in a heap. In the half-darkness they winked and glowed. Scooping some up in his hands, and shouldering a golden battle flag, Wiglaf hurried back to his earl. He hoped to find him still alive.

The king had slumped. With eyes closed he struggled to catch each breath. The poison welled out of his throat. Wiglaf brought more water and finally roused his earl.

"I have not much longer among you," sighed Beowulf. Then his eyes fell on the wealth that Wiglaf had brought from the cave. "I am glad. This gold shall be for my tribe. Will you ask our oldest warriors to build me a barrow? Ask them to climb this headland and build me a death pile high on its top. Let my deathbed rise high above Hronesnesse. So in other years will incoming ships take their bearings by its shape against the sky, and follow its beacon into harbor. This will be my last deed for the Geats."

Then slipping his golden collar from his shoulders and his ring of kingship from his finger, he handed them to Wiglaf. He said:

> "Du eart endelaf
> Usses cynnes
> Wœgmundinga
> Ealle wyrd forspeof

Mine mazas
To metod-sceafte
Eorlas on elne
Ic him æfter sceal."14

"You are the very last of my kin, the only son left of the
House of Waegmunding. Wyrd has swept them all before
her. They were all warriors mighty and true. I shall go
after them ... now."

Those were the last words of the dying Beowulf, king of
the Geats. Wiglaf's heart broke to see his earl slacken and
drop to the wet sand. Not far from Beowulf lay the charred
remains of the worm, eaten by the fire that had fed it. He
would never again streak fiery-tongued across a midnight
sky spreading death and shuddering fear. There he sprawled
on the ground, brought low by the hand of a hero. What
man do you know who has fought such a fight for his people?

Beowulf had scarcely died before the faint-hearts came
crawling out of their burrows. Still and ashamed, they crept
up beside Wiglaf. That earl had not budged from the body
of Beowulf. Bent with grief, he stood staring down at the
mighty king whose soul had fled to its Maker. Finally Wiglaf
noticed that the warriors stood round him.

"Look here," spat Wiglaf, looking them scornfully in the
eyes, "you can tell the truth to the others. You were here at
least. You saw our king stride forth alone to the battle. You
saw him stand up to the fiery worm that burned the flesh
from his body. With all the true men of the Geatish tribes
ready and eager to help him, why did he have to pick you?

"Did you stand shoulder to shoulder with Beowulf at the
hour of his death? No.... You let him drain the cup
alone. You hid and watched Beowulf die. You saw that I
tried to fight, but my puny arms could do nothing. Do your
greedy eyes catch the glints of the gold he won? Yes, Beowulf
won this for you, but I say it shall never be yours!

"You are hereby stripped of your ranks and your lands,
from this day henceforward. Your sons will be penniless!
Your children shall wander from here to there and never
find a dwelling to shelter their nakedness! Your craven hearts
shall be loudly sung through all of our mead halls! For a
warrior death is much better!"

The shrill sound of the war horn blared the news of Beowulf's death inland to his people. Men shuddered throughout
the land. Women wailed and bemoaned their loss. Folks

14 Verse 5621.

knew there would be wars now that no dauntless leader
breasted the foemen for them. They recalled with fear how
the Franks and the Frisians had fought them of old. They
knew the Merovingian lords would be only too happy to sail
proudly up to their towns with fire and with sword. The
Swedes too would come hungrily over to harass them, to
steal their crops. The Swedish kings would darken the land
with their scaffolds and run them through with their swords,
as a pastime.

"Let us bear our king to his barrow. Let us lift the body of
Beowulf and raise it high on the wood we have piled. Our
warrior will hear no more the sweet sound of the harp. Let
not the raven brag to the eagle how he plucked out his eyes,
or how he grew fat and sleek on his flesh. I say to you now,
'Let us lift up our earl. Let us take him in our arms for the
last time. He was a ring-giver, mighty and true!' "

The Geatish warriors gathered beside the cave. In sorrow
and hot tears they gazed for the last time on Beowulf. They
saw by his ashes the length and breadth of the dragon. He
had been fifty feet long at least. Long had he flown through
the air. He never would quiver again. For one thousand
years he had lorded it over the hoard. Beowulf had laid him
low.

How amazing it is to wonder on what day, on what shore,
a warrior will find his death. Even an earl of world-wide
song cannot sit in his mead hall forever. Even he cannot
know when the time will draw near. So was it with Beowulf.
He had not foreseen it either.

The chiefs of the Geats, wise and white-haired, passed
beside the barrow. They muttered queer oaths through their
beards. "May the man who treads on this hoard be swallowed. May he who soils this holy spot be tied to the stone
slabs of the olden gods. May he be hurled into hell. May
he be eaten by bloodsuckers. For our earl-king was not
greedy for gold. If he gathered wealth, it was not for himself. Our king was not a hoarder, but a giver of golden
rings."

Then Wiglaf spoke to them. "You see where our earl lies
dead through the sin of one man. We could not stop Beowulf
from grappling hard with this worm. Let us search out this
hoard, load it in wagons, and carry it all to the headland."

A crowd of carls had been gathering timber for the barrow at the very edge of Hronesnesse Cliff. Around its sides
were stacked the helmets and shields that Beowulf would
never wear again. The body of the dead earl was sorrow-

fully placed at the peak. Then the fire was lighted. Sobs came from the warriors who watched their earl vanish. The wind was hushed. Huge clouds of smoke rose straight up into the heavens. Men moaned as they heard the heart of Beowulf burst.

An old woman with disheveled hair began weeping and singing a doleful song of the sorrows that would soon befall them all. She sobbed and sang of the bloody wars that would burst upon them, of the Viking raids from the stormy sea, of the yoke of serfdom they would all likely wear. The smoke from the burning barrow faded into the blue sky.

During the following weeks the Geats built a stone light-house on the spot where the barrow had stood. For ten days they worked, piling it high and making it strong so that sailors in after years could sight it from the sea even when they were still afar off. They surrounded the whole with a wall. Under this lighthouse they dug a hole and buried the hoard of the worm, the rings and the sparkling stones, all the wealth that their earl had ever won. They gave back to the earth what had been stolen from her in the bygone days. They wanted the gold to become sand again, and the gems to return to stone. There it still lies today, as worthless to us as it was to them.

As night fell, when the sun was only a thin, red streak on the western rim of the world, twelve of the worthiest earls moved in a line around the tomb, singing the Song of the Hero.

They boasted of his might as a warrior should who holds his king as peerless. They sang the song of Beowulf as kinfolk will do to cheer their dead king as he leaves this world, as his soul rushes out to fly through the sea wind. They said that he had been among all the kings of the earth the kindest and sweetest. They said he had been the most beloved of them all, of his people. They said he had been watchful to save his good name and theirs. They said he had never broken an oath nor ever recoiled from a needful deed. They said he was not a taker, but a giver.

They said their King Beowulf had walked upright down the paths of his life like a true man and a hero, that the light of his life should rightfully shine far out over the north-ern sea and be a beacon to others.

2

Wales: Peredur, Son of York

INTRODUCTION

THE STORY OF THE HERO Peredur belongs to the Cymry or
Welsh, one branch of the Celtic-speaking peoples. The Celtic
languages may be divided into three groups: Gaulish,
Brythonic (Welsh, Cornish, Breton), and Goidelic (Gaelic,
Irish, Manx).

A hero named Peredur, who died fighting the Angles in
580 according to a Welsh chronicle, was buried near Picker-
ing, Yorkshire. Celtic tradition has always associated Peredur
with King Arthur and his knights; but, although Peredur
may have been a contemporary of Arthur, his story is much
older. It was told by Welsh bards, or *storiawr*, long before
the Arthurian legends of the Round Table developed.

There are, in fact, elements of the Peredur hero myth that
are common to other Indo-European heroes such as Perseus,
Cyrus, Theseus, and Romulus and Remus. However, there
are elements in it that also recall the revenge motif of the Isis-
Osiris religion in Egypt as well as the death-and-birth of the
seasons in the Ishtar or Venus-Adonis stories. Still another
interesting feature of the Peredur myth links it to European
folklore, particularly to that of another Celtic people—the
Irish.

Wales has a poetic tradition that is well documented. Poems
in Welsh, or Cymraeg, date from the sixth century when four
of their great poets lived: Aneurin, Taliesin, Llywarch Hen,
and Myrddin (the Merlin of Arthurian legend). As early as
the ninth century the bards of the Cymry held song festivals

51

or eisteddfods. There was a great flowering of Welsh literature during the reigns of Rhys ap Tewdwr and Gruffyd ap
Cynan, who came to Wales from Brittany and Ireland respec-
tively in 1077 and 1080. Geoffrey of Monmouth had written,
or translated into Latin, his *History of the Britons* by 1135.
Into this work later writers would delve for material on
Arthur, who kept growing in importance with the passage of
time, particularly among the Celtic refugees in the French
province of Brittany.

The four ancient books of Wales are the *Black Book of
Caermarthen,* the *Book of Aneurin,* the *Book of Taliesin,* and
the *Red Book of Hergest.* This last book contains eleven tales
or *Mabinogion,* among them the Peredur story, long known
and told in the area around the Irish Sea. By the twelfth
century the story had found a great number of skillful adapters
in France, in Holland, and in Germany. Thanks to their
efforts we have from the primitive, Celtic Peredur the most
famous of medieval knights, Sir Percival of the Holy Grail,
and the German Parzifal.

Then in the thirteenth century authors had moved on to
subjects other than those that glorified chivalry. Scholars
have speculated as to why such a popular hero as Percival
should so suddenly have been abandoned. Miss Jessie L.
Weston in her book *The Quest of the Holy Grail* (London,
1913) wondered if this sudden loss of interest could have
had anything to do with the dissolution of the powerful order
of the Knights Templars, and whether any of their mysterious
rites had some direct relation to Percival.

Miss Weston has suggested two theories of this Peredur
myth that seem to stand close examination very well. She
believed that the original story was Druidic and not Christian,
and that it concerned a secret initiation ceremony. All the
adventures of Peredur were examinations which the hero
either passed or failed.

The association of Peredur with the Grail was a French addition to the original story, as were later ideas about his
chastity. Such subsequent heroes as Galahad, Lohengrin,
and Sir Launfal seem to have been patterned after Peredur.

This story is very similar to the rites of primitive cultures
celebrating the death and rebirth of vegetation. The reader
will note how often Peredur rides through a wasteland and
through snow, how the women wail as in the ancient festivals
of Adonis or Tammuz, and how we assume that Peredur can
heal and restore life to the earth. These ancient cults were
called mysteries. As the reader will see, Peredur's is a
very mysterious story. It is moreover a traditional one, the

real meaning of which may even have been forgotten by the time the *Red Book of Hergest* was actually written.

The following is a fairly close but somewhat abridged translation from the Welsh version. Miss Mary Williams of the Universities of Wales and Paris has commented upon the Peredur story at great length in her dissertation of 1909. Her suggestion that it falls into three parts has been adopted. Her study reveals that Parts I and III do resemble accounts of Percival as told on the Continent. Part II, however, which occurs neither in the French nor in the German account, probably represents the original Welsh myth. In Part II references to Irish folklore are numerous, and Arthur's role less apparent. Here Peredur is the real hero who keeps the vassals he conquers for himself.

Not only was Peredur-Percival-Parzifal the most distinctively human and also the best beloved hero of the Middle Ages. His myth has had a strange fortune and a strong influence upon European letters, apparently even having traveled into Spain, where Cervantes seems to have taken material from it. The idea of this myth has been regenerated very recently in twentieth-century fiction, particularly among such French novelists as Samuel Beckett and Robbe-Grillet. For this reason his story may be of very special interest to us now.

Owing to the very unusual nature of the hero Peredur, one has more than an inkling about a medieval ideal that could have been patterned after the teachings of Jesus Himself. Peredur is the pure in heart. He is simple, honest, modest, guileless, a child in the hands of his motivator. There is a pathetic quality about his story that strikes a responsive chord. He makes one wonder if there did not live once during the Middle Ages a person who was the living example and spiritual descendant of this traditional hero whose story was so widespread that it became almost a way of life. There is a strange, haunting quality in Peredur that reminds one of Joan of Arc.

THE CHILDHOOD OF PEREDUR

THE COUNT OF YORK owned estates in the north. He did

not maintain himself principally by his revenues, however, but rather by tournaments, combats, and wars. As usually happens to him who seeks, the count was killed as were six of his sons. His last son was named Peredur. He was the youngest. Since he was too young for combats and wars, he survived. Otherwise he would have been killed along with his father and brothers.

Peredur's mother was an intelligent and resourceful woman. She thought a great deal about her son's future and about his domains. She finally decided to flee to an uninhabited, out-of-the-way spot. Besides her only surviving son she took with her only women, other children, and peaceable, industrious men who were either unable to fight or indisposed to do so. None of these people ever dared mention either horses or weapons in Peredur's presence for fear he would acquire a taste for them.

The little count used to go out into the forest every day to play games with lances he had cut out of holly[1] wood. One day he saw his mother's herd of goats with two does near them. Peredur was surprised to see hornless animals. He decided they were goats that had strayed alone so long that they had lost their horns. He rounded them up with the herd and shut them all up in a forest enclosure. Then he went home.

"Mother," said Peredur, "I just saw an astonishing thing! Two of your goats went wild and strayed so long in the forest that they lost their horns. You can't imagine what a trouble I had to drive them into the pen with the others!"

Immediately everyone went to look. Their amazement was great to see that any child could have had the courage and agility to drive wild deer into a pen!

Another time three knights rode along a forest path. It was Gwalchmei,[2] Gweir, and Owein. They were following the trail of a knight who had shared apples[3] at Arthur's court.

"Mother," asked Peredur. "Who are they?"

"Angels, my boy," she answered.

"Then I am going with them as an angel," said Peredur, and followed them into the woods.

"Tell me, my soul," said Owein to Peredur, "did you see a knight go by here today or yesterday?"

"I don't know what a knight is."

"What I am," said Owein.

---

[1] Holly and mistletoe are druid symbols.

[2] Gwalchmei is Sir Gawain.

[3] "Apple" is *avalla*, from which comes *"Avalon,"* say some.

"If you would tell me what I ask, I would tell you what you ask," replied Peredur.

"Willingly."

"What is this?" asked Peredur, pointing to the saddle.

"A saddle," answered Owein.

Then Peredur questioned him about all his equipment and harness until he had learned their names and their functions. Owein explained them completely. "Ride forward!" Peredur told them. "I saw the sort of man you are seeking. As for me, I shall follow you as a knight. Right now. Today!"

When Peredur returned to his mother he said, "Those were not angels. Those were *knights*, Mother!" Peredur's mother fainted away.

Then Peredur ran out to the yard where the pack horses were kept, those that carried firewood on their backs and brought back food and drink into the deep woods. He picked out a sway-backed gray nag which was bony and thin, but in his opinion the strongest of the lot. He threw a pack saddle over it and then returned to his mother.

"Well," said she. "You want to leave us?"

"Yes," said Peredur.

"Wait first to hear my counsels."

"I'll wait. Talk fast."

"Go straight," said she, "to the court of Arthur, where live the best, the most generous, and the most valiant of men. Whenever you see a church, say a *Pater* near it. If you see food and drink that you need and if no one is courteous enough or good enough to offer it, then help yourself. If you hear screams, go in their direction; there is no yelp more distinctive than that of a young woman. If you see a beautiful jewel, take that also and give it to somebody else. That way you will acquire a reputation. If you see a beautiful girl, make love to her. Even if she doesn't want you, she will consider you more courteous and more powerful than as if you hadn't seduced her."

With sticks and branches Peredur managed to imitate the various accouterments of a knight, as he had seen them on Owein's saddle. Then he left home, holding in his hand a bunch of pointed spears just in case.

For two days and two nights he rode through various wild and uninhabited forests without either food or drink. Then as he passed through a dark and solitary wood, he saw a little glade. Since there was a lodge in its center, Peredur dutifully recited a *Pater* as if it had been a church. Then he rode toward the lodge. The door was open. Near the door was a dark-haired girl seated on a golden chair. She wore on her head a diadem of gold set with precious stones and on her finger a heavy gold ring.

Peredur dismounted and entered. The virgin greeted him kindly and made him welcome. Inside the lodge was a table set with two flagons of red wine, two loaves of white bread, and some slices of milkfed pork.

"My mother told me," said Peredur, "that in whatever place I saw food and drink, I was to take it."

"Go to the table, Prince," she said, "and may God bless you."

Peredur went to the table, ate half of the bread, drank half of the wine, and left the rest for the girl. When he had eaten, he stood up and walked over to her. "My mother," said he, "instructed me that whenever I saw a beautiful jewel, I was to take it."

"Take my soul, if you like," said she. "Don't think I'd hinder you!"

Peredur took her ring. Then he bent his knee before her, gave her a kiss, jumped on his horse, and rode away. No sooner had he left than the knight who owned the glade arrived. He saw the hoofprints of Peredur's nag.

"Tell me," said the Knight of the Glade to the maiden, "who was here after me?"

"A strange man, sir," she answered. Then she told him in detail about Peredur's lamentable equipment and the aim of his travels.

"Tell," he replied, "whether he had you."

"On my word," she said, "he did not."

"On *my* word, I don't believe you. And until I meet him and avenge my anger and shame, you won't sleep two nights in the same spot." Then the knight arose and set out after Peredur.

PEREDUR AT ARTHUR'S COURT

Now PEREDUR was still riding toward Arthur's court. Upon his arrival there, he saw a strange knight ride up and give a gold ring to a groom for holding his horse. The knight

clanked into the hall where Arthur and his attendants, and
Gwenhwyvar and her ladies, sat in state. A bedchamber
page was just holding a goblet out to Gwenhwyvar.

The strange knight seized the goblet from the queen's
hand. Without saying a word, he dashed its contents over
the queen's face and her bosom. Then he slapped her cheeks
and said, "If there is anyone who wishes to dispute with me
over this goblet and avenge the insult to Gwenhwyvar, let
him follow me into the meadow. I'll wait for him there."
Amid a dead silence the knight strode from the hall.

Then the courtiers bowed low their heads for fear they
would be asked to avenge Gwenhwyvar's injury. It seemed
to them that no knight would have dared such an outrage if
he did not possess such strength and valor—or else have such
power in sorcery and enchantments—that he was proof
against their lances.

Just then Peredur made his way into the hall, still mounted
upon his bony gray nag with his makeshift, clumsy trappings.
Kay was standing in the middle of the hall.

"Hey! you long fellow over there," called Peredur. "Where's
Arthur?"

"What does the likes of you want with Arthur?" said Kay.

"My mother told me to go to him and have myself dubbed
a knight."

"My word," said Kay, "you are too ill mounted and too
ill armed!" Even as he spoke the courtiers began to laugh and
to mock Peredur. They threw sticks at him, happy that such
a fellow should have turned up in time to change the subject
from Gwenhwyvar.

Then came into the hall a dwarf, who had sought refuge
there the year before for himself and his female. During
the whole year neither one nor the other had ever spoken a
word. As soon as the dwarf spied Peredur, however, he
cried, "Ha! Ha! May God bless you, fair Peredur, son of
York, leader of warriors and flower of chivalry!"

"Truly, valet," said Kay to the dwarf, "one would have to
be ill advised to have spent a whole year dumb and mute at
Arthur's court, free to choose one's companion for chatting
and drinking, and then to go call, in the presence of Arthur
and his train, a man of this sort 'leader of warriors and flower
of chivalry.'" Kay gave the dwarf such a blow on the head
that he sent him reeling and unconscious the entire length of
the hall. Then the female dwarf arrived.

"Ha! Ha! May God bless you, Peredur, fair son of York,
flower of knighthood and light of chivalry!"

"Truly, woman," said Kay, "that's what I call stupid, to

have remained mute for an entire year at Arthur's court, without saying a single word to anyone at all, and then today, in the presence of Arthur and his warriors, to call such a sight the 'flower of knighthood and the light of chivalry.' " Then he kicked her so hard that she fell in a faint.

"You long fellow, over there," insisted Peredur. "Point out Arthur to me, I said."

"Hush your song," replied Kay. "Look, why don't you go after that knight who waits in the meadow! Take the goblet away from him. Unseat him. Then, you see, you can keep his horse and his armor. After that we shall talk about your becoming a knight."

"Long fellow, I'll do it," said Peredur. He turned his nag about and outside to the meadow. There he found the knight riding up and down, very proud of his strength and his effrontery.

"Tell me, boy," said the knight, "did you see anyone from Arthur's court following me?"

"That tall fellow there ordered me to unseat you, to capture the goblet, and to take your horse and your armor for myself."

"Hush up, silly. Go back to the court and command Arthur from me to come out and fight. And if he doesn't come right away, I won't wait either."

"Upon my word," said Peredur. "You can choose. Whether by your leave or by force, I have been told to take your goblet and your armor." At this, the knight charged Peredur so furiously that with the butt of his lance he hurt the youth between the neck and the shoulder.

"Ah, man," said Peredur. "My mother's people didn't play like that with me. Let's take turns playing that game!" So he hurled one of his holly spears. It pierced the knight's eye so deeply that it came out the nape of his neck. The knight fell over backward dead on the grass.

"In truth," said Owein[4] to Kay, "you were badly inspired to send that young fool after the knight. Either one or the other: he got tumbled off his horse or killed. If the knight threw him, he will count him among the gentry of the court. The result will be eternal shame for Arthur and us. If he killed the boy, the dishonor will be the same, with one more sin for you. May I lose my own honor if I don't go see what happened."

Owein went to the meadow. When he arrived, he was

---

[4] Gwalchmei accompanied Kay in most versions. The knight is the Red Knight, he who killed Peredur's father. The Red Knight's mother is a witch.

amazed to see Peredur dragging the strange knight the length of the field. "Ah, sir!" said Owein. "Wait! I'll help you off with his armor."

"Never," answered Peredur. "This iron dress is a part of him. It will never come off."

Owein showed Peredur how to take off the armor and the rich robes of the knight. "These are for you, my soul," he said. "Wear them in joy to Arthur's court with me."

"May I be disgraced if I go," said Peredur. "You carry the goblet for me to Gwenhwyvar. Say to Arthur that in whatever place I may go, I am his man. Whatever service or advantage I can achieve for him, I shall do it willingly. Add that I shall never go to his court before I have met that long fellow who was there, so that I may avenge the injury to the dwarf and his she-dwarf."

Owein returned to the court and narrated this adventure to Arthur, to Gwenhwyvar, and to the courtiers, without forgetting the threat against Kay. From time to time a vanquished knight rode up to the court from Peredur, and told the same story.

THE FISHER KING, OR THE NEXT EXAMINATION

PEREDUR RODE FORTH until he came to a vast wasteland. There on the edge of the wilderness he found a pond on the other bank of which was a tall castle, surrounded by massive ramparts. By the edge of the water sat a white-haired man on a cushion of gold brocade. His valets were fishing from a rowboat.

When the man saw Peredur, he stood up and returned to the castle. He limped badly. Peredur followed him into the courtyard. The door was open. They entered the hall. There the old man sat on a cushion of gold brocade. The great fire in the hearth had been lighted.

The attendants in the castle all rose courteously to greet Peredur. They assisted him from his horse and lifted off his armor. The old man patted the cushion with his hand, thus inviting the youth to sit by him. They sat beside each other, and they talked. When the time came, the tables were set, and they ate. Peredur sat beside the master. After dinner he asked Peredur if he knew how to use a sword.

"I believe," answered Peredur, "that if I were taught, I should know. He who can use a staff and buckler should know how to fight with a sword."

The old man had two sons, one blond and the other dark. "Stand up, young men," said the man, "and fight with the staff and buckler." They skirmished.

"Tell me, my soul," said the man to Peredur, "which one is better."

"In my opinion, the blond could draw blood whenever he wanted."

"Then take the dark one's weapons and draw blood from the blond, if you can."

Peredur struck the blond youth such a blow that one eyelid fell over his eye and his blood flowed in torrents.

"Good, my soul," said the old man. "Now come and sit by me. You are the most skillful in all this island. I am your uncle,[5] your mother's brother. You will stay with me a while to learn courtesy and manners. Give up your mother tongue. I shall dub you a knight. This is what you are to do from now on: should you ever see something extraordinary, do not inquire about it so long as no one has the courtesy to explain it. The blame will never fall on you, but upon your teacher."

THE SECOND KING AND HIS EXAMINATION

THE NEXT MORNING Peredur arose early, saddled his horse, and with his uncle's permission set out on his quest. First he came to a lonely wood and a flat meadow beyond which he saw a huge fortress and a magnificent palace. The door was open, so he entered. On one side of a large hall sat a majestic man with white hair. Pages surrounded him. They arose to greet Peredur ceremoniously. They seated the youth beside the old man. After dinner the man asked Peredur if he knew how to wield a sword.

"If I were taught, I should know," Peredur answered.

[5] Beowulf was also a king's nephew.

There was in the hall a great iron bar, so large that a man's hand could not grasp it. "Take the sword," said the old man to Peredur, "and strike this iron ring." When Peredur struck the iron bar, he broke it and the sword into two pieces. Then, following instructions, he fitted the pieces together and joined them. Again he struck the bar, and broke it and the sword, and fitted them together. The third time, however, although he broke both the ring and the sword, he could not make them stick together.

"Very good, young man," said the lord. "You may come and sit down, and may God bless you. I see, however, that you have only two-thirds of your strength; you still have to acquire the remaining third! When you have your strength entire, no one will dare to oppose you. I am your uncle, and the brother of the lord who received you last night."

On the heels of these events, there came into the hall two men bearing an enormous lance. Three streams of blood flowed down its head to the floor. At this dreadful sight all the company began to lament and to moan so bitterly that it was unbearable to hear them. Despite all this, the nobleman did not interrupt his conversation with Peredur. He gave no explanation of this occurrence, nor did Peredur ask for one.

After a moment of silence two maidens entered holding between them a huge platter upon which was a man's head resting in a pool of blood. Again all present began to weep and to scream so pitifully that it was embarrassing to be in the same hall with them. Finally they grew still and began to drink as much as they could hold.

PEREDUR IN DISGRACE

THE NEXT MORNING with his uncle's consent Peredur set forth again. He came to a wood from the depths of which he heard screams. Riding in that direction, he came upon a dark-haired gentlewoman standing beside a caparisoned horse. In her arms she held a man's corpse. Every time she pushed the body into the saddle, it fell stiffly to the ground. Then she screamed.

"Tell me, Sister," said Peredur, "why you are screaming."

"Oh, it's Peredur, the excommunicated!" she cried angrily. "Little help we have ever had from you in our sorrow!"

"Why do you say I am excommunicated?"

"For one thing, you caused your mother's death by leaving home against her wishes! Then the two dwarfs you saw at Arthur's court you failed to recognize. They used to belong to your own father! You and I had the same wet nurse; I am therefore your sister. This is my husband, who was killed by the knight of these woods. Don't go near that knight, for he would like to kill you too."

"You are wrong to blame me," protested Peredur. "Now I *shall* have trouble killing him because I have lingered so long with you! If I had stayed longer, I never should have been able to kill him. As for you, stop that screaming. It does no good! I'll bury your dead. Then I'll follow your knight. If I can get revenge for you, I'll do so."

Peredur followed the knight, met him in a clearing, charged and unseated him. When the knight asked for mercy, Peredur said, "I grant it on condition that you take this woman as your wife, and that you leave in her hands all the wealth you owe her as an indemnity for having murdered her husband without reason. Then you will go to Arthur's court. You will tell him that I vanquished you in Arthur's name. You will add that I shall never go to his court before I have met the long fellow and avenged the wrongs to the dwarfs."

The knight lifted the lady into his saddle and rode to Arthur's court. There he told his story without forgetting the threat to Kay. The latter bore the reproaches of Arthur for having caused such a courageous man as Peredur to shun the court.

"This youth will never come to court, nor will Kay ever leave it," said Owein.

"By my faith then," cried Arthur, "I shall search him out in all the islands of Britain until I find him. Then let the one do his worst to the other!"

DAMSEL IN DISTRESS

PEREDUR RODE FORWARD until he came to a lonely wood

where he saw no traces of man or beast, only wild grasses
and bushes. At the end of the wood was a tall castle of rich
exterior surrounded on all sides by massive, high towers. Before its entrance the grass grew thickest.

A scrawny, red-haired boy stuck his head over the battle-
ments and called down, "Choose, lord. Either I open the door
myself or I'll go notify our master that you are at the gate."

"Tell him I am here. If he wants me to enter, I will."

The boy returned at once, unbarred the gate, and preceded
Peredur into the hall. There Peredur saw eighteen skinny
valets all in red,[6] all about the same age and size, all dressed
alike. He praised their skill and courtesy in disarming him.
Then they all sat down and talked.

Later five maidens entered. There was one more noble in
bearing than the others. Peredur was sure he had never seen
such a beauty. She wore an old dress of precious brocade
which had once been elegant but which was now so tattered
that you could see her bare skin through it. Her skin was
whiter than a flower of white glass. Her hair and brows were
blacker than jet. On her cheeks were two red spots, redder
than the reddest red you ever saw. The maiden greeted
Peredur. Then she threw both her arms about his neck and
drew him down on the cushions beside her. Soon afterward
Peredur saw two sisters enter, one bearing a crock of wine,
and the other six loaves of white bread.

"Lady," they said, "God knows there was nothing but this
to eat at the convent tonight." Everyone sat down to supper.
Peredur noticed that the maiden wanted to give him a larger
share of food than to the others.

"Sister," said he, "it is I who will apportion the bread and
the wine."

"Not at all, my soul. It is I."

"Then shame on my beard," he answered, "if I don't!"
Peredur took the bread, cut equal shares for all, and gave
each one his phial of wine. After the meal he called for a
room and went to bed.

"Listen, Sister," said the valets to the damsel, "here is what
we advise."

"What?" she said.

"Go find the youth in his chamber and offer yourself to
him, as a wife or as mistress, whichever he wills."

"That's very improper," she answered, "that I who have
never had anything to do with a man, should give myself to

---

[6] The color red plays a prominent part in Welsh tales.

Peredur before he has even courted me. I wouldn't hear of such conduct for anything in the world!"

"Then let God be our witness," said they, "that if you don't do it, we'll abandon you here to your enemies."

The maiden, weeping floods of tears, rose and went into Peredur's chamber. The squeak of the door awoke him. He saw her standing there with tears rolling down her cheeks.

"Tell me, Sister, why you weep."

"I will tell you, sir. My father owned this castle and the richest fiefs all around. The son of another count asked my father for my hand. I would not go to him willingly, nor would my father force me. Since I am an only child, I inherited all these lands at my father's death. Then I wanted this suitor even less. Therefore he declared war on me, took all my lands, leaving me with only this castle. Thanks to my valiant servants I have been able to resist. Now our food is gone. For the last few days we have lived on what the sisters have been able to forage in the country around us. Now even they have nothing more to eat. Not later than tomorrow the count will renew his attack. If he captures me, he will throw me to his stableboys. Therefore I come to offer myself to you, if you want me, so that you will rescue us all or help us defend this castle."

"Go, Sister," said Peredur, "to bed. And nothing of that sort." The maiden went out of the room and to bed.

Peredur remained with the damsel until he had vanquished her enemies and re-established her authority. On his way from her castle he also met and overcame the Knight of the Glade. After that he met the witches of Kaer Loyw,[7] who took him to their castle for three weeks in order to perfect him in the art of chivalry.

THE RED, THE BLACK, AND THE WHITE

TOWARD DUSK ONE DAY Peredur came to a valley where dwelled a servant of God. This hermit welcomed Peredur to his cell. The next morning the youth set out through the fresh

[7] Gloucester.

snow that had been falling all night. He saw before him a
hawk that had just killed a wild duck. At the sound of the
horse's hoofs, the hawk flew away. Then a crow settled down
on the duck. Peredur reined in his horse. In silence he medi-
tated on the sight of the dead bird. He gazed upon the blackness of the crow, the whiteness of the snow, and the redness
of blood. He recalled that he had seen these three colors
upon the lady he loved the best. Her hair was blacker than
the crow's feathers, blacker even than jet. Her skin was as
white as snow. Her two cheeks were as red as red blood.

Just at that moment Arthur and his courtiers came into
sight.

"Do you recognize that knight of the long lance, he who
is stopped in the woods?" asked Arthur.

"Sir King," said a page, "I will go see."

Peredur was so deep in his trance that he neither heard the
page ride up nor his question. When the page pricked him
with his lance, Peredur turned and absently toppled the page
over his horse's ears into a snowbank. He did the same to
the twenty-four knights who came up, one by one, to ask
who he was.

Then Kay trotted up to Peredur. His questions were sharp
and rude. Peredur caught Kay under the chin with his lance
and threw him to earth so hard that Kay's arm and shoulder
blade were broken. Kay lay there, unconscious in the snow.
His horse, snorting and rearing, galloped back to Arthur.
At first the king and his courtiers thought that Kay was dead.
Then they decided that if a good doctor could be found, the
bones could be made to knit and heal. They carried Kay to
Arthur's own pavilion, for the king loved him dearly.

Peredur still did not awaken from his deep meditation.
Gwalchmei remarked that no one should trouble a knight so
inopportunely when he was sunk in reverie. He observed
that the strange knight had perhaps suffered a loss, or that
he was thinking of the lady he loved. "The knights who
importuned him probably did it rudely. If you wish, Sir
King, I will ask if he is ready to leave off his meditation, and
if so, whether he would not like to come along nicely to
see you."

Gwalchmei found Peredur still leaning upon the shaft of his
lance, still lost in thought. Gwalchmei said quietly, "If I
thought it would be as welcome to you as it is to me, I would
ask you to speak with me. Two of Arthur's men have already
come to invite you to his pavilion."

"I know," said Peredur, "but they introduced themselves
in a very displeasing fashion. They quarreled with me because

I was upset. They disturbed me during my meditation. I was reflecting on the lady I love the best.

"This is how the memory came upon me. I was gazing at the snow, the crow, and the drops of blood from the duck that the hawk had killed on the snow. I recalled that her complexion had the whiteness of snow, that her hair and brows were as black as these black feathers of the crow, and that her cheeks were as crimson as these drops of blood."

"Such a meditation," said Gwalchmei, "has, indeed, a certain character of nobility. It is not at all astonishing that you did not wish to be withdrawn from such a lofty subject."

"Will you tell me if Kay is at Arthur's court?"

"He is. You fought with him last. He has no cause for self-congratulation. You broke his arm and his shoulder."

"Good. I am glad thus to have begun my revenge for the dwarfs."

Gwalchmei recognized Peredur. He threw both arms around the youth's neck and swore his friendship. Then Gwalchmei and Peredur rode side by side to Arthur, joyful and merry. Arthur welcomed Peredur and bade him remain at his side. Peredur returned with Arthur to Caerleon.

Part II

THE VALLEY ROUND

DURING HIS FIRST EVENING, as Peredur was exploring Arthur's castle, he met Angharat of the Golden Hand.[8] "On my honor," Peredur told this damsel, "you are a charming and quite delicious young girl. I could bind myself to love you more than anybody, if you so desired."

"I give you my word," Angharat answered, "that I do not love you and that I shall never desire any part of you."

Peredur replied, "As for me then, I swear that I shall never speak another word until you realize that you love me and long for me more than any man alive!"

[8] Law Euraw.

Next morning Peredur set out. He followed the high road
as it wound along the crest of a mountain. When he had
crossed its heights, he saw below him a circular valley with
a rocky, wooded rim and a flat, green bottom. Fields and
plowed lands alternated. In the center of the forested area
was a group of houses crudely built of black stone. As he
wound past a rocky spur, he saw a lion hitched to a chain.
The sleeping beast barred the path. Behind it was an abyss
filled with the white bones of men and animals. Peredur
unsheathed his sword and dealt the lion such a blow that it
dropped into the chasm. Then he cut the chain from which
it dangled and watched the huge beast fall on the pile of
bones.[9] After that Peredur led his horse down the winding
path into the valley.

There he came to a beautiful castle. In its courtyard sat a
gray-haired man, the tallest man Peredur had ever seen. A
dark-haired youth and a blond one were flipping knives. Their
knife handles were made of whalebone. When the old man
saw Peredur, he growled, "Shame on the beard of my porter!"
Peredur knew he referred to the lion.

At supper they were joined by a lady and her daughter,
both taller than any ladies Peredur had ever seen. During
the meal Peredur and the girl chatted until her face became
clouded and she fell silent. She whispered to Peredur that
she had fallen in love with him and therefore feared his
death in the morning. When Peredur asked for her help, the
girl managed to have his horse and armor left beside his lodging that night. The next morning he arose early, armed himself, and vanquished in succession the giants who dwelled
in the crude stone buildings, the two youths, and then the
lord of the castle. He sent the white-haired man to Arthur's
court to swear homage and be baptized.

"I thank God," Peredur said to himself, "that I did not
break my oath not to speak a word to a Christian!"

PEREDUR'S WOUND

As PEREDUR RODE FORTH AGAIN, he saw only a forlorn and

---

[9] Sir Walter Scott observes in *Ivanhoe,* Chap. 35, that the phrase *Ut
Leo semper feriatur* (Let the Lion always be struck—or killed) seems
to be a signal word of the Order of the Knights Templar.

barren country. The only house he found was a poor cottage. There he heard of a huge snake that crouched over a golden ring. This snake would allow no one to live within a radius of seven miles. Peredur sought out the snake. H fought him furiously, tirelessly, and with glorious success. He killed the snake and took its golden ring. Then for a long time Peredur lived a wanderer's life without ever exchanging a word with any kind of Christian. This was why the color faded from his cheeks, and he lost his great beauty. His pallor was the result of the extreme sorrow he felt not to be at Arthur's court, near the lady he loved the best, and near Gwalchmei. Finally he rode toward Caerleon.

Along the road he met the people of Arthur, riding with Kay at their head to deliver a message. Although Peredur recognized them all, he was so thin and so pale that not one of them recognized him.

"Where are you coming from, sir?" said Kay. He asked Peredur the question again and a third time. Peredur said not a word. Kay then struck the youth with his lance and pierced his thigh.[10] Since he would not break his vow, Peredur passed on without avenging the injury.

Then Gwalchmei protested, "By me and by God, Kay, you behaved badly in mistreating that youth as you did, only because he could not speak!" Gwalchmei escorted Peredur to Arthur's court and said to Gwenhwyvar, "Princess, do you see with what cruelty Kay has treated this boy who could not speak? For God's sake and for mine, have him attended by doctors until I return. I shall repay this service!"

While Peredur was living, still unrecognized, at Arthur's court, a knight rode up to the meadow at Caerleon. He wanted to fight. And he found what he sought. However, this knight overcame every opponent for a week. There he strutted in the meadow, vanquishing his one knight per day!

One morning as Arthur and his knights were coming from church, they passed this saucy knight in his meadow, his battle standard raised to invite combat. "Ah! my courageous ones," sighed Arthur, "by your valor I shall not leave this spot until I have had my arms and my horse brought to me so that I can fight this oaf!" As pages were leading Arthur's horse to him, they passed by Peredur. Still without speaking, Peredur put on Arthur's armor, mounted Arthur's horse, and rode across the meadow.

Then everyone, seeing the mute knight mount and ride to combat, climbed on the roofs of the houses or on the hills

[10] A euphemism.

to look. Peredur gave a sign with his hand that the challenger
could begin the combat. Even when the knight charged him
full tilt, Peredur never budged from his place. Then it was
Peredur's turn. He spurred his horse across the meadow,
furious and valiant, terrible and mighty. He gave the knight
such a sharp, poisoned, hard, and searing blow under the
chin—a blow worthy of a knight that has three-thirds of his
strength—that Peredur lifted his challenger clear out of his
saddle and hurled him a good distance away. Then Peredur
trotted back, returned the horse and armor to the squires,
and trudged on foot along the dusty road to the court. People
lined the way and called him "the mute youth."

As Peredur entered Arthur's hall, he met Angharat of the
Golden Hand. "By me and by God," said she, "it is a great
pity that you cannot speak. If you could, I should love
you more than any other man, and upon my word, even
though you cannot speak, I will love you even so, the best
in all the world!"

By his faithful love for Angharat was Peredur recognized.
He remained in the company of Gwalchmei, Owein son of
Urien, and all those of Arthur's court, and he lived at Arthur's
court, at Caerleon on the Wye.

THE EMPRESS OF CRISTINOBYL

DURING THIS TIME Peredur accomplished successfully the
quest of the one-eyed Black Knight. On his way to kill
the Serpent of the Cairn he met the most beautiful damsel
in the world. She gave him a magic stone and told Peredur
that if he wished to find her, he could ride in the direction
of India.

Holding the stone in his hand, Peredur rode toward a valley
which was traversed by a river.

*Ac ynteu a doeth racda6 parth a dyffryn avon. A
gororeu y dyffryn oed yn goet. Ac o pop parth yr avon
yn weirglodeu g6astat. Ac or neill parth arall y g6elei
kad6 o defeit duon. Ac val y brefei vn or defeit g6ynyon
y deuei vn or defeit duon dr6od. Ac y bydei yn wen. Ac*

*val y brefei vn or defeit duon y deuei vn or defeit
g6ynnyon dr6od ac y bydei du.*[11]

Its slopes were wooded, but from the two banks of the
river stretched even meadows. On one bank was a flock of
white sheep; on the other a flock of black ones. Every time a
white sheep bleated, a black one would cross the river and
become white; whenever a black sheep bleated, a white one
crossed and became black.

At this river's edge stood a tree which was on fire from
roots to tip on one side, but green and leafy on the other
side.

Through the amazing virtues of the stone Peredur overcame the reptile. He won vassals for himself, including a
Red Knight who loved the Countess of Prowess. Then he
rode forth in search of the beautiful maiden who had given
him the magic stone.

Peredur rode eastward until he came to the prettiest river
valley he had ever seen. There were pitched many brilliantly
colored pavilions; but more strange, the valley was dotted
with watermills and windmills. The first man Peredur met
was tall and swarthy. Although Peredur took him for a car-
penter, the man said he was the chief miller of all the windmills.

"May I find lodging with you?" asked Peredur.

"Willingly."

Once Peredur was lodged in the miller's house, he borrowed
money from his host to provide food and drink for the household, saying that he would earn the sum in the tournament
before he left. He asked the miller why there were so many
pavilions of knights and such crowds of people.

"Either one or the other," answered the miller. "Either
you come from far away, or you are not in your right mind.
There resides here the most beautiful lady in the world. She
is the empress of Cristinobyl the Great, the lady who will
only have as her husband the most courageous man in the
world, for she has no need of riches. That is why you see
so many mills; we have to provide food for all her suitors."

The next morning Peredur, clad in full armor, set out for
the daily tournament. On his way he spied his beautiful girl,
she who had given him the magic stone. She was looking
out of a silk pavilion. Peredur had never gazed on one so
lovely. The longer he stood and gazed, the deeper in love he
fell. He stood without moving or speaking from early morn-

[11] From the manuscript Peniarth 4; 6=the letter *w*.

ing until noon, and from noon until evening. When that day's tournament ended, he returned to his lodging, obliged to borrow more money from the miller. The miller's wife was displeased, particularly when Peredur spent the second day as entranced as he was the first.

On the third day as Peredur still stood enthralled, gazing upon the exquisite beauty of the lady, the miller came up behind him and cracked him on the shoulder with a hatchet handle. "Do one or the other," the miller told Peredur. "Either clear out of here, or go enter the lists."

Peredur grinned at the miller and went forth to joust. When he had overcome all his opponents, he sent them as presents to the empress. With the horses and their trappings he was able to repay the miller's wife. Peredur returned each day to the tournament until he was the sole remaining knight on the field. Then the empress sent for him. Peredur paid no attention to her summons the first time. She sent again. Still he ignored her. The third time she dispatched one hundred knights with orders to bring Peredur to her feet, by force if necessary.

Peredur played straight with the one hundred knights. He trussed them up as one would a kid and tossed them all into the moat. Then the empress in despair sent a wise old man, who politely requested Peredur to call upon the empress. He told Peredur that the empress loved him passionately. That time Peredur went to her hall, but he took the miller with him. Peredur sat down on the first seat he came to, so the empress was obliged to walk across the hall to him. After he had exchanged the time of day with her, Peredur returned to his lodgings.

The next day he waited upon the empress again. No seat of honor had been prepared for him, for no courtier could guess where he would choose to sit. As the lovers were chatting, a black man entered. He carried a golden goblet filled with wine. Falling upon his knees, he entreated the empress to bestow the cup only upon that man who consented to fight him for her hand. Peredur took the goblet, drank the wine, and tossed the goblet to the miller's wife.

Then an even taller man entered, bearing a horn goblet filled with wine. Peredur took that one also. The third man was even bigger than the first two. His hair was curly and red. His goblet was made of crystal. The next morning Peredur left his lodgings, killed the three warriors, and sat down in the empress' hall.

"Beautiful Peredur," said the empress, "do you remember

that you promised to love me more than any other lady if I gave you the stone that helped you to slay the crocodile?"

"Princess," he answered, "it's the truth. I remember." Then Peredur stayed in Cristinobyl and governed with the empress for fourteen years.

THE BLACK GIRL AT CAERLEON

FOUR KNIGHTS—Owein, Gwalchmei, Howel, and Peredur of the Long Lance [12] were seated on a brocade carpet in the main hall of Arthur's castle when the Black Girl entered. Her hair was black and curly. She rode a yellow mule which she slapped with thick leather thongs. Her appearance was uncouth and ugly. Her face and hands were blacker than the blackest iron dipped in pitch. Even that was not the most striking aspect of her.

The most striking aspect of the Black Girl was her body. Her cheekbones were too high, and her chin was too long. Her nose was too short, and her nostrils were too wide. One of her eyes was a shiny greenish-blue. The other eye was jet black and sunken in her skull. Her teeth were long and yellow, yellower than the flowers of the furze bush. Her belly was pointed and so high it met her chin. Her spine was as crooked as a scythe handle. Her thighs were wide and bony over legs like sticks. Her knees and feet were huge.

The Black Girl greeted everyone at the court politely, except Peredur. "Peredur," she said accusingly, "I won't greet you because you don't deserve it! Destiny was certainly blind when she allowed you to become favored and famous! When you went to the Court of the Lame King, when you saw the bleeding lance brought in before you, when you saw with your own eyes the three streams of blood and other prodigies too, you neither asked the reason nor the cause of them. If you *had* asked, the Lame King would have recovered his health for himself and prosperity for the land. Because of you there will always be wars and famines, women left widowed, and damsels without wealth or food! All these winter calamities just because of you!"

[12] Baladyr Hir.

Then the Black Girl shamed Arthur with her sad stories of beleaguered castles, damsels in distress, and five hundred and sixty-six fierce knights still to be overcome. Gwalchmei and the other knights hastened to right these wrongs. There was a bustle of departure and a clanking of armor in the hall. Horses were saddled posthaste. Only this time Peredur was not duped. He remained thinking. "Upon my word," he said finally, "I see that I must not sleep until I have solved the mystery of the bleeding lance!"

Peredur set out on this quest through all the islands, hunting night and day for news of the Black Girl. Finally in the valley of a strange river he met a priest of whom he requested a blessing.

"No, unhappy Peredur," said the priest, "you don't deserve my blessing. Nor will it ever bring happiness to wear armor on a day like this!"

"Why, what day is it?"

"It is Good Friday."

"Please don't reproach me," cried Peredur. "I didn't know it was spring. I have then been wandering a year to the day!"

Peredur walked along the forest paths until he came to the Bald Castle. There in the hall he met the priest again. This time he received the Father's blessing. For three days the priest instructed Peredur, and taught him how to find the end of his quest. He directed Peredur to a nearby castle where he could inquire about what he had always sought, Castle Marvelous!

CASTLE MARVELOUS

PEREDUR FOUND THE Castle Marvelous, which he had sought so long, in the middle of a lake. Its gate stood open. When he entered the hall, he saw a chessboard where the pieces were playing all by themselves. He sat down and helped one side, but his side lost. Then the winners all began to boast and to shout so loudly that Peredur lost his temper. He grabbed the chessmen and tossed the board into the lake.

He had no sooner done this than the Black Girl appeared.

She was very angry. "May God never forgive you!" she screamed. "You're always doing everything wrong!"

"*Now* what do you expect of me, Black Girl?" asked Peredur.

"Look what you just did! You threw the princess's game away. She wouldn't have that happen for all her vast empire!"

"Is there any way that I can recover it then?"

"Well, yes, if you went to Kaer Ysbidinongyl. There's a black man there who is laying waste the domains of our princess. If you killed him, you could win back her chessboard. However, if you go to Kaer Ysbidinongyl, you will be killed."

"Will you serve as my guide to that place?"

"No," said the Black Girl, "but I *will* show you the road."

Peredur traveled all the way to Kaer Ysbidinongyl, where he overcame the black man, who in exchange for his life promised to return the chessboard. Peredur rode back to Castle Marvelous only to find the Black Girl angrier than ever.

"Now may the curse of God fall upon your head for your trouble, for having let live such an accursed ravager. Now he will continue to ruin our lands and our crops! I told you to kill him!"

"I left him his life," replied Peredur, "so that he would put back the chessboard."

"Well, it's not in the same place as it was before," she retorted. "Retrace your steps, and this time, kill him!" Peredur went all the way back and killed the black man.

Then when he had returned to Castle Marvelous, he insisted upon seeing the Princess. "By me and by God," said the Black Girl, "you won't see her this time either unless you kill the demon that haunts our forest."

"What sort of demon is it?"

"It's a deer as fleet as the swiftest bird that flies. It has in its forehead one horn as long as the staff of a lance, and as pointed as the most pointed lance there is. He nibbles up all the branches of all the trees and eats all the grass in all the forest glades. He kills every living animal he can find, which doesn't matter so much because those he doesn't hunt out die of starvation anyway. Worse even than that, he comes down every evening to the fish pond. He drinks all the water in it so that we have no fish to eat either. Even the minnows die before fresh water can seep into the pool."

"Maiden," said Peredur, "will you show me where this creature is?"

"Certainly not," she retorted. "I have helped you enough. Not a soul has dared go into the forest for over a year. You may take the princess' little spaniel with you, however. He will drive the wild beast toward you, and then you can kill it."

The little dog scented the animal, and drove it toward Peredur. The beast with lowered horn attacked furiously. Peredur side-stepped, let it rush past him, and as it did so, cut its head clean off with his sword. Before Peredur could lift up the head, a lady on horseback galloped up to him, crying, "Ah, Sir Knight, you have conducted yourself in a most unchivalrous fashion in so destroying the most rare jewel in all my domains." Then she settled the dog in the folds of her cloak and the deer's head, with its brilliant red collar, next to her body.

"I was asked to do it," replied Peredur. "Is there no way at all for me to win your friendship?"

"Yes. Go up to the summit of that mountain you see over there. Then hunt for a bush under which lies a flat stone. Call aloud three times for a champion to fight you. Thus you will deliver us all."

This time Peredur did exactly as he was told. Out of the ground beneath his feet rose a black knight with antique, rusted armor. He rode a bony, emaciated horse. Every time Peredur struck him from his mount, the aged knight vaulted to the saddle again. Finally Peredur dismounted and drew his sword. Then before he even saw what happened, the rusty knight disappeared before his eyes. He took Peredur's horse with him, and also his own.

Peredur set out on foot down the steep mountainside. As he walked, he saw across the valley a castle with massive towers. When he arrived there, the door was unbarred, so he entered. In the hall sat of all people the gray-haired king who limped. Seated by his side was Peredur's friend, the knight Gwalchmei. Then Peredur noticed that his own horse was stabled beside that of Gwalchmei. Both the Fisher King and Gwalchmei greeted Peredur with great joy. The king made room for Peredur on his other side.

Soon afterward the youthful blond youth entered and knelt before Peredur, begging his friendship. "Sir," he said, "it was I who traveled to Arthur's court disguised as the Black Girl, and I so disguised also when you threw away the chessboard of the princess, and when you killed the dark man of Ysbidinongyl, when you rid us of the devouring deer,

and when you combated the wintry knight at flat rock. It
was I also who carried the bleeding head on the grail, and I
who showed you the lance with its stream of blood the
length of the blade.

"The head was that of your first cousin, he who was slain
by the witches of Kaer Loyw. It was they who also crippled
your uncle. I am also your cousin. It was written that you,
Peredur, would avenge all these wrongs."

Peredur and Gwalchmei decided to send for aid to Arthur's
court. Then all the knights of Britain campaigned against
the witches. One witch tried to kill a knight, but Peredur
prevented her. A second time she also wanted to kill a knight
before Peredur, but he prevented her. The third time a witch
did kill a knight before Peredur. Then Peredur unsheathed
his sword. He struck her such a blow upon the point of her
helmet that he bent it inward, cut through the metal, and slit
it in two.

With a piercing scream the witch ordered the others to
retreat. "It is our pupil Peredur, he whom we instructed in
chivalry. It was written ages ago that he would kill us!"

Then Arthur and his knights began to wield their swords
through the air, right and left, as the witches whirred past
them. They fought until they had killed every last one.

That is the story they tell of Peredur in Castle Marvelous.

3

France: The Song of Roland

INTRODUCTION

The Song of Roland is probably the most famous piece
of medieval French literature. Its renown is due in great
part to the enthusiasm it created among the French Romantic
poets of the nineteenth century. It is a curious fact that, although the enormous and largely unknown body of literature
produced in France from 1000 to 1500 is vastly more extensive than that of any other European nation, by the French
it is still held in a disrepute that dates from the Classical
seventeenth century. Where England has the one great epic,
Beowulf, France has eighty of them. The *Roland* poem belongs to one cycle of epics centered about the life of Charlemagne.

Because of the great popularity of the *Roland,* the epic
became one of the chief literary forms for those writers who
wished to compose in French. Latin was the language of
education in all the western European countries. Latin literature continued to develop side by side with works in the
vernaculars, and popular pieces such as the *Roland* were
translated into Latin so that everyone could read them. Although the *Roland* is not the oldest extant literary document
in the French language, it is the oldest masterpiece.

France dominated the European literary scene during the
Middle Ages. The reader will see how the themes from
Beowulf as well as those from the story of Peredur appear
in French literature, vastly polished and developed during
those centuries when Old French was also the language of

England. Into France, the center of learning and culture, hundreds of stories converged, were treated, and then radiated throughout Europe.

The author of *The Song of Roland* is unknown; its date (*c.* 1100?), its origin, and its purpose are still highly disputed. It seems obvious from the tone and language of this poem, however, that it was composed by one man, and that he was not only a great poet, but also well educated. He knew not only certain classics, but also a great deal about history and geography. He was patriotic, religious, and chauvinistic. He certainly did not attempt to write about Charlemagne with any degree of exactness, for that emperor's engagement at Saragossa was not the brilliant victory the poet pretends. Like all artists he has transformed his initial situation. Régine Pernoud, one of the most distinguished of modern medievalists, points out that using the subject as a pretext is a characteristic of medieval art.

As the reader will see, our poet is partial to certain localities in northern France, and also to those churches and monasteries along the pilgrims' route to Saint James of Campostella. This was noted by the greatest scholar of this epic, Professor Joseph Bédier (1864-1938).

Upon the barest framework of historical fact—his Charlemagne was a real king—our author has given us a picture of a cultural and national ideal, the imaginary Roland. He was writing at a time when the great nobles of Europe were embarking upon that fantastic series of foreign wars they called the Crusades. The First Crusade lasted from 1096 to 1099. It is also true that Charles Martel had stopped the spread of Islam into France at Poitiers in 732. He is supposed to have fought an army of 90,000 Mussulmans.

In *The Song of Roland* we have a kind of meshing of the earlier themes—the horn, the sword, and the lance—which will be further expanded, by such great writers as Chrétien de Troyes, into the final Grail stories and Arthurian legends. There is no longer any trace, in the *Roland,* of either resistance to Christianity, of survivals of Scandinavian gods, or of Druidism. France was devoutly Christian; her Vikings or Normans outdid the rest of France in religious fervor. France was, indeed, the right arm of the church. The scene is already set for Saint Louis and the subsequent Crusades.

The religious aspects of this poem, its prayers in particular, have been exhaustively studied by Sister Marie Pierre Koch in her dissertation published in 1940 by the Catholic University of America Press. No definitive explanation has been given, to my knowledge, of the letters *AOI* that occur in the text. Scholars have suggested that they have a religious significance, such as has the word "Alleluia."

As *Beowulf* testified to the earliest known origins of feudalism, so the *Roland* explains the operation of a feudal court where the king is only a vassal among his vassals, where appointments are made by nomination, and where the majority vote prevails over the king. Here is Act I of the great drama between the Roman concept of divine right of kings and the equally well entrenched Germanic system that will succumb under Louis XIV. His absolute monarchy entailed the swift destruction of that institution in France.

The *Roland* is written in Old French, a beautiful language with a vocabulary much larger and far more expressive than that of modern French. Many of its most picturesque words and expressions were systematically reduced by the French writers and scholars of the seventeenth century. A great many of these words remained, however, in English, and it is much easier for the American student to read Old French than would be imagined. Some of its themes and attitudes were also saved for us by our foremost medievalist, Shakespeare, who could very well have agreed with the author of the *Roland* that lyric poetry and epic poetry harmonize, and that historical events make the finest setting for the development of a poet's political and personal convictions.

Although the fifteenth-century French poet who is known to English lovers of poetry as Charles of Orleans said "Roland and Saint Louis" when he thought of the heroes of France, the "Roland" poem was "discovered" at Oxford University by a French scholar, Francisque Michel, in 1837. Another copy dating from the fourteenth century was later found in Venice, for Roland—renamed Orlando—was wholeheartedly adopted in Italy.

Among the legions of great authorities on this poem, aside from M. Bédier, are Gaston Paris, Maurice Wilmotte, Gustave Cohen, Ferdinand Lot, Ernest Curtius, Camille Jullian, and Dean Arthur Sideleau of the University of Montreal.

It may be of interest to readers of my *Ancient Myths*[1] to note that the *Chanson de Roland* is contemporary with the *Shah Nameh* of Persia.

---

[1] New American Library, New York, 1960.

ROLLANZ

Carles li reis, nostre emperere magnes,
Set anz tuz pleins ad estet en Espaigne:
Tresqu'en la mer cunquist la tere altaigne.
N'i ad castel ki devant lui remaigne;
Mur ne citet n'i est remes a fraindre,
Fors Sarraguce, ki est en une muntaigne.
Li reis Marsilie la tient, ki Deu nen aimet.
Mahumet sert e Apollin recleimet:
Nes poet guarder que mals ne l'i ateignet.   [Verses 1-9]

Carles the King, our great Charlemagne,
Seven full years has campaigned in Spain,
Up to the sea has conquered proud domains.
There is not a castle that before him remains,
Not a rampart nor city has he to gain
Save Saragossa, which is on a mountain.
King Marsilie hoids it whom God disdains;
He serves Mohammed and Apollo acclaims
Marsilie found *they* were not sovereign!

[V. 815] High are the peaks and the valleys dark! The
Pyrenees tower into the clouds above their dizzy passes. All
day long Carlemagne[2] and the Franks ride northward through
the mountains in such great numbers that the very earth
shakes. Straining their eyes, the knights gaze across the
foothills, hoping to catch their first sight of France. Thoughts
of their home and families whom they left seven years before
bring tears to their eyes. More than his knights is King
Carles full of grief, for behind him, at the gates of Spain, he
has stationed his nephew Rollanz. The twelve peers of
France and twenty thousand knights are still back in Spain
to assure the rear guard!

   [2] Proper names have often been left in Old French because of their
musical effect: Rollanz, Carles, Carlemagne, etc.

Now Carlemagne weeps; he cannot hide his tears. "I feel danger behind me!" says the king. "I fear Rollanz is in danger, for Guenes named him to command the rear guard. . . . If I lose Rollanz, I shall never have exchange!"

[V. 999] Clear is the day in Spain, and radiant the sun! Four hundred thousand Sarrazins, under King Marsilie of Saragossa, spur their horses northward! Crimson, blue, and white flash their banners in the sun. A thousand trumpets shrill as they ride in serried ranks. Their clarions call through the thin mountain air, and alert the rear guard of the Franks, who are almost at the pass.

"Sir Companion," asked Oliviers of his friend Rollanz, "can it be that the Sarrazins have followed?"

"If they have," Rollanz answered Oliviers, "then it is the will of God. We shall make our stand here. Every vassal knows what he must suffer for his king—distress, and heat and cold. Let every baron strike great blows for Carlemagne!"

Oliviers climbed a hill to look toward the south. There he saw such a host of Sarrazins coming that he could not even count them. Their helmets glittered in the sun and their shields; their satin banners floated over a sea of rhythmic, mounted knights. "Rollanz, sound the horn!" cried Oliviers. "Carlemagne will hear it and come back!"

"I shall not call for aid! I shall not sound the horn!" Rollanz answered his friend. "In doing so I would lose my good name in my beloved France. Durendal will run in blood today up to its golden hilt! Let the pagans spur northward to the portals! I swear to you here; they are bent unto death. May neither God nor the angels suffer shame because of us! Halt! Let us wheel about and fight them!"

Among the twelve peers was the Archbishop Turpins. Standing on a hillock, he called the Franks to him. "Dismount and pray, for the battle draws near." Then he blessed the valiant knights and gave them absolution. "As penance I command you to strike a blow for God!"

The sunny-faced, the smiling Rollanz reviewed the peers. He rode his swift war charger and brandished high his lance. Its pennants were pure white with long, streaming tassels. "Sir Barons, before evening we shall have won a wealthy prize. These pagans that spur after us are seeking martyrdom." As Rollanz, sheathed in armor, cantered Veillantif down the line of the Franks, their battle cry "Mountjoy" rose from twenty thousand throats. They knew Guenes had sold them to King Marsilie of Saragossa. Then Guenes had appointed

Rollanz to the rear guard. They knew they were betrayed.

Opposite the Franks lined up the hosts from Spain, vassals and allies of Marsilie of Saragossa. "Cowardly French, ride forth and tilt with us! Today your Carlemagne will lose his *right hand*. Foolish was your king to leave his nephew Rollanz at the pass! Do you know you were sold and betrayed into our ambush by your own Baron Guenes?"

Rollanz struck the first blow that day at Roncevals. With his sword Durendal he split the taunter's body. "No, son of a slave, our King Carles knew whom to trust! No shame shall fall on him, on us, or on our gentle France!" Second to Rollanz, Oliviers marked out his man, dug his golden spurs into his horse's flanks and charged the pagan foe. Third into their ranks lumbered the Archbishop Turpins, marked out a prince of Barbary, and slew him with his boar spear. Then the good Sir Gerin sent a heathen's soul to Satan. Gerin's friend, the Knight Gerier, next pierced a pagan peer. Duke Sansun attacked next, and after him Anseïs. "That was a worthy arm," cheered Rollanz. Then Engelers of Gascony, Oton, and Berengier accounted for three more. Of the twelve Spanish peers, only Margariz and Chernubles still lived a few minutes more.

The twelve peers of France fought like lions on that field. With each blow Rollanz split a Sarrazin's skull, sectioned his body, and severed the horse's spine. He swung about him in scythe strokes. At one moment he passed Oliviers, who was braining enemies with his shivered lance. "Where's Halteclere, your sword?" Oliviers had been too busy to unsheathe it! . . . By hundreds, then by thousands, they strewed the field with pagan dead. Many a gallant French knight also gave up his young life at Roncevals.

Across the Pyrenees all France waited. All France knew that it was a tragic day. From the Mont-Saint-Michel to Saints, and from Besançon to Ouessant, walls crumbled in every house! At noon there grew a darkness in the sky and a great hush broken only by streaks of chainfire and thunder. A hollow wind swept from mountain to seacoast. Huge chunks of hail rattled on the thatch. People crowded together for comfort. They spoke only in whispers. "Here has come the day of judgment and the end of the world!" They did not know and therefore could not say the truth: it was grief sweeping across fair France for the coming death of Rollanz!

Even as the Frankish peers stood masters of the field, they heard a distant rumbling like the waves of the seacoast. Then hove into sight the main body of the Spanish army,

twenty battalions on the double, and seven thousand trumpets
sounding the charge. At their head galloped, his dragon pennant streaming in the hot summer sun, Abisme, the daring
leader of the infidels. The Archbishop Turpins marked him
well. "That Sarrazin is a heretic. Much better I should kill
him, for I have always hated cowards!" Turpins spurred his
yellow-maned Danish charger and smashed his lance into the
amethysts and topazes that gleamed on Abisme's shield. Turpins ran him through. Then he wheeled back and encouraged
the Franks, "Sir Barons, go not with somber thoughts! Beyond this last day we shall live no more on earth. Therefore
strike your blows today for God and for France! I am here
to guarantee you all a seat in Paradise."

Then a count of Saragossa, Climborins by name—he who
had kissed Guenes on the mouth for his treason—unhorsed
and killed Engelers of Gascony. What a loss was that for
the Franks! Oliviers saw it and took revenge. Then the
heathen Valdabrun—he who had taken Jerusalem by treachery, violated the temple of Solomon, and killed the Patriarch
before his fonts—slaughtered the distinguished Duke Sansun.
"God! What a baron was he!" moaned the Franks. Rollanz
struck down Valdabrun, split his skull, his byrnie, his jeweled
saddle, and his horse's spine. Then charged from the Spanish
ranks an African son of a king, who cut the vermilion-and-
azure shield of Anseïs, killed that noble baron. "Baron
Anseïs, what a pity is your death!" moaned the Franks. Then
from the middle rode out the Archbishop Turpins. Never
tonsured priest ever did such deeds of prowess. "You have
just killed a baron whom my heart regrets," said Turpins
as he struck the African dead.

Grandonie, the heathen son of Cappadocia's king, crushed
the crimson shield of Gerin, then killed Gerier his companion, and after them Berengier. "See how our numbers
dwindle!" moaned the Franks. Rollanz saw those heathen
blows. Grandonie had never seen Rollanz in his life, and
yet he recognized him. Despite the noise and confusion of
battle, Grandonie knew Rollanz at once. Rollanz was the
open-faced, proud-eyed, the graceful, handsome knight. All
at once Grandonie was afraid. Rollanz did not let him
escape. With one stroke of Durendal he slit the helmet of
Toledo steel as far as the nose, then cut through the teeth and
lips, unthreaded the chain mail, ripped through the silver
pommel, and crushed the horse's spine. Then cried the
Franks, "Carles's *right hand* guarantees us!" Drops of bright
blood trickled through the green field of Roncevals.

In the Book of Deeds it is well written that the Franks had

killed up to this moment four thousand of their foes. They stemmed the first four attacks, but the fifth one cost them dear. All the Franks were dead, except for sixty knights whom God had thus far spared. They saw what there was to do: they must fetch a high price!

"Sir Knight and dear companions," shouted Rollanz to Oliviers, "with all these knights dead, France will remain a desert! I shall now wind the horn!"

"To sound it now would be unworthy of us all! . . . How bloody are your arms, dear Rollanz!"

"I have been dealing bloody blows. . . . Why are you angry with me now?"

"All this carnage is your fault! You outstretched yourself today. If you had listened when I spoke, King Carles would be here now. You have lost us by your pride, Rollanz. Before evening you and I will say farewell."

As Rollanz and Oliviers stood quarreling, the Archbishop Turpins came between them. "Sir Rollanz! Sir Oliviers! By God, I beg you to stop! The horn can no longer save us. Yet, on the other hand, it would still be better for Rollanz to sound it. Why? Because the Franks will return with our army. They will gather up our bodies and carry them over the mountains. They will not leave us as carrion for wild dogs and wolves. They will inter us in the crypts of our cathedrals."

"Sir, well spoken," answered Rollanz. He lifted the horn to his lips and blew with all his might, until his temples burst and the salt blood burst through his throat.

High are the peaks and loud the voice of the horn! For thirty leagues around its shrill tongue blared. Far up on the passes of the Pyrenees, Carlemagne heard it and halted. "Our men do battle!" cried King Carles.

"No," answered the traitor Guenes. "You know how playful Rollanz is. He'd blow his horn all day on the track of a hare. Who'd dare to attack our rear guard? Let's ride forward into France."

"Listen," commanded Carles. "That horn was winded long!"

Duke Naimes agreed with Carles. "Rollanz does battle. I am sure of it. And that man, Guenes, beside you, Sir King, has betrayed him! God, Sire, do you hear that desperate horn?"

"Answer Rollanz," cried Carles. "Sound the horns and arm yourselves all!" In haste the Franks dismounted, slipped on their mail shirts, grasped their spears, and mounted their war horses. Under their breaths they prayed Rollanz would

live to see their avenging arms. What is the use of words?
They were too late.

Already the vesper shadows crept down the mountain
slopes. At the head of his army Carlemagne galloped hard,
his face intent and angry as he leaned forward on his horse's
neck. Before turning southward, Carles had ordered Guenes
seized and put in the guard of the cooks and kitchen knaves.
"Watch him closely," commanded the king, "for he is a
base felon! He has handed one of mine over to the enemy
today!" The kitchen boys pulled out Guenes's hair and his
whiskers. They fastened a peg and chain about his neck, the
sort a bear wears. Then they hoisted him on a pack animal
and beat him with switches and sticks.

[V. 1830] High are the hills and shadowy and dark, the
valleys deep and the torrents swift! Rollanz looked over his
shoulder toward the mountain peaks and then at the dead
lords of France who lay at his feet. "I saw you lay your
sweet lives down for me, and yet I could not save you. May
God bear you all to Paradise. May he rest your gallant souls
in sainted flowers! Greater barons than you have I never
seen." Then Rollanz returned to battle, so terrible and swift
that the archbishop gasped to see him drive the heathen
like packs of yelping dogs before him.

"That's what a true knight should be," thought Turpins,
"either strong and proud like Rollanz, or else I wouldn't give
four cents for him. Either let him be like Rollanz, or let him
go to a monastery and pray for our sins." Rollanz gave no
quarter that day and took no prisoners. Through the thick
of battle he spied the King of Saragossa. "May God damn
you!" cried Rollanz as he struck off King Marsilie's right
hand. Then he cut off his prince's head. At that one hundred
thousand pagans, screaming to Mohammed for aid, fled from
the field of battle. . . . Call them, as you will! They will not
return!

Then Marsilie's uncle, a king who held lands all the way
from Carthage to Ethiopia, led his troops against the Franks.
His warriors were black and fierce; only their teeth showed
white under their helms. When Rollanz saw them coming,
he knew that he was lost. They were gallant, those men!
Rallying the few remaining Franks, however, Rollanz plunged
dauntlessly into their midst. As the African king rode past on
his sorrel, he struck Oliviers a deathblow in the back. Before
he fell, however, Oliviers turned and killed that king. "You
shall never go brag to some lady how you killed Oliviers,"

he cried. Then he summoned Rollanz, for he knew he soon would die.

Hurrying to Oliviers' side, Rollanz scanned his friend's face sadly. Oliviers' cheeks were already pale and bloodless. Great clots of blood dripped from his body to the ground. Rollanz' eyes blurred, and his head swam at the sight. Oliviers did not even recognize Rollanz. Thinking he was an enemy knight, Oliviers swung his sword at him and dented his helmet. When Rollanz spoke, then Oliviers came to his senses, knew the voice, and asked forgiveness. "I have no injury, Oliviers," said Rollanz gently. "I pardon you here and before God." Then each knight bowed to the other. So did Rollanz and Oliviers part in their lifetimes.

"Sir Companion," murmured Rollanz in farewell, "what a pity for one so brave! Together have we two been both in years and in days. When you are dead, it is pain for me to live!" In his grief Rollanz would have fallen from the saddle if his golden spurs had not held him upright.

There were only three French barons left alive. One was Gualter of Hum, who had fought all day on the mountains. Now, a sole survivor, he rode down to the plain toward Rollanz. "Where are you, gentle Count? Where are you, Rollanz? I was never afraid when I could fight beside you!" Side by side, Rollanz, Gualter, and the Archbishop Turpins of Rheims faced the Sarrazin host. None of them would abandon the others. Forty thousand mounted Sarrazins face them, and one thousand on foot. No pagan stirs a foot to meet them. Instead, they shower volleys of spears, lances, arrows, and darts; Gualter falls. The archbishop's horse falls. The archbishop's body is pierced through with four spears!

Yet the gallant archbishop still struggled to his feet. His eyes sought Rollanz. He gasped, "I am not defeated! I do not surrender!" Then the huge Turpins advanced boldly toward the enemy, swinging his sword about his head in a frenzy of anger and will to defy them. The Book says he injured four hundred more, and so says the eyewitness, the Baron Gilie who built the monastery at Laon. Anyone who doesn't know this, understands nothing about History!

Count Rollanz stood alone. He trembled from fatigue, from the heat of battle, and from his bursting temples. He still did not know whether or not Carlemagne had heard his call. He tried once more to sound the horn, but his strength was almost gone. Even so, the emperor heard the feeble notes. "Sirs!" called King Carles. "That was my nephew's last breath! I can tell by the sound that he is near death! Ride on, whoever wishes to see him yet alive! Sound all our horns at once!" Then sixty thousand trumpets blared full-tongued through the hills and echoing vales.

On the plain of Roncevals the pagans stopped to hear that blast. "Carles will soon be upon us! Then there will be havoc. If Rollanz lives one hour more, we are lost and so is Spain." Then four hundred banded together and advanced toward Turpins and Rollanz.

Count Rollanz of France, nephew of the king, drew himself up cold and haughty. He clenched his teeth and waited. He would never retreat an inch while breath stayed in his lungs. "I am on horseback while you have lost your mount," said Rollanz to the archbishop. "Therefore let Durendal bear the brunt. Know only that I am beside you, whatever happens."

Turpins laughed and answered stanchly, "He is a felon who will still not strike them hard! Carles is coming. He will avenge us."

The four hundred Sarrazins stood face to face with Rollanz. Not a man of them dared attack, and yet there was not a moment to lose. Even then they could hear the advance body of the Franks thundering down the mountain. The blaring war cry "Mountjoy" floated to their ears. Instead of rushing the two French barons, the Sarrazins let fly another volley of spears, arrows, lances, and beribboned darts. Then they turned tail and fled for their lives across the field.

Rollanz stood alone on the field of battle. His armor, his helmet, his mail were pierced and shattered. His valiant war horse Veillantif was dead of thirty wounds. Rollanz turned to the archbishop. As gently as he could, he lifted off his armor and stanched his wounds. Then raising the prelate in his arms, Rollanz laid him on thick grass. "Take leave of me, gentle sir," pleaded Rollanz. "All our friends and companions, all are dead. I shall go and carry their bodies here before you. I shall lay them in a row here on the sod."

Still the archbishop lived and so did his great heart. "Go and return, Rollanz. This field is ours, thank God—yours and mine!"

Rollanz walked across the battlefield. He searched through the vales and he searched through the hills. First he found Sir Gerin and Sir Gerier, then Sir Berengier, Sir Anseïs, and Sir Sansun. Then he found the body of that great hero Sir Gerard of Rusillun. These he laid at the archbishop's feet so that they could be blessed. Then Rollanz sought and found his dear friend, Sir Oliviers the Wise. As he carried Oliviers in his arms, Rollanz spoke soft words to his friend, and wept. After he had laid Oliviers on the earth, Rollanz could endure no more. His face became drained and white. He sank to the ground.

"How I pity you, Baron," said the Archbishop Turpins. The compassion he felt for Rollanz was the sharpest pain he had felt all that day. Unsteadily the worthy prelate rose to his feet. He wanted to bring water for Rollanz from the little stream that flows at Roncevals, but he had lost too much blood. Before he had traversed the length of an acre, his heart faltered and stopped beating. The throes of death gripped him. He fell forward on the grass.

As Rollanz struggled to regain consciousness, he saw the archbishop join his hands and raise them to the heavens imploring God to give him Paradise. Then his head fell, and he died. Through many great battles, and many fine sermons, he had campaigned all his life against the pagans. May God grant him his sainted benediction! AOI[3]

Rollanz was alone. Sensing that his own death was near, he prayed for the archbishop. He saw how he lay, his beautiful white hands crossed on his breast. "Ah, gentle man, knight of illustrious ancestry, I recommend thee today to the celestial Glory. Never will any man do more willingly Your service. Nor has any prophet equaled thee since the Apostles in keeping the faith and attracting men to it. May your soul suffer no hardship. May the gate of Paradise be open when you come."

Rollanz feels death very close. His brains bubble out through his ears. His every thought is a prayer to God to summon to Him the dead peers of France. He prays to the Angel Gabriel, who is near. Then taking his ivory war horn in one hand, and his sword Durendal in the other, Rollanz walks in the direction of Spain toward a hill where there are four marble steps. There he falls over backward on the green turf.

High are the peaks and very tall the trees. Four marble steps there were shimmering and white. On the bright green grass the Count Rollanz falls fainting. Now a Sarrazin, who had smeared his face and body with blood, pretending to be dead among the dead, had all this time been watching Rollanz. As soon as he sees the count lying alone, the heathen in his pride and folly rushes over to him. He tugs at Durendal. Rollanz feels his hands and recovers his strength long

[3] See Introduction.

enough to strike one last blow with his war horn, so true that
the pagan's brains come oozing out his eye sockets.

Rollanz' one thought is for his sword. He cannot risk its
falling into enemy hands. Ten times he brings the steel
blade down upon a rock, but in vain. It neither blunts nor
breaks. "Holy Mother, help me! Ah, Durendal! How sad
I am for you. With you in my hand how many lands, how
many kingdoms have I subdued that Carles of the curly white
beard now holds in sway! You must never fall into the grasp
of a man who would flee before the foe!" Even though he
strikes the blade full against brown chalcedony, it neither
shivers nor cracks!

Rollanz gazes at the twinkling sword, murmuring to himself, "Ah, Durendal, how beautiful you are, how you shine,
how white you shine! How against the sun you gleam and
return fire for fire! How well I remember that day God
commanded Carlemagne to bestow you upon a count and
captain. Then gave he you to me, King Carles the Great.
Together we have conquered Anjou and Brittany. Together
we have won Poitou and Maine, and fair Normandie, Provence and Aquitaine, Lombardy and Romagna,⁴ Bavaria and
Flanders, and even Burgundy! Together we have won Constantinople and Poland. Saxony. Scotland. England. All
these lands does Carles hold, who has the whitest beard. For
you, Durendal, I feel such heavy grief. May France never
have to say that you are in pagan hands!"

Desperately Rollanz strikes the brown rock with all his
power and might. The sword neither splinters nor breaks,
only bounces away from the rock. Rollanz speaks to it
again, "Ah! Durendal, how lovely and how holy art thou!
Thy hilt holds the most holy relics: Saint Peter's tooth, Saint
Basil's blood, Saint Denis's⁵ hair, and a precious remnant from
Saint Mary's own robe. No pagan must ever lord it with
you! I pray that a coward's hand may never defile you! By
your aid I have conquered so many fair lands!"

Now Rollanz feels that death, stealing its way from head
to heart, creeps over his whole body. He runs toward a
tall pine tree, where he falls face downward on the ground,
his sword and horn safely under his body, his face pointing
toward the enemy. He confesses his sins. In atonement he
holds out his gauntlet toward God. "*Mea culpa. Mea culpa.*
Forgive me my sins, the great and the small, throughout my
life from birth to death." Again he offers his right gauntlet

⁴ Or Rumania.
⁵ Patron saint of France.

to God. . . . The angels from heaven hover softly over him.
AOI.

Count Rollanz of France lies under a pine tree. Toward
Spain he has turned his sweet face. All his memories surge
through his mind—how many lands he has won, his beloved France, the strong men of his lineage, his liege lord,
and King Carles who raised him and fed him from childhood
at his own table. "True Father, Thou who never lied, Thou
who called back Lazarun from the dead, Thou who saved
Daniel from the lions, guard my soul from perdition despite
the sins of my life." Rollanz holds forth his right glove to
God. . . . It is Saint Gabriel himself who stoops and takes
the glove from the hand of Rollanz. Then, and only then,
Rollanz drops his weary head to his arm. Hands joined, he
goes to his end. God sends his angel cherubim. He also
sends Saint Michael-of-the-Peril. With them comes Saint
Gabriel. Together they bear the soul of Rollanz to Paradise.

[V. 2397] Rollanz is dead. God has his soul in Heaven.
. . . Now the emperor reaches Roncevals. There is not a road
or a path, not an ell or an inch of ground where does not lie
a Frenchman or a pagan. Carles cries aloud, "Where are you,
my fine nephew? Where is the Archbishop? Where is the
Count Oliviers? Where is Gerin, and Gerier, and Berengier,
the Gascon Engelers, Duke Sansun, the worthy Anseïs, and
that great hero, Gerard de Rusillun the Old? Where are my
Twelve Peers of France whom I left at the pass? No matter
how I call, will no voice answer mine? Answer me! . . . How
greatly am I dismayed that I was not here when this battle
commenced!" King Carles tears at his beard, so appalled is
he. His twenty thousand Franks kneel upon the sod and
weep.

Upon the field of Roncevals the Frankish army weeps.
They mourn aloud their sons, their brothers, and their
nephews. They weep for dear friends and honored liege lords.
Then Duke Naimes first of all speaks to Carlemagne. "Sire,
lift your head. Do you see that cloud of dust not two leagues
away? That's the pagan host retreating! Let us first avenge
our grief."

"That far away already?" mused King Carles of France.
"Grant us this grace, O God. These men have stripped from
me the gentlest flowers of France." Then Carles summons
four knights, "Guard this field of combat, with its hills and
its vales. Let these dead be, exactly as they lie. Let neither
beast nor lion come near them. Let neither squire nor servant
lay a finger on these dead! Let no man touch a one of them

until God lets me return." A thousand knights patrolled and mounted guard.

Bugles sounded. Ranks formed. Carles rode to the head of the columns and signaled them to ride. He set a hard pace against the Sarrazins' backs. Not until vespers did the army slacken speed. Then the king dismounted in a meadow to pray. He knelt and touched his forehead to the earth. There he asked *his* Sovereign Lord to hold back the night, to stretch out the day. Then came to Carles that angel who communed with him and directed his prayers. The angel's words were rapid and clear: "Carles, mount. The daylight shall not lack. God knows you have just lost the finest flower of France. Vengeance is yours today upon these criminals." The emperor set out at once. AOI

For Carles the king, God made a mighty show. He held back the sun, as it was. Less than two leagues ahead the pagan host rode hard. Carlemagne followed harder. Mile after mile the Franks closed the gap. In the Valley of the Shadow⁶ the Franks caught up with the Sarrazins. With bursting hearts they wielded swords and axes upon their backs. Detachments forged a circular path ahead on either side and barred the main road and the paths to the south. The pagans were trapped with the dark waters of the Ebro River behind them. The stream was deep and marvelously swift; there was neither barge nor ferry nor warship standing by with ready oar. The pagans called upon their god Tervagant to help them. Then they plunged into the Ebro.

No god helped them. Those who wore rich armor and mail sank first, swifter than rocks, to the bottom. Others floated downstream, gulping great draughts of river water before they drowned in agony. The Franks lined the riverbank and cried aloud, "Ah, Rollanz, what grief we feel for you!"

As soon as Carles was certain that not a pagan lived, that all had perished either by sword or by water, he dismounted and like a noble king lay on the ground to thank God. His men looked about them. They were astonished at the amount of riches that strewed the field. By the time Carles had finished his devotions, the sun had set! He spoke then to his knights, "Let us find shelter here for the night. It is too late to return today to Roncevals. Our horses are weary and worn. Unloose their girths, lift off the saddles, and unfasten their golden bridles. Let them graze in these fields."

"Sire, you speak well," answered the Knights.

⁶ Val Tenebrus.

The emperor took lodging there by the Ebro waters. His Franks dismounted in that wasteland, lifted off the ornate saddles, and slipped the bridles from their horses' heads. Then they turned the animals loose to pasture. They could give them no more attention than that.[7] The knights were so tired that they slept there on the ground. Not even a guard was set on their camp.

The emperor also slept in that meadow, his boar spear close to his head. He would not even disarm. He slept in his white hauberk, his jeweled helmet still tightly laced and his massive sword Joyous cinched to his belt. The great sword of Carlemagne lay in beauty, it that changed colors thirty times a day. In its pommel lay encased the point of the lance which had pierced Our Lord on the Cross. Because of the treasure it enclosed, the sword of Carles was called Joyous. It was this joy that the Franks were remembering when they called their battle cry, "Mountjoy!" This is the reason that no people can stand against them.

Clear is the night and the moon glimmering. Carles lies on the ground grieving for his nephew Rollanz. His heart is heavy too for Oliviers, for the Twelve Peers of France, and for the French knights whom he has left dead and blood-smeared on the field of Roncevals. He cannot change his nature; therefore he weeps for them and laments. He begs God to guarantee their salvation. The weight of his affliction wears him so sorely that he finally falls asleep. Even the horses have lain down. Those that have the strength to eat, champ the grass where they lie. *Mult ad apris ki bien conuist ahan*—that man has learned much who has known agony deeply.

Carles sleeps like a man in travail. Then God sends Saint Gabriel to watch over the emperor. All night long the angel stands close by his head. He sends Carles a dream of a great battle he will fight, and of the deaths he will still see. Then in his dream Carlemagne sees mighty cold winds and frosts, storms and marvelous huge tempests, and a monstrous wall of fire and flame that engulfs his whole army. As the ash and apple-wood spears catch fire in the hands of the men, Carles groans. Then the bucklers catch fire up to their golden hasps. The boar-spear shafts explode! The steel and mail and helmets curl and buckle in the flames. Carles sees his knights in torment.

Then the scene changes. Bears and ravenous leopards leap out of the woods and devour the Franks. Serpents and fabled

[7] See Rustam and his horse, Goodrich, *Ancient Myths*, p. 135.

vipers, dragons and demons come to feed on the bodies! More than thirty thousand winged griffins swoop down upon the host! Carles's Franks cry out to him frantically, "Carlemagne! Help us! Help!" The king, though wracked with grief and anxious to go to their aid, is hindered. Finally from a wood lumbers a huge lion, enraged, lordly, treacherous, dauntless. It leaps upon the emperor himself! They fall to the ground, struggle, tumble, fight. Carles cannot tell which one is uppermost. . . . Even through this dream Carles does not awaken.

Then the scene changes. In his next dream Carles is in his castle at Aix. There he sees before him a bear held by two chains. All of a sudden, from the forest of Ardennes he sees thirty bears burst! They seem to speak in the language of men, for Carles hears them say to him, "Sire! Give him back to us! It is not just to keep him any longer! He is our relative. He deserves our succor!" Even as the bears grow angry and threaten, a greyhound runs down the palace steps toward them, darts between the chained bear and his relatives. It leaps for the chained bear's throat. The two fight furiously, but Carles cannot tell which one is vanquished. . . . All these presages the angel of God shows the noble king. Then Carles sleeps dreamlessly until the broad daylight.

[V. 2845] The next morning at the very break of day Carlemagne awakens. Saint Gabriel, who has watched him all the night, makes his sign over the king's head. Carles stands up. His first act is to lay down his weapons and to divest himself of his armor. All the Franks watch him and do likewise. Then they mount their horses and return by high road and byroad to Roncevals. They are going to see by morning light the terrible damage there where the battle was. AOI

When Carles finally comes to Roncevals itself, he can no longer refrain from tears. Holding up his gauntlet, he stops the troops behind him. Then he turns in the saddle and tells them, "Sirs, advance at a walk, for I myself must go ahead of you, especially now. I should like to find my nephew's body first. I remember one day at Aix there was a splendid feast day. My knights were boasting of their chivalry, of their great battles, and of the escarpments they had stormed. Then I overheard my young nephew Rollanz talking. Rollanz said, 'If ever I trespass, if ever I die in a strange land you will know where to find me. You will find me lying farther into enemy territory than any other man in our ranks. You will find me lying in death with my face turned not away, but full toward our foes. Thus in the very act of conquering, I swear I shall die like a baron.'"

The emperor of the Franks walked his horse forward, not much farther than one could throw a stick. He climbed a mound. The flowers of the field, between his horse's feet, were every one stained with scarlet blood. Tears ran down the old king's cheeks. He rode slowly along until he came to two trees. There he saw on the brown stone the cuts from Rollanz' sword. There he saw stretched in death upon the greensward his nephew Rollanz.

A shudder ran over the king. He dismounted and ran toward his nephew. In his two hands he held the knight's body and rocked back and forth in bitter convulsions of grief. When his sobs had begun to subside, Duke Naimes, Count Acelin, Geoffrey of Anjou, and his brother Tierri lifted the king from the body and bore him under a pine tree. From there Carles looked down upon his boy and said to him softly, "My friend, my Rollanz, God have mercy on thee! For no man ever saw a knight like thee joust and tilt so nobly in such awful wars. *La meie honor est turnet en declin* —my honor is turned to its decline."

The four knights clasped the old king's hands. Again he spoke to Rollanz, "My friend, my Rollanz, may God put thy soul in flowers, in Paradise, among the glorious! Not a day shall henceforth dawn but I shall suffer because of thee. No one now will uphold my honor. I have not a friend left on this earth. Relatives perhaps, but none noble like thee.

"My friend, my Rollanz, I shall go from here to France. When I am in my own estates at Laon, foreign vassals will inquire, 'Where is your count, the Captain?' I shall have to answer that he died in Spain.

"My friend, my Rollanz, valorous and beautiful knight, when I am at Aix in my Chapel,[8] men will come to me asking for news of thee. Then I shall have to say to them, 'Dead is that youth who conquered so many domains for me.' Then will rise up the Saxons, the Hungarians, the Rumanians, the Bulgars, the Poles, the Italians, the Africans, and those of Califerne. . . . I wish that I were dead."

Geoffrey of Anjou said to the king, "Do you not, Sire, abandon yourself entirely to your grief. Let us seek our knights, our priests, our abbots, and our bishops, and let us inter them honorably according to our rites."

Carles stood by as the bodies of Rollanz, Oliviers, and the Archbishop Turpins were opened, their hearts wrapped in silk, and their bodies enfolded in deerhides. He ordered them placed on three carts and draped in silk gauze.

He had hardly taken these dispositions when messengers

[8] Aix-la-Chapelle.

from Saragossa announced the approach of the Sarrazin reinforcements from Arabia. Carles turned toward them and
pursued the war.

[V. 2980]

THE VENGEANCE OF CHARLEMAGNE

[V. 3633] WHITE IS THE HEAT and high the clouds of dust.
The pagans are in flight, and the Franks press them hard. The
chase lasts right to the gates of Saragossa.

To the highest tower of the palace Brandimonie, wife of
King Marsilie of Saragossa, has climbed. With her are her
scholars[9] and her canons of the false faith, those who are
neither tonsured nor ordained. When Brandimonie sees the
Arabian forces so confounded, she screams aloud, "Mohammed, help us! Ah, gentle Marsilie, they are vanquished,
our men! Our emir has been killed, to our great sorrow. And
you have been wounded by Rollanz, to our great shame!"
Upon hearing her wild words Marsilie turned his face to the
wall. He shed tears, his face clouded over, and he died of
sorrow. Loaded as he was with sin, he gave up his soul to
living devils.

The pagans are finally dead, and King Carles has won
the war. First he orders the portals of Saragossa to be burst
wide open. He knows perfectly well that it will not be defended. He takes possession of the city. His troops file
through its streets and find lodging for the night. Proud
is King Carles of the flowerlike white beard. From Queen
Brandimonie herself Carlemagne receives the towers and the
dungeons, the ten large and fifty small ones. He whom God
aids can carry out his plans.

That day passes, and the night is full of stars. The emperor
of the Franks has captured Saragossa! By orders of the king,
the pagan idols are destroyed so that neither evil nor sorcery
can work any more harm. The bishops bless the waters and

[9] *Clerc* is "scholar" or "intellectual" in Old French; *clergie* is "learning"
or "scholars."

convert the heathen. If any man protests, he is burned or
put to the sword. More than one hundred thousand listen to
exhortations and accept the faith. Carles makes exception
for the Queen Brandimonie. She will be carried captive
back to France. Carles wishes her to be converted also, but
through love. Swiftly sped the night, and dawned a cloud-
less day. Carles left one thousand trusty, proven knights to
rule the city in his name. He garrisoned its towers. Then
mounting at the head of his troops, taking beside him Brandimonie—to whom he only wished well—Carles set out happy
and joyous. On the way home he seized Narbonne and
passed by. Then he came to Bordeaux where he left in the
Church of Saint Seurin the ivory war horn which pilgrims go
to see even today. He crossed the Gironde on great ships.
He bore his nephew's body, that of his highborn friend and
companion Sir Oliviers, and that of the Archbishop Turpins
to the Church of Saint Romain at Blaye. In white sarcophagi
he laid them to rest, the valorous barons. Then over mountain and down dale he journeyed, without stopping, to his own
city of Aix.

As soon as Carles arrives in his capital, he orders the presence of ponderous and learned judges from all parts of his
empire. He requests the instant attendance of ambassadors,
both authoritative and wise, from Bavaria, from Saxony, from
Lorraine, from Friesland, from Germany, from Burgundy,
from Poitou, from Normandy, from Brittany, and from
France (they are the wisest). Then he declares in session
(October 16) the court that will sit in judgment upon Guenes.

[V. 3705] The Emperor Carles has returned home from
Spain; he has made his way to Aix, the chief seat of his
empire. He climbs the degrees to his throne, where he sits in
regal state. Then hastens to his presence the lovely damsel
Alde. "Where," Alde asks the king, "where is Rollanz, our
noble captain? Where is he who swore to take me as his
wife?"

Tears come to Carles's eyes. Averting his eyes, he pulls
at his long, white beard. "Sister, dear young friend, after
whom do you inquire?"

"Rollanz."

"Do you seek from me a dead man? My nephew Rollanz
died in Spain. I will grant your suit, however, in the person of
my son Louis. I can do no more than that for you, dear lady.
Accept my son and heir Louis, a count of the marches."[10]

Alde replied to Carles in swift, breathless words, "Your

[10] Marquis.

answer rings strangely in my ears, O King. May it please God. May it please the Saints. May it please the angels in heaven that after Rollanz, I do not remain in this world at all. . . ." Color drained from Alde's cheeks, and she slipped to the marble floor at the king's feet. She was already dead, this promised wife of Rollanz. God have mercy on her soul.

Carles the king did not know that the damsel had died. He thinks she only swooned. He is so sorry for the pretty maiden that he weeps. He rises from the throne and chafes her hands. Then he lifts her in his arms. Only when her head droops on his shoulder does he realize that she is dead. Carles summons four countesses. He orders the maiden's slender body borne to a minister, laid in state by an altar, and waked by nuns. He has Alde buried there. He can do no more to honor this maiden.

The emperor Carles has returned to Aix from his seven-year campaign in Spain. The felon Guenes, attached to a stake, has been brought before the palace. Serfs have tied his hands with deerhide thongs; they beat him with sticks and switches. Guenes has not merited better treatment. There the traitor awaits the commencement of his trial. As the Book of Deeds records, Carles has summoned his leading vassals, who have convened in the Chapel at Aix. It is the high feast day of that great baron of France, Saint Silvestre. On that day begins the judgment to which the traitor Guenes has been carted.

"Sir Barons," says Carlemagne the king, "judge me the case of Guenes. He was in my host all the way to Spain. He stripped from me twenty thousand of my Frankish warriors, and my own nephew whom your eyes shall never more behold. He caused the death of Sir Oliviers, the chivalrous, the courageous. He betrayed my Twelve Peers for goods and for gold."

"Felon indeed," shouted Guenes defiantly, "if I hide that fact! Rollanz did me wrong both in goods and in gold. It was for that I sought his death and his distress. But treason, no! That did I never do!"

Answer the Franks, "We will take it under advisement."

Before Carles the king stands Guenes on his feet. He is a strapping fellow with a high-colored face. If he were only loyal, you would call him a noble man. He holds the gaze of all Franks and of his judges. Thirty of his family have come to be with him. Then Guenes shouts loudly, in a very deep voice, "Sirs, I was in the host when the emperor whom I serve still with fidelity and love received hostages from Marsilie of Saragossa. We all suspected the Sarrazin was lying. Carles asked for a messenger from among us to send into Spain, into almost certain death, since our previous heralds had been slain. His nephew Rollanz proposed me for the post. I went, since I was so named and commanded; and I managed to survive. Before all the host, I openly swore vengeance upon Rollanz. I got my revenge, but there was no treason in that!"

Answer the Franks, "We shall see."

Guenes understands that upon their decision hangs his life. Thirty of his relatives are there, but one among them is most reliable and influential. This is the knight Pinabel, who knows not only how to plead well, but also how to compose an excellent brief. Pinabel, in addition, is courageous. He handles weapons extremely well. Guenes tells him, "Friend, get me off. Get me out of here, out of death and calumny!"

Pinabel reassures Guenes, "You will certainly be saved. If any French baron here present casts his vote for your death, rather than see you hanged, I shall meet him sword to sword, my body for yours. In such a trial I shall demonstrate your innocence. Never fear." Guenes bows low to Pinabel.

Judges from all the territories of the Carolingian Empire debate what they are to do, and lower their voices when Pinabel is present. They are finally unanimous in their verdict, all except the young Count Tierri. This count and his brother Geoffrey of Anjou had lifted the body of Rollanz on the field of Roncevals. Tierri voted for the death of Guenes.

The judges advance to Carles, saying, "Sire, we beg you to call it quits with Count Guenes, who will henceforward serve you in all good faith and honor. Leave him his life, for he is a very gentle man. You cannot have back Rollanz, not for lands or for gold."

The king replies, "You are felons!" When Carles sees that they have all failed him, his heart and brow grow sad.

Then steps before the king the younger brother of Geoffrey of Anjou, the youngster Tierri. He is a slender youth and not very tall. His skin is dark, and his hair very black. He says courteously to Carlemagne, "Sire, great King, do not lose your spirits so. You know how long and how willingly I have served you. According to the tradition of my ancestors, I am bound personally to uphold your accusation before this court. No matter what the forfeits of Rollanz to Guenes may have been, the Count Rollanz acted in your service, which should therefore have guaranteed his safety. Guenes, in so betraying Rollanz to his death, broke both his feudal oath and our laws. Let him therefore be viewed and treated as a perjurer. If he has a champion from among his family, let that man advance

with his sword against mine, let us put the innocence of
Guenes here to trial again before this court and our king.
Accordingly, I also claim my right. I ask to challenge
Guenes."

Answer the Franks, "You have spoken well."

Then strides before the king the tall, strong Pinabel. He
is a valorous baron. He says, "Sir King, this court has convened at your instance to judge your accusation. Let this
affair make less stir. I see before me Tierri, and I hear his
request. I cancel his vote, and herewith ask to fight him."
Pinabel strips off his right gauntlet of deerhide and hands it
to the king.

Carles says, "I require now a guarantee. Who will give
his word and bond for this man!" The thirty relatives of
Guenes step forward.

"I shall set you at liberty on your oaths," announces Carles.
Then he assigns guards to watch them. When Tierri sees that
there will be a trial by conflict, he also presents his right gauntlet to Carles and gives bondsmen who are placed under like
surveillance.

The king orders four benches to be set up before the palace,
and there the challengers and their bondsmen to sit. In due
procedure and plain sight of all, the quarrel is provoked. The
great hero, Ogier of Denmark, bears the challenges from each
to the other. The knights ask for horses and arms. When they
are dressed, they each confess and are absolved. Each one
makes generous bequests to the ministers of his preference.
Both bow before the king. They wear spurs, white hauberks,
gleaming helmets, and shields with coat of arms. Their swords
are sheathed. Their boar spears are ready. Then each is
raised to the saddle of his war horse. One hundred thousand knights weep for love of Rollanz and pity for the young
Tierri. What the outcome will be, only God knows.

Before the palace at Aix, the meadow is very wide. There
the two knights meet to render justice. They are both great
vassals and both of them valorous. Each one mounts a horse
that is savage and aggressive. Both knights spur forward, slackening the reins. Each one strikes the other with all his strength
and might. At the first well-aimed blow the shields are shivered, the hauberks split open, the girths broken, the cantles
turned, and the saddles thrown to the ground. The spectators
weep to behold this awful sight.

Both knights fall heavily to the ground. Quickly both rise
to their feet, however. Pinabel is much swifter, lighter-footed,
and more agile. Each one looks about for the other. Their
horses are gone. They unsheathe their swords with golden

hilts and strike great, ringing blows at each other's heads.
Both helmets are crushed and pierced. The Franks who watch
moan aloud. "Oh, God," says Carlemagne, "may the right
triumph!"

Pinabel speaks first. "Tierri, call off the fight. I will
be your vassal in all love and faith. At your pleasure I will
give you my wealth. Only let Guenes be reconciled with
the king."

Tierri answers, "I take no thought of what you propose.
May I be dishonored if I consent to such a thing! Between
us two today must God *show* who is right. You, Pinabel, are
chivalrous, strong, and brave. This I know. Your body is
well molded. The peers hold you as a peer among them.
Therefore do you break off this combat. Such Justice will be
done to Guenes as men will remember every day of their
lives from now forward."

"May God not so please," replies Pinabel. "It is my duty
to uphold my family. I will never unsay myself for any
man alive. I prefer death to dishonor."

Then they renew their struggle so violently that sparks fly
from their swords. No man can come between them. They
are fighting to the death. Pinabel of Sorence is of very great
valor. On his helmet from Provence he strikes Tierri so hard
that sparks land in the grass and set fire to it. He thrusts the
point of his sword in Tierri's face so fiercely that he cuts a
gash the length of the young knight's cheek. He slits open
Tierri's hauberk down to the belly.

Tierri feels the hot blood running down his face. He sees
it dripping into the grass. Then he strikes Pinabel a blow that
severs the nosepiece from his helmet and lets the sword pierce
his skull. Tierri stirs the blade about in the brain and so kills
the valiant Pinabel. The Franks cry loudly, "It is a sign from
God! Let Guenes be hanged and also his relatives, who
answered for his good faith!"

Carles, accompanied by four of his greatest knights—Duke
Naimes, Ogier of Denmark, Geoffrey of Anjou, and Guil-
laume of Blaye—strides to Tierri and enfolds him in his arms.
With his own sable tippet Carles wipes the blood from Tierri's
face. Squires hasten to disarm Tierri gently. Then they place
him upon an Arabian mule and lead him among great shouting to the palace.

Again Carles sits in session with his judges, of whom he
enquires, "What is your will for those I hold in bond? They
came to swear for Guenes."

Answer the Franks, "Not one of them has the right to live."

Carles orders all of Guenes's relatives strung up on the

hangman's tree. One hundred sergeants carry out this sentence promptly. The man who betrays, kills others along with himself.

The court then turns its attention to Guenes. Their verdict is that he should die in the most excruciating agony. Four horses are brought. Guenes is tied to each one by his hands and feet. Then four sergeants whip up the horses, driving them toward a stream. Guenes dies, indeed, in great pain. When a man betrays another, it is not right that he live to brag of it.

Then Carles asks the court its pleasure concerning the captive Queen Brandimonie. "I have in my palace a noble lady prisoner. She has heard so many sermons that she desires to be baptized."

Answer the Franks, "Let godmothers be found. Receive her into the church." They rechristened her Juliane. Then the judges were dismissed.

Carlemagne retires to sleep in his high-vaulted chamber. As he rests, Saint Gabriel descends to him, saying, "Carles, arise! Call up your army! Christianity needs you and cries aloud for you!"

Carles did not want to rise. "O God," prayed the king, "you see how painful is my life!" Then he pulled at his long, white beard and wept.

CI FALT LA GESTE QUE TURDOLDUS DECLINET.[11]
[V. 4002]

---

[11] This is the last line of the Oxford manuscript. It is highly controversial. It seems to say, "Here ends the Deeds [poem] that Turold recites [or composes, or writes]."

4

France: Berta of Hungary

INTRODUCTION

THE WORD "minstrel" and the special function of that medieval person, who was so closely allied to three art spheres—poetry, music, and drama—are well known. It is unusual, however, to read and to know a composition actually written by a minstrel; for very few such compositions have come down the centuries to us. The following story was written by a Belgian minstrel who has also left us three other poems. His name was Adenes li Rois—Little Adam, King of Minstrels. Although his tale—it is neither a true epic nor a true romance, but halfway between the two—is usually classified with the Charlemagne cycle, it is not particularly historical, so far as one can say. The Queen Berta about whom the story revolves died in 783. Our poem of 3,482 verses dates from about 1270.

In the *Roland* epic we have had a view of medieval life from an aristocratic level. That author, learned, pious, conversant with the attitudes and manners of the great nobles, looks *down* into only one level of medieval culture, and seems to know well only one area of northern France, such as that near the Mont-Saint-Michel, a new church in his day, only about 350 years old. Adenes li Rois, on the other hand, looks *up* toward the nobility from his humble station and birth. He therefore brings constantly into what he writes a social awareness of the people around him—the peasant, the citizen of Paris, even the coal miner—which is new in literature. Medieval romances and their descendants, our novels, will continue to present and later to plead for social reform and for justice.

Just as scholars compute that the *Roland* must have been composed between the conquest of England (1066) and the capture of Jerusalem by the Crusaders (1099), so one can say also from internal evidence that Adenes wrote during the Crusades and at a time not too distant from the discovery of the New World. The reader will note that our celebrated

102

minstrel was a man of the world, that he knew women and understood well their intimate fears, that he traveled, and that he took real joy and pride in his artist's eye for the evocative image.

His technical skill is wonderful! He chooses a rhyme and then ends every verse on it, sometimes for pages at a time without exhausting his store of words. One can easily see how such a talented man must have been as loved by medieval lords and ladies as our own actors are cherished by millions of us today. One thinks of Adenes li Rois adding a new poem to his repertoire and then delighting audiences in Brabant and France with it. A good word for such an artist is "virtuoso."

Not only is his poem different from the *Roland* in tone and viewpoint; it also differs in subject matter. Great forests, already noticed and described by Julius Caesar, stretched across northern and central Europe. Small groups of people lived in scattered towns where they were not safe from plagues and wars. One feels the dread of the forest in the *Berta* poem, similar to the dread the early settlers in America felt after they had crossed the Ohio River and plunged into "the trees," to use the term of the novelist Conrad Richter.

The sort of story Adenes tells will give encouragement to thousands of fairy tales throughout Europe. In France it will be followed by "Sleeping Beauty" and "Rose Red and Snow White," which seem so close to our story. Similarly, its themes—known to both high and low—will be repeated in other languages than French. There is a medieval students' song that comes to mind in connection with the Princess Berta:

> *Rosa rubicundior*
> *Lilio candidior*
> *Omnibus formosior;*
> *Semper in te glorior!*

(Redder than a rose, whiter than a lily, shapelier than all others; I'm always delighting in [or boasting about] you!)

The reader will see many of our previous symbols as well as new ones, understandable and familiar to us because of Freudian studies. One which will gain in importance is the *rose*. Certain scholars of ancient history and architecture— and a comparison of myths seems to corroborate this opinion —believe that the rose was imported by the Crusaders, from Persia. One realizes the significance of this symbol in the cult of the Virgin, which is coming into prominence as Adenes writes. Along with this emphasis upon the Virgin we shall see in France an emphasis upon women, and the code of chivalry which they in large part designed. The rose windows at Chartres and Notre Dame de Paris are ample evidence of the importance of this symbol. Our poem further testifies to this trend by the emphasis upon the relationship between Berta and her mother.

The king and queen of Hungary, Berta's parents, are themselves the subject of a very beautiful medieval poem.

In reading this text the English-speaking person feels very close to that superb poet who above all others has taught us to be at home in a medieval setting, he who may also have read before us the *Berta* poem—Geoffrey Chaucer.

BERTA OF HUNGARY

TOWARD THE END OF APRIL, on the kind of day which is soft and warm, when the green grass has sprung up all over the meadows and every little tree is longing to be crowned with flowers, I thought one Friday morning I would take a trip to Paris. I wanted to say prayers of thanksgiving in the Church of Saint Denis.

It was there that I became acquainted with a monk named Savary who, as we got talking, invited me to his library. He very kindly showed me a storybook which he allowed me to read. I was so fascinated that I stayed there reading a certain tale until the following Tuesday; and here that story is—not misunderstood as some apprentice minstrel or unskilled writer would tell it, but so rhymed and so truly recounted that the uninitiate will be amazed and the sophisticated reader delighted.

At that time when my story begins, there was in France a royal king named Charles Martel, who had accomplished many deeds worthy of renown, such as: enemies overthrown, hauberks slit, peace assured. The king had two sons. Both were with him in Paris about Saint John's Day when roses are in bloom. The older, named Carlemans, had already been dubbed knight for about four years; he later took holy vows and retired to an abbey. The second son was named Pepin.

Pepin was little, only five feet, six inches tall, but daring!

One time the king his father and the court were dining in
the garden when a fierce lion, belonging to a Norman gentleman, escaped from his cage, killed two attendant nobles, and
forced King Charles and the queen to retire. Pepin rushed
inside for a sword. In a twinkling he had faced the beast—
not only faced him, actually killed him!

"Beautiful boy and very sweet son," his mother said to
Pepin, "how could you even think of approaching such a
hideous creature?"

"Lady," he answered, "when one is destined for kingship,
one must not doubt one's powers to avert danger!"

Now Pepin was only twenty years old at the time! I'm
sorry. I didn't mean to digress. I know you haven't all day
to sit about and listen.... Well, Charles Martel passed away,
so did his fair-faced queen, and Pepin was crowned as the
legitimate heir of France. He fought many wars, tumbled
many a castle, and married a noble lady. However, he could
not get an heir from her no matter how often they slept together. Finally she passed away. God rest her soul.

Then Pepin assembled his barons. The question was:
Where should he find a wife? One of his nobles began to
talk about a certain girl. "Sire, I know of a maiden who is
supposed to be the most exquisite female creature from here
to beyond the seas! She is the Princess of Hungary. I hear
that she is named Berta the Debonaire."[1]

"Sir," assented Pepin. "She is the very one for me! I'll
take her as my wife and my queen."

The very next day Pepin sent a large party of knights into
Hungary to make a formal request for the hand of the
Princess Berta. They arrived on a Tuesday in time for dinner.
Queen Blancheflor of Hungary summoned her daughter.
When the French knights, who were all connoisseurs of
feminine charms, saw this maiden they were stunned! She
was so pink and white, so mantled in long, blonde curls, so
winsome, so slender and so dimpled, that they could hardly
wait to snatch her away for King Pepin. It was agreed, the
princess consenting, that they might take her back to France
to make her a wife and a queen.

Berta's farewells were tearful. "Daughter," counseled her
father, "try to resemble your mother. Be sweet and gentle
to the poor. She who does good about her will be amply re-
compensed. Be kind. If you show them in France that you
are debonaire, you then will be truly beautiful. My dear
daughter, I recommend you to God's keeping."

In those days it was the custom for every lord and baron

[1] Original meaning in this case: "highborn."

to keep French tutors in his domains, so that Berta had learned this language of culture as a child. In any case, her mother and father, King Floire and Queen Blancheflor, had learned French in Paris. They had been born and raised in this suburb of Saint Denis. They decided to send with the princess three of their own servants—an old woman named Margiste, her daughter Aliste, and their cousin Tibert. "Take care of these servants," counseled Blancheflor, "because I ransomed them from slavery out of my own pocket. Therefore I know that they will serve you faithfully. Moreover, the serving girl Aliste looks so exactly like you that her beauty will second yours."

"Lady," promised Berta, "they shall never lack. More than that, I shall arrange for Aliste to be well married in France."

When the Princess Berta was seated on her bay palfrey, her mother, weeping, asked her daughter for the little ring she wore on her finger. When Berta had given her mother the ring, Blancheflor said, "Daughter, may God take good care of you for me! Try to ingratiate yourself with the scholars and intellectuals, for they are very troublesome in France."

"Mother, I promise. Oh, how can I leave you both? I feel as if someone were piercing my belly with a knife!"

"Daughter," comforted Blancheflor, "be smiling and merry. What is this talk about knives! Remember, you are going to be married, and traveling into France on this lovely, sunny day. My heart is really at peace for you. There are no gentler, finer people in all the world than the French!"

The pretty maiden wept so pitifully at leaving her mother and father that she drooped in the saddle and almost fainted away. However, the party finally finished their farewells and set out on their journey. They passed through Germany, crossed the Rhine at Saint Herbert,[2] and rode safely through the great forest of Ardennes.[3] At the crossing of the Meuse they were entertained by the fabled hero, the Duke Naimes, in whose honor the city of Namur was named. They rode into Paris early on a Sunday morning.

Pepin, escorted by seventeen hundred gaily bedecked cavaliers, jogged up to meet the Princess of Hungary. Church bells tolled merrily. There was not a street in all Paris that was not adorned with banners and spread with carpets. Bands of young girls in holiday finery strolled singing carols and strewing flowers. Pepin bowed low to his bride and she to him. Dashing young knights spurred their horses to get a

[2] Near Cologne.
[3] The setting of Shakespeare's *As You Like It.*

closer look at the princess. "Oh, ho!" cried the French
nobles. "Have we a springtime mistress!" and "Look at
young youthfulness in person!"

Pepin married Berta on a day in mid-August. It was such
a magnificent ceremony, without a raindrop or a breath of
wind. The king was garbed in Eastern silk with a crown on
his head worth at least 100,000 marks, maybe more. Berta
was as pretty as a pink flower on a grafted fruit tree. A
master tent was set in the palace garden for a hundred and
thirty guests. Minstrels played violas, lutes, and harps. Many
young ladies were presented to the queen. Everyone fought to
be noticed by Berta. She had already charmed the younger
knights, who envied Pepin's possession of her. Berta was
radiant—but soon she will be sent down a path that will cause
her rosy cheeks to be furrowed with tears, all because of that
rotten old bitch of a Margiste. May the Lord God confound
her!

When the king rose—for he did not wish to delay the con-
summation of his marriage any longer—dukes, counts, and
princes escorted the new queen to her bedchamber so that
she could be disrobed. After Berta was arrayed for bed, her
maid Margiste kneeling began to whisper to her. "When the
King Pepin comes to you this night to do what a man in all
firmness does to his wife, I have heard from a friend of mine
that he intends to kill you. He has a knife. I have trembled
so to tell this to you!"

As the innocent Berta heard these words, she began to
shake and to cry. The old hag consoled her, however. "Lady,
there's no use weeping. After the abbots and bishops have
come in to bless your bridal bed, I'll put Aliste in it instead
of you. If one of you is to be murdered, let it be she! I've
already told her how she must perform. God knows, as I
swear, that I'd much rather have her die than you. You know
what your parents did for me." Then Berta was as relieved as
if someone had given her all the gold of Montpellier!

Margiste trotted to her daughter's room. "Aliste," she said,
"please God and Saint Peter, you shall be Queen of France!
All we have to do now is to dispose of Berta. That won't be
too difficult!"

"May God hear your prayer," chirped Aliste. "Go fetch our
cousin Tibert, and we'll finish her off!" Fast as a greyhound
the old woman ran to find the ruffian Tibert.

That night the unsuspecting Pepin covered the serving
girl in bed, so thoroughly that before morning she had conceived. All this time Margiste kept Berta in her room, and
laughed. Berta read a book while her husband did all his will

and kingly duty, to Aliste, in the next room. In the morning,
following Margiste's directions explicitly, Berta entered the
bridal chamber and stabbed Aliste in the thigh with a little
dagger Margiste had shown her how to use. Aliste screamed
so sharp she awoke Pepin. Then Margiste cried, "Oh, look,
Sire, my daughter has tried to murder your bride!"

Pepin sat up in bed and began to curse. "Have her destroyed, Sire," begged Margiste, "for I disown her utterly!"
She cuffed Berta hard and shoved her out into the hall where
Tibert swathed her in a cloak and pulled her away into Margiste's room. He forced a gag into her mouth, as one would
a bit on a horse, tied her hands behind her back, and threw
her on the bed with a sheet over her.

Soon after breakfast three sergeants were dispatched by the
king secretly—for this attempted assassination was a nasty
business—to escort Tibert out into the forest where Berta
could be quietly beheaded. When they stopped at an inn for
the night, they laid Berta on a bed. Tibert stood by her with
drawn sword threatening to chop off her head if she made the
slightest sound. After she had drunk some water, he replaced
the gag and retied her wrists.

For five days they traveled in this fashion, Berta wrapped
in a dark cloak and bundled on a pack animal, until they came
to the lonely dark forest of Mans.[4] There they halted under
an olive tree.[5] Tibert pulled Berta to the grass and unwrapped
the thick cloak. The three sergeants gasped to see that the
criminal they were hauling to execution was a fragile, winsome, blonde princess. Berta stood trembling before them,
her long golden hair falling almost to the ground. She wore
a white silk tunic and a white cape. She gazed at the four
men so imploringly that they pitied the poor girl, especially
the King's sergeant Morans. Then when Berta saw Tibert's
sword drawn to behead her, she fell to her knees and began to
pray. The gag kept her from wailing. She could only moan.

"By God, Tibert," cried Morans, the first sergeant, "your
heart is as hard as a rock. I'd sooner kill you right here and
now, and never return to France, than let you touch a hair
of this maiden." The three sergeants grabbed Tibert, and
forced him to his knees. Then Morans untied Berta's hands
and the gag. "Fly, Beauty, and may God help you," he said.
After Tibert saw that Berta had escaped through the trees,
even in that extremity he thought of a way to save himself.

[4] This forest, like Sherwood in England, plays its part in medieval fact
and legend. It was here that Charles VI went violently insane.
[5] Olive tree, symbol of peace—Sir Oliviers the Wise in the *Roland*. I
never saw an olive tree around the city of Le Mans.

He and the three sergeants killed a pig, cut out its heart, and carried it back to Margiste. She and Aliste rejoiced at the sight of what they thought was the heart of Berta.

Sobbing from fear, Queen Berta stumbled through the great forest. Night had fallen. All around her owls hooted from the treetops, and wolves howled in the distance. Streaks of lightning flared through the black tree trunks before the thunder shook the earth under her feet. Rain fell along with hail whipped by an icy wind.

"Sir God," wept Berta, "surely you will show me the way as you did to Gaspar, Melchior, and Balthazar when they sought the Virgin's Son." On and on through the rainy woods she fled, tripping over slippery stones, switched by low-hanging branches. The wolves howled after her. "Alas, how could you have been so cruel to me, old woman?"

This was the Queen of France who stumbled through a black forest, without a roof over her head or the rudest couch to lie upon, her dress torn and ragged and her pretty white hands scratched and bleeding. In the beating rain and darkness she came once to a river; but when she knelt to drink, the water was as cloudy as ale. Then she sped wearily on, bumping into trees and fighting her way through thorns that pulled at her cloak, darting down one path to the right and another to the left, as the lightning showed her an opening in the dense woods, not knowing which was the right road to take. When a huge, gnarled branch clutched at her breast, she screamed for her mother. If Queen Blancheflor could have seen her darling child, her precious Berta whose cheeks were as red as the rose and whose skin was as white as the lily, how she would have wept too!

"Somebody, help me! Answer me! I'm afraid!" screamed Berta in terror as she turned about in the forest maze. "I am lost! Find me, somebody! . . . Oh, I thought I was mounting a throne when they sent me to Paris. Now I see the truth. I have only gone from bad to worse since I arrived in this land. Saint Denis! Help me! The wolves will surely eat me alive! Saint Catherine! Open the door of Paradise to me!"

The royal Berta finally made herself a bed of leaves in a hollow spot. No body has ever slept on the cold ground so pitifully, all the way from Wales to Thessaly! She broke fronds from the ferns beside her. These were her blanket. Her pillow was a stone. There it was she finally fell asleep, lost and forlorn, this maiden so tender. Berta was at this time not more than sixteen years old. She slept soundly, however, because the harder was her lot, the more she trusted in God,

laying her sorrow at his feet. Toward morning the rain ceased.
Then it grew clear and bitter cold under the thick trees.

Berta woke up shivering. In the cold morning light she
saw how dense the woods were and how forsaken. "Please
God," she prayed, "to show me where to go, and I promise
that I will henceforth be humble. *I will never tell who I am,*
either that I am the daughter of Hungary or the wife of
France. Only God grant me that I keep my maidenhood,
... and I hope that Tibert dies for the injuries he has done
me."

During the early daylight hours Berta wandered along the
forest paths. Her body was blue with cold, for her silk
chemise and cloak were wet and thin. She came to a spring
of clear water. After she had drunk enough to quench her
thirst, she grew even chillier. Then following a beaten path
for some distance, she came to a hermit's cell. She beat upon
his door with the wooden knocker that hung from a cord.
The hermit slid open his wicket and peered at her.

"May I come in and warm myself, holy hermit?"

"Oh, by God," he replied, "I could never allow the enemy
to gain such power over me! What is such a Beauty as you
doing in these leafy woods? You must be the Devil come to
tempt me! But God has promised me sanctity, and I shall
never let you enter—you or any female creature!" Then
he quickly made the sign of the cross.

"Oh, don't misunderstand me. I also have vowed my heart
to God."

"Who are you then, and who are your parents?

"I am only a poor girl. Please may I come in? I am so
cold."

"Beauty," insisted the hermit, "I can let no fiend in, neither
in summer *nor* in winter!"

Berta stood shaking with cold in front of his door. She was
so frightened and so hungry that she began to wail again. In
pity the hermit passed her a piece of black bread through the
wicket. It was soggy and full of chaff. Berta thanked him,
but her sobs wracked her so that she could not even taste it.
She just stood and cried. It had begun to rain again.

"Beauty," called the hermit, "I know what you could do.
You could go to the house of Simon and Constance. They
would give you shelter."

"But I don't know the way if no one is here to show me."

"Don't be frightened, Beauty. Just keep straight down
this path. It is not far."

"But I don't know what path you mean. As true as God
sees me here, I am dead and gone forever if I have to sleep

another night in these woods. Even if the Virgin Mary were
to give me twenty lives, I would wear them all out before
tomorrow morning."

At these words the hermit grudgingly consented to unbar
the door and set her on the right path. Berta almost died of
panic a little way down the trail when she saw a huge bear
coming toward her. Her faith in the Virgin was upheld, however, for the bear lumbered off the road and disappeared into
the trees. Finally Berta met the Sheriff Simon himself. He
dismounted, amazed to see a shivering maiden trudging along
the lonely road. It was Simon's duty to patrol the roads in
this area of the forest.

"Beauty, who are you?" he inquired.

"Sir," Berta replied, "I am only the humble daughter of a
vavasor from Alsace. I ran away from a stepmother who beats
me. I have been wandering a long time in these woods. I am
so cold and so hungry."

The warmhearted Simon took Berta to his manor house,
where she was made welcome by his wife Constance and his
two daughters, Ysabel and Aiglente. Within a few days the
slender princess had become one of the family. Her new
sisters marveled at Berta's beauty. They loved to comb her
long curls, which were longer than Elaine's.[6] They knew her
name was Berta, but they all believed her story of how she
had escaped through the forest. Berta and her foster sisters
loved each other dearly. They spent long hours together working with silken and golden threads, which Berta taught them
how to do. It occurred to none of them to wonder why the
strange maiden was so often pensive and generally silent
about herself.

Ysabel and Aiglente often told their mother that if Berta
ever ran away from their house, they would accompany her.
"Berta is sweeter than the wild rose in May," the girls never
tired of saying. Berta lived in Simon's house as his niece for
nine and a half years. Everyone agreed she was the most
virtuous maiden, the most stainless young girl in all that lonely
forest.

Pepin was living meanwhile with Aliste as man and wife.
They had two sons, Rainfrois and Heudris, who were treacherous boys. The Hungarian queen, whom everyone believed
was Berta, was loathed by her subjects because of the taxes
and tolls she levied upon rich and poor regardless, even upon
priories and abbeys. She and her mother Margiste collected
taxes upon the sale of pepper, cumin, spices, and wax as well

[6] Apparently the Elaine of Lancelot. Chaucer also uses this comparison.

as upon wheat and wine. Both bent every effort to amass
treasures by the power they had wheedled from Pepin. Aliste
often sat playing with her treasures, counting them, and
laughing; if she had been wiser, she would rather have cried
to see them pile up about her!

In the meantime both Berta's brother and sister had died,
so that King Floire and Queen Blancheflor were faced with
the lack of an heir to the throne of Hungary. They sent a
messenger to Pepin to request that he dispatch his younger
son to them so that Berta's child could be trained for kingship
also. Although King Pepin was disposed to accept this honor,
Aliste returned word that she could not and would not be
deprived of one of her sons. Floire could hardly believe his
ears when the messenger returned this answer.

That same night Queen Blancheflor, sleeping beside
her husband, had a terrible dream. She dreamed that a wild
bear was eating her ribs, her right arm, and her buttocks,
that its claws were ripping her cheeks. She awoke from this
nightmare weeping. As the king tried vainly to comfort her,
Blancheflor told him that she felt her dream announced
danger to Berta. She pleaded to be allowed to journey into
France at holiday time. She had not seen her daughter for
eight and a half years.

"How could we who love each other so dearly live so long
apart?" asked the king; but Blancheflor replied that her
mother's heart knew there was something amiss with Berta.
He finally consented to her departure, since he hoped she
would bring back with her one of Berta's sons. The king
ordered one hundred knights to accompany Blancheflor. "I
want you to be splendidly escorted. You know how haughty
the French are and how they judge by appearances."

Blancheflor had not penetrated very far into French soil
before she began to hear the unpleasant reports about her
daughter. "How could my Berta be so hated?" wondered the
mother. "She never saw either rapacity or greed as a child.
I know my own daughter's heart as every mother does who
has trained her child's character. If this story is true, I shall
certainly take her to task, and make her return at once all
the monies and treasures she has extorted."

Once Blancheflor met a poor peasant. "Lady, I complain
to you about your wicked daughter," said he, grasping her
mount's bridle. "I too once owned a horse that carried
thatch and faggots into town. This Queen Berta we have in
France confiscated my animal, our sole means of livelihood.
Now my wife and little ones are starving. By the Lord who
made Adam and Eve, I shall curse her from evening to day-

break, and call upon God to avenge me." The queen gave him
her purse.

Blancheflor and her retinue arrived into Paris on a Monday.
Pepin was overjoyed to hear of it—not so Margiste, nor
Aliste, nor Tibert! Those three sat on their cushions and wondered what to do. Margiste proposed that Aliste should pre-
tend to have fallen ill suddenly, that she should go to bed,
and be drawn out of it under no pretext whatsoever. Margiste also knew how to brew a poison that could be fed to
Blancheflor in a pear or some cherries. Aliste preferred
flight.

"I'm afraid," said Aliste, "because of my feet. You know
my feet and heels are not half so wide as Berta's were. Let
us load our wealth on mules and have Tibert lead us out of
the country—into Sicily, perhaps. There we could get rich
even faster through usury." They decided, however, to adopt
Margiste's plan. They stopped up the windows with tapestries.
After the room had been darkened, Aliste climbed into bed,
pulling the covers up even over her chin, her nose, and her
eyes.

Shortly the news of the queen's illness spread through the
city; it caused a general rejoicing. Pepin started out from the
palace, accompanied by his two sons, to meet Queen Blancheflor in Montmartre where she was hearing mass. Pepin bowed
to his mother-in-law and embraced her. Blancheflor's first
words were, "Tell me in the name of Jesus, how is my
daughter?"

"Why, she was so overjoyed to hear of your arrival that
she became ill. As soon as she sees you, however, I know
that she will recover."

Blancheflor fell silent. Although Pepin tried to cheer her,
she would not smile. When he presented his two sons to her,
Blancheflor only nodded coldly to them. She looked each
boy up and down without seeing in either face any family
trait. She could not understand why Berta had not sent a
personal message. With a white, stern face she looked down
the hill of Montmartre at the fair city of Paris spread out in
the valley below her. It would have charmed her eyes, had
her heart been less heavy. She saw the high, square towers
of Montlhéry castle, the broad Seine meandering between
the vineyards, the cities of Pontoise, Poissy, Meulan along
the highroad, Marly, Conflans, and Montmorency among
their meadows, and many another large city that I will not
even name. The queen sighed to see such a lovely countryside
and wondered again how her daughter could have earned in
this fair land such a black name.

Pepin escorted his mother-in-law across the marble court-yard of his palace. Then Margiste rushed up to her former mistress. She was as wild-eyed as a devil and had self-inflicted scratches on her cheeks.

"Margiste," commanded Blancheflor after she had raised the servant and embraced her, "where is my daughter? Have her shown to me at once."

"Lady," answered Margiste, "she was so overjoyed at your arrival that she fell into a dire illness. Let her sleep until vespers."

The queen was so rebuffed and so disappointed that she grew pale and silent again. To Pepin's attempts at consolation she replied, "The King Floire loves our child Berta more than anything in the world. I had thought also to take home her younger son to adopt him as our heir."

"Lady," said Pepin, "do it forthwith. I grant the request." Four hundred knights sat down to dinner in honor of Hungary's queen. At the end of the evening Margiste again asked Blancheflor to delay awakening "Berta."

"Willingly," answered the mother. "But by the will of the Almighty God, however, I shall sit myself right here—and hear you that I speak truly—nor leave this spot until I have seen with my own eyes the pretty body of my child and kissed her pretty lips." There Blancheflor sat from early morning under an espalier tree in the courtyard, sad and worried. Once again she summoned Margiste. "Tell me why my daughter suddenly became so covetous of gold. Both young and old complain about her. It is not only unseemly conduct in her, but it is a trait of her nature that I as her mother do not recognize."

"They have only told you lies, and cursed be their hides," affirmed Margiste. "No kinder lady ever wore a golden ring!"

"Tell me," persisted the queen. "Where is your daughter Aliste?"

"Lady, I will tell you. She died suddenly one day as she was sitting on her stool. I don't know what disease she had on her cheek. I guess that in the end it was leprosy. Know that my heart under my breast was sore, for she was frank and vivacious. I had her buried in an old chapel, secretly, so the word would not spread."

For two whole days Blancheflor sat before that chamber door so vigilantly and so faithfully that the old hag could neither come nor go. Tibert and the bitch figured out pre-texts to keep Blancheflor from Aliste's chamber. Then just before supper one evening, as dusk was falling, Queen Blancheflor lost her temper. She refused to endure one instant longer of not seeing her child. She called a young servant girl to fetch a candle, and despite Tibert's objection she forced her way into the bedroom.

All was dark inside. Like a cat Margiste struck the servant so hard that the poor girl fell in a pool of blood to the floor. The candle went out. Then Queen Blancheflor's suspicions about Margiste were confirmed. She walked straight to the bed and began to run her fingers over the coverlet.

"Mother," said the false Berta in a very plaintive voice, "how nice that you could come. How is my father whom God blesses?"

"Daughter, he was well when I had to leave him."

"May God be praised. . . . I regret not to be able to entertain you with festivities. It makes me so miserable that I think I shall die. I should like to divert you . . ." Aliste was so frightened and trembled so under the covers that she had lost all her taste for laughter. She twisted her head away from the queen and squirmed out of reach of her fingers.

"Daughter," said Blancheflor, "my heart breaks to see you so ill, as you say."

"Mother," whispered the servant Aliste, "I am suffering such martyrdom that I fear my white skin will become as yellow as wax. The physician tells me that light makes me worse, and talking too. Nothing is more aggravating to my condition. Therefore I cannot have visitors. Believe me, I am very annoyed, for my heart longs for gossip about Father. I don't know what to do. I am so discomfited. Let me rest; and may Jesus thank you for it, because . . ."

When Blancheflor heard those mewing words, her heart sank to her toes. "Help me, dear God," she said, "who never lied; for this is not my daughter whom I have found in this bed! Why, if my daughter were half dead, even then she would have kissed me and shown me her love!" Blancheflor opened wide the door to the corridor and summoned the household. "Come here at once, all of you! Come running in the name of God! I have not found my daughter in this room, and I shall prove it to you promptly." Then she ordered the servants to strip the cloth-of-gold hangings from the windows. With her own hands she pulled down tapestries and draperies from the vaulted ceilings.

"Lady," shrieked Margiste, "for the love of God, do you want to kill your daughter? She hasn't slept for three days!"

"Shut up, old woman," snapped the queen. Neither Margiste nor Tibert could think of a further trick to thwart her anger.

Clear light from the setting sun flooded into the chamber.
Aliste had pulled the covers up over her head. When the
household had collected, Queen Blancheflor stepped up to
the bed. With both hands she grasped the coverlet and
pulled it entirely off the bed. Her eyes fell accusingly on
the serving girl's feet. They were little, only half the size
of Berta's.′ The queen cried in anguish and grew deathly
pale. Quickly the agile Aliste pulled a sheet over herself and
leaped for the door. Blancheflor caught her by her braids
and threw her to the carpet.

"Halloo! Come here! Help! Help! This is no child of
mine! Alas, and woe is me! This wench is the child of Margiste, whom I fed from babyhood. They have murdered my
sweet Berta whom I loved more than life!"

When Pepin heard that news, he also ran into the chamber.
"French King," accused Blancheflor, "what have you done
with my daughter? Where is my child, so blonde, so sweet,
so courteous, so well educated? Where is Berta the Debonaire?
If I don't have word of her at once, you will feel the weight
of my rage!"

Pepin was so astounded that he grew red with fury. He
beckoned four sergeants to seize the old hag and hold her up
before him. "Hag, you will burn for this, by the body of
Jesus Christ!" Then Pepin retired to his throne room, followed
by his barons. As the old hag was dragged before him, it
began to storm and thunder. Pepin shuddered at the loathsome old woman who had forced her daughter upon him
for so long. "She is the Antichrist!" he said. They put her
to the torture, twisted her thumbs with screws until she was
ready to confess to all her crimes, including the poison. She
was condemned unanimously to the stake.

Then the rough Tibert talked fast. "Sir King, as far as I
know, Berta is dead; for we left her in the forest where bears,
lions, and wild boars roam. If it had not been for Morans,
I would have cut off her head." More than seventeen hundred courtiers began to weep.

A great fire was kindled with thorns. Some piled on brush
while others fanned it until the flames were white-hot. Then
the rotten old bitch was thrown into it, and well had she deserved it! When her daughter Aliste saw this, she groveled
on the floor before Pepin. Then Tibert was tied to horses and
dragged outside the walls of Paris to the hangman's field at
Montfaucon, where he was left dangling in the wind. And
that was good for him!

′ This poem of Adenes is entitled *Bert aus Grans Pies*, referred to in
English somewhat unpoetically as *Bertha Broadfoot*.

The peers advised Pepin, "Do not take the serving girl's
life, if you wish to follow our counsel. Let her live it out
since she has borne you children. However, from this day
forth, she must never approach you again nor maintain con-
tact with any noble of France."

Pepin sighed when he heard their verdict. "Sirs, she deserves to be stoned and destroyed; but I shall not counter-
mand your decision."

Aliste pleaded with the king. "Sire, allow me to withdraw
from the world to a nunnery in Montmartre. I know how to
read and sing. Let me also take my wealth as a dowry. As
for my sons, keep them with you, have them knighted, and
find them rich wives. Remember our nights in bed together!"
Pepin disdained a refusal, so disgusted was he!

It took eight days to transport all of Aliste's belongings to
Montmartre, so much gold and silver was there, and that's
not counting all her other divers and sundry riches which I
won't trouble to list. Let me go on with the story.

Pepin was disconsolate. There never ruled in France a
king with such a soft heart. He did his best, as a gentle
man, to console Blancheflor; neither one of them could smile.
Pepin ordered two of his most treasured palfreys brought. He
helped Blancheflor into a litter that had been attached to the
horses, for Berta's mother was too despondent to ride a horse.
Followed by throngs of Parisians, some weeping for their
lost queen, and others cursing Aliste and grumbling because
she had not been executed and her wealth given to the poor,
Pepin escorted Blancheflor all the way to Senlis.

"How shall I tell her father that his sweet child is dead?"
moaned the queen. "Just imagine how he will tear his beard!
There will not be such grief from Friesland to the sea.[8] How
is it that my heart under my breast does not break? I wish
that I were dead and gone." There was general mourning in
every Hungarian town. Then was hair pulled and palms
beaten against each other! In every street people wept for
Berta the Debonaire.

Pepin summoned Morans to his presence. "Hear my
thought," said the king. "I know that without you my wife
would have been murdered. I think she was probably eaten
alive by wild beasts; otherwise she would have returned. I
want you to search the Forest of Mans. Ask every inhabitant
throughout that region. See if you cannot find at least a
piece of her dress. Know that I shall love her as long as I
live. Know that I would kiss her evening and morning too."

[8] Outremer, or the Holy Land.

For fifteen days Morans and his men beat the countryside. They found no trace of Berta—nothing.

The Sheriff Simon heard what had happened in Paris. He and his wife Constance were thoughtful. After some discussion they called Berta, told her the startling news, and asked, "Berta, are you the lady King Pepin is seeking?"

Although Berta grew pale with fright, she would not break her vow. "It is not I. Believe me, I deny it." When her foster parents replied not a word, Berta argued, "Do you think that I prefer a manor house in these woods to the king of France's palace?"

"Sire," reported Morans to Pepin, "we sought Madame with all our hearts. We questioned every knight, every bourgeois, every peasant, every serf. We asked every plowman, every coal miner, every belabored varlet. We stopped at each church and each chapel by the road. We even asked those sick-a-bed for news of the queen. We know no more today than nine years ago." Morans was so depressed, so sorrowful for his past deed that he made a pilgrimage outremer to do penance for his failure to save the queen of France. His two companions accompanied him, but only Morans lived to see France again.

Pepin did not recover from his sorrow even when the young Duke Naimes rode in from his lord, the Duke of Bavaria. Young Naimes and twelve nobles had been sent to request Pepin to ordain them as knights. Naimes gave Pepin very good advice. It was decided that the court would remove to the city of Mans, where at Pentacost the German knights were ceremoniously dubbed. During this celebration the Duke Naimes asked Pepin why he did not take a new bride.

"Sirs," replied the king, "that shall I not do. . . . I loved the Princess Berta, whom I only saw for a few precious hours. Then I was tricked and disgraced by a serving girl. When I think of my wedding day in Paris and of the gentle princess who was stolen right under my eyes, I feel like taking my own life. I dream only of caressing her fair body from evening until daybreak." The virgin knights were bewildered, for they did not know love.

On a Thursday morning the king rode into the forest to hunt deer; but because he was melancholy he preferred to ride alone, apart from the hunting party. For hours he let his horse bear him wherever it willed, up one path and down another, until he came to that chapel where Simon and his family performed their daily devotions. Berta had remained in the holy place after the departure of the others. She had prayed very long that morning, asking God to give her special

strength so that she could resist revealing her true identity
and thus breaking her vow. She had just left the chapel, carrying her psalter and Book of Hours[9] in her hand when Pepin
rode up the path toward her.

"Beauty, don't be alarmed," smiled Pepin. "I am a knight
and vassal of that king to whom this whole sweet France belongs. In truth, I have lost my way, which pains me not a
little. Is there a manor or fief in this vicinity where I could
get redirected?"

"Sir," replied Berta, "the Sheriff Simon, I believe, could
do so."

"Why, thank you, Beauty." The more Pepin looked at her,
the more he observed how crimson and white were her cheeks
and how blonde the little curls under her hood. Only then
did he realize that quite by accident he had stumbled upon
a very young and very desirable damsel. Without another
word he dismounted; and before she could even gasp, he had
pressed her close against him. When he felt to his surprise
that she was struggling in his arms and twisting away from
his lips, he urged her to answer his desires. "Look," Pepin
whispered in her ear, "love me, Beauty. Make love to me. . . .
You shall come back into France. Will you love me? Why
don't you give in? . . . You won't? Look, I will buy you any
jewel that your little heart desires. I don't care how much it
costs. . . . Won't you? Very well. I will settle a rich estate
upon you." Pepin still held her close against him. He pushed
back her hood. "Not a person will do you harm. . . ." The
more he urged her, the harder she struggled. Berta didn't
care a mint leaf for all his bribes. Pepin saw that this girl
was actually terrified of his caresses and the strength of
his arm.

"Oh, please," begged Berta. "Please let me go. My Uncle
Simon will come looking for me. You must let me go. My
Uncle Simon has to journey up to Mans today to carry vic-
tuals to the king."

"Beauty, tell me what you were doing alone in this wood."

"I was praying in the chapel, but a little angel came down
to hear my pleas. I overstayed the mass."

Pepin scanned her face narrowly as she talked. It seemed
to him that if he could not take her by force, he would be
obliged to win her through love. Have her, he must. In his

[9] A Book of Hours was one of the most valuable and prized possessions
of the Middle Ages. One that belonged to the Duke of Berry is at the
Cloisters branch of the Metropolitan Museum of Art, New York City.
Even an ordinary book would have been worth several thousand dollars
in modern currency.

eyes she became more lovely every second. With her cape askew, he saw her lovely breasts, and that her golden hair flowed in curls to the ground. "Beauty," pleaded Pepin, "I must make love to you. . . . I will honor you afterward. I promise I will take you back to France. I will give you so much wealth that no desire you have shall go unfulfilled. I am going to make you do my will anyway, whatever it may cost; so you may as well yield right now."

"Sir, I forbid you to touch me!" replied Berta with great distinctness. Tears came to her eyes and slowly rolled down her cheeks. "I order you to step back, Sir Knight. You have offended me greatly. I am no ordinary damsel. I am the wife of Pepin, king of France. I am the daughter of the king and queen of Hungary. . . . Do not venture a step further in my direction. Know that I am the queen of France!"

Pepin was so amazed that he grew pale. He could not, indeed, take a step. He could not even speak. For several minutes he just stood and stared at her. Then he gulped and swallowed, for there was a lump in his throat. "Beauty," he said then softly, "if what you say is true, I wouldn't harm your person for one thousand marks in gold."

Berta walked along the forest path toward Simon's house while Pepin, leading his horse, followed her. Hard as he questioned her about herself, the maiden would not reply or volunteer any corroboration of her story. Simon greeted the strange knight and wondered at Berta's flushed face. He and Constance saw there had been an attempt at rape, but they could tell it had not succeeded. Pepin introduced himself as the king of Paris. He was very gallant toward Constance and her two daughters. The family saw that their strange guest was a nobleman.

As soon as an apt occasion presented itself, Pepin drew Simon aside to inquire about Berta's chastity. At once Simon called his wife. That lady scolded Pepin roundly, "Sir, our niece has been complaining about your conduct. It seems you tried to take her virginity. Our dear child is frightened. This was very unknightly of you."

Then Pepin decided to take them into his confidence. "Your Berta has just told me something, that, if it is the truth, will bring down upon your heads the blessings of France. She told me she was the queen of France! Say what you know about this maiden, and beware of my ire if you lie to me."

"Sir," answered Simon, "all we know is that I found her wandering in the forest. She was blue with exposure and half dead from fright and hunger. We can both bear witness to her purity and honor. As far as we know, she came from

Alsace. . . . In all this country she is the most pleasing and
most gentle maiden. To this I can and will swear before you
and before God."

"Simon," replied the king, "Let us go all three of us and
talk to her."

"Sir," answered Simon, "do you know what I suggest? If
I were you, I would hide behind this curtain and listen to
what she tells my wife and me. She will be frank and open
with us."

Simon took Berta by the hand and led her into the hall
where Pepin was concealed. "Berta," he told her kindly,
"this noble knight has revealed your words, what you told
him in the forest. They are very wonderful and joyous. Why
did you hide your rank from us?"

"I beg you, dear Berta, to tell us the truth," urged Constance.

"I had to tell the knight that I was Berta the queen," she
replied. Berta was so embarrassed that she could not meet
their eyes. "It was the only way to save myself from being
raped in the woods."

Constance led the slender Berta from the hall. Then she
told the strange knight, "I do not know what to think now.
Our niece would be delirious to hide such a fact from us
who love her. She cannot be the queen of France!"

Pepin, with somber thoughts and wrinkled brow, took leave
of his host and hostess. He had chased enough for that day.
As soon as he arrived in Mans, however, he dispatched a
messenger to bring Simon to him. "Simon," said Pepin, "you
did not recognize me. I am Pepin the king."

"Oh, Sire," replied Simon, bowing low to show his awed
respect, "had I known it was you, I should have made you
many times more welcome in my home."

"Your reception was sufficient," sighed Pepin. "I am
distraught because of my dear wife Berta, who was stolen
from me so many years ago. I cannot sleep nights because
of my desire to hold her in my arms." After some delibera-
tion between the two men, Pepin concluded, "Do you know
what to do? You will return home and mention this occurrence to no one at all. My heart will not be denied. My
heart tells me that the maiden in your house *is* my lost bride,
although the fact that she continues to deny it grieves me
deeply."

"I can never believe either," mused Simon, "that this girl
is not your wife whom you love so deeply. My idea is that
when she found herself, so chilled and so famished in the
deep forest, she made some vow which she now fears to

break. Such a virtuous girl as she is would not endanger her salvation for all your gold and all your fair domains, not even for the kingdom of France."

"Simon," concurred Pepin, "I really think you have solved this mystery; on the other hand, you know how I was deceived by a scheming woman. You will understand my desire for proof. Therefore, since I must put my mind at rest, I shall send word to Hungary to ask her mother Blancheflor." Pepin called a chaplain, to whom he dictated a letter.

Great was the rejoicing in Hungary when King Floire and Queen Blancheflor broke the seal of the king's missive and read his words. Early next morning they set out for France, traveling so hard that within a few days they had arrived in Paris. Pepin urged them not to delay, but to set out at once for Mans. He was so eager to see Berta again that their whole party arrived in the city of Mans one day for dinner. However, Queen Blancheflor could neither eat nor drink, so anxious was she to clasp her beloved daughter in her arms.

Simon, summoned to the royal presence, asked, "Has Queen Blancheflor come?"

"Yes," replied Pepin, "only she is so upset that she can neither eat nor sleep."

"I am more and more certain our niece is your queen," said Simon. "Every time I mention your name, she hangs her head, blushes, and grows silent. Have no fear for her nature. She is the most honorable maiden in the land."

King Pepin and his royal guests were secretly escorted by Simon out of the city, through the forest, and into his home. "Where is Berta?" asked Pepin breathlessly.

"She is in my chamber repairing an altar cloth that was torn," answered Constance.

The whole party, excited and eager, burst through the chamber door, and saw Berta sitting before her embroidery frame. As soon as her eyes fell upon Blancheflor, the maiden Berta rose to her feet. She ran across the room and sank down on her knees, burying her face in her mother's skirts. All could see that she had swooned.

"May God be praised," cried King Floire. "We have found our priceless daughter!" King Floire raised his child gently, drew his Berta into his arms, enfolded his slim daughter, stroked her hair, and kissed her face.

"Oh, God," cried Pepin, "who made heaven and earth, be praised for this our destiny. You have rewarded me so today, oh God, you have so changed my sorrow into joy, that any happiness I ever felt before is a hundred times doubled. May

this day be honored long, the day when I again found my
Lady!"

The news sped swiftly to Mans. All the church bells began to toll paeans of joy. Their peals carried through the trees
into the room where Berta was being kissed and caressed by
her parents. Then Pepin went up to her, bowed low, and
said, "Sweet friend, for God's sake, say something to me. I
am King Pepin, and I here crave your forgiveness for all the
pain and the frights I have caused you."

Berta marveled deeply to hear his gentle words. Like a
highborn princess she answered becomingly, "Sire, since it
is really you, I thank the Holy Virgin who gave birth at
Bethlehem."

Pepin called for his sergeant Henri, his marshal Gautier,
and his chamberlain Tierri. "Ride into Mans and bring us
tents and pavilions. Provide for our comfort here; here it
was that I found all my joy, and here it is our pleasure to
remain. Ask the Duke Naimes and the new knights to join
our company." So the court convened there in the forest,
and that was on a Monday.

That night in the royal pavilion Pepin at long last slept
with his wife, and there also the three following nights. He
caressed her from evening to morning. In the morning he
dubbed Simon a knight at Berta's request. It was the Duke
Naimes who buckled on the spurs, and Pepin who extended
the sword, struck Simon on the shoulders, and ordained him
knight. Simon kissed the king's foot and leg. Then Pepin
raised Simon, and kissed him on the cheeks. Afterward
Pepin bestowed on his new knight a thousand pounds of in-
come per year in lands. He also gave five hundred pounds a
year to each of his daughters. He ordered their coat of arms
to be field-blue struck with white and a golden fleur-de-lys.
Their heirs still bear this device today.

"Constance," said Berta, "you and your daughters shall
accompany me into France. It is not right that I should have
such honors and you such humility." Constance replied that
they would all do her will gladly.

The royalty and their train of nobles made a solemn entry
into the city of Mans on a Tuesday morning. Berta rode
between the king and the Duke Naimes. They were met by
the clergy, lay and ecclesiastical, who bore in their hands
caskets containing holy relics, silver and gold censers, cloth
of gold and silken fabrics. Ladies and nobles of the area
thronged to be presented to the queen about whose distress
they had long heard. The festivities lasted for eight days.

Then Pepin ordered their return to Paris. Near Berta rode

Ysabel and Aiglente. The three young ladies were gay and
merry all the way. The sun shone down over the beautiful
fields of France. Through every hamlet and burg people
crowded close to the queen. Many had journeyed long distances on foot and on horseback to glimpse her loveliness.
They saw that she was *noble and humble*,[10] and they blessed
her mother for having brought her up so well. Minstrels accompanied them with lute and merry song all the way to
Paris.

> *Grant joie orent en France li joene et li chenu.*[11]
> *Encontre Pepin vinrent si ami et si dru,*
> *Et encontre lor dame dont grant joie ont eü;*
> *De ce qu'est retrouvée gracient moult Jhesu.*
> *Tant vont que de Paris ont maint clochier veü;*
> *Paris ert acesmée c'onques mais si ne fu,*
> *Car moult furent la gent de grant joie esmeü*
> *Pour le bien que il voient que Diex leur a rendu.*
> *Ne remest en la vile ne chauf ne chevelu,*
> *Ne moine ne abé, ordené ne rendu,*
> *Qui à pourcession ne soient tuit venu.*
> *Sachiez cel jour i ot maint grant destrier coru*
> *Et i ot lainte lance brisie sor escu;*
> *Berte la debonaire ot cel jour maint salu.*

> Great joy was had in France by young heads and
>   hoary
> Who greeted Pepin so friendly and so merry,
> Then met his sweet lady whom they hailed joyfully;
> People thanked Jesus she'd been found in safety.
> They filed through Paris under tower and belfry—
> Paris never was adorned so beautifully.
> So moved were the people they turned prayerfully
> To thank God above that they should so honored be.
> There remained in the town not a bald nor a curly,
> No monk nor abbot, no ordained nor renegee;
> But joined the procession and the ceremony.
> Be sure great chargers spurred before the canopy.
> Long lances and bright shields were shivered
>   gallantly
> For the debonaire Berta their homage and her fee.

The king and queen of Hungary were happy and comforted

----

[10] This phrase occurs often in manuscripts which describe the queens of
France or great princesses.
[11] Verse 3329.

to watch this reception given to Berta by the Parisians. After
eight more days of celebration, during which Pepin outdid all
previous records for grace, entertainment, and hospitality,
Floire and Blancheflor returned to Hungary. They founded
and endowed an abbey for sixty nuns in honor of their
daughter's fortunate return to her rightful place upon the
throne. This was not the only joy they carried back into
Hungary with them. Within a few months Queen Blancheflor
gave birth to a baby girl, who was named Constance in honor
of the fine lady who had rescued Berta. This is the Constance
who in good time became the queen of Hungary.

Pepin and Berta ruled happily in France. When the unfortunate Sergeant Morans returned from outremer, Berta
asked her husband to receive him. She pardoned him herself
and thanked him; for, as she told him publicly, he had really
saved her life. She further requested Pepin to confer knighthood upon Morans, and it was so done.

The first child born to Berta and Pepin was a lovely daughter, who was gentle, teachable, and mild. This girl grew up
to become the wife of Sir Milon d'Aiglent. Her son was the
great hero Rollanz, he who never knew cowardice, he who
was daring and bold, he who was the finest flower of chivalry.

The second child of Berta and Pepin was a boy. He it was
who led great wars against the pagans, who upheld and en-
forced the laws of God, who drove the infidels out of many a
fertile field, who pierced many a helmet, crumpled many
a buckler, broke many a hauberk, cut off many an enemy's
head, and fought his whole life long with all his mighty heart
for his lands of France, so valiantly, indeed, that the wide
world mourns his passing even to this day. The second child
of Berta and Pepin was named Carles.

He was great Charlemagne.

5

Austría: Sifrít

INTRODUCTION

THE FOLLOWING CHAPTER summarizes the first sixteen adventures from the *Nibelungenlied*, an Austrian poem of unknown authorship, composed about 1200. This work centers about the life of Sifrit, the Siegfried of the Wagnerian operas, who became the best-known hero of German and Scandinavian literature.

The *Nibelungenlied* is an amalgam of stories from three principal sources: actual history of the invasions of the fifth century, Scandinavian mythology—which in turn comes largely from Icelandic manuscripts—and Oriental legends partially remembered from Asia, the original home of the Indo-Europeans. As a historical document this poem corroborates the importance of certain kings and queens such as the Hun Attila who had 500,000 men under his command at one battle, men collected from Kiev to what is now Vienna.

In 430 Attila defeated and killed a Burgundian king named Gundicarius, the Gunther of our story. Attila himself, according to unproved suspicions of the time, was murdered in 453 by his Burgundian wife, Ildico, perhaps the Chriemhilde (*Chriem* = grim-grief; *hilde* = bearing) of our story. Our poet treats one of his characters, the knight Dietrich, with great respect; historians have seen in him Theodoric the Great, king of the Ostrogoths, who in actual fact reigned some fifty years after Attila.

The first half of this poem takes place at the court of Burgundy. The Burgundians were Germanic tribes, who added to their domains until in the fifteenth century their alliance with Henry V of England prolonged the Hundred Years' War. When their empire was dismembered at the close of that century, its western half fell to France while its eastern half went to the husband of the Duchess Marie of Burgundy, a hitherto unimportant prince named Hohenzollern. Sifrit is said at first in our poem to have come from the Low Country

126

at the mouth of the Rhine, a territory held by the Franks and called Austrasie. The Franks considered themselves descendants of the Trojans of Asia Minor. One character in the story, Hagen, comes from Tronje (New Troy) in Alsace. Sifrit comes from Santen (Troia Francorum).

Sifrit himself, however, seems rather to resemble Achilles. Both were young and courageous, both were invulnerable except in one spot, both fought a warrior maiden, and both were murdered. The tradition of the warrior maiden—in our present story she is Brunhilde (Brun = brunie-byrnie)—derives also from antiquity. Not only was there Penthesilea and Camilla, but also that Persian maiden named Gurdafrid, whom we meet for a brief moment in the *Shah Nameh*. Brunhilde's original name in Scandinavian mythology was Sigrdífa. In those stories Sifrit was a descendant of the god Odin, or Woden (for whom Wednesday is named), recognized by the Romans as Mercury. (Wednesday is called *Mercredi* in French, and in Italian, *Mercoledi*.) Odin, like Sifrit, was closely associated with a galloping horse of gigantic size just as Suhrab and Rustam were in Persian legend.

The poet of the *Nibelungenlied* presupposes a certain acquaintance with Scandinavian legend, which tells of the Valkyrie Brunhilde lying in a magic sleep surrounded by fire; she is rescued and awakened by Sifrit. The poet gives no details of the Nibelungen treasure. Apparently the Nibelungenland was somewhere in the North, and a Nibelung was he who possessed this fatal hoard. The idea of gold bringing death we have seen in *Beowulf*.

The following adaptation follows closely a two-volume translation of the *Lied* into French, made in Russia in 1837 by a French schoolteacher, Mme. Charlotte Moreau de la Meltière. Her work has been checked against an original German text and also against two subsequent French translations of 1866 and 1909.

Mme. de la Meltière dedicates her book to Catharine the Great of Russia.

SIFRIT AND CHRIEMHILDE

IN THE MOST ANCIENT LEGENDS are recorded the names of the lovers Sifrit and Chriemhilde. In song and poem are commemorated their story—tales of his valor, of their undying love, of the festivals their presence graced, the pageantry of her tears and the wrongs they suffered, side by side with the prodigious exploits of bloodthirsty warriors.

There grew up in the pleasant land of Burgundy, protected and cherished by three mighty chiefs who were her brothers, this tender maiden whom we know by the name of Chriemhilde. Her beauty was so exquisite, so fragile that its fame and the prestige of this princess were celebrated by wandering bards throughout lands even beyond the Rhine. Chriemhilde, they said, declined to requite the love proposals of any suitor; they told how her reluctance was due to a dream.

She had once dreamed that two eagles, swooping down from the skies, devoured a sleek falcon which she had raised, loved, and trained diligently. What a sorrow to the gentle girl was this presage! The maiden's mother, Queen Uta, explained to her child that this dream meant only that her pet bird was that great lord who would become her husband, he who would be torn apart by eagles if he were not carefully safeguarded.

"No," cried Chriemhilde. "I shall never marry. I see how great the sorrow of married women is."

"Make no hasty decisions," answered the queen. "Only the love of a man can transport you above all other joys. You are very beautiful. We shall hope for that great knight who surpasses all others for your husband." While she awaited her knight in shining armor, Chriemhilde lived in peace, hidden safely from rough warriors in her brothers' palace of Worms-on-the-Rhine.

On the lower reaches of this river, in the realms of the Franks, ruled a fabled king named Sigmund[1] and his queen, Siglinde. Their son was already a hero. He was Sifrit. Although this youth had only been dubbed at the summer solstice, he had already worked fabulous deeds. He had fought a dragon, had bathed in its blood so that his skin had become as tough as horn, had stolen the magic cape[2] which made its wearer invisible, and had seized the golden hoard of the Nibelungen. The young Sifrit, whose laughter and sunny beauty had already made him the object of amorous glances, had not felt love until he heard of the beauty of the hidden Princess Chriemhilde. Her inaccessibility seemed a challenge sufficient to his strength, particularly since her oldest brother Gunther ruled as many vassals and owned as much wealth as did Sifrit's own father in the Niderland. Therefore, overruling his parents' protests and refusing the aid of a host, Sifrit, accompanied by eleven knights, set out from Santen

[1] See Chapter I, *Beowulf*, page 31.
[2] Tarnkappe.

magnificently attired in golden armor and squirrel-skin robes
to win all by himself the hand of the Princess Chriemhilde.
Within seven days he had arrived at Worms.

King Gunther of Burgundy looked out his palace window
to see the twelve strange knights in his courtyard. Their
golden helmets flashed in the sun. He saw that their battle
swords reached to their spurs. They were magnificently ap-
pareled. Gunther called for his Uncle Hagen, for Hagen was
bold and experienced. In the course of his adventures this
dark knight had visited many lands and known many foreign
kings.

Hagen leaned out the window and recognized the strangers.
"I believe it is Sifrit of the Niderland," he said, "although I
never saw him before. He won the treasure of the Nibelungen
that was hidden under a mountain. He conquered the dwarf
Alberich and made him a slave. From this hoard he took his
mighty sword Balmung, and from Alberich the magic cape.
He also killed the dragon that lived under the linden tree,
bathed in its blood so that his skin became as hard as horn.
No weapon can harm him.[3] Let us receive this fair hero so
kindly that we turn him into an ally, certainly not into an
enemy."

Gunther, his brothers Gernot and Giselhers, and their
Uncle Hagen welcomed Sifrit into their hall and inquired
about his voyage. "I am a warrior destined one day to wear
a crown," boasted Sifrit. "I have heard that you Burgundians
are valorous. Whether you like it or not, I have come to de-
prive you of your possessions and also to subdue your towns
and villages."

"Why should I be stripped dishonorably of those lands
which my fathers so long ruled honorably?" asked Gunther.

"I am sorry to see that you have come here for a quarrel,"
said Hagen.

"Sifrit, welcome to our lands," cried Giselhers, the youngest
brother. "Let wine be brought to this hero!"

At his words and the subsequent welcome of Gunther,
Sifrit became friendly. "All that we have is yours, royal
guest," said Gunther. "We shall share our wealth with you.
Only ask any favor of us, and it shall be granted."

The Burgundian lords entertained Sifrit at feastings and at
tourneys, where with lance, sword, and javelin Sifrit was
every time first. The royal Princess Chriemhilde watched him

---

[3] This repetition, as here in conversation, of material previously given in
straight narrative, is so characteristic that one might say it authenticates
the poem. The medieval authors may have done this because their works
were meant to be read or recited aloud.

secretly from her windows. She gasped at his beauty and skill. She knew he was the hero of the Franks, and felt in her secret heart that he would be her one and only love. Sifrit did not know that the princess had seen him, or even that she had heard all about him. Inexperienced at intrigue, he could think of no way to meet her or to acknowledge his passion.

Their dalliance and their tourneys were interrupted by messengers from the two northern kings of the Saxons and the Danes. "Within twelve weeks our kings will pay you a visit, Gunther of Burgundy. They will come at the head of their hosts. Their purpose is conquest. Prepare to do battle!"

In Gunther's council it was Hagen who suggested that their guest Sifrit be notified of this threat. The young prince of the Niderland volunteered his aid at once. "Calm your fears," said Sifrit. "Even if the Saxons and Danes attack with thirty thousand men, I will meet them with only a thousand!"

Gunther's forces were assembled. They set out from Worms with the minstrel-knight Folker bearing the silken banner and Hagen in command of the columns. They passed through Hesse, burning the villages and pillaging until they came to the frontiers of Saxony. There Hagen remained with the army while Sifrit, followed by chosen companions, led the attack into the enemy. After a bloody contest Sifrit took the Danish king prisoner and sent him back to Gunther at Worms. Three times Sifrit cut a path through the Saxon ranks until his arms ran in enemy blood from wielding his magic sword Balmung. When the Saxon king learned that his brother had been taken prisoner, and when he saw the design of the crown on the strange knight's buckler, he knew that his foe was the hero Sifrit. At once he ordered his banner to be lowered in sign of surrender. He too was ordered to Worms as a hostage. Stretchers transported the wounded into Burgundy, along with the five hundred captives. Runners carrying the news of this victory were dispatched to the Rhine.

Chriemhilde the Beautiful asked a messenger for news. "If you say good words to me, I will give you so much gold that you will be rich. Speak the truth, if you crave my favor. How did our Burgundians pursue the war? Which knight did the greatest exploits? That is what you are to tell me!"

"Since I must tell you, gracious Queen," replied the messenger, "it was in verity the arm of Sifrit alone that accomplished prodigies. The deeds of Hagen were nothing but the wind in comparison to those of Sigmund's great son. He has caused such grief among the Saxon women that they

have now only to mourn and lament their whole lives long.
Wherever he struck, the blood bubbled crimson and hot.
Learn also that he overcame two battle-wise kings single-
handed, and that he is sending them as hostages to your
brother Gunther. Great was the fury of the young Sifrit!"

As Chriemhilde listened, her glowing cheeks became as
red as the rose. "You shall have ten marks and new livery,"
she replied. (One recites messages willingly to such rich
ladies.) The damsels of Gunther's court hid behind their
windows and watched the roads that led into the palace. Gunther greeted his victorious vassals, first the band of warriors
who bore many a sword, many a captured shield, many a
trophy. Then came the wounded and prisoners; only sixty
Burgundians had been lost in that war. Gunther lodged his
men in the town, without forgetting to provide for the captives so that his magnanimity in victory would be remembered.

Gunther then began to plan a festival as a reward to his
loyal subjects. Queen Uta opened chests and wardrobes so
that the young ladies of her court could be splendidly attired.
She heard that many noble warriors would be presented to
her. Day after day knights arrived to do honor to the Burgundian royalty. Each was given rich robes and red gold for
his love. Tiers of benches were built along the Rhine and
places assigned according to each visitor's rank.

By Pentecost thirty-two princes and five thousand knights
had jogged into Worms, each more nobly outfitted than the
other. The Burgundians took Gunther aside and advised,
"If you really wish this festival to be the most memorable
ever attended, allow your noble guests to glimpse your sister
Chriemhilde. What else warms the heart of a warrior? What
greater compliment, what more suitable reward could you
offer them than to let the knights parade before our hidden
beauty whom no man has ever seen, but about whom all have
heard? The poets sing her praises!"

Then did an excited princess and her damsels open the
cases where the treasures of the kingdom were laid safely.
More rich fabrics were ordered from the merchants. Wide
ribbons were unrolled; jeweled clips, bracelets, pendants, and
buckles were unwrapped and polished. Many warriors considered that the sight of this princess was, indeed, a boon
far to be preferred to wealth and domains.

Gunther commanded one hundred knights with drawn
swords to form an escort for his sister. The great hall, packed
with thousands of knights, waited in silence as the procession
of royal ladies ascended the stairs. First came Queen Uta, followed by one hundred noble dames clad in satins and gleam-

ing with jewels; then came Chriemhilde surrounded by a bevy of smiling young girls.

Chriemhilde walked into the hall, that gracious and shy young beauty, as pink as a morning sunbeam on drops of dew. Her cheeks were even brighter than the precious stones sewn over the skirt of her gown. She gleamed more luminously over the damsels in her train than does the moon over its surrounding stars. Sifrit, seeing for the first time her whom he loved, felt pride swell in his heart. Chamberlains ordered the cheering knights to step back so that no one approached the princess too closely.

"Brother," said Gernot to Gunther, "now is an opportunity to pay homage to Sifrit, and thus bind this hero to us forever. Let the Princess Chriemhilde greet him! All present know that she has never greeted a knight in her life before. Let Sifrit approach, and bid her acknowledge him." Gunther so instructed his sister.

Others told Sifrit, "Approach. King Gunther is about to do you an unparalleled honor before all his court."

Sifrit, growing pale and red at the same time, advanced to the princess, and bowed before her. To the delight of the court the princess—she who had up until this day lived a virginal life far from the sight of men—spoke to Sifrit. "Dear lord," she said, "good and noble knight, welcome." Sifrit bowed low before the maiden, but when he raised his head, their eyes locked.... Perhaps he disobeyed protocol and took her white hand. That would not be surprising, for joy ran fast through the heart of Sifrit those days in May.

Certain is it that Sifrit, escorting her from the church door one morning, whispered in her ear, "I shall serve you forever. I shall never rest until I have won your good graces. If I live, my life shall be consecrated entirely to you."

On the twelfth day of the festival Gunther consulted Sifrit about his two royal prisoners, who were recovering from their wounds. "What do you think, Sifrit?" asked the king. "They will swear never to bring war parties into my lands again. They offer me all the gold that five hundred horses can carry in exchange for their freedom."

"To accept their gold would be acting dishonorably," replied Sifrit. "Ask them only to give you their hands on it that they will refrain from war. Take no gold from them, nothing. Give them their freedom, outside of Burgundy."

The Danish king took his leave, for the festival had drawn to a close. The Saxon king also took leave of Gunther and of his noble captors. Knights and vassals retired happily to their lands. Sifrit would have returned home to the Niderland, but he remained at Worms-on-the-Rhine because he had won the love of the Princess Chriemhilde.

Sifrit had won that love which meant death . . . the love of the Princess Chriemhilde. Through her undying love Sifrit was to find his death. In this love King Gunther of Burgundy also found death, and also Chriemhilde's two brothers Gernot and Giselhers. Yes, even Giselhers, who was only a boy at the May festival given in honor of that war, also found death. Because of this love the minstrel-knight Folker, he who loved Hagen, also found death. Because of the love of Sifrit and Chriemhilde the terrible, black knight Hagen himself found death, far from home, in the burning palace of the awesome Attila, king of the Huns.

Such was the fate of them all because of the sleepless, passionate love the Princess Chriemhilde of Burgundy bore Sifrit.

SIFRIT AND BRUNHILDE

MEANWHILE Gunther, king of Burgundy, had no bride for himself. He and the members of his royal court often heard tales of the extraordinary beauty possessed by princesses in exotic, distant lands, so much so that Gunther resolved to court one of those faraway beauties himself. Both his heroes and his warriors approved his decision, especially when Gunther's thoughts turned to that princess who was by all reports the most hazardous to win, and the most glamorous.

Far across the sea, according to Gunther's informants, there reigned a foreign princess named Brunhilde. No lady had ever been like her, for she vanquished her suitors by feats of arms.

Den stein warf si verre,   dar nâch si wîten spranc.
  swer ir minne gerte,   der muose âne wanc
  driu spil an gewinnen   der vrowen wol geborn:
  gebrast im an eime   er het daz houbet verlorn.

A stone she heaved far   and reached it with one bound.
He who sought her love   had dauntless to confound
In three knightly tests   that maiden so well bred;
If he failed one trial   then forfeit was his head.

All the suitors of Brunhilde had thus far, indeed, lost their heads. Gunther, however, would not be dissuaded. The more dangers his informers painted for him, the more eager was Gunther to pit his strength against such a fierce and heartless maiden.

"No matter what may befall," concluded Gunther, "I shall cross the western sea. I shall make my way to Brunhilde. I shall risk my life to win her love; even if I die in the attempt, I want her united to me in wedlock."

"I am opposed to such an enterprise," said Sifrit. "This queen has such barbarous customs that he who desires to serve her must pay dear for such an honor. You shall not find in me any encouragement for this sea voyage of yours."

"Hear now my opinion," said Hagen. "You must solicit from Sifrit himself help and counsel in such an immense voyage. I advise you this, for Sifrit knows many things about this Queen Brunhilde."

"Sifrit, beloved friend," pleaded Gunther, "will you assist me to seek out this fabled Queen of Beauty? . . . If you accept, as I beseech you to do, and if Brunhilde ever falls into my possession, I shall place at your feet both my honor and my life."

Then Sifrit, son of Sigmund, replied, "Let it be as you desire. If you will give me your sister, the lovely Chriemhilde, I shall ask for no other guerdon."

"Here is my hand and oath on it," shouted Gunther. "Let once Brunhilde set foot in Burgundy, and Chriemhilde is yours. How joyously will you live with such a gentle beauty as my sister!" Sifrit laughed in anticipation of that moment while in the back of his mind he was remembering that he would need the magic cape which rendered him invisible and gave him the strength of twelve men, if ever he was to surpass Brunhilde in agility and supernatural strength.

"Tell us then, Sifrit, how we shall arrange to appear before this barbarous queen in all our royal pomp and splendor. How many warriors shall we need? Will thirty thousand be sufficient, do you think?"

"No matter what your numbers, how valiant their hearts, or how strong the temper of their swords, they would all die in her fierce land," mused Sifrit. "That is not the way to capture her. Rather let us float down the Rhine in a small band. . . . Allow me, in accordance with the laws of chivalry, to name those valiant few who shall accompany you. I shall be one; you shall be second, Gunther; Hagen shall

be third; and his brother Dankwart the fourth. Full thousands
will not withstand our virtue and cunning."

"Tell me also, Sifrit, how I am to observe etiquette in her
court, so that during our passage I shall be able to prepare
my words and gestures."

"Believe me, Gunther, the most splended attires that the
minds of men could invent have already been paraded before
her. However, let us be richly dressed so that the women of
her court will not shame us when they gossip at their windows."

"Since that is the case, I shall ask my mother, Queen Uta,
to choose for us that raiment which will do us the most credit
and earn for us the greatest glory," replied Gunther.

Then Hagen interrupted brusquely, "Why go to your
mother, Gunther? It seems to me you would do better to
ask for the Princess Chriemhilde's opinion. She would know
best what would delight a maiden."

Chriemhilde was notified in sufficient time of their desire
for audience so that she and her court were attired radiantly.
She led Gunther and Sifrit by the hand to seats of state
beside her. While she had displayed before them cuts of
richly painted silks, heavy with gold thread, she and Sifrit
exchanged looks of love secretly.

"I should be pained before all ladies," assured Chriemhilde,
"if ever you were to appear at a disadvantage before another
queen. Moreover, do not plead for my assistance; order me
to advise you, for I shall always hasten to fulfill your com-
mands joyously. Ask your servants only to bring me precious
stones laid on a shield so that my women may set them in
these silks, which, as you see, are plentiful in my court. Who
are these warriors I am to attire?" she inquired.

"There will be four of us," answered the king. "We shall
each require three sets of garments, each one more ornate
than the preceding." After he and Sifrit had bowed from
her presence, Chriemhilde summoned thirty skilled women
to work the jewels into the silk fabrics. She cut the heavy
cloth herself, choosing Arabian silk as white and thick as
snow, and green silk as bright and glossy as green clover
leaves. She used sealskins and beaver for the hems and
cuffs. For seven weeks Chriemhilde and her court worked
on these magnificent garments, choosing other gold brocades
from Libya and Morocco, which they edged with ermine. By
the time that the ship which would bear the royalty over
the ocean was launched on the Rhine, the women were
sick from overwork.

"Brother," wept Chriemhilde, "you can still remain here. You will find just as beautiful a wife here in Burgundy." Her tears fell upon the gold of her dress and tarnished it in long streaks. "Sifrit," she sobbed, "I entrust my brother to your protection and recommend him to your vigilance. Let no shadow blacker than death creep over him in the barbarous land of this Brunhilde."

"While I live, Chriemhilde," he replied, "you need never fear. I shall bring him back home to you. Be sure of that."

As the young beauties of Burgundy watched from their windows, a breeze caught the sail of the king's ship and bore it swiftly downstream. "Who will be our pilot?" asked Gunther.

"I," replied Sifrit gaily, "for I know the sea paths." Sifrit took the rudder then while Gunther leaned to an oar. Their horses were well stowed in the hold of the ship. Their food— many dainties, too, and their Rhine wine were well battened down. The cables strained. The canvas bellied out to catch the wind. Before nightfall they had journeyed twenty miles, and at the end of the twelfth day they had come within sight of the dreadful Isentein Castle[4] in the kingdom of Brunhilde, a country known only to Sifrit.

"One word of caution before we arrive," warned Sifrit. "We must all tell the same story and never gainsay it, any one of us. Otherwise, there will befall awful disasters to each one of us. We must tell Brunhilde that Gunther is the king, and that I am only his vassal. If we make her believe this, and keep to our story, I have no doubt that we can take her alive. You must all give me your words now not to fail me in this." When they had pledged their solemn oaths as knights, Sifrit reminded them that he had undertaken this peril not for the sake of Gunther, but because he wanted to win the hand of Chriemhilde.

Their vessel floated so close under the many exterior ramparts of Isenstein Castle that the warriors could look up into the faces of the maidens who crowded its black walls and who gazed down upon them. Gunther exclaimed over and over at their exotic beauty.

[4] In Icelandic *is* = ice; *steinn* = stone. If Sifrit approached Iceland from the east, he would have seen cliffs of dark basalt (since Iceland is a volcanic island) rising 3,000 feet into the air from the sea. On the eastern coast, near the town of Eskifjördur, are beds of Iceland spar, a transparent and vitreous mineral that can be seen from long distances and from the sea probably looks very much like ice.

"Quick," he urged Sifrit. "They are all so lovely! Tell me, I urge you, which one is Brunhilde."

Sifrit threw back his head and laughed. "Look them all over carefully, Gunther," he teased. "Pick out the one you would have as your wife in bed with you, and I will then say if she is Brunhilde."

After a careful scrutiny Gunther pointed upward and excitedly showed Sifrit the direction of his gaze. "Do you see that tall one, the maiden dressed in the long, white robe, as white as the driving snow, as majestic as a queen? That is the one I would choose. Is she the Queen Brunhilde?"

"Your eyes have not deceived you," laughed Sifrit. "That beautiful maiden is, well enough, the noble Brunhilde, the very woman your heart, your courage, and your virility have set out to master!"

When Brunhilde saw that the strange mariners were pointing at her, she withdrew haughtily from the walls and commanded her attendants to do likewise. At once her ladies rushed to deck themselves in finery. (Women are all vain, and that is their custom. When they meet heroes, they wish to be admired.) Some ladies disobeyed Brunhilde and continued to peek through the narrow windows.

As soon as the ship touched land, Sifrit led out two of the fine war horses they had brought, holding the head of one so that Gunther could mount. No one of the maidens missed a part of the proceedings! That was probably the first time that a king's son like Sifrit had ever held the stirrup for anyone! Then Sifrit mounted. Both knights wore the snow-white costumes. Both their horses were also pure white and mettlesome after their long sea crossing. And still the women watched from their windows. Both knights cantered up to the palace, the little golden bells on their saddles tinkling merrily. They had come to Brunhilde's throne, just as they had intended.

Brunhilde covertly watched them approach. She marked their splendid attire, their newly sharpened lance points, their battle swords that hung to their spurs. Hagen and Dankwart advanced behind Gunther and Sifrit. Their costumes were as black and glistening as a raven's plumage. Their shields were brand-new, very wide, very polished, very solidly smithied. Upon their vestments gleamed precious gems from India. Brunhilde knew that they had moored their vessel casually upon her shores, with no one to guard it. Carelessly also had they penetrated her massive fortress, black rock piled tier on tier beneath eighty-six towers, three palace courts, a throne room constructed of marble as green as grass.[5]

Courtiers and servants threw open the great hall of Iceland as the four from Burgundy clanked down the fortress corridors. When valets came to take their arms, Hagen refused angrily until Sifrit persuaded him by explaining that this was the Icelandic custom.

Brunhilde sent them the following greeting: "I wish to be informed without delay who these unknown warriors are who tramp through my palace so proudly, why these knights-at-arms have sailed to my shores."

One of her counselors advised, "None of them has been recognized, save one, who resembles Sifrit. Let us make that one welcome with zeal and prudence. Another one is praiseworthy, I should say. He could be some great king who possesses vast domains. That is probably the case, for his bearing is haughty. The third is extremely tall, but sinister of aspect. I can tell by the somber lights of his eyes that he is fierce and arrogant. The youngest of the four appears to be courtly. As a matter of fact, I admire the way he carries himself, modestly and gracefully as one who has just finished his apprenticeship as page and squire."

"Bring my reception attire," said Brunhilde. "If the mighty Sifrit has come to this land for love of me, he shall not escape with his life. I am not afraid of him, even so much as to think he may force me to become his wife."

Then escorted by five hundred Icelandic barons, each one with drawn sword in hand, Queen Brunhilde crossed the marble floor to the strangers. "Welcome in this land, Sir Sifrit. What is the purpose of your voyage?"

"Many thanks, sovereign Queen, most noble daughter of a king," he replied, "for greeting me first; but I must yield precedence to my liege lord here present, of whom I am only the vassal. He is the king of Rhineland. What more can I say but that he has crossed the sea desiring your love so ardently that he will never renounce it. His name is Gunther, this wealthy and dreaded sovereign. After he has vanquished you, no wish of his remains to be fulfilled. No wish on

[5] While it is possible that the description of Brunhilde's castle could be a poetic memory of Iceland, the green marble of its floors seems altogether inexplicable. There are no real castles or ruins of real castles in Iceland. However, a historical Brunhilde (or Brunehaut), daughter of the Visigoth king of Spain, did marry in 566 Sigebert, king of Austrasie. In our story Sifrit also came from Santen in Austrasie. In Spain there is a green marble called *marbre Campan*.

earth! He demanded my presence on this voyage, which I
would rather of my own free will have declined."

"Are you, Sifrit, this king's vassal?" queried Brunhilde.
"Is he your liege lord? Have you sworn fealty to this King
Gunther? Does your lord know of the three trials he must
undergo?"

Then Hagen cried rudely, "Woman, what are these so
onerous trials? My king will bend every ounce of his great
strength before he lets a woman defeat him!"

"First he must tilt with me. Then he is to throw a boulder,
and then leap to it. Do not be so rash; for if he loses, so you
will all lose your heads!" Brunhilde spoke eye to eye with
Hagen. She was superb in her arrogance.

Sifrit whispered to Gunther to accept the challenge forthwith. "I am ready to contest you, magnificent Queen," said
the king, "and either win you or die."

While judges of the bout were drawing a circle for the
meet and taking their places, and while the seven hundred
or more Icelandic knights were preparing to witness it duly,
Sifrit slipped down to the ship, put on his magic cloak, and
returned to Gunther's side, invisible. Brunhilde meanwhile
had been attired in coat of mail, red-gold helmet, and shield
upon which green stones had been set, stones greener than
grass. (On my word, he was a daring man who thought to
oppose her!) When Hagen saw the Icelandic queen easily
lift her shield, cunningly fashioned of three thicknesses of
gold and metal plate, even Hagen was daunted. He tried to
discourage Gunther.

"What do you say, Sir Gunther?" cried Hagen, more and
more intimidated. "This woman is the devil's bride, no
other!"

Gunther himself fell back when he saw three servants
staggering under the weight of Brunhilde's lance, so thick
and broad, so powerful and pointed, so long and heavy and
filed to a needle point was it! "If only I were home in Burgundy now," thought Hagen, "this barbarian could rule forever safe from my pursuit!"

Hagen's younger brother, Dankwart, thought to himself,
"Has it come to this, that we must all perish because of a
woman?" Despite himself Dankwart looked backward toward
the palace, trying to think of a plan whereby he could retrieve
his own weapons and those of the swarthy Hagen.

There was nothing bashful about Hagen; he spoke his
defiance aloud. "If only I had a sword, we should see whether
this proud woman should not find her temper softened!"

Brunhilde smiled when she heard him. At her command courtiers returned their weapons to both Hagen and Dank-wart. The younger brother blushed until he grew purple at this contemptuous gesture, but Hagen respected her for it.

As Gunther set his feet to receive Brunhilde's spear, he felt a hand on his arm. At first he could not imagine who had touched him, but hearing Sifrit's voice he grew reassured. Sifrit slipped his left arm into Gunther's shield strap and grasped Gunther's lance with his right hand. Even so, even the strength of both warriors together could not stop the force of her lance. With a clap like thunder it rang on the metal shield. Red sparks burst like blinding sunlight at the point of impact. The lance pierced the shield through and through, and clanged on Gunther's helmet. Its force threw both Gunther and Sifrit over backward to the earth!

Sifrit scrambled to his feet. Now it was Gunther's turn to throw the lance, and Brunhilde must fall also or they were lost. Sifrit drew back the lance until his hand was well be-hind his right shoulder. Then, leaping forward, he hurled it—he who had the strength of twelve men—so unerringly and so powerfully that Brunhilde in her turn spun around and fell to the earth. Opposite her Sifrit vomited pools of blood from his effort, and yet the onlookers saw only Gun-ther.

Trembling violently, Brunhilde, on her feet again, called across the lists, "Many thanks to you, Gunther, for such a fine blow!" It did not occur to her that Gunther had not aimed that lance, or even that he was far from capable of such a feat. Red with anger at her first defeat, the noble maiden strode with big steps up to the round boulder that no man alone could lift. Inspecting her arm bands to see that they were tight, she bent down, grasped the stone, set her feet, and then to the Icelanders' delight lifted it gracefully and hurled it a good distance from her. Then, feet close together, she leaped well beyond it, landing with a great ringing of armor.

In utter silence Gunther and Sifrit raised the boulder in their turn. The later heaved it over seventy-two feet, and leaped well beyond it so easily that he was able to carry Gunther along with him.

When she recognized by these deeds that she had been fairly beaten, Brunhilde said to her subjects in low tones, "Approach, relatives, friends, warriors. You have just become the subjects of this Burgundian king." Then all present laid down their arms and knelt before Gunther. All believed he had vanquished their queen justly, by virtue of his superior strength.

Brunhilde took Gunther's hand and acknowledged before her courtiers that all her lands and wealth had also become his property. Of those present Hagen's face was the most triumphant. He grew even more pleased when he observed that the Icelandic queen received Gunther in her palace with every sign of honor and respect that she could make to his chivalry. Hagen's hatred of Brunhilde vanished.

After the agile Sifrit had run toward the ship and hidden his cloak, he entered the hall and asked the king respectfully, "When will the trials begin? Whom are you awaiting, O King? Let us find out the result!" So did the guileful Sifrit behave as if he knew nothing of what had transpired.

"How does it happen, Sir Sifrit," asked Brunhilde, "that you did not witness those games and did not see your liege triumph?"

Quickly Hagen answered, "Noble Queen, when you so impressed us with your overwhelming strength and superb skill, our Sifrit was at the ship."

"I am very happy to learn that my liege has won. That is good news, indeed," cried Sifrit. "Now is your pride humbled, Brunhilde. Now do your recognize your lord and master! Now, noble maiden, must you accompany us to Burgundy!"

Brunhilde dispatched messengers throughout her domains. When her friends and relatives had all assembled, she turned over her kingdom to an uncle. Then amid the tears and wails of her subjects she chose two thousand warriors, eighty-six matrons, and a hundred maidens to accompany her. It was decided that her wedding would be celebrated at Worms-on-the-Rhine. The voyage to the mouth of that river was long and perilous. Queen Brunhilde never saw her native Iceland again.

The double wedding took place at the palace of Gunther, where at the banquet Brunhilde wore the crown of her new kingdom. She wondered sadly why Gunther should have bestowed his sister upon a mere vassal like Sifrit, but promising that he would one day explain why he had conferred such an unparalleled honor upon the Niderland hero, Gunther refused at the moment to reveal his secret. During the wedding supper Brunhilde watched Sifrit and Chriemhilde sitting together, wrapt in their love. Despite her efforts to resign herself, the Icelandic queen's face grew dark; and once tears came to her eyes.

That night Sifrit made to Chriemhilde the supreme offering of his love. They became one in flesh.

In the nuptial chamber of Gunther, however, there was another story! Once the servants and knightly escorts had withdrawn, Gunther hastened to close the door. Then he blew out the lights just as Brunhilde in her fine white linen nightgown walked toward the bed and lay down. "Now," thought Gunther, "I shall obtain what I have desired for so many endless days!"

Although not so beautiful as the Princess Chriemhilde, Queen Brunhilde was still splendid in her virginal loveliness. Gunther lay on the bed beside her and clasped her body close to him. His joy was great. He had already begun to open her robe and to caress her naked body when to his astonishment Brunhilde addressed him in tones of hatred and loathing!

"Noble knight, you must immediately renounce what you intend this night with me! I forbid you to touch me! Know once for all that I have decided to remain a virgin until I learn the secret you and your vassal Sifrit have between you. It concerns me too deeply, and I see that it also concerns your sister Chriemhilde, who has greeted me so affectionately and so regally here in your land. Why have you married your sister to a vassal? It humiliates me even to think of it!"

Gunther, thinking that he could quell her by sheer force, now that she was undressed and weaponless, knowing also that once she yielded to him and lost her virginity she would also have lost her unnatural power both as a warrior maiden and as an individual reigning sovereign, gave no thought to her words. Instead he opened her gown and continued his caresses. Brunhilde, however, had not yet lost her power. Indignantly she wrenched off the braided silk rope she wore about her waist and despite Gunther's attempts to catch her hands, Brunhilde tied the sash tightly about both his feet and his hands. Then she carried him, bent double and trussed up firmly, to the wall, where she suspended him from a hook. Once she had disposed of King Gunther of Burgundy, Brunhilde straightened her robe and climbed back into bed.

"You can stop speaking love words to me, Gunther," she called across the dark room to him, "and stop disturbing my rest also!"

King Gunther was so tied, his head hanging down almost

to the floor, that he could only gasp in mortification and pain, "Untie me, O Queen, I beg of you! Let me go. I swear that I shall never again try to vanquish you, and that I shall only rarely approach your couch."

Brunhilde then walked over, untied him and stood him up on his feet. She allowed him to stretch out on the side of the bed so long as he did not touch her. She never would have endured his wrinkling and disarranging her white linen nightgown.

A radiant, merry Sifrit met only sour looks from Gunther the next morning. At Sifrit's request for information about his wedding joys, Gunther replied that Brunhilde had left him hanging from a hook all night long, right in his own palace!

"Oh, well, I'll take care of her once for all," laughed Sifrit. "I shall see that tonight you sleep so close against her that she never again dares to refuse your love. I shall use the magic cape. What you do is this: be sure to send away the chambermaids and the bedroom pages for the night, so that we shall have neither witness nor any of her people about to whom she could call for help."

"In truth," said Gunther, "assist me in subduing her, for I have led a raging fiend into my bed."

"When you see the candle flames blown out tonight," continued Sifrit, "you will know that I am in the room. I shall quell her proud spirit so that she will lie patiently under your caresses from this night onward!"

"If you would do that, Sifrit," smiled Gunther, "then perhaps I could recover from my humiliation. Only don't go too far! Don't deflower her yourself! Whatever you invent to do, whatever way you choose to whip her will please me —only let me be the one to break open her body."

"On my honor, I don't want to make love to your Icelandic queen," laughed Sifrit. "You need not worry about that! Your lovely sister satisfies me completely, above all females!"

That day seemed as long to Gunther as thirty days. He could hardly sit still during the long banquet and actually dismissed the noble guests early. Sifrit was sitting holding hands with Chriemhilde when all at once he disappeared. "Where did King Sifrit go?" Chriemhilde asked her attendants. "He was here beside me just a few minutes ago. I didn't even feel his hands slip out of mine!" The Lady Chriemhilde, however, was wise enough to keep silent and to retire to her chambers. Sifrit joined her later.

In the royal chamber, as soon as the tapers were extinguished, Gunther hurried to double-bolt the heavy door. Then what screams and what cries came from the bed where Sifrit tried to hold down Brunhilde! Gunther's heart rose joyously and then sank when through the darkness he could tell that the maiden had thrown Sifrit off her!

"Go away from me. Go far away from me!" Brunhilde screamed. "Gunther! You shall be terribly chastised for this!"

Sifrit disguised his voice and in Gunther's tones ordered her to submit. From all the thrashing and gasping on the bed, Gunther could be sure that Sifrit was not consummating the marriage. Once Brunhilde threw Sifrit off the bed so violently that he cracked his head on a bench. After a deep breath Sifrit leaped on her again, pinning down her hands at her sides. Another time she escaped and stood up beside the bed.

"It is unseemly that a royal lady, a queen and the daughter of a king, should have her white shift torn from her body! You shall suffer for this outrage you do me, unfortunate wretch! You shall pay for this before you die!"

Then the struggle began afresh with even greater violence. When Brunhilde tried to tie Sifrit and hang him from the wall, she found that she could not hold him as she had so easily been able to do the preceding night. She squeezed his wrists so hard that the skin cracked and the bright blood ran down his fingers. In trying to untangle her belt so that she could tie at least his hands, she caught her own wrists. Then Sifrit held her on the bed. Then what vengeance did he take while Brunhilde screamed. . . . She trembled from head to foot, and then grew quiet, while Gunther consummated the marriage.

Once her strength was gone, Brunhilde knelt on the floor beside the bed and begged that her life be spared. She promised to be yielding and gentle henceforth, and never to refuse her love. "You have shown me that you are my master," she confessed to Gunther.

Sifrit then released her and stole from the room carrying her braided sash and her golden ring that he had taken by force. With a merry laugh he gave both the ring and the belt as gifts to his beloved Chriemhilde.

After fourteen days the wedding celebrations drew to a close. Sifrit and Chriemhilde prepared to choose retainers and retire to their own Niderland kingdom. They could have required the attendance of Hagen, but that dour lord re-

plied, "Do you not know the tradition of the heads of my
house? My place shall always be, as it has been for my ancestors, close to the queen of Burgundy. I am henceforth
a vassal of our Queen Brunhilde."

No princess was ever so joyously welcomed as was Queen
Chriemhilde by Sifrit's parents in the Niderland. There they
lived happily for many years.

SIFRIT

BRUNHILDE MAINTAINED an outward calm in her new life,
but her thoughts were troubled, for Gunther had never revealed his secret. Nor could Brunhilde understand why Sifrit,
who she still believed was their vassal, never fulfilled his
duties toward them, but on the contrary lived in far-distant
Norway. Tortured by doubt, Brunhilde finally persuaded
Gunther to invite them all to a tournament. To her delight
Sifrit and Chriemhilde, as well as Sigmund and Siglinde, accepted the urgent and loving invitation.

During the course of this magnificent tournament, it happened one day that the two ladies Chriemhilde and Brunhilde
were seated side by side at the table.

"All the lands of the earth should really belong to my
handsome husband," sighed Chriemhilde. "Just see how gallant he is."

"That, of course, could never occur while King Gunther
lives," replied Brunhilde in astonishment.

"See how my Sifrit shines like the moon among lesser
lights!" boasted Chriemhilde.

"Shine as he may," answered Brunhilde curtly, "he cannot
surpass my lord. I have heard your Sifrit swear with his own
lips that he was the vassal of Gunther."

Chriemhilde answered furiously, "I shall have to ask you
to cease such lies! Do you for a moment think that my
brothers would have married *me* to a vassal? Moreover, you
must well have observed that we never pay you any homage
of fealty!"

"We shall see how high you have risen, my fine lady!"
hissed Brunhilde, "and whether or not you are prompt in
acquitting yourselves of those duties!"

"Indeed," taunted Chriemhilde, "I shall show you today
which one of us takes precedence over the other at the church

door! I tell you, I am above all the queens who ever wore crown in this world!"

Each lady imperiously summoned her attendants and ordered them to outdo themselves in the splendor of their attire. Each lady walked confidently between the ranks of waiting knights, who were amazed to see them arrive separately for the first time, up to the portals of the church. Each queen wore her jewels and her most sumptuous gown. Chriemhilde was the more dazzling, however, because of the Nibelungen treasure her lord Sifrit had wrested from the dragon under the linden tree.

Raising her hand majestically, Brunhilde commanded, "Back, *vassal*, and stay far behind me! A mere vassal does not precede a queen into the minster!"

Then Chriemhilde cried in such a loud voice that the knights and courtiers all heard her clearly, "You would do better to curb your tongue, *concubine!* How can one man's concubine be the wife of an honorable king?"

"Whom are you calling a concubine?" gasped Brunhilde.

"You!" shouted Chriemhilde. "Sifrit, my beloved husband, possessed your body first. You were not a virgin when Gunther possessed you! Oh, no! It was not my brother Gunther who took your virginity!"

"On my honor," said Brunhilde, "I shall ask Gunther himself about that!"

"Do so," hissed Chriemhilde. "You have been blinded by your own ignorance. Your calling me a 'vassal' has so kindled my anger that you have lost my friendship forever. Now go into the church and do penance for all your sins!"

While Brunhilde stood weeping at the church door, Chriemhilde swept past her with her train of attendants. When the service was ended, Brunhilde still stood at the minster door waiting for Chriemhilde to emerge. Brunhilde stopped her and said, "Do you still call me a concubine? If that fatal word is true, prove my crime to me now!"

"You would have done better to let me pass," replied Chriemhilde, "because I have the proofs right on my person. Here they are. This golden ring, which I am wearing on my finger, was a gift from my beloved Sifrit on the second day of my marriage."

"That royal ring was stolen from me," cried Brunhilde. "Now do I recognize the traitor who took it! It was you!"

"I did not steal your ring," affirmed Chriemhilde. "My husband Sifrit wrested it from your hand, and this braided

sash also, as proof that he was in your bed. Yes! My beloved Sifrit slept with you first!"

Chriemhilde swept haughtily away to her court. Brunhilde
remained still weeping at the church door until Gunther
could be notified. When the king, distressed and appalled
at his wife's dishonor announced so publicly, inquired of
her what reparation she demanded, Brunhilde assured him
that if he did not avenge her, she would not receive him in
her arms again.

Gunther assembled his court and required the presence
of both queens and of Sifrit. Before his nobles he accused
Sifrit of having vaunted the possession of Brunhilde. Before
the black faces of the Burgundian nobles Sifrit swore that
he had never done any such thing. The courtiers stared
ominously at him. Gunther, however, believed Sifrit and
pardoned him publicly. Sifrit then swore to silence his wife,
and he suggested that Gunther do likewise. Both queens
withdrew from the presence chamber, but Brunhilde hung
her head in grief and shame. She now understood Gunther's
secret. On her way out, she met the dark knight Hagen.

"Who has made my noble Queen weep?" questioned Hagen
angrily. Sobbing, Brunhilde admitted her shame to him.
Hagen's answer was solemn. Bending his knee before her,
Hagen swore, "Chriemhilde's lord will bear the penalty for
your dishonor, or I shall turn my back on the joys of this
earth."

Several of the Burgundian knights during their next council
thought also that Sifrit should be punished for Brunhilde's
disgrace. Gunther did not consent, however; for, as he pointed out, Sifrit was too powerful an adversary for them to
encounter. Like a refrain Hagen kept whispering to Gunther, "Just think, King, how many lands you would encom-
pass, however, if he *were dead.*" Gernot, one brother of
the king, voted openly for Sifrit's death. Giselhers, the
youngest brother, thought on the contrary that no woman's
quarrel was worth the price of a man's life.

"My honor also is involved," argued Hagen. "What tar-
nishes the queen of Burgundy's name also defames me.
Think, King Gunther, of Sifrit's Nibelungen treasure. It could
all be ours. Think of the gold!" Because of Hagen's reasons it was agreed that he should kill Sifrit, lure him to his
death by treachery even, if necessary.

The conspirators subsequently either withdrew or lost interest in the plot, all except Hagen. He arranged to have
false messengers come from the Saxon and Danish kings to

declare their sovereigns' intentions of making war on Burgundy. As Hagen had foreseen, Sifrit volunteered to serve Gunther as he had done previously. Then the implacable Hagen called upon Chriemhilde.

"How can I serve you best in this coming war, Lady?" he inquired.

"First you must not blame Sifrit for Brunhilde's anger," she replied. "Only protect my lord, for the fault was not his. It was mine, and he has chastised my body severely enough as my punishment."

"Tell me how I must protect your lord," Hagen urged. It was common knowledge that Sifrit's horny flesh was invulnerable. "I am your relative," Hagen reminded her, "and as such I only wish your lord all goodness."

"I should not worry at all," confessed Chriemhilde, "if someone during the battle were to curb his thirst for combat."

"Do you worry that some person could wound Sifrit?" persisted Hagen. "If so, you should tell me how I can safeguard him."

"My lord is daring, as you know; and he is wonderfully powerful. When years ago he vanquished the dragon on that mountain, brought that foul worm to his death under the linden tree, Sifrit then bathed in the dragon's blood. What a great hero he is! Ever since that day my lord has been invulnerable. No arm, no weapon can pierce him. All the same, I worry when he rides impetuously through the crush of battle. Then do I tremble in fear that I shall lose his dear life. What anguish grips me then!" (Chriemhilde should have said no more!)

"Hagen, I shall confide in you because you are my uncle. I enjoin you to keep faith with me, for I shall now reveal to you alone that one place on his body where Sifrit could be pierced, even to his death! That day when the red blood gushed from the dragon's dying carcass, as my Sifrit gloriously bathed in its crimson floods, a leaf from the linden tree dropped to his shoulders and adhered. Only in that one place can his body be wounded!"

The faithless Hagen then replied to Chriemhilde, "Embroider then, O Queen, a cross on the back of his robe so that I can see plainly, even through the clouds of dust, the place I must watch as I ride close behind him."

"That is exactly what I shall do," exclaimed Chriemhilde in relief. "I shall choose strands of silk and trace a mystic cross. May your protecting arm keep my lord safe for me!"

"Never fear, Lady," promised Hagen. "I shall not forget."

The next morning the Burgundian knights, led by Gunther, Sifrit, and Hagen, attaching red streamers to their lances as was their custom in time of war, rode gallantly out of the city to battle. They had not gone far, however, when they were met by messengers who announced that the Saxon and Danish kings had revoked their warlike decisions. Despite their relief, the Burgundian knights were crestfallen. Rather than remain idle in their court, Gunther suggested that they prepare for a hunting trip into the Odenwald Forest. Gunther knew that Hagen was waiting for an opportunity to murder Sifrit.

The young Niderland king welcomed the suggestion of a royal hunt and listened to Hagen's clever description of bears and wild boars that roamed the deep woods in great numbers. They returned to the court to notify gamekeepers, masters of the hunt, and to loose the packs of dogs. Brunhilde prepared baskets of food which she sent ahead of them to a spring deep in the forest.

Chriemhilde wept bitterly, however, and pleaded with Sifrit to remain with her at the palace. "Last night I had such a lamentable dream. It was as if two fierce boars had pursued you over the heather. Then I saw the little flowers stained red with—! Ah, I have good reasons for my tears. I have a premonition—every now and then a shudder runs through me—that some implacable enemy is hovering over us with a hatred that no deed of mine can mollify."

"My beloved," comforted Sifrit, "no one hates us here. I have earned the ire of no man! These good warriors are our friends."

"No. It's not true, Sifrit. No, last night my dreams were black and funereal. It seems I dreamed two huge mountains toppled down upon your dear body. If I were never to look upon your face again, do you know what torture would burn into the depths of my being?" Sifrit held her in his arms and then left her chamber rapidly without another word.

When the royal huntsmen had come into the forest, Hagen suggested that he, Sifrit, and Gunther hunt separately so that he who brought down the largest game could be adjudged the winner. "Let us divide the valets and the dogs," proposed Hagen. "He who proves the most skillful forester shall receive our compliments."

"Oh," laughed Sifrit, "that's an excellent idea. Just give me one bloodhound, one which can scent the spoor of a bear through these dark trees, and I'll track down your Burgundian game for you!"

Then Sifrit spurred his fleet horse along the paths, over fallen tree trunks, urged him over streams so dexterously that no game raised by the hound was lost. He speared a fierce wolf-dog, and soon after felled a lion with one of his well-aimed arrows. The beast leaped thrice and rolled over dead. Then he killed a wild bull, a bison, and a buffalo.[6] He also bagged several stags and does. Still his agile horse bore him swiftly through the tangled undergrowth. At last he killed, swinging his war sword with both hands, a monstrous boar as it rushed him, tusks lowered.

The master of the hunt recalled the hounds and ended the chase. The Burgundians laughed as Sifrit rode up to them. "Let a few of our animals live," they teased. "You have denuded our forest of game today." Sifrit laughed merrily with them. They rode together toward the sound of the horn that announced Gunther's camping area. On the way they spotted a huge bear.

"Loose my hound again," said Sifrit. "We'll have some fun with this old fellow." Then Sifrit dismounted and approached the bear, which was trapped by the hunters on all sides of it. Easily Sifrit tied the bear's claws and slipped a noose on it, forcing the animal to trail after him like a dog on a leash. Thus Sifrit rode into Gunther's camp, leading a bear by the neck!

Sifrit's hunting costume was so splendid that there probably never was seen one so sumptuous in all Burgundy. His robe was of a thick, rich black. His toque was of sable, as costly, surely, as the fur straps of his quiver. Wild panther skins decorated the quiver. Over his robes he wore a collar of white lynx scalloped with gold. He bore his fabled sword Balmung in his hand. From his quiver protruded arrows with shafts of gold.

As he rode into the circle where the king and his nobles reclined on golden chairs, while under the trees the cooks and kitchen boys roasted game over spits and spread delicious food on embroidered cloths, Sifrit released the bear that he had hauled behind him. Then he roared with laughter to see the fierce beast lumber between the campfires. The cooks fled clutching their utensils! The nobles holloed for the dogs to be untied, or called for their swords. Kettles and chairs went flying! Dogs barked and servants yelled. Then, still laughing, Sifrit killed the bear with one stroke of Balmung.

[6] Buffalo (*urus*) is one of the rare animals mentioned in the text. It is found in the annals of Charlemagne's hunts, and also in connection with the Valhalla warriors.

Everyone agreed that he should be praised for his impromptu diversion. They complimented him on the blow that had slain the bear.

The nobles took places at the magnificently appointed tables, where they were served the rich food that Brunhilde had ordered for their enjoyment. However, the wine stewards still had not arrived! Otherwise, no one could do anything but compliment Gunther upon his feast.

"Your cooks keep serving me one delicious roast after another," called Sifrit, "but where are your wine stewards? Either treat hunters better than this, or I shall leave off the chase altogether! Haven't I deserved a better reward than this?"

"Indeed, we shall repair such an oversight," called Gunther to Sifrit. "Besides, it is not I but Hagen who is responsible for this misdeed!"

"Truly, honored lords," apologized Hagen, "I thought we were going to hunt in another direction today. I sent our wines to that rendezvous. Therefore if we are all so thirsty already, I hope they will find us before long!"

"And I hope your body is torturing you with thirst also," replied Sifrit. "What we need here is seven draft horses heavily laden with mead and wine. Otherwise, we should have camped closer to the Rhine."

This was what Hagen had carefully planned.

"There is a pure, crystal-clear spring not far from here, if you are so thirsty, Sifrit." Then as the Niderland king prepared to ride to the spring, Hagen continued, "Your noble Chriemhilde is always boasting of how fleet of foot you are, Sifrit. I for one should certainly like to race you."

"And I too," added Gunther.

"Very well," agreed Sifrit. "I'll race you both. And it shall be recounted afterward how you stripped down while I outpaced you both loaded with my heavy hunting suit, my sword Balmung, and my quiver full of arrows." As he spoke Hagen and Gunther were disrobing until they stood ready in their white shirt sleeves.

At a signal all three set off through the woods toward the linden-tree fountain. Sifrit won easily. He arrived long before them. Even so he would not commit the discourtesy of drinking before Gunther. To while away the time Sifrit unbucked his sword, stripped off his quiver and shield, and tossed them on a bed of moss. He laid his lance against the trunk of the linden tree; its point disappeared among the green leaves.

As soon as the others had arrived, Gunther threw himself face down beside the clear, limpid spring and drank. Then after him Sifrit did likewise. Behind him Hagen, marking well the cross, drove his lance at it and through Sifrit's body so carefully that the blood shot up from Sifrit's heart and wet Hagen—all over his white shirt. The lance stayed bolt-upright in the wound. That was the first time Hagen ever fled, and the last time.

Shielding his eyes from the horrible sight, Hagen rushed away from Sifrit. . . . Sifrit raised himself to his knees, then to his feet. The iron tip of the lance protruded from his chest. His eyes sought his sword Balmung, but he could not reach it in time. All he could reach was his shield. This he heaved across the clearing at Hagen. Hagen fell to the ground, stunned by the impact. The precious gems from the shield rolled into the green moss. The clang re-echoed through the forest.

His blood poured from Sifrit. He tottered to his feet. Clots of red blood from his opened heart flowed upon the forest flowers at his feet, staining them all scarlet. Sifrit's knees buckled. He slipped to the ground.

"Misfortune upon both your heads, cowardly and faithless warriors. How have my exploits, accomplished at your request, served me? I kept faith with you, for which I now receive your payment. You have today betrayed also my wife, who is your relative. All your children will be held accursed for this your deed today. Your names shall be scratched from the roll of the valiant and honorable."

Little by little the other knights came by twos and threes to look upon the dying Sifrit. At their lamentations Gunther also began to weep. Sifrit taunted him then, "Let the author of this deed weep; that shall not efface his guilt. He could have renounced this plot."

"Ah," cried Hagen in disgust, "what are you all sniveling about? Our cares are over! Glory be to me who ended his domination!"

Desperately Sifrit struggled against death. "The day will come when you will regret my murder," he told them. "You can believe the dying words of him you have slain."

Carefully the warriors raised the corpse of Sifrit and laid it on his shield. They prepared to bear him through the trees. They debated what story of accident to invent for Chriemhilde and how to protect Hagen from her wrath.

"Bah!" snorted Hagen, picking up Balmung and buckling it to his own belt. "I myself shall carry Sifrit. I myself shall

set his body outside his wife's chamber door. Let her find
him at dawn when she starts for matins in the church. Let
her weep! What do I care for the tears of a woman who
brought shame to Queen Brunhilde of Burgundy?" '

Chriemhilde mourned Sifrit all the days of her life. Sigmund and Siglinde returned to the Niderland without her.
She asked them for the Nibelungen treasure. When she had
received her fabulous dowry, she thought to use it to buy
knights who would avenge Sifrit; but Hagen stole the key to
it. When Attila, king of the Huns, asked for her hand in
marriage, Gunther consented, glad to have her malevolence
far in eastern lands, far away from him and his court.
Although Hagen thought it was a mistake to let her assume
such new riches and honors, Gunther allowed Chriemhilde
to marry Attila.⁸

Years later when Chriemhilde sent messengers to Worms-
on-the-Rhine assuring them all of her pardon and undying
affection and inviting them to a tournament at Attila's court,
Hagen opposed their acceptance. Gunther, Gernot, and the
youngest brother Giselhers, who had always adored Chriemhilde, accompanied by Hagen, Folker, and their most valiant
knights, traveled royally down the Danube. There Chriemhilde sat in royal state, awaiting them.

Her Huns murdered the Burgundians for her sake, all but
Gunther and Hagen. Chriemhilde incited the Huns to chop
down the Burgundians right in her mead hall; and when she
saw that some were still alive, she set fire to the hall, trying
to burn them alive. They became so parched with thirst that
to survive they had to drink blood from the corpses. Finally,
only Gunther and Hagen remained. The great warrior
Dietrich brought them tied to Chriemhilde, on condition that
she spare their lives.

Chriemhilde broke her word to Dietrich. First she had
Gunther beheaded. She carried his bleeding head to Hagen.
"Now tell me where my Nibelungen treasure is," she ordered,
"you loathsome devil!"

"Only I know, Lady, so be sure you will never find out for
all your cruelty and treachery." Hagen had thrown the
Nibelungen gold to the bottom of the Rhine. Wielding Balmung in both her hands, Chriemhilde beheaded Hagen herself. The Huns were so horrified from all the days and nights

---

' The section that follows is a summary of Adventures 17 to 39 of the
Nibelungenlied.
⁸ Attila is called Etzel in the text; Etzel is also a name for the Volga.

of carnage this fierce queen had caused in their land that one of them stepped forward and slew her where she stood.

Attila of the Huns watched her die. What happened after that I cannot say . . .

. . . But if you wish to see the linden-tree spring, walk through the forest of Odenwald, near the village of Ottenheim. This fountain still flows limpid and pure, just as I tell you. Do not doubt me. You will find it.

6

Germany: Tannhäuser

INTRODUCTION

TANNHÄUSER IS THE HERO of a strange and mysterious myth that has haunted the pages of German literature ever since the high Middle Ages.[1] This legend has been treated by the best of the German Romantic poets as well as by such writers and musicians as E. T. A. Hoffmann in his *Tales*[2] (c. 1815 ff.), and Richard Wagner in his opera *Tannhäuser* (1845). The same medieval myth is also found in northern Britain, in the Italian Apennine mountains, and near the volcanoes of Vesuvius and Etna. However, Tannhäuser's presence—and his disappearance from the earth—have been commemorated most often in those areas that are now Germany.

Quite plainly, the story of Tannhäuser bears witness to the fact that in certain areas Christianity replaced the old religion of Europe only with great difficulty, for, like the Roman Emperor Julian, Tannhäuser is an apostate.

The myth would have us believe that a medieval pagan priestess vied with the leader of all Christendom, that her worship continued throughout the Middle Ages, and that she still resided in the megalithic temples of western Europe, which were old before the Greeks invaded Greece. Although her rites were officially forbidden, her worship was celebrated

---

[1] The version given here is from "Le Paradis de La Reine Sibylle" (Paris 1897, 1930), or The Paradise of Queen Sibyl.

[2] "Serapionsbrüdern." See also Johann Tieck, Ludwig Beckstein, and H. V. Ofterdingen.

on magical mountains throughout Europe. She came to be
confused with the classical goddess Venus, and her magic
mountains were called Venusbergs in Germany, where the
written versions of the Tannhäuser myth seem to have origi-
nated. Her worship was celebrated at several real mountains:
Hörselberg, Waldsee, Freiburg, and Wolkenstein, as well as at
peaks in Italy and Scotland. The legend was related by various medieval writers, among them, Thomas of Erceldoune,
Vincent of Beauvais, Gervase of Tilbury, Antoine de La Sale,
and Andrea de Barberino. Their material came largely from
the German *ballade* called "Tannhäuserlied," and from the
adventures of an actual thirteenth-century German knight,
poet, and crusader (1205-70) named Tannhäuser. He is said
to have waited upon Pope Urban IV (1261-64) before retir-
ing permanently into his magic mountain (*Zauberberg*).

The version of Tannhäuser's story which follows is excerpt-
ed from the French of Antoine de La Sale (c. 1388–c. 1462)
and to my knowledge has not been previously translated.
La Sale is better known for his *Fifteen Joys of Marriage*
(trans. 1926, 1959) and his other work of fiction, *Little John
of Saintré* (trans. 1931).

His telling of the Tannhäuser myth is very interesting for
several reasons. From the point of view of literature we have
in La Sale a modern writer of prose fiction whose world is on
the verge of the Renaissance, but still darkened by the
Hundred Years War. Nonetheless our author has a new sense
of purpose and of craft. We watch him struggle with a novelist's problems, although the novel as a literary form does not
yet exist. Renaissance writers will soon invent it, and Cervantes will use it to describe a similar descent into an underground cavern in *Don Quixote*. The reader will see how, in
his opening remarks, La Sale wrestles with credibility, point
of view, the reader's skepticism, and the difficulty every
creative artist has in *persuading* and capturing his audience.
Throughout the work, La Sale purposely befuddles his reader
by changing pronouns: "I," "we," "you," "he." In this way he
draws the reader out of his reality and into that of the writer.
He works hard upon the reader's sense of drama and mystery, upon his presumed fear of height, assuming that the
reader shares the medieval hatred of mountains for the haz-
ards they posed. Artfully he entices the reader with his per-
petual "I cannot . . . I can," hoping to change the world with
mere words.

It is so rare for a medieval writer to observe and report
upon a physical landscape that the modern reader hardly

dares believe what a treasure he has in La Sale. The mountain he describes, with its subterranean caverns, lacks only twentieth-century technical and archaeological terminology to become what it surely is: a megalithic chambered tomb very similar to the long barrow of West Kennet in Wiltshire, England, within its complex of the Avebury group. Such a Neolithic gallery-grave is not medieval, of course, but dates from c. 3000 B.C. Like the cave in our tale, the West Kennet barrow has a facade or outer wall of stone, an approach passage, and north and south chambers, some of which are cubes; the transepted gallery described by La Sale also occurs regularly throughout European multiple tombs.

Thus, the mountain and cave of La Sale were parts of a temple complex from Neolithic days when goddesses like the Delphic Oracle (see my *Ancient Myths*[3]) and her associate, the Cumaean Sibyl, not far from Mount Vesuvius, reigned throughout Europe. According to the old religion, an initiation ceremony allowed the candidate to descend into an underground chamber, simulate death, undergo great trials, and experience a rebirth into a new life. The early Christian Church continued this custom, calling such pagan shrines "purgatories." The most celebrated purgatory during medieval times was the one at Lough Derg (Red Lake) in County Donegal, Ireland, to which pilgrimages were made in the twelfth century in honor of a Patrick, for whom the purgatory was named. Although Pope Alexander VI ordered it closed in 1497, it was still being used in 1790. Medieval accounts of the Patrick's Purgatory make no reference to a pagan goddess, however.

As is the case in all the Tannhäuser myths, the Queen Sibyl whom we meet in La Sale's version is the goddess Venus. In both Roman and Greek mythology, Venus (or Aphrodite), the daughter of Jupiter (Zeus), was the goddess of love. Although she often killed her lovers—Adonis, Hippolytus, and Paris, for example—her reputation improved among the Romans because, as lover of Anchises, she became mother of Aeneas, the founder of Rome. The Middle Ages celebrated her love affair with the war god Mars (see Jean de Meung, *Romance of the Rose*, v. 13,847 ff.), a liaison which seems to have established the format for the famous triangular myth of adultery which later surfaced in such stories as that of King Mark, Queen Isolde, and Tristan. In her role as moon goddess, Venus was the protector of lovers: among them, Cu-

[3] New American Library, New York, 1960.

pid and Psyche, Atalanta and Hippomenes, Hero and Lean-
der, Pygmalion and Galatea, Pyramus and Thisbe, Pluto and
Proserpine, Paris and Helen, Aeneas and Dido. From this list
of love stories the medieval writers of romance found major
sources of material, to which they added their own original
ingredient, romantic love.

It is as moon goddess that Venus becomes connected in
medieval literature with a real priestess of the old religion,
the Cumaean Sibyl. The Sibyl's shrine in Italy was at Cumae,
near dark Lake Avernus, at the opening of a cavern or underground temple, and it was here that she led heroes down
into the underworld, her most famous initiate being Aeneas
(see Vergil's *Aeneid*). The rituals associated with her sanc-
tuary bequeathed a formula in European letters: a goddess or
priestess, a golden wand or golden bough, a mountain or vol-
cano, a dark lake, underground passages, ordeals of initiation,
metal doors guarded by monster(s), strange noises or groans,
a narrow "perilous" bridge over a rushing stream, lighted tapers, white-clad priests, and paradise after purgatory.

Like the Cumaean Sibyl, Venus resided on or near mountains. Her husband was the black god Vulcan, who, according
to Homer, was also a son of Jupiter. This blacksmith of the
gods ruled fire and forges and had his metal workshop underground near volcanic Mount Etna. There were priestesses of
Venus at many of the places Ulysses is said to have stopped
or been seduced: Scylla lived near Etna, Circe in the Gulf of
Gaeta, the Sirens at Stromboli or north of Messina, and
Calypso on Malta.

Antoine de La Sale, who wrote his version of Tannhäuser
before 1440, knew Provence well, since he was for some time
tutor to the court of Count René d'Anjou (later King of Sicily). "Good King" René and his close friend, the Visconti
Duke Charles of Orleans, helped to introduce the pagan
themes of the Italian Renaissance to western Europe. It is
possible that La Sale received their expert advice as he composed his work. In any case, his material is well presented
and the pagan symbols artfully displayed. The author pretends innocence, expecting the reader to collaborate or add
associations: peacock = the bird of Venus; horses = the common pagan sacrificial animal; rocking stone = dolmen; wealth
= possessions under the earth; magical numbers = 9, 30, 330;
"popular tradition" = paganism. The cord that one unravels
as one descends into a cave refers back to the legend of
Theseus on Crete, for his was one of the earliest (i.e., proto-
typical) descents into the underworld. Very few heroes de-

scended and returned alive. As Vergil warned, only the descent was easy: *"Facilis descensus Averni."*

La Sale seems to have been unaware of any source, such as the German Tannhäuser, or unwilling to admit such a source, for his hero remains unnamed. On the other hand, his proper names are thoughtfully chosen. The character whom he calls Anthony Smoke or Smokey reminds us of the blacksmith of the gods, Vulcan. The name of his mountain, Monte Moynaco, is of suitably difficult etymology. Perhaps it derives from the Latin *moenia*, which means fortified mountain, or even prehistoric hill-fort.

La Sale is retelling an ancient, pagan myth. The most memorable ancient heroes who precede Tannhäuser are: Ulysses, Hercules, Orpheus, Theseus, Aeneas, and Plutarch's initiate into the mysteries of the underworld, Thespesios.

THE ASCENT

To CLIMB TO the top of the mountain, there are two routes, one to the right, and one to the left. The latter, to the left, is actually much shorter, which is why I came back down that way; but it is a much steeper climb going up, since it is precipitous and full of rocks, and surely no horse alive could ever climb it. Along this road there are two very pretty springs of clear water, as cool and fresh as anyone could hope to find. They say even that they never harmed either man or beast, no matter how much they drank, no matter how overheated they were.

The other way, the one on the right hand, is quite a bit longer, but a much easier climb, for it has several switchbacks. A man could, if he really wanted to do so, ride his horse to the very top, but since that would be very hard on the animal, I went up on foot, leading my horses behind me. The length of this road there is not a drop to drink. But this route rambles on so long, this way and the opposite, that finally you come out on the other side of the mountain, right across from the summit which is called the crown of the peak, where the entrance to the cavern is, as has already been indicated.

From there to the summit you have thereabouts two thousand paces, or perhaps about two thirds of a mile ... One thing I am more definite about is this: if there is any wind at all, you stand in very great danger of your life.

And, even with not a breath of wind blowing, still what a hideous sight it is to look down into valleys on all sides! This is most confoundingly so on the left-hand side; for there the summit literally falls away from you, and so steep, and so far down that it is totally unbelievable. Whoever went up there on horseback would have to be insane. Horses will allow themselves be taken up if they are led by the bridle, however, as we have seen, all the way to the very summit of the mountain; for at the very top there is a little smooth plot of ground, just as green as any meadow.

This so-called crown of the mountain actually is a rim of rocks sculpted all around, at a height of about three lances. That is on the side of the mountain where you come out on the summit after having gone up the larger path. And all the rest of the mountain top is about six thousand feet high, or more, and just as straight up as a rock wall. And into this crown of rock there are two passageways which lead onto the crest, where the entrance to the cavern is.

One thing I will swear to, for sure, that the better of these two passageways is sufficient to strike such fear into the heart, which knows in any case how awful the fear of the superhuman can be, and most confoundingly on the way down. For if by some mischance the foot were to slip, there is no power on earth to stop it safely there, beyond God's.

And just to *look down* into that terrible, deep, hideous chasm, there is not a human heart that could stop pounding.

At the foot of this precipice, which is called the crown of the mountain, there lie strewn about several huge boulders, which can, if pushed by many people, be rocked. This I absolutely swear to you: if one of these rocking stones is rolled toward the edge, even ones not bigger than a wine keg, in a flash it will be lost to sight, and supposing it's a clear, still day, you will hear it as plain as anything, when it strikes rock and bounces, and strikes, all the way down. Even so, there are several fairly wide clearings on this mountain where the country people come to cut grass, which they fashion into haycocks too, and tie with braids and then just let roll down-

hill. Also on this mountain several herds pasture, and some
sheep graze there too, both because of the particularly lush
herbage that grow there.

The lower summit and the regal crown, or true summit,
are separated from each other by a saddle which goes up
about another hundred and twenty feet to the higher peak.
And there is the entrance to the cave, on the right-hand side.

The entrance is small, shaped like an oblong shield, that is,
pointed at the tip and widening at the top. There is a stone at
the entrance so that anyone wishing to enter is obliged to
squat all the way to the ground and squeeze in on all fours,
and inch down the passage foot by foot until you come out
into a perfectly square chamber, situated on the right-hand
side of the bottleneck, where there are seats carved into the
rock, on every side. The chamber measures something like
eight or ten feet, as wide as it is long, and of that same
height. Within this chamber there is another, round passage-
way, about the dimensions of a man's head, which lets in a
very little daylight, probably that faint because of the great
thickness of the mountain. In order to advance farther, one
has to turn right again and descend feet-first, because otherwise it is not possible, the tunnel becoming narrow and the
incline so steep that it goes straight downward.

THE DESCENT

As FOR THE REST of it and the other marvels that were to be
seen, I personally can no longer relate with authority, not
having gone farther than that, my chief business not requiring
me to do so, for any good reason. Even if I had wanted to go
farther on into the cave, which I did not want to do, I could
not have done so without great danger to my person. To tell
the truth, I could not myself say another thing about it at all,
just that I went there with a scholar of that region. This was
Doctor Jehan de Sore, who actually guided me and some
people from the town of Monte Moynaco, no more nor less.

They and I also heard a shrill voice call from down below in
the caverns, sounding very much like the screams of a
peacock, seeming to come from afar off.

The people said it was the call of the Sibyl, ... from Paradise.

As far as I am concerned, I cannot believe a word of it. I
think it was probably the whinnying of my horses, which I
had left at the foot of the mountain. They were away down
there in the distance, and very far off from me. Thus, I do
not actually know from my own experience a single other
thing, except what the country folks and the people from that
town told me.

Some people just make fun of it altogether, while others
put their full trust in it because of the ancient knowledge of
the ordinary country people. Add to this the account of five
men from the above-mentioned locality, Monte Moynaco,
who personally explored this cavern more in depth than any
people are known to have done up to this time. Now, I myself spoke personally to two of the five who, having much
enjoyed the fellowship of those telling and listening to the stories and adventures connected with this cave, undertook to go
themselves all the way to the metal doors which hang on
their hinges night and day, as I will shortly make clear to
you.

Therefore they made provision of coils of rope, of both
heavy and light cord, that were twelve thousand yards long
each, and they tied one end to the entrance of the cave
so that they could feel their way back, if worse came to
worse. Then too they prepared lanterns, candles, flints, guns,
provisions for five days, and other necessities. Then in they
went.

They calculate that the first narrow cave extends about the
range of an arrow that is shot from a crossbow. After this
distance, it widens until men can walk comfortably in single
file, and in some place two abreast, in other places three
abreast. They passed through this wide cave, the way still going downhill, maybe a distance again of a half mile, they
thought. Then they came to a fault in the earth, which cut
across the cave, out of which blew such a fantastically violent
and unimaginable draft of wind that not a man among them
dared set one foot into it, or even a toe. Every time one of
them stepped close to it, he felt sure that such a force would
sweep him quite away. They were so frightened that they
made the decision to turn back at that point. So they turned

hastily around there, actually leaving behind them most of their equipment. The sort of thing they did is what idle young people often take on, when they have nothing better to do for amusement.

THE PRIEST AND THE GERMANS

DOUBTLESS, there are many strange and marvelous sights within this cavern, at least according to popular tradition and local beliefs, obviously nothing that a man could believe in as far as fact if it were not for the testimony of several church men and others in the neighboring castle of Monte Moynaco. There resided a certain priest named Don Anthon Fumato, who was called Sir Anthony Smokey. After several bouts of lunacy, he was never really in his right mind again. During his illnesses he came and went around the area, telling of the sorts of marvels which people sick with this type of illness customarily tell, but without harming anyone in any way.

This priest several times swore uphill and down, without varying his story in any detail, that he had been inside this cave, all the way to the metal doors, which night and day swing ajar, slam shut, and swing open again. However, since he was often out of his mind altogether, as we have already explained, very few people believed that what he swore to was fact.

For instance, they say that this priest kept saying that he had once guided two men from one of the counties inside Germany, and that they had continued past the metal doors. Before they undertook this expedition to the cavern itself, however, they asked to hear about the adventures, which the priest told them word for word, reassuring them, especially the one who wanted to be the first to have gone through those portals and beyond. So they made up their minds to go, and they went.

When they came to the metal doors, and before they actually proceeded beyond them, they requested the priest to

await their return to that point for the space of twenty-four
hours, the length of a natural day. He told me that he did
this, exactly as he undertook to do, but that while he was
awaiting their coming, he fell asleep.

While he still slept, he seemed to see them returning, each
one bearing in his hand a lighted taper which threw out a
peculiarly brilliant light, and it seemed to him then that they
spoke to him and asked him to wait for them a little while
longer, for they would very shortly return again. At these
words the priest awoke, wondering if he had not been dream-
ing a dream which had in actuality really occurred.

Then he knew not what to do, whether to go after them or
to wait, as he had just that instant been requested to do, and
as he had given his word to do. He decided therefore to wait
a little longer, which he did, he recalled, for the period of another half day, or for twelve more hours. They never returned.

Then he left, exiting in the same way as he had entered,
and came out of it altogether. And from that day to this, not
a word of news about these two men has ever been heard, as
to whether they remained inside, or whether they departed
from there as he had dreamed they did. Everybody he told
about these events asked him to tell more about the marvels
of this cave, and what he had found there.

What he told about the entrance corroborates what we already knew, up to the downdraft of wind, which gave more
credence to whatever else the priest recalled. After the cutting
in two of the cave by this rushing wind, he said that this current rushing through the fissure lasts no more than thirty feet.
Actually, it blows hardest at the outset, for if a person were
to take only three or four steps forward into it, he could
quite easily pass through the rest. After this wind, a person
can advance as much as a distance of eighteen hundred feet
without encountering any new peril, still going downhill all
the time.

Then you come to a bridge so strange that you cannot tell
what sort it is; it seemed to me anyway that it was hardly a
foot wide but extremely long. Below the bridge is the most
awful, yawning chasm, at the bottom of which there flows a
huge, rolling river, which makes such a loud noise that everything seems from all sides at once to be melting into it, so
marvelous is its huge attraction. As soon as you set your two
feet upon this bridge, however, it becomes wide enough, and
the more you walk forward on it, the wider it becomes and

the less it sags in the middle, and the less roars the rushing water underneath. Once past the bridge, the road stretches out plainly enough before you, wide and straight, and at that point the cave appears to be not naturally made, but constructed to be that way, or made by artificial means.

The way goes along, crossing this well-lighted, fairly wide cave for quite a distance, but which it is difficult to approximate with any degree of accuracy. However, at the opposite end of this chamber there stood two dragons, one on either hand, who were not real but artificial. In reality, I was not sure but that they were alive, except that they stood very still, because their eyes were so fiery that they actually cast light from them. After these two dragons, you enter a very narrow chamber, where the passage requires single file again, but it lasts for only about a hundred feet.

Then you come into a small, square antechamber. It is here, at this point in the cave, that the two doors swing open and clang shut so continuously that a person has no difficulty perceiving that whoever enters can only do so at the cost of being twice welcomed, and all battered. This was the trial, which completely daunted the two Germans, about whom we have already heard, and which also convinced the priest never to venture beyond the antechamber. They were so terrified that more than once they were about ready to give up the adventure.

Nevertheless, one of them thought it over, and told the other that really they should be ashamed to return then, considering how much they had already ventured, and that he firmly believed that the swinging doors presented no greater danger than the risks incurred in the windy draft, or at the perilous bridge, or at the sight of the hideousness of the dragons, all of which had finally proved easy to undergo. So they agreed that the speaker would go first, because at each of the other tests the priest had gone first, since it was he who was their guide, he, as it were, who had been guaranteeing their safety.

Therefore the speaker entered first, all at once, at such a burst of speed as would take a person across a green meadow, and the second German followed close after, but not before having requested the priest to await them there, which he did.

From the other side of the swinging doors not a ray of light whatsoever shone forth. There could only be heard a loud humming noise, like the murmur of a great many voices

talking all at once. As far as the other marvels beyond these
metal portals are concerned, as we have mentioned earlier,
there is not a mortal of our age, so far as I have been able to
discover, who knows more of them than the priest has already disclosed.

Many people put no faith at all in these marvels, particularly because of the priest's weakness in the head, which often causes him to have periods of madness, as we have
already explained. Because of which, some people say he saw
all such visions in the first place. Just the same, during the
times when he was in his right mind, he swore to all of it.
Then he was quite the gentleman and of most pleasant acquaintance. In any case, whatever he said about the places up
to the downdraft of wind had been corroborated by the others who had ventured that far.

As far as the rest, for what lies beyond the metal gates, not
a person can be found who knows anything at all. Exception
must be made, of course, for the old folks of the area who,
by general consent and common knowledge, tell all about it
and claim to possess the truth. Individually and collectively,
they tell some tales which are pretty hard to believe, although, to be sure, I have heard the same account elsewhere,
perhaps not so coherently presented, however.

They say, for instance, that once upon a time there was another knight, also from one of the territories of Germany,
where people are generally great travelers and great questers
after the adventures in the world. This particular knight
heard tell of the adventures of this mountain. He decided to
go there, and go he did. From this knight were learned more
of the perils and marvels of this kingdom of Queen Sibyl. He
told about the fissure where the wind whistled past, about the
dragons, and the metal doors, and other things which the
priest reported. His account certainly adds more proof to
what the priest has claimed.

THE COUNTRY PEOPLE vouch for the fact that the abovestated German knight, he and his servant, actually entered the underground. They subsequently told of it, saying that when they came to the place beyond the metal doors, they saw a most splendid, richly adorned, gleaming door which lit up the whole chamber, until it sparkled like crystal. And after they had looked carefully around them, they realized how long they had remained silent, without hearing the slightest sound. They were quite amazed at this, because when they were in the outer chamber, in front of the metal doors, they had heard a very loud sound like the murmuring of many people, it had seemed to them at the time. Now that they were inside, they no longer heard any sound whatsoever.

They remained standing still for quite some time, wondering what to do. Their thoughts were interrupted by the sound of a voice, coming from quite near the door. Then the knight gathered enough courage to cry out. Not long thereafter he was answered and asked what he was seeking and from whom he came. He replied to the voice that he was a knight from one of the territories of Germany, and that he had journeyed there in order to see the marvels of this world, as his condition obliged him to do, if he would acquire the honor and glory of chivalry. He was then asked and most humbly requested to grant them of his own kindness a short delay until the Queen could be notified of his arrival and presence.

Shortly thereafter there appeared before him a great number of people of the most honorable rank, who asked him the same two questions, to whom he gave the same replies. Then they caused the door to be opened before him, bidding him a cordial welcome, and then receiving him most respectfully with proper ceremony. However, before they had him pass through still another door, which was more beautiful and ornate than the one before it, they ushered him into an intimate chamber, which was hung with costly tapestries. There they assisted him to disrobe, both outer and inner clothing being taken from him down to the skin. Then they robed him in other most luxurious garments. Then, to the sound of melodic music played on instruments, they led him through gardens, halls, and chambers, each one more beautifully furnished than one could imagine. At the entry to each room and each gallery, there were large groups of ladies and damsels, of knights and squires, all superbly dressed and most expensively too, all having gathered to receive him with proper dignity.

Before all this company he was taken to the Queen. She was seated on her tribunal, and attended by many persons, just as if she were the sovereign of earth, such were the appearances of those about her in all their indescribable elegance, so magnificent that one could never dream of becoming so wealthy. She greeted the knight as a knight deserves to be greeted, like a man who recognizes worth and pays the proper respects to honored ladies and men of distinction. By all then in their turn, he was most honorably received and with sweet affection, as persons of breeding know how to do. The Queen greeted him in true sovereign fashion, taking pleasure in his acquaintance, like one who much desired to keep him in her service forevermore.

Therefore after having greeted him with due ceremony, and after having inquired about his name, his rank, and his quest, she asked him from which of the German marches he came and from what country. For this Queen and all those ladies who live within know how to speak all the languages of the earth. As soon as they have spent the period of three hundred thirty days inside, they know all languages, and as soon as they have been inside for a year and nine days they understand all languages as well as they do their own native tongue, although they cannot speak them all until the whole term is past. The knight told her what his name was and the name of the marches from which he came.

Then she asked him what he thought of this country and of the sights which he was seeing, and if over beyond, they had so many handsome subjects and such immense wealth as she had. And the knight told her that they did not, nor ever could have, for he could not believe that even in ten worlds there could be such treasures as she had in hers alone.

"Still," said the Queen, "there will be even more of them here, for we shall continue to increase in wealth as long as the century lasts."

"Truly, Madame?" said the knight. "Therefore you are, you and your people, the most fortunate of all the ages. And when the world shall come to an end, Madame, what will happen to you?"

To this she replied: "We shall become what it has been ordained that we become. Do not seek to know more than that. Instead, examine all these unattached ladies whom you see present, and select the one most to your taste for yourself. I will give her to you."

At this point the knight bent very humbly before her to show his gratitude, saying that truly he had only journeyed there for the purpose which he had already stated. Then the Queen explained to him their customs, and set for him the term of his residence, for a period of eight days, on the ninth day set for his departure. If he did not wish on the ninth day to depart, then he could not leave until the thirtieth day. And in the event that on the thirtieth day he did not take his leave, he could not depart until the three hundred thirtieth day, and if it happened that on the thirtieth day after three hundred he still did not wish to leave, the prevailing usage required that he never thereafter depart.

With these three terms of residence the knight was very pleased, and he chose the first; but afterwards, the second; and from the second, the third. For so great was the endless pleasure which he experienced there, that one day was to him more like an hour.

However, before he could decide as to whether he should stay or leave, and when, he was called upon to elect the one lady the most to his taste. The same was true for his squire, who was therefore equally delighted. Thus, this knight lived there for a period of three hundred days, counting them carefully as they sped past. Thinking of one of his past relationships one day, however, he suddenly began to feel a pain in his heart. From this sad thought, he began to love God so much that he turned to considering for what fellowship he had decided to scorn His Creator, acting in worldliness against His will and His commandments. He then thought preponderantly of the very horrible sin in which he lived, because of which for a period of three hundred days he had put God out of his life.

Thus, he went to confess his most abominable sins, most of which so darkly offended the Lord. When the Father heard that he had yielded to the suggestions of the Fiend, and for so long a time, he stopped his words and refused to hear an-

other syllable, for the Father had no power to grant either
penance or remission. He therefore sent him on to the Pope,
as he who is Vicar of God, but he exhorted him to repent
truly, as he truly was repentant, and to trust in the mercy of
God. He thus took leave of his confessor.

The knight went before Pope Innocent in the year 1352,
although others say it was Pope Urban, named Grimouault,
in the year 1362, and still others say it was Pope Urban of
Limouzin in the year 1377. It was a Pope who excommunicated many ... who attacked necromancers and had them
break up the walkway around the crown of the Sibyl's Mountain so nobody could climb up there any more, and the entrance to the cavern blocked up with stone and fill ...⁴

However, to return to my story, the Pope was notified that
there had arrived by the sainted grace and power of God a
knight who was more damnable than any other man, and that
he was suing for admittance in order to confess his most
abominable sins. When the Pope heard this, he marveled
much. Then he had them admit the knight, of whom he
asked who he was, what he sought, and where he was raised.

"Holy Father," said the knight, "who I am and from what
origin you will know soon enough. But I come to you, Vicar
of God, to seek pardon from you and mercy for the offenses
which I have committed against my Savior." Then he related
in true confession the sum of his sins, as he recalled them,
from the hour of his birth to the day when he left the cave,
all about his enslavement to the Fiend, from whom he
brought a golden wand that had been given him there. When
he had recounted in detail all the ways in which he had disobeyed his Creator's commandments, especially the great de-
lights and worldly pleasures which he had enjoyed over a
period of three hundred thirty days, as we have seen, then the
Pope was both angry and grieved, although on the other hand
His Holiness delighted that his repentance was also sincere.
Nevertheless, he had no inclination whatsoever to pardon the
knight nor to absolve him. Thus, sternly he drove him from
his sight, a lost man. It was not so much that he could not
have pardoned him, nor that he did not incline to do so, but
more that he wanted others to comprehend the enormity of
such sin as that in which the knight had lolled so long, being
enfolded, as he was, in the pleasant vanity of this Queen Sibyl. Others must be made to profit from this example, must

⁴ Section omitted discusses the Babylonian Captivity of the Papacy.

be chastised too, so that they too should in advance despair
of forgiveness.

Thus, the knight departed in the manner you know, so disconsolate that not a heart could help pitying him as they saw
and heard him go. In plaintive lament he cursed the day he
was born. Then he met a Cardinal, who felt such sorrow for
him that he received him in audience, and, as gently as he
could, he drew him out of the deepest of his despair by assuring him that he would intercede and work toward obtaining a
pardon. Thus, true to his word, he appeared several times before the Pope on the knight's behalf, but to no avail, there
still being no hope for mercy in this grave affair.

By this time the knight repented so bitterly that there was
no action he would not have undertaken to get a pardon. He
came and went often before Cardinals, other Church digni-
taries, all sorts of other personages, to try to obtain a pardon.
Meanwhile the Enemy, who is very subtle, and who night and
day plots only to undo the friends of God, placed in the heart
of the squire such a desire to return that he was hardly an
hour without desiring and regretting the absence of all those
great benefits which he had left and which night and day tor-
mented him, so much so that he hoped the knight would soon
weary at the delays and despair altogether of receiving a pardon. Even so, the knight would have continued to stay and
suffer if his squire, who by means of the Enemy's assistance
had first converted him, had not again begun the same operation.

The squire hit upon a clever solution. One day he ran
toward the knight, pretending that he was being pursued, crying, "Oh, sir, for God's sake, let us run for our lives! I just
ran into some of your friends, so-and-so too, who are looking
for you. They assured me that the Pope has proceeded
against us in court, that he has sent for us, to arrest us, and
put us to death. Sir, do you take this for idle gossip? Do you
not clearly see that if the Pope had wanted to pardon you, he
had the power? He would already have pardoned you, if ever
he intended to do so, after all the entreaties and briefs which
have been filed on your behalf. But he has had only one wish,
and also the power, which is to put us to death. Believe your
friends therefore, for otherwise I'm going to save my own
skin, and, thus, I bid you adieu."

WHEN THE KNIGHT heard this news, of his condemnation to death, like a desperate man out of his wits he left, taking the most direct route he knew, straight back to the cave. Shortly thereafter the Pope sent for the knight. He had had him on his mind, and had decided to pardon him. Nobody knew where the knight was, nor what had happened to him. Finally the Pope suspected that the knight had left the city for good; he further understood that if he had, indeed, departed, he had done so out of desperation; the Pope therefore felt personally responsible. He had them seek the knight all over town. Later he went even further and had him sought in places where he had resided, and then even along the highway to the cave, so that he could surely be turned back to the Pope.

All these measures were a little too late, for by this time the knight had already arrived back in the cave. This was corroborated by shepherds who were guarding their sheep upon the mountainsides. The knight had stopped and spoken to them in these words: "My friends, if you ever hear of people who are seeking a knight, one who once repented more sorely his terrible sins, a knight whom the Pope refused to pardon because he had been inside this cave of Queen Sibyl, tell them that I am he. Even though I was not able to save the life of my soul, I wish not to lose that of my body. Whoever henceforth wants anything from me will find me in the entourage of the above-named Queen."

After having addressed these words to the shepherds, the knight gave them a written message, drawn up for the Captain of the city, but drafted for the general public:

> To whom shall concern news of him whom the Pope did not wish to pardon. He may be found within the Paradise of Queen Sibyl.

172

Then weeping very bitterly, he commended them to God. Both stepped inside the cave. Thereafter they were never seen nor heard of again.

You may be sure that I asked to see the letter which he had left, because in it I hoped to learn their names. Unfortunately, I was told that it had been taken to the Pope, as he had ordered it to be taken, and that he personally had burned it.

And so, not long after the knight's departure, the message and word from the Pope, which he so longed to receive, really arrived. The messengers were told how the knight had reentered the cave, and they picked up his announcement. They were very sorry, because they felt certain that their messages were the very ones he so long sought. They had already spoken to the knight, so that they knew his sorrow, and now they anticipated the Pope's displeasure. However, having done their errand, they returned to him, who was so grief-stricken that he could hardly have been more so. But his repentance was too late.

The Pope ordered immediately that the entrance to the cave be blocked so thoroughly that no man ever again could return there. Furthermore, by formal edicts he forbade all men henceforth ever to enter.

Nonetheless, whoever went and whatever they did as a result, the entrance is still open, as I have certified. And it is the truth, furthermore, that within the first chamber after the entrance, where the passage allows some light and air to penetrate, there are carved the names of several persons, in a writing which it is very difficult to decipher. Even so, among these names, I made out the name of a German, which is carved into the stone like this:

HANS WAN BANBORG INTRAVIT.[5]

There is also the name of someone else, which makes me think he came either from some part of France or England. The language is French or English,[6] and the name is either Thomin de Pons, or Pous. Several other names almost cover the whole surface of the stone.

Therefore, to follow suit, I also cut my name and my crest on the rock, not without a good deal of trouble, for it was very hard. Now others will say that I, Anthoine de La Sale, have been inside also. Please God, I wish I hadn't.

[5] In Latin, with Gothic lettering: "HANS etc. entered."
[6] Anglo-Norman, presumably.

[The author seems not to know the ending of the Tannhäuser legend since he has allowed Queen Sibyl to win the knight's soul by default. In the primitive legend the Queen gives the knight (Tannhäuser) a green wand. The Pope tells Tannhäuser that he can no more be pardoned than his wand can grow leaves again. Three days later, the Queen's wand puts forth leaves. Thus, Tannhäuser rejoins her because her magic prevails.—NLG]

7

Ireland: Cuchulain

INTRODUCTION

THE MEDIEVAL MANUSCRIPTS of the Gaels of Ireland describe a savage world of ancient peoples, virtually untouched by Roman or Christian influences. Without this literature in Gaelic, we would know very little about Neolithic Ireland. The old Irish literature speaks imaginatively and at great length of a barbaric world whose social forms, political institutions, and way of life have vanished from the earth almost without trace. Only these great works of art survive . . . entire.

The epics of Ireland, the most famous of which, the life and adventures of the hero Cuchulain, appears in the Book of Leinster, are generally believed to be the oldest in western Europe, and are considered by many to be the greatest. They have preserved what Giraldus Cambrensis, the twelfth-century churchman and historian, called "the old religion." Despite the fact that Christianity was introduced to Ireland in the fourth century, St. Bernard observed with great regret that before 1130 there was hardly a true Christian in all of Ireland.

Archaeologic evidence[1] confirms that a megalithic culture flourished in Ireland from at least 2000 B.C., and that its religion entailed the sacrifice of men, animals, and plants. Gods were worshipped in human and animal form. Terribly savage rites were performed by vast numbers of people to guarantee

---

[1] Robert A. S. Macalister, *The Archaeology of Ireland* (New York and London, 1931).

that winter would end and that the sun of spring would arise,
like a brown bull with crescent horns, from the northeast, en-
suring fertility for crops, cattle, and man. Assemblies were
held at various times of the year, and dancing, singing, pro-
cessions, and ritual acts were performed to the din of drums,
pipes, and other noise-makers.

We know from the epics that there were five ancient provinces: Ulaid, Laigin, Connachta, Mumu, and Mide (the
present Ulster, Leinster, Connacht, Munster, and Meath).[2]
Our hero's story comes from the Ultonian (Ulster) Cycle; the
site of the palace where he was raised (Emain Macha) can
be visited today near the present city of Armagh. The hill-top
dunns, or dry-forts, of these ancient peoples can also be seen
today throughout Ireland and Britain.

Their society centered about a king (rí) and his people
(tuath), both under a High King (Ardrí) at Tara. In our
epic, the king is the legendary King Conchobar, also called
Conor mac Nessa. A High King was *Dagda-Mor*, whose harp
flew through the air to him at Tara, much as the lyre flew to
the Greek god Apollo. Probably Apollo, who visited the Hy-
perboreans every nineteen years, is the heavenly father of our
hero Cuchulain.

Ancient Ireland possessed four supremely sacred treasures
in its four great cities. At Falias was the Lia Fail, or stone of
destiny. At Gorias was the invincible spear of Lugh (Apollo's
Gaelic name), who was in Gaelic described as Lam Fada
(Long-Arm). In Finias lay another magic spear, and in
Murias the cauldron of the Dagda. The cauldron, which
would not cook food for a coward, was an inexhaustible
source of food; many scholars believe that it was the prototype of the Holy Grail. At the time of our epic, the supernatural elements in Gaelic mythology had not yet been entirely
rationalized, or explained and reduced to commonplace hap-
penings.

According to the bardic legends of Ireland,[3] the history of
the Irish people goes back to the Flood of Noah, at which
time the first man arrived on the island. The fourth race to
arrive were called the Dedannans, or Tuatha De Danann
(peoples of the goddess Dana). Their presences haunt our
story:

[2] Myles Dillon, *Early Irish Literature* (Chicago, 1948).
[3] P. W. Joyce's *Old Celtic Romances* (London and Dublin, 1920) is
the best book I know on the subject of Irish mythology and literature.

Mannanan Mac Lir = the sea god,
Fand = his wife,
Dagda = "the great good fire," who reigned as first High
    King, or Dagda Mor,
Angus = son of the Dagda, who lived at Brugh-on-
    Boyne,
Nuada Silver Hand = the next supreme ruler,
Lir of Sidh Finnaha = the father of the children of Lir,
    or "King Lear,"
Dianket = the great physician,
Armedda = his daughter, also a physician,
Gobnenn = the blacksmith of the gods, and
Lugh Lam Fada = the Dedannan ruler after Nuada.

The old poets wove their legends, histories, romances, and epics about these personages. The Ulster Cycle centers around
the Red Branch heroes of King Conor or Conchobar, while a
later Fenian Cycle tells of the adventures that occurred during the long reign of King Finn. The manuscripts were lost
during the Middle Ages because of the Danish invasions of
Ireland, and the Anglo-Norman invasion after 1066. Since
1900 they have been preserved at Trinity College, Dublin,
and at the Royal Irish Academy in that city.

The early gods and rulers were defeated by a subsequent
Celtic invasion of Ireland, and some deities (the sea god, for
example) migrated. The other Dedannans were assigned palaces (i.e., chambered burial mounds) underground in Ireland.
These mounds may be visited today, precisely where the epics
say they are. These palaces were called *sidhe* (pronounced
shee-hee), and Dedannans were called *Aes Sidhe*, people of
the mounds. (The word "banshee" comes from *Bean-Sidhe*,
meaning literally "a woman of the mounds.") Armagh, Gal-
way, Longford, Donegal, Turan, and Meath are famous for
these *sidhe*. The mound (*sidh*) of the Dagda was at Brugh-
on-Boyne, or New Grange (Meath). Old verses say:

Behold the *sidh* before your eyes,
It is manifestly a king's mansion,
Which was built by the Great Dagda.
It was a wonder, a royal court, and
    an admirable hill.

The Book of Invasions assumes that in Ireland the gods ruled
as earthly kings until 1700 B.C. Others say they were con-

quered by the Gaels around 3303 B.C.[4] Their own dead gods
slept underground in eternal sleep, much as Kronos, the Greek
father of the gods, did. The Irish bards believed that the Tuatha De Danann must have come from outer space, so intelligent and so learned were they. It is difficult to be precise and
consistent in the world of mythology. And yet the myths of
Ireland have a basis in fact, for the mounds and dolmens
they mention can be found where they were placed by
Cuchulain and other heroes.

As a child the mythic hero is associated with a sacred animal which he subdues in order to gain the attributes of that
creature: Hercules—serpents; Samson—a lion; Rustam—an
elephant; Sifrit—a dragon; Cuchulain—a guard dog. Cuchulain
is also, like Ireland, closely linked to the horse; at the end of
the epic, the sacred animal is sacrificed with her master. Our
hero stands against a matriarchal society whose queen he will
depose; the day of women warriors ends, for a while, with
this epic. Like his father, the sun god Apollo (Lugh), Cuchulain resembles the sun. His victory brings an end to winter,
but like the winter sun, he dies in order to give birth to
spring.

The reader will doubtless note the close parallels between
the Cuchulain legend and the Persian epic, *Shah Nameh* (the
death of Sohrab), as well as *Sir Gawain and the Green
Knight* (the beheading game). There are many close connections between this material and the stories involving King
Arthur, Sir Tristan, and Sir Percivale, not the least of which
is Morrigan, who becomes Morgan le Fay in Arthurian
legend. Here also the epic is interwoven with tragedy, for the
hero is doomed to kill his son and to die in war. Like Roland, Cuchulain believes that posthumous glory is the reason
and purpose of life. The Gaelic bards seem in many cases to
have inspired the *Song of Roland*. Similarly, in *Erec et En-
ide*, the French poet Chrétien de Troyes also follows a pil-
low-talk episode between husband and wife that resembles the
talk between Queen Medb and her consort. During this conversation, the idea of capturing the Brown Bull occurs to the
Queen, i. e., the war is conceived. The idea of couvade (page
180ff) occurs also in the thirteenth-century French story *Au-
cassin and Nicolette*. Peredur's golden ring is explained here
(see Chapter 2).

[4] E.g., Jean Markdale, a contemporary French authority on Celtic
literature in Ireland and Brittany. See his *L'Epopée celtique d'Irlande*
(Paris, 1971).

The following account of Cuchulain is not a translation. Although many episodes, such as the childhood incidents, the guarding of the marches, the meetings with Morrigan, the rout of Murthemney, the combat with Ferdiad, the recovery of Ulaid, and the battle of the bulls are abbreviated from the Book of Leinster (*Leabhar Laighneach*), the story which follows is a compilation of other accounts, among them, the Book of Invasions (*Leabhar Gabala*) and the Book of the Dun (*Leabhar na hUidre*).[5]

Translations of these Irish manuscripts began to appear throughout Europe from 1872 on, perhaps the most famous being those by O'Looney, Jubainville, Hall, O'Curry, O'Daley, Sullivan, and Lady Gregory.[6]

The English equivalents of Gaelic proper names are so varied that a person may feel free to choose any one of them, as fancy dictates; thus, although Queen Medb's name was supposedly pronounced "Maeve," I have preferred the distinctiveness of the transliteration. Cuchulain is pronounced Koo-hoó-lin.

THE COMING OF CUCHULAIN

THEN QUEEN MEDB OF CONNACHT consulted her druid priest, for she needed enlightenment from him and an augury for the future. "There are now many beside me," she said, "who bid farewell today to their clan, and other relations, and companions. Now for my sake, and for the possession of the Bull of the East, they leave home, land, father, and mother. Should they never return here, then they will heave sighs in my direction, for I have called this host. Nor am I any less

---

[5] See Donald MacKinnon, *A Descriptive Catalogue of Gaelic Manuscripts* (Edinburgh, 1912).

[6] For a complete version, see Lady Gregory's *Cuchulain of Muirthemne; the Story of the Men of the Red Branch of Ulster Arranged and Put into English by Lady Gregory. With a Preface by W. B. Yeats.* Foreword by Daniel Murphy (Great Britain, 1902, 1903, 1907, 1911, 1915, 1925, 1933, 1975, 272 pp.).

dear than them, to myself. Pray, discover for my army whether we shall ever or never return westwards again."

The druid of Queen Medb answered her: "Whoever fails, thou shalt not."

Leaving her druid, the Queen's charioteer carefully drove her back, observing proper ritual by making *right* turns only. He too sought good omens. As she was being driven back to the host, the Queen caught sight of someone strange. An unknown chariot swiftly approached. The driver was standing alone in the vehicle. His passenger stood balanced on the hindpole, not in the basket. In her right hand she held up a golden wand. She was a tall girl, wearing a flowing green mantle, a heavy gold brooch at her bosom, and a red woven hood and tunic. Her face was open and fair, but her forehead very prominent. Her eyes were gray-blue, but with three pupils each. Her eyebrows were black, like her lashes, which cast curved shadows on her cheekbones. Red-lipped and sweet-voiced was the maiden; snow-white was her delicate skin so it shone through her silken garments. Three braids of long, golden hair she wore, two turned about her head, one falling to her calves, almost to her golden sandals.

The Queen ordered her charioteer to pull up. After examining the maiden, the Queen inquired, "Why have you come here now?"

"To tell thee the future," the maiden replied. "The four mighty provinces of Ireland have massed against the East. You have called up the Host of Erin."

"Who art thou, maiden?"

"I am a prophetess and a poet," she replied. "My name is Fedelm, and I come from the *sidh*."

"And before that?" asked the Queen.

"From Scotland, where I studied prophecy. Now I can divine the future."

"Then, tell me, Fedelm, what you see for my host and of me."

"Crimson and bloody red. Bathed in it. Ill-fated."

In vain Queen Medb argued with the poetess, pointing out how the Easterners were sick in bed with stomach ache, all doomed to couvade as a result of the goddess Macha's curse. They would not even be able to don armor, nor mount a horse, nor stand in their war chariots, nor wield a spear. The eastern Ultonians had been cursed by Macha, for they had forced her, not knowing it was the goddess, to run a foot race just as her labor pains were commencing. She ran, but in anguish and against her will, and she won, dropping to the

earth at the finish line just as her baby was born. Therefore
she cursed the men of eastern Ireland, making them, all but
two, sick with labor pains for four days.

In vain Queen Medb argued for the force of her provinces,
for the strength of her heroes, for the loyalty of her
fortresses, and for her requirement: the Brown Bull of
Cooley, the dark horns of the rising. Her own bull was red-
and-white, going far down each evening into the western
ocean, over toward paradise and the fountain of youth in
Brazil.

Then Fedelm unfolded her knowledge, her story being in
verse, and called "The Coming of Cuchulain."

These are the heroic ancestors of Ulaid, from the reign of
the first King Conchobar [Conor.] His best palace is still
called the "Red Branch" because of its nine halls of red yew
and its walls of red bronze. His capital is still Emain Macha,
in eastern Ireland.

Princess Maga, daughter of the Dagda, wedded Ross the
Red. Her grandson is the present King Conor. Ross the Red
also wedded a maiden named Roy whose son became until
then the greatest Red Branch hero, Fergus Mac Roy (son of
Roig or Roy). In second place, Princess Maga wedded the Chief
Druid Cathbad, and another grandson of hers became King
Conall of the Victories. By this second marriage she also bore
a Princess Dectera, during the reign of King Conor.

One day Princess Dectera, along with her fifty maidens-in-
waiting, wandered away from the royal palace and was never
seen again, or for a period of three years. Then one day a
large flock of birds flew down upon the fields thereabouts,
picking at the fruits, damaging the crops. King Conor and the
great champion Fergus attacked the birds with stones shot
from their slings. They pursued them until they found themselves lured away and close to the great *sidh* of the Dagda
Angus on the Boyne River. Darkness by then had dropped
upon the land. The King had no roof over his head, until
someone found a hut. Later, however, another attendant
came upon a strange palace standing not far from the Boyne.
The attendant was greeted at the portal by "the-most-splendid-youth," and by his lady, and then by the other fifty
maidens, who so long had been lost to King Conor's court.
Obviously, there was the Princess Dectera. The lord of the
palace was, of course, Lugh Lamfada, Ethlinn's green-clad
son, . . . "the-most-splendid-youth."

King Conor sent for Dectera at once, but she requested a
short delay, not feeling at all well that evening.

Upon awakening, King Conor's warriors discovered, lying
among them in the early light of the hut, a male infant newly
born. Thus, Dectera rewarded her land and compensated for
her long withdrawal. The baby was carried home to the Red
Branch. Shortly, he was allotted his inheritance to have and
to hold: the lovely Plain of Murthemney, and the fort
(dunn) of Dundalk. When King Conor's druid saw the child,
he broke into a chant:

> The mouths of men will praise him . . .
> Charioteers, warriors, kings, and sages will
>   sing his praise . . .
> This child will be loved by all the Gaels.
> This child will redress wrong . . .
> Fight alone at the fords . . .
> Decide quarrels . . .
> He will be our champion and our hero!

The druid doubtless knew what was sometimes forgotten:
that Princess Dectera was one day seated at her wedding
feast, near her bridegroom, an Ultonian chieftain named Sualtam. All of a sudden, a mayfly apparently dropped into her
wine cup, for she swallowed it, in any case. Later that afternoon she felt so heavy with the wine that she fell asleep. In
her dream the glorious Lugh Lamfada appeared before her in
all his green and radiant beauty. What she swallowed was his,
he said, so he was inside, waiting to be born. The Princess
awoke not as her former self, but as a bird among her fifty
maiden birds. They it was who lured the Ultonian warriors to
the great *sidh*, Brugh-on-the-Boyne.

The baby was taken to Emain Macha, and his mother Dectera married his father Sualtam. The baby was temporarily
named Setanta.

Some knew what else was forgotten: that King Conor himself arrived in the meadows about the *sidh*. When he heard
the celestial music of the ancient gods, he wished not to lie
alone in his hut that night, but also to lie with the beautiful
girl of the god's palace. His courtiers brought her to him,
even though she asked to be excused because she was not
feeling well at all that evening. At daybreak the King found a
newborn babe between them, swaddled in his own royal
mantle. This was the third birthing of the wonderful child
Setanta.

Years later, after Fergus had left Emain Macha and joined
the adversary Queen Medb, he warned her host: there will

come out of the East a ravening lion, the doom of the world, the conqueror of the host, the chief vassal of Ireland, the mangler of warriors, the destroyer of rulers, the torch of the East . . . one now named Setanta, son of Sualtam.

"I have three gifts, by magic," the child used to say. "I the first time received the gift of sight, then the gift of understanding, and the third time I received the gift of calculation."

King Conor customarily spent the second third of each day watching the boys play and train in the meadows before his palace at Emain Macha. There little Setanta longed to go. He pleaded with his mother until she allowed him to depart, trudging along, carrying his toy weapons—shield, hurley and ball, javelin, and staff. The little child failed to request, or to be assigned, an older brother to protect him from the wild, older players. One hundred players stopped to see the small, strange urchin, who entered the play with mere toys, who played without assignment, or permission, or admission to the troop. They hurled one hundred fifty silver balls at his head. Setanta warded them off.

Suddenly every hair of his head stood up like a rod. A crown of red fire blazed about his ears. One eye closed until it became as small as the eye of a needle, while the other eye opened until it was as wide as the mouth of a goblet. His lips widened from ear to ear, and parted until the red of his gullet showed. Thus, for the first time, the champion's battle frenzy seized the youth. The boys froze.

Fifty kings' sons then fled screaming before Setanta, who leaped after them in pursuit. King Conor stopped the boy, however, and made him request formal protection from the older boys. However, when next the King looked, he saw that Setanta had hurled fifty princes' sons unconscious to the earth. "Why so, Setanta?" asked the King. "They gave you their protection."

"They had better have asked for mine," answered Setanta. Before others could play with him, they had each one to ask his permission and his protection.

"This youngster did all this," said Fergus to Queen Medb, "and after only five years from his births."

"Truly," said King Conall of the Victories, "we do well to make his acquaintance, for he is one of our foster sons."

* * *

Then the King's son told of Setanta's adventure with Culann the Smith.[7] It was King Conor who had been invited to a feast by Culann, and asked to bring only his closest retainers, since the Smith was not wealthy in lands, only by his own toil. Before setting out at dusk, the King therefore chose fifty chieftains of the chariot force and went to bid the youths farewell. He was again astonished at the force of Setanta. The lad could strip his one hundred fifty playmates of every stitch of their clothing, without so much as losing the gold brooch at his own shoulder. Therefore the King invited Setanta also to the feast, when his games were finished for the day.

As soon as King Conor arrived at the dunn of Culann the Smith, he was welcomed, made comfortable with fresh rushes under his feet and fresh straw to tread upon. Then beverages were served and tidbits to whet the appetite. Before sitting to the feast, the Smith asked the King if he had set any rear guard, or if any armed escort had followed him. The King said that he had not, nor did he remember the boy Setanta.

The Smith then informed the King that he would loose his guard dog. "I have a superb Spanish bloodhound," he said, "which knows only me, and which must be handled with three men and three chains. I loose him at night so that he can guard our fortress round about, and protect the livestock."

"Let him be loosed," agreed the King, "and patrol the household all about."

Thus, the chains were loosed, and the guard dog freed to lie on the mound where he could see all about the fortress. There he lay, his head on his paws, as wild and savage a dog as could be found anywhere.

Soon enough, the hound saw the young Setanta approaching, throwing his silver ball in the air and batting it before him. As the dog rose to spring, however, he was brought low, for the boy hit the silver ball down his gullet. Then he grabbed him by the hind legs, and whirling, beat his head against the huge pillar stone which marked Culann's boundary.

From within the hall King Conor heard the hound bay, remembered the boy, and dreaded to see Setanta dead. "Alas!" he cried. "This feast is bad luck for us all."

At once, the mightiest warriors of the East rushed out the

---

[7] That is, Vulcan. His dog guards the entrance to Hades, and in classical mythology is called Cerberus.

door. As one person they hurried to the palisade. Fergus arrived there first. The great hero lifted little Setanta to his shoulder, bore him in triumph down the hall, and set him on the King's knee. Then the great hue and cry, that the son of the King's sister had been killed, was hushed.

When Culann the Smith reentered the dunn, however, his head hung low. "I welcome thy coming, youngster," said the Smith, "in honor of thy parents, not for thyself. Because of thyself, I wish I had not offered my feast. Thou hast robbed me of my dog, which tended my herds and my flocks. He was my friend and my protector."

"Let me pass judgment," said the boy.

"What judgment?" asked Conor.

"First to raise and to train a puppy from that dog, until he can replace his sire. Meanwhile, O Culann, take me for thy hound. I will safeguard this Plain of Murthemney meanwhile."

Then King Conor's druid rose to speak. "Shall you not, then, from this day forth, be known as the 'Hound of Culann'?"

"No," said Setanta.

"Yes," said the druid. "The men of Ireland and the men of Alba [Scotland] shall record thy names in their annals."

"Whatever," said the boy. "Whatever names you will."

In this way, at age six, Setanta received his real name, the one by which Queen Medb would know him: the Hound (Cu) of Culann, or Cuchulain.

* * *

The day he first took arms was a day which the druid Cathbad recognized as the moment a hero would begin his short and glorious career. Cuchulain therefore selected that day. He chose his life.

Upon another such auspicious day Cuchulain first found the only war chariot strong enough to hold him. That very day also he made a circuit of eastern Ireland, sweeping, conquering, killing, capturing not only a flight of swans from the sky, but a herd of swift, untamed deer. They had been bounding at full speed. Still possessed with battle fury, his chariot hung with the bloody heads of the champions he had defeated, Cuchulain bore down upon Emain Macha. As he sped, he hurled threats ahead of him.

King Conor understood that the boy could not stop. He therefore ordered all the women to strip naked, to form a line before his chariot, and to face him. Cuchulain then stopped, for shame. Then warriors lifted him from the vehicle and plunged him into three vats of cold water, one after the other. Each vat boiled at the heat in him, but finally he grew cooler.

Cuchulain then dressed for court in crimson and royal purple. He had seven toes to each foot, seven fingers to each hand, seven pupils to each eye, four patches of down on each cheek, fifty strands of golden hair, and a clean-shaven spot on his head where the King could kiss him and stroke him. He also wore a green mantle over his tunic, and a cloth of gold, and a silver brooch. On his arm he bore a purple shield, on his head, a golden coronet. Then was Cuchulain seven years old.

Cuchulain was seventeen years old when Queen Medb summoned her host, and consulted her druid, donned her armor, and mounted her war chariot, and invaded his land.

THE HOUND OF CULLAN

Cuchulain possessed many gifts, which endeared him to the women of Emain Macha, but he loved none of them. He played chess and checkers very well. He told fortunes pleasingly. He acted prudently. He was kind to all. His defects were threefold: too young, too reckless, too handsome.

Cuchulain loved none at the court, no maiden suggested by the King, no maiden at all, in truth, until he saw Emer. Her gifts were six: beauty, voice, language, needlework, wisdom, and chastity.

Emer welcomed Cuchulain at her father's fortress, and refused him. She found him too young, too uneducated, too unaccomplished. Only the greatest deeds could win her love, she said. The two promised to love only each other, forever.

The young hero decided to complete his education, since complete it he must, with the greatest warrior and teacher of warriors, Queen Skatha of Skye. He prepared his ship for departure across the sea to the Outer Hebrides. There south of

Isle Ornsay rose her Dunscaith Castle. It overlooked Loch Eishort. Here Skatha the Wise received those pupils who gained admittance across the sea chasm twenty feet wide. It defended her fortress.

After crossing the windy sea to the north, after fighting gales and ice, quicksand, and glacial pools, Cuchulain landed. He crossed the Isle of Skye to the Plain of Misfortune. That seemed impossible to cross. He sank in the mire at each step. As he wondered what to do, he saw coming toward him the most handsome green youth, with a face too dazzling to look at with the naked eye. The youth rolled a huge wheel up to Cuchulain and showed him how to use it. Cuchulain rolled the wheel before him, and as it sizzled and burned, it made a dry, solid path for him to walk.

Between him and Queen Skatha's castle there now lay the Bridge of Leaps. It crossed the chasm before the castle, but no student could cross it until he graduated. Queen Skatha sometimes taught two last lessons: how to cross the bridge, and how to use the terrible harpoon. Before the bridge, her other pupils trained and practiced their exercises. Cuchulain recognized his old friend Ferdiad. "No student dares cross the bridge before the teacher has taught the secret," he said. Looking down, Cuchulain could see hungry fish swimming back and forth in the sea. For a while he rested.

Later that evening Cuchulain rushed upon the bridge, which twice buckled in the middle and sent him reeling backward. The third attempt almost succeeded, and the fourth time he crossed the chasm. Skatha accepted him as her student, and kept him with her for one year and one day. He spent the time pleasantly, studying feats of arms, developing his control of the world, and learning to write with twigs and with notches on wands, as the druids wrote, or using the Ogham alphabet. He and Ferdiad became ever closer friends.

While Cuchulain was still at Skye, he saw Queen Skatha prepare for war against a band of women warriors. They fought so fiercely under Princess Aifa, their skilled leader, that even such a warrior as Skatha was afraid. To protect her pupil, she administered a sleeping potion to Cuchulain. Despite its power, the youth awoke in time to accompany the Queen to war. They set out for Aifa's country, the Land of Shadows. There Cuchulain fought alone against the Princess and by a stratagem diverted her attention. Then he lifted her from her chariot, carried her away, and became her lover.

When Cuchulain left Skye, he gave Aifa a golden ring for the child she would soon bear. "Teach him three lessons," he instructed her, "that he shall never reveal his name, that he shall never yield the right of way to any man, and that he shall never refuse combat. He shall be named Connla."

Then Cuchulain returned home to Ireland and prepared to take Emer as his wife. Her men defended the dunn of Forgall against him, but the hero killed eight with each blow. The rest died, clumsily trying to imitate the teaching of Skatha, the "salmon-leap," which they saw Cuchulain perform. Only graduates from Skye had learned, however, how to pole-vault over the ramparts of the hill-forts such as that at Forgall. On the way home with Emer, Cuchulain also killed one hundred men who awaited his chariot at each river ford.

Despite his love for Fand, whom the sea god allowed to woo him in Dundalk, Cuchulain never married again. Fand finally despaired of taking him to her palace across the western ocean. Emer was Cuchulain's one and only wife.

* * *

Cuchulain became acknowledged champion of Ireland in the following way. A certain warrior named Briccriu proposed a test. First he prepared a lavish feast for warriors and their women. Then he summoned Terrible from his home under the waters of a black tarn. The hideous giant appeared suddenly before the eyes of the horrified revelers. He challenged the three bravest heroes to cut off his head, and then put their own heads on the block. Only Cuchulain dared accept the challenge. Making a prayer and spell over his sword blade, he raised it and drove it down with such force that the giant's head was cleanly severed. To everyone's horror, Terrible rose from the floor, lifted up his bleeding head, and strode from the hall.

The next day he returned, whole and sound, but carrying his giant's axe. "Lie down," he commanded Cuchulain. Proudly, showing no fear, the hero complied. "Stretch your neck more," Terrible ordered. "Make it easier for me." Cuchulain stretched out his neck. The giant raised his axe as high as his two huge arms could lift it. Then he swung it down, but he missed. He raised it, swung again, and missed. A third time he raised the axe, swung, and brought the butt of the axe down upon the chopping block. "Rise," he told Cuchulain. "You are the boldest man in Ireland."

Cuchulain became the champion of the East, and the poets were encouraged to record his points of excellence, as follows: excellence of body, shape, and build. His grades in the following skills were also excellent: swimming, horsemanship, checkers, chess, and competitions of various sorts. In combat he was, as we have seen, unmatched in all Ireland, and this despite his very average height and weight. Among the Gaels, excellence in speech was always prized, and Cuchulain had therefore been carefully trained to speak in public. He was equally excellent in counsel, a skill he displayed in early childhood, as we have seen. His bearing was excellent, his poise was absolute. Nobody could shake him, and no thing. He was also excellent in burning enemy fortresses, in seizing enemy goods, property, and treasure.

Many stories recorded by the poets demonstrate the dedication of Cuchulain to his people.

A high festival was once called for eastern Ireland, during which King Conor and his retinue happened to take a stroll along that beach which is now called "the Strand of the Footprints."

Looking out across the Irish Sea, they saw a small craft approaching over the choppy water. As it drew nearer, they saw that it was made of bronze. Only one person stood in the craft, and he held oars which gleamed like bronze in the light. As he drew nearer to land, he could be made out. It was a tall and very handsome boy. Although his ship danced on the swells, the lad stooped every now and then, selected a stone from a pile at his feet, placed it in a sling, and shot at a gull. Each time the seabird fell dead at the boy's feet. King Conor's men were astonished at such skill. The King was shaken. "See what a boy from across the sea can do. What would happen to us if such boys, grown to manhood, invaded Erin?"

The King was right too, for the lad landed and soon had conquered and bound with leather straps some of the bravest champions who happened to their sorrow to be on the beach that day. "Then send for Cuchulain," King Conor commanded. Messengers sped to Dundalk.

When Emer heard what had happened, and that the lovely boy had come over the Irish Sea from Scotland or Skye, she begged her husband not to go. "This may be your son," she pleaded, "and the son of Princess Aifa. He was told to seek you as soon as the ring fitted his thumb."

"No," said Cuchulain. "The youth must die for the safety and honor of my land and myself. Even if it is Connla." When Cuchulain reached the shore, he saw the youngster tossing his weapons in the air and catching them, and performing many feats of dexterity.

"It is very well to play," Cuchulain told him, "but now let playing cease. Who are you? Where is your home?"

"I am forbidden to say," the boy replied.

"Then prepare to die," Cuchulain told him.

"So be it," the youth answered.

Thus, Cuchulain slew his own son under water, at a beach called, after the strong feet of the youngster, "the Strand of the Footprints." The weapon which Cuchulain hurled into his son's abdomen was the magical harpoon. Its barbs crept into every crevice. Its use was the one lesson Skatha taught to Cuchulain alone.

A pillar stone was erected there in memory of Connla. People mourned for three days, and animals moaned too, for during the three days no calves were allowed to suckle.

QUEEN MEDB OF CONNACHT

(*Taín Bó Cúalnge* = The Cattle Raid of Cooley)

KING, QUEEN, MEN, AND STRIPLINGS, all mustered in the West to invade King Conor's realm. Each host marched with its ruler, each troop with its captain, each band with its leader. Each host chose its own route across country, and its own halting spot at nightfall. Fergus was chosen as liaison officer between them and their foes because, although he had lived in the East for seven years, he had fallen out because of the lovelorn Deirdre and had resided in Connacht, some say for seventeen years. Out of love for both armies, however, he moved the forces slowly and evacuated people from the lands ahead of them. Daily he warned Medb against the dread Blacksmith's Hound. While the Ultonians lay ill with stomach ache, Cuchulain and his earthly father Sualtam roamed the marches and patrolled the fords.

"Tell our men," Cuchulain told his father, "to move up into the woods, and wastelands, and steep pastures of our province, for the enemy will travel on the smooth plains."

Then Cuchulain stepped into the forest and with his axe

cut an oak sapling, which he twisted into a wreath. Around the center of this ring he cut a message in Ogham script. He then thrust the ring down upon a pillar stone where the enemy must pass the boundary line. When the nobles of Erin arrived at the marker, they saw where horses had recently champed the grass. Fergus himself read the message to Queen Medb after her company had come to a halt. The message said: "Let no one pass east of this boundary unless he can, with one hand, make such a ring from an oak sapling. Exception is made for Fergus alone." The host of Erin might have halted, but the Queen led them to shelter in the forest. Thus, all passed the boundary.

The Queen asked Fedelm what future events she saw. The maiden could not see, she said, because of the forest. "Then we'll cut it down," decided Queen Medb, "and make plow land of it."

Nevertheless, no one made camp that night, nor built a shelter for himself. No fires were lit. No meals were prepared. Nobody drank a drop. In silence the host crouched in the forest. It began to snow. By morning the snow lay deep and cold up to the chariot poles, up to the flanks of the horses, up to the shoulders of the troops. The army moved forward in the morning sun, two warriors with their charioteers reconnoitering.

Cuchulain caught their scouts at the ford. Bathed and rested, he had already counted the host from their tracks, which is considered one of the three best calculations in Ireland. He had also already cut a four-pronged fork and driven it into the ford in such a way that chariots and drivers would be impaled when they attempted to drive across the river. He beheaded the scouts and sent their horses, all streaming with the blood of the corpses, back to the main body of the host. The four heads he impaled on his forks. The van of Queen Medb's host came upon this terrible sight. They awaited the host. All turned in consternation, upon each other.

Fergus again read the Ogham sentence which Cuchulain had cut on the stick: "Go not past this point unless one of you can hurl this forked stick with one hand, as I have done." Fourteen chariots were broken in attempts to pull out Cuchulain's forked stake.

"Who did it?" he was asked.

"Who else but my former nursling, the wolf-dog of Culann the Smith?"

"We are not impressed," said the Queen. "He has but one life, and he has not yet even been wounded." She was determined to seize the Brown Bull of Cooley. She counted no cost. The winter was deep upon them all.

Then Cuchulain made a threat at her directly, saying that as soon as he saw the Queen he would cast a stone whistling close to her ear. West of the ford he sent one which killed her pet bird as it perched on her shoulder. When she turned east of the ford, he sent another that killed her pet squirrel, as it sat on her shoulder. One after another, her warriors fell silently, their skulls split by his stones. "That man will kill two-thirds of your host," Medb's King told her. Nevertheless, he and the warriors, while Fergus worried and looked anxiously over his shoulder, harried and laid waste the plains.

The great (goddess) Morrigan came from the *sidh* and perched on a standing-stone and drove off the Brown Bull of Cooley. Fifty grown youths leaped somersaults on his back. She said:

Restless Brown Bull of Cooley
  Knows not the really terrible battle . . .
The raven croaks, for it will not conceal that
The host ranges across the sunlit fields, that
The troops raid the pastures.
I have a secret that you shall learn.
The grasses wave. The flowers glow golden.
The goddesses three low like kine.
The raven Morrigan herself is wild for blood.
The men of Ireland are dead;
Their tale is woe.
The battle storm of Cooley for ever and ever is to the
  death of all their mighty sons.
Brothers look on the deaths of brothers.

Queen Medb drove now surrounded by a retinue of chariots on all sides of her. When she walked, she had her warriors hold a canopy of shields over her head. When she wished water, she sent her maidens to the river. One maiden wore the Queen's golden diadem on her head. Cuchulain killed her with one stone, and every night one hundred of Erin's warriors. He would come to no terms with her herald Mac Roth, but he did come to terms with Fergus, that a champion was to meet him every day.

Behind Cuchulain's back, Queen Medb ravaged the land. Every ford she crossed is named "Ath Medba," Medb's Ford. "Dindgna Medba" is each Medb's Hill. "Pupall Medba" is Medb's Tent. "Bili Medba" is Medb's Tree. Finally she cap-

tured the Brown Bull of Cúalnge, along with his fifty heifers,
which he covered every day. Queen Medb made a circuit to
northwards, also laying waste by fire and sword the homeland
of the Picts. She bore fifty noble women captive into Dalri-
ada, where she had them hanged and crucified. Cuchulain
also would come to no terms.

Queen Medb then sent him her daughter to wife, but
Cuchulain cut off her braids and thrust a standing stone
through her cloak, and left her there pinned to the earth and
snow. Thereafter no talk of truce any more.

Cuchulain still fought alone against them all, except for the
boy troop from Emain Macha. They decided to go to his aid.
Without telling him, they marched forth upon the plain, bran-
dishing their boy's clubs and spears. The host saw them ad-
vancing. They waited. When they had the boys close enough,
they slaughtered them at one shot. Not a boy escaped.

Then Cuchulain entered his real battle-frenzy, where before he had been able to keep somewhat cool by sitting naked
in the snow. When enflamed by his great courage, the slight
youth became distended with contortions so terrible that once
a hundred warriors dropped dead just at the sight of him. He
quivered. His calves, heels, and buttocks shifted to the front
of his body. His feet and knees switched to the rear of him.
His muscles swelled until they looked like skulls. One eye
protruded. His mouth stretched from ear to ear. Foam as
thick as the wool on a sheep rolled from his open jaws. His
heart pounded and roared like a lion's or a hound dog's
heart. A halo played about his head, shooting sparks and rays
above him. His hair stood up like red and tangled wires. As
he grew hotter, torrents of blood spouted from him toward
the four cardinal points of the horizon, and fell back to earth
about him like red smoke, or red rain, or solar storm clouds.

Even while Cuchulain roamed sleepless and solitary,
guarding the fords and the marches, fending off war parties
from the Plain of Murthemney, he was tempted. He saw a
young woman coming toward him at the ford. Since she wore
a dress of *all the colors* of the rainbow, he knew that she was
the very highest personage. She was most beautiful that day.

"Who art thou?" Cuchulain asked.

"I am Morrigan, daughter of the Eternal King," she replied. "I have come to be thy love," she said, "and love thee,
and give thee my cattle, and give thee my gold."

"No," said Cuchulain. "Not now. I am weak with warfare,
with hunger, and with lack of sleep. I cannot."

"I have come to help."

"Not for a woman's love," he said. "We do not fight here for that."

"Then," said she, "watch thy fortunes fall. In the next fight I shall intrude, in the form of a eel. I shall seize thy feet in the ford and trip thee."

"Then I shall seize thee," he replied, "between my toes and squeeze thee, until thy bones crack, and so on and so on."

"Then afterwards," she said, "I will turn myself into a gray wolf and stampede the cattle into the ford, and crush thee."

"Then I shall fit a stone to my sling and crush thine eye right in thy skull. Thou shall be blinded, and so on and so on."

"Then I shall turn myself into a red-and-white heifer, like the cattle of the underworld's king, and lead the herd over thee, and stomp on thee in the waters and the lakes and the black bogs, and never shalt thou see me in time."

"I," said he, "shall hurl a rock at thee to break off one of thy legs under thy body, and thou shalt remain lame, and so on and so on, until I have a change of heart, and break the spell."

Then Morrigan flew up and was gone, blackness and all.

After her departure, Queen Medb broke her agreement to send only one champion per day against Cuchulain. Thereafter she sent them in ambush and under flags of peace, by sixes and dozens. Then in one great fight in the ford, Morrigan fiercely attacked also, as eel, as wolf, and as heifer. Here, although Cuchulain broke her bones and put out her eye, still he was wounded through and through. He despaired of continuing alone to guard his land.

That night he tossed and worried, wounded and burning with thirst. Then an old hag approached, dressed in black, withered and lame, halt and blind, dragging by its halter a red cow with only three teats. She milked her old cow one teat at a time and, as he suffered from thirst, gave the milk to Cuchulain, and so on and so on, until the cow's bag was empty. For each drink Cuchulain gladly thanked the crone, thus breaking his own spell and healing the very wounds he had just managed to inflict. Once her wounds were healed, she taunted him. "Well, well, Cuchulain," she said, "and I thank thee."

"Had I known it was thee, Morrigan," he cried, "I should never have healed thee." Into the tree she flew, then, as a black, croaking crow. "Ah," said Cuchulain, "it is a fearful sight to see one black crow there, for 'One crow sorrow . . .'"

He was right, for just then one hundred warriors from

Queen Medb fell upon him. He killed them all in the ford, which henceforth bore the name of "Ath Cro," or Bloody Ford. The river henceforth was called "Glass Cro," or Bloody River. These names were well chosen, for truly, the gore and the blood turned all those waters red.

Some say that as Cuchulain lay exhausted beside the bodies of the dead, peering wearily beyond the river at the bright fires of the host preparing their evening meal, and drying their clothing, and making up their beds for sleep, that then he despaired. Leaning on his elbow, he watched their countless spears flash and gleam in the firelight. His eyes swam with lack of sleep for so long a time.

Then from the shimmering firelight Cuchulain saw the handsome youth, the one who had brought him the wheel at Skye. The lovely green stranger walked unseen through the middle of the host. His tunic flashed with golden glints. His mantle flowed green above their campfires. His silver brooch shone like a beacon. In one hand he carried a black shield, in the other, two spears.

Coming close to Cuchulain, the stranger spoke softly, "Sleep now, my Cuchulain, sleep. Close for three days thine eyes. All this time I shall take thy place and sleepless defend the ford and the marches against the host of Queen Medb."

Cuchulain dropped into a dreamless sleep. The stranger then anointed his wounds with powerful medicines of which only the ancient gods of Ireland have the secret. The wounds closed and healed. Cuchulain regained his strength. In his sleep, however, he recognized the great god Lugh, who had come out of the chambered undergrounds of Tara where dwell the fourth race of gods who settled Ireland. They are the glorious and golden giants, Tuatha De Danann.

These people of the goddess Dana first used gold and silver in an Age of Bronze. They first cleared the land, first drained the swamps. They built the great temples of stone like the one they sent to Britain—Stonehenge. When conquered, they retired to their underground barrows, or *Sidhe* where they still live today.

Cuchulain knew that Lugh of the Tuatha De Danann was his real father.

AFTER THE HOST had passed the boundary stone into Ross, they made camp for the night. Queen Medb exhorted them to furnish a great champion, but the warriors refused. "My people do not owe you a victim," each said. "It shall not be I."

Therefore the Queen had recourse finally to Fergus mac Roig who, having formerly been king in the East, was her general-in-chief. At first Fergus too refused, alleging Cuchulain's youth, and the fact that Fergus had fostered him. "He was my foster son," he said, "and used to sit on my knee in the Red Branch."

Therefore the Queen had them serve heavy wines to Fergus all evening, and had many persons keep questioning him, "Are you going?... Is it true?..." At dawn Fergus was awakened by them. Reluctantly he had himself dressed, and he called for his chariot.

Cuchulain smiled to see him come, for neither he nor Fergus could ever, by wine or whatever else, be persuaded to combat each other. Then, in addition, Fergus was still wearing the wooden sword which Queen Medb's consort had imposed upon him. The consort had, about a year ago, found Fergus making love to the Queen one day, trysting with her on a hillside. He stole his real sword.

"Dangerous, master," said Cuchulain, "to travel without a sword, if you come near me."

"Not so, dear son," answered Fergus, "for had I my sword again, I should never draw it against thee. As you respect your first teacher," he added, "take to your chariot in flight before me."

"Hardly," Cuchulain replied scornfully.

"Understand me," said Fergus. "That will avoid confrontation today, and I swear that on the day when I see thee pierced with a thousand wounds, and sore and bleeding, that then I will turn my chariot about and flee from thee. And when that day comes, all the men of the four provinces of Erin will take not a thought for Queen Medb and her consort, but will follow me forthwith."

The host cheered when they saw this unexpected event: Cuchulain in broad daylight mounting his chariot, not to combat Fergus, but to fly at top speed, and with every sign of fear and confusion, across the plain.

"After him, Fergus," the Queen cried.

"No," he called out to her. "I'm not bound today for a lover's tryst. This partner is too fast for me."

This encounter of Cuchulain was called the White Combat, since no blood was shed on either side. "Now, then," swore Fergus, "I shall never again go against that Hound of Culann!"

Day after day Cuchulain met the champions of Erin at the ford, and he conquered them singly, if they came singly, or accompanied by twelve warriors as Ferchu came, or accompanied by his twenty-seven sons and his grandson, as Calatin the Bold came—and their weapons were dipped in poison. Cuchulain alone, or with the secret assistance of Fergus upon occasion, killed them all. Standing stones were raised, one for each body, and the heads were placed upon them.

Meanwhile a terrible accident occurred to Cuchulain's father Sualtam, as he rode about the East, trying to rouse the warriors of King Conor. Sualtam accidentally fell over his own shield and decapitated himself. Fortunately, however, his head kept on talking and exhorting the sick warriors to rise from their beds. Sualtam knew that Cuchulain was reaching the end of his strength.

The leaders of Erin consulted seriously with Queen Medb, for whom now should they send against Cuchulain? The answer appeared obvious, since Fergus had solemnly sworn never again to combat him. The only man alive who could reasonably be expected actually to defeat Cuchulain was his old classmate and dear friend Ferdiad.[8] In addition, Ferdiad mac Daman came from one of the four heroic races of Ireland, from the lands of Erris, in Domnann (County Mayo). In all the west of the northern world, the combat of Cuchulain and Ferdiad would be the greatest imaginable.

Ferdiad mac Daman was called the "Horn-skin of Erris" because of the hide which he wore over himself. He was also called the immovable rock and the irresistible force. He was Cuchulain's foster brother. He and Cuchulain were the same

---

[8] Pronounced Fer-dee-ah.

age and had received the same training and fosterage. Both
had trained finally with Queen Skatha of Skye, so that their
methods of attack and defense were identical. No champion
in the world would fight Ferdiad, except perhaps Cuchulain.
To fight Ferdiad would resemble attempting to fell an oak
tree with a bare fist, or subdue a den of lions, or thrust the
hand into a viper's nest. Ferdiad could set his shield upon
any ford of any river whatsoever. No one would touch it.

Ferdiad acknowledged one weakness, however. He had not
learned the use of the terrible harpoon, or *Gae Bulga*
(Hooked Spear), from Queen Skatha. He fully trusted in his
horn coating, however, even against the harpoon.

Messengers were dispatched from Queen Medb and the
host to Ferdiad. He sent them back posthaste. He ignored the
summons. He knew they needed him if they were to kill
Cuchulain.

After the messengers with their invitations there came the
druids of Queen Medb, and her poets, and her propagandists.
These people camped at his doorstep and satirized Ferdiad,
reviled him, called him coward and worse, until in exasper-
ation he yielded, and called for his chariot, and drove to
Queen Medb's camp. As well be riddled with man's weapons,
he reasoned, as become the butt of every rhymster.

What a triumph for Queen Medb and her consort! What
extreme joy possessed them! To welcome Ferdiad. To have
him walk into their tent and into their hands! They entrusted
him to their most skilled people. Ferdiad was wined and
dined. He was bowed down to, and waited upon, and fawned
over like the noblest king. The best-tasting, strongest beverages were set into his hand. He became merry and very
drunk. Then the Queen offered him all sort of rewards and
promised great promises, if he would agree to meet Cuchulain. "Do you know, dear Ferdiad, why you have been invited here?"

"No, truly," he replied, "except to be a warrior among the
noble warriors of Erin. Why should I not be invited here?"

"Truly, rather to take a new chariot worth the price of
fifty serving maids, and the robes of a dozen warriors, from
stuffs of all colors, with the Plain of Ai as your domain. It is
equal and more to the Plain of Murthemney, as all know. Invited here so that wine may be poured at all moments. That
your family should from this day forth be freed of all duties
toward the royal house, i.e., freed forever of military service,
and of rent, and of tribute. This to the end of time and all
life in Ireland. Ferdiad, take this golden brooch, of massive

gold, as my sign that all this is yours, plus my daughter, Finnabair to wife, not to mention my friendship forever more."

"These gifts suffice," concurred the warriors. "Enough. Enough."

"It will go hard with me tomorrow," Ferdiad said then. "I am not to be spurned, but Cuchulain handles weapons like nobody else I know. My wounding will be hard. It is no soft task to stand up to him, and to that. Our struggle will be terrible."

"Take me as lover," the Queen urged him. "Swear. Make an oath."

"I swear."

"Then take my brooch," she said in ratification. "All my treasures shall be yours. Finnabair to wife, when you have slain him."

"Were I to receive the Plain of Ai, and have Finnabair, and dwell with her on those lands forever, I still would not face the Hound. We are equals. One will not win. We were raised by the same nurses. They taught us the same lessons. I feel no fear of Cuchulain. Rather, my heart bleeds with love for him."

"Horses. Lands. Estates. Domains. All yours. But fight," she said.

"Nothing," he answered. "None of it. I will go, if I go, only because Queen Medb asks me to go, and only because the poets will sing of it."

"Then, Mac Daman," she said, "go, for fame eternal lies upon him who fells the Hound. It will be known as Ferdiad's Ford."

"The gifts suffice," the warriors affirmed. "They are high gifts."

"Yes, granted that they are high," concluded Ferdiad, "but I will not take them. I will leave them all here, beside Queen Medb's person. If they are given for combat, if they are bestowed because I am to kill my foster-brother, the only man equal to me in skills and accomplishments, then I will not accept them. Cuchulain is my friend, my ally, my associate, my beloved companion."

Then Ferdiad turned to poetry, reciting a long complaint in ballad style, each stanza presenting a theme:

"I would rather fight two hundred men, than Cuchulain.
The Hound and I sadly will butcher each other.
Blameless each of us, we shall meet because of a woman.

If I kill Cuchulain, then I shall kill myself afterwards, with
my sword, or by springing over the horizon.
If I kill Cuchulain, I shall turn in his place on this host,
and lie buried beside him, in one grave.
Let me die, not him, let not him feed croaking birds.
Let the Hound know! Skatha foretold my death at a ford,
in Ireland,
by the hand of Cuchulain.
Woe upon Medb. She has brought me here to fight the
Hound, face to face. How hard that combat will be."

Entirely as if she had listened to none of Ferdiad's lament,
Queen Medb, adroit at dividing friends, asked if her men had
heard Cuchulain's last word.

"What last word?" asked Ferdiad.

"He said he expected you to fall, unequal as you are, he
said, to him in combat," she replied, lying to all.

"Then he spoke unjustly," Ferdiad told the warriors. "I
have never belittled him. I said no ill of him. I swear that if
he has scorned me, I shall be first to correct his opinion. And
yet, I would meet him only with the greatest reluctance."

Thus, in the presence of the Queen and the warriors, Ferdiad ultimately pledged his word to meet Cuchulain on the
morrow. All were duly witnesses. He could no longer break
his promise, or seek excuse, without being publicly shamed as
coward and liar.

"My best wishes," said Queen Medb, "for victory. Cuchulain defends his mother's land, and you defend Connacht,
being yourself a king's son of Connacht."

Among all the warriors of Erin there was present, however,
one wonderful man, namely Fergus mac Roig. After the oath
of Ferdiad had been witnessed and sworn, Fergus retired to
his tent. "Alas," he told his household, "for the deed that will
come in the morning."

"What deed?" they asked.

"The death of my foster son, Cuchulain."

"Who will slay him?"

"Who else but his foster brother?"

Since no one else dared accept to carry a message, Fergus
himself went to find Cuchulain, hoping to persuade him to
leave the ford before Ferdiad could arrive.

Cuchulain saw Fergus coming, and recognized him because
of the royal size of his chariot, more like a copper-and-
bronze moving fort, and because of his kingly appearance
and long, curly beard. "He is easy to recognize," said Cuchu-

lain. "My old master has come to warn me, I am sure, and to place me first in his heart, before all Erin and its four provinces." He walked out of his camp to welcome Fergus.

"Be welcome, dear master," said Cuchulain. "All I have is yours. From the birds of this meadow, have one and half another. From the salmon of this river, have one and half another. Take from my hand sprigs of fresh watercress, and fronds of red laver, and a taste of sweetgrass. We shall wash it down with cold water from the clean sand here."

"That is the portion of an outcast, my son," said Fergus.

"It is mine," Cuchulain told him.

"I have come to inform thee," Fergus told him, "who will challenge thee at the ford tomorrow morning."

"And I will hear his name from thee," said Cuchulain.

"He is Ferdiad Mac Daman Mac Dare, friend, comrade, brother, thine equal in education, in feats, and in prowess."

"I should almost prefer to die at his hands," said Cuchulain sadly, "rather than he should die at mine. My love for him is great, was always great."

"I have come with many warnings," said Fergus, "as master and foster father to pupil and foster son. Be on guard. Fear him. Dread him. His hide is horn and his belt is stone. Neither has ever been reddened with his own blood. In the hour of battle he roars like a lion, falls like the fist of doom, clutches like an incoming tide. He mangles, crushes, swallows."

"Let him come," said Cuchulain. "Here I stand day after day on guard at this ford. Here I have warred alone from harvest to springtime. Not a night have I been absent for fear of weakness on the morrow. Not a foot have I yielded yet. I think not to run before him either."

Long Fergus argued with him and lessoned him, as he had always been accustomed to do. Cuchulain answered his old master freely and openly, as he had been taught. He was anxious, he admitted, but not from fear. His dread of Ferdiad arose from love only.

"My reward, as thy teacher," concluded Fergus, "will be to have thee carry off tomorrow the victory over Ferdiad." Fergus bade farewell to Cuchulain then, not wishing to have his absence noticed. Having said what he intended, he left the future in the hands of his former student.

After the departure of Fergus, Cuchulain's charioteer asked his master, "What plans for this evening?"

"Well, what?" asked Cuchulain. Then his charioteer Laeg entreated Cuchulain to spend the night at home with his wife

Emer. "Tomorrow Ferdiad will be splendid beyond belief," said Laeg. "His hair will have been plaited and combed by the women, and he will be fresh from his bath, and dressed fit to kill. He will be driven across the field, watched and admired by the four provinces of Erin."

Cuchulain took his suggestion and spent that night at home in Dundalk. His wife Emer was famous for the beauty of her own hair.

Ferdiad returned from Queen Medb to his own tent. His people there made no pretense to lightheartedness. Frankly, they were downcast and fearful. On the morrow the two champions would meet. One of them must die, and probably both of them would die, either at once or during the day. Since one of the two had to die, it would be, they reasoned, their lord Ferdiad. Meeting the Hound of Culann and surviving was probably not possible, certainly not likely.

Soon after supper Ferdiad fell into a deep sleep, which lasted throughout the early part of the night. Hours before daylight, however, he awoke and was unable to fall asleep again. The logic of his situation was inescapable. If he did not meet Cuchulain on the morrow, he had given his word to fight six champions. If he did meet Cuchulain, then he would lose Medb's daughter and all the treasure the Queen had promised. Ferdiad was certain that he was going to his death. Therefore he chose not to fall asleep again.

As soon as it was light, he called for his charioteer and asked to have his horses hitched and his chariot yoked. In vain the charioteer pleaded with his master not to go. "Not go," cried Ferdiad, "when before the Queen and her consort and her daughter, and before all the nobles of Erin, I have sworn to meet Cuchulain?"

"It would still be better not to go," said his charioteer.

"I will hear not another word, boy," ordered Ferdiad. "As for Cuchulain, let him kill me so I shall not kill him. For were I to kill him, then I would turn my fury against both Medb and Erin. They deserve no better. They exacted oaths from me when I was drunk and happy. Therefore hush, boy, and let's hasten into our future."

It was not even broad daylight when Ferdiad stepped proudly into the car of his chariot. At once they started to move away from the camp. At the last moment the warrior instructed his driver to turn around and make three triumphal sweeps before the host, so that all could admire the champion and his equipage.

"Eh, consort," Medb yelled from her tent, where she was

taking care of her private duties. "Wake up, our future son-in-law is bidding us a fond farewell."

"Is he, now?" the consort shouted back to her.

"He won't return on the same feet," she said, laughing.

"So long as Cuchulain falls," said the consort, "and yet truly I wish him no misfortune, especially."

"Can you see Cuchulain?" Ferdiad asked his charioteer, when they had pulled up at the ford.

"No," he answered. "He has not yet arrived."

"Then unhitch the horses," said Ferdiad, "and make me a bed here of hides and cushions so I can sleep off my heaviness." While the master slept, the charioteer stood guard.

As for Cuchulain, he took particular care not to awaken until the full light of the sun had streamed over Dundalk. After everyone else had arisen, Cuchulain then lazily drew his hand over his face and casually called for his chariot. Carefully and slowly he moved so as to show no sign of nervousness or anxiety. "Come, boy," he said to Laeg. "Our friend Ferdiad rises early, as we recall. He may grow tired of awaiting us."

The horses were stamping. The chariot was ready. Cuchulain stepped in, Laeg only raised his whip, and off they whirled. No sooner had the horses broken into a gallop, carrying the redsword hero, the erlking Cuchulain, than the godlings flew from their underground palaces, and swirled through the air about him. Always escorted by the Tuatha De Danann with their otherworld beings, and goblins, and elves screaming their ghostly screams about him, Cuchulain's equipage howled across the land as if the hounds of hell were baying full-voiced behind him.

From his sentry duty at the ford, the charioteer of Ferdiad heard the unearthly chariot and crew approach: bodies rushed through the air, shields whistled in the wind, javelins clanked, swords struck, helmets crashed, spears rang upon metal, cuirasses creaked, weapons crashed upon weapons, ropes twanged, wheels whirled, the chariot groaned, the hooves of the horses thundered, speaking to warriors the stern words of war and of the business of killing.

The charioteer awoke his master by placing his hand as gently as he could on Ferdiad's shoulder. Ferdiad sprang to his feet and quickly buckled his tunic and his broad war belt.

"Woe to you," cried the boy as he stood there before Ferdiad. "I knew it last year, and I told you too. The Hound will defeat us. I know it."

"Come now," laughed Ferdiad, "he is not paying us to sing

his praises. Let us cease magnifying him. As we recall, Queen Medb prophesied our victory. Now is the time for us to help each other and ourselves . . . Why are you silent, boy? . . . What do you see?"

"Behold Cuchulain," the charioteer replied, "and behold his wondrous chariot. It is made of crystal and yoked in gold. Its side plates are copper inlaid with silver. Swiftly it speeds toward us. Perfect is its balance and short its turning radius. The car is roofed with a green sunshade and painted all about with the deeds of heroes. The lord himself rides seated, his seven weapons laid in order beside him. The two wheels are shiny and black. The pole is red enamel over tin. The bridles are leather, chased with gold.

"Two horses pull the hero's chariot. Both are swift, alert, agile, and furious for combat. Their heads are small, their ears large, their snouts are short, their chests are broad, their nostrils are flared, their hearts are quick, their flanks are high, their hooves are broad, their limbs are slender, their manes are long. The lead horse is the famed Gray of Macha.

"She steps small, the broad-hipped wonder. Fearless and resolute she speeds in one of the yokes of the chariot. The other one of the pair is a broad, fast horse named Black of Sithleann.

"The pair pull the chariot like hawks dropping through the March wind after their prey on the highlands, like a stag pounding through the leafy woods with the hounds just catching his scent. The earth rumbles under their hooves and shudders at their fierce speed.

"I see a man now standing in the chariot, his hair is long and fair and curly. He is folded in a long silken cloak of Persian blue. In his hand a flaming spear glows red and silver along its honed edge. His hair is three-colored: light brown near the scalp, red in its mid length, and golden blond on the ends. Thus, he seems to wear a golden crown."

Truly, Cuchulain was fair whenever he went to display his youthful self, either to the ladies, or to a host, as today. His hair seemed three heads of hair: brown, red, and yellow. Three braids were wrapped about his head, holding from his face the long, waving, golden mass of curls that blew lightly back from his shoulders. At his neck the brilliant golden coils of his torque collar and breast-plate flamed and gleamed before him. Suspended from the crown of his head were one hundred silken cords from which dangled one hundred garnets. On his cheeks were painted four balls: yellow, green, blue, and royal purple.

When the day was fine, he wore his fair-weather dress: fringed purple mantle which fell about him in five pleats, white breast-plate of pure silver inlaid with gold, war trousers of red, royal silk brocade, body tunic of soft silk fringed with golden tassels. His purple buckler bore on it as escutcheon five golden wheels, indicating the circling rays of the sun. In his girdle, ready to hand, he carried a keen sword with a golden hilt and ivory guards. In his chariot were laid long spear and short spear, plus thongs and rivets for use in hurling. Usually he carried by the hair nine severed heads.

When Cuchulain paraded in full-splendored panoply, then the maidens and the women begged to be lifted so that they could feast their eyes on beauty. They would sit on the flats of the warriors' raised shields and gaze and gaze upon Cuchulain. He was a marvel to behold, a shining sight one could never forget. Like the sun rising above the horizon, he almost hurt the eyes.

The king-hero's battle dress this day consisted of twenty-seven layers of hides, which had remained stiff, and which were then waxed and pounded into one tunic, and strengthened by cords and ties. Over that he wore the champion's war girdle made of the toughest leather cut from seven thicknesses of ox hides. The girdle reached from his slender waist to his armpits. The soft lower parts of his body were covered first with soft silk trousers, over which he wore a kilt of stout leather, and over that another girdle of cowhide. Thus attired, the king-warrior Cuchulain stepped into his chariot.

The war chariot was open in front, curved at the rear where the seat was, the car made of wickerwork, mounted on two wheels and hitched to two horses side by side, with two single-trees between them. The chariot was scythed with iron sickles, thin blades, barbed hooks, and long spikes. To its poles were affixed sharp nails and trailing hooks on thongs. With it, the champion performed easily his "thunder-deed," killing and lacerating a hundred men, or two hundred men in a few minutes, wheeling at top speed down the enemy ranks and through their camps.

For driving the chariot, Laeg wore first of all a simple cowled dress of softened deerskin, so stitched and so fitted that it left ample room for his arms. Over this he put on, for great occasions, such as today, a long cloak of black raven's feathers, in honor of the goddess of war. He wore a fitted battle cap which confined his jet-black hair and assured his vision, unlike his master Cuchulain, who wore the crested battle helmet with its long, trailing plumes. As sign of the charioteer, and so no enemy rushing at full speed upon him from the front would have difficulty distinguishing him from the warrior, Laeg pressed upon his forehead a wide gold stripe which had been especially molded to fit his head. Last of all, the charioteer loosed the hobbles from the horses' feet, grasped the reins in his left hand, leaped aboard, and set to using the silver goad in his right hand.

The horses wore golden coats of mail over their heads and backs, the mail cleverly lined with thin iron sheets. Laeg usually drove Cuchulain abroad under a magical veil of invisibility.

Today Cuchulain drove directly to the north side of the ford. On the opposite bank Ferdiad stood waiting. "Welcome, Cuchulain," he said with a smile.

"I no longer trust your words of welcome," Cuchulain answered. "Not now. How can you think to welcome me? I am at home here. You are not only a stranger in my land, but, even worse, an armed intruder. Do you find it proper for you to welcome me into my own lands? How do you explain your presence, your coming to my lands to fight me? My people fly before you. My women run from their homes. You drive off my grazing horses, and run off my livestock, and my yeomen."

"Very well," answered Ferdiad, "and how do you explain it? Have you not driven here to do battle with me? As I recall, when we were students of Queen Skatha, you were my squire, who made my bed and polished my weapons."

"True, indeed," agreed Cuchulain. "I was younger and much smaller then, and much kindlier. My disposition has taken a different turn with the years. Today, mind you, there is in the world no champion whom I cannot drive from this ford."

With that, each one stepped into the water until they met in the middle of the stream. There to each other, no longer having to shout, they went to the business of serious insults. "Eh, Cua," Ferdiad said contemptuously, "this is a champion you think of meeting, not a boy any longer. You'll never see home again."

"I have come only because I must prove to you my valor," said Cuchulain. "I will fight you a hundred battles, if necessary. You are foolhardy."

"Your people can count you as lost, now and forever. Your head is as good as on a spit already. You must lose, for the guilt of this combat is your guilt."

"Ah, Ferdiad," sighed Cuchulain. "You have come here because of Queen Medb's maiden, who has already lost many suitors. You have come for the rewards and for the domain which the Queen of Erin has promised. Many others before you, believe me, have been lured here by the same bait and the same lying words. Return, O Ferdiad. Do not combat me. Else I shall make a bed for you, and final resting place. Can you, alone of all men, escape from me? Why you? The Queen's daughter Finnabair will never be your wife. She is the lure that has blinded you, I see.

"O Ferdiad, never break your oath of friendship to me. Do not break this bond between us. Do not break your promise to love me forever. Go not back on your bond. Do not come near me today. No nearer.

"Before you, fifty men have been promised Finnabair as their bride. All fifty died at my hand. I would never break my bond to you, for the sake of a maiden already plighted to fifty dead men. She is a chattel, not a pure maiden ... Remember the old days of our boyhood. We were friends. We sought valor together, side by side, all those years ... Would you combat me, Cuchulain?"

Turning to poetry for most of his arguments, Cuchulain then continued: "Once we were closest friends, true friends, truly pledged to be friends, forever. We shared the same bed. We trod the same forest paths. We slept the same deep sleep after toil. We fought side by side, me for you, and you for me. We studied and practiced together, day after day."

"O Cua, you have become a great champion. The days that are past are past and gone. Treason has come between us, and your wounding. We are no longer whole. Our trade was a hard one. Speak to me no more of friendship. Think no more today that I am your friend. Cua, it is useless.

"We have battled too long with words," Ferdiad concluded sadly. "What weapons shall we next take up?"

"The choice is yours today, Ferdiad, for you arrived first here at the ford."

"Do you remember the commencement rite at Queen Skatha's school, and with which arms it is fought?"

"I remember. Let us begin with them, then." Then, taking care to choose weapons which were in every point equally matched, they set to work. Each had a large shield, plus an octagonal targe for catching darts. Each selected eight darts, eight swords decorated with walrus teeth, eight spears decorated with ivory. They aimed and threw. Their small weapons soared straight and buzzed like the flight of a bee. Every one struck the target.

Neither man missed the target. Every dart struck and every spear and every sword thrust, but the shields and targes withstood, growing only more pierced and more dented. The morning hours wore away. Neither had the advantage. They were equally matched, as equally matched as ever. At noon Ferdiad suggested they call it quits. Cuchulain agreed.

"We shall come to no decision with these arms," said Ferdiad. "Let us choose others."

"If that time has come," replied Cuchulain.

Then Ferdiad chose long spears, the ones with cords of flax. Each one took a new, harder shield. All afternoon, until the setting sun shone yellow across the fields, they hurled their spears at each other, never missing. Each one finally was completely reddened with the blood which streamed or oozed from countless cuts and scratches. "Shall we make a truce now?" asked Ferdiad.

"It is your choice today," replied Cuchulain. Thus, they both ceased at sunset. Their charioteers caught the weapons as they were tossed to them. Then both warriors stood in the middle of the stream, locked in an embrace. Each one placed his hand on the other's neck and gave him three kisses in love and memory of their boyhood friendship. That night the four horses were hobbled in the same paddock. Both charioteers shared the one fire. Fresh beds of rushes were made for the warriors and supplied with special pillows used for wounded men. The healers came and applied their medicines and their bandages. Cuchulain was treated, of course, by the great sages from the *sidhe* of the Tuatha De Danann. He sent these specialists with their age-old remedies to Ferdiad also, however, where he too lay in his pools of gore.

Ferdiad for his part sent to Cuchulain all the succulent dishes that his host prepared for him, and they were many. On his eastern side of the ford, Cuchulain was attended by only a few of the persons left alive on the Plains of Breg. These faithful friends dared come to him only after dark.

Ferdiad allowed Cuchulain to choose weapons the morning of the second day. "Let us take lances today," Cuchulain said, "for they will hasten this decision more than our casting of yesterday. Let us also mount our war chariots and combat from over our horses."

This day they never halted from dawn until dark. Hour after hour they drove as fast as their chariots could go, hurling lances with all their skill and strength. Birds, flights of birds, could have passed through each hero's body, so torn and gashed were they now. Large pieces of torn flesh hung from their untended wounds.

"Our charioteers are weary, and our horses are exhausted," said Cuchulain. "Why should we not be exhausted also? Shall we halt for the night? ... Our combat is a fight between giants, but we may spare our chariots, I think. Let us hobble our steeds and let the din of metal cease."

"If that hour has come," called Ferdiad. Thus, they both ceased at sunset. Their charioteers caught the weapons as they were tossed to them. Then both warriors stood in the middle of the stream, locked in an embrace. Each one placed his hand on the other's neck and gave him three kisses in love and memory of their boyhood friendship. That night the four horses were hobbled in the same paddock. Both charioteers shared the one fire. Fresh beds of rushes were made for the warriors, and supplied with special pillows used for wounded men. The healers now could do little except watch over the wounded champions, staunch the bleeding where it was possible, and apply whatever magical cures they knew: potions, charms, spells.

Ferdiad for his part sent to Cuchulain all the succulent dishes that his host prepared for him, and they were many. On his eastern side of the ford Cuchulain was attended by only a few of the persons left alive in the Plain of Breg. These faithful friends dared come to him only after dark.

When daylight came and they met again on opposite banks of the ford, they looked across at each other. Ferdiad seemed, to the eyes of Cuchulain, to be much altered. "You have an evil look today, O Ferdiad," he called. "Your hair has grown darker. Your eyes look clouded. Your body seems to slump. Your face is unrecognizable. You walk with a new, strange gait."

"I do not from fear or dread of you," answered Ferdiad. "I am still the champion of Erin."

"Alas, that you are," replied Cuchulain. "Is it not a pity now that you fight to the death with your oldest and truest friend, the companion of your childhood! And all because of a woman's interference."

"It is a pity," Ferdiad agreed, "but should I lay down my arms now, I would henceforth be scorned by all Erin, and cast out by Queen Medb and her nobles."

"It is a pity," Cuchulain repeated, "because for my part no woman in the world, and no man either, nobody but you yourself, could persuade me to attack you. Even now, my heart rises up in me at the thought of it."

The two champions then addressed each other in verse, Cuchulain lamenting the certain doom of Ferdiad. The latter in verse bowed his head before his tragic fate, knowing that he was betrayed by Medb, but accepting to die rather than to desert, like a coward. "Therefore," concluded Ferdiad, "it is useless for you, gentle Cua, to find fault with the color of my hair. Will you choose weapons?"

"Not I," said Cuchulain.

"Let us take swords today, then, and smite each other. Hopefully we shall by nightfall have arrived at a decision."

"As you wish," Cuchulain replied.

The shields which they chose this day were long ones which covered them fully. Then they struck and sliced with their heavy swords, cutting through defenses and fabric particularly on each other's shoulders, shoulder-blades, and thighs. They cut pieces of flesh from each other as large as a child's head. All day long, without ceasing, they heaved the mighty blades down upon each other, until darkness fell. Then Ferdiad called the halt. Both champions threw their equipment to their charioteers.

That morning they had met cheerfully and bantered with each other. This evening they, each one, turned from the other and parted without word or sign. The grooms dressed down the horses separately and hobbled them in separate paddocks. The squires cleaned the armor and weapons separately. Each charioteer sat by his own fire. Ferdiad sent no delicacies to Cuchulain, and the latter sent him no medicine.

Even before dawn lightened the eastern sky on the next day, Ferdiad was awake and busy. Even before dressing, he towered over the host—wide-awake, fully conscious of the significance of the day, sternly concentrating upon the business at hand. He recognized the day of decision. Three outcomes appeared most probable: Cuchulain would fall, he would fall, both would fall.

This morning he set about dressing in his finest clothing. Next to his fair skin he pulled on silken trousers with borders of flecked gold. Over these, he wore a brown leather kilt cleverly sewed. Over his abdomen he placed a flat, round stone of adamant which he had brought from Africa.[9] He laced it tightly to his body. No cutting edge or spear point could

[9] Irish tradition often refers to Africa as the place from which early settlers of Ireland in remote antiquity emigrated. Certain of the stones of Stonehenge likewise were said to have come from Africa.

crack that. Over these he laced a second kilt of flexible metal
plates, strong enough to deflect Cuchulain's dreaded harpoon,
if he should use it. Over his head he drew his crested helmet,
which was a pure work of art, studded with carbuncles,
enameled red, and accented with the red-and-white fires of
crystals and rubies. For his right hand he chose his sharpest
spear. He hung his scythe-shaped falchion on his left side,
shining and whetted to a thin line, inset with white gold and
red gold. Over his broad shoulders he flung his most massive
shield, made of buffalo hide, with a central boss of red gold.

As he waited at the ford for Cuchulain to arrive, Ferdiad
amused himself and the host of Erin by performing wonderful feats of dexterity; tossing his murderously keen weapons
high in the air and catching them in his bare hands, juggling
perilously there in the sunlight.

Cuchulain then came down to the water's edge and stood
quietly admiring Ferdiad's feats and the beauty of his splendid war dress. "Master Laeg," Cuchulain said to his charioteer, "keep a close watch on our combat today. If you see me
lag and fall before him, then taunt me and encourage me to
greater effort. But if you see me victorious, or well on the
way to killing him, then by all means be so kind as to praise
me and tell me that I am doing the right thing." Then Cuchulain stepped forward and in his turn showed his strength and
skill and demonstrated how he would pierce Ferdiad's defense, defeat his plan of battle, catch him unawares, force
him to the ground, and behead him with one stroke.

"What weapons, Ferdiad?" Cuchulain called.

"It is your day for choosing," Ferdiad replied.

"Then let us move to the 'Deed of the Ford,' " Cuchulain
proposed. Although he dreaded this ritual more than any
other form of combat, Ferdiad could only accept. This was
Cuchulain's ultimate maneuver, his deadliest battle tactic, the
one during which he had up until now killed his strongest opponents.

In all the annals of the champions, this battle of "Ferdiad's
Ford" has remained the most amazing, the most terrifying,
the most celebrated. Here were the two supreme heroes, each
one a champion of his native land. They were the two most
accomplished chariot warriors in the west of the northern
world. Both were veterans of various sorts of combat, both
seasoned and tempered with years of experience. Their personal bravery was apparent now as during the whole of their
lives. Northeastern vs. western Ireland met there at the ford,

in their strength and will to fight, and in their mutual acceptance of death.

Without a further word, they began the ritual combat, hurling at each other weapon after weapon, ceaselessly until the
sun was overhead. Then at noon, instead of stopping for rest,
each champion entered into a new and more desperate effort.
Each one drew closer and closer to his antagonist.

Suddenly Cuchulain leaped high in the air, landing on top
of Ferdiad's buffalo shield. Thence he sought Ferdiad's head,
attempting to catch it against the shield rim and sever it from
his body. But Ferdiad, in a mighty surge of strength, heaved
the lighter Cuchulain off his shield, across the stream, and on
to the opposite bank. A second time the Hound sprang,
leaping lightly across the water and catching himself again
upright upon Ferdiad's back. But again Ferdiad raised both
shield and warrior, used his left knee as a ram, and tossed
Cuchulain upon his back on the river bank.

"What are you there," Laeg called to Cuchulain, "a child?
Are you a helpless toddler some mother shakes off? Are you
a cup tossed out of the dishpan? Are you malt ground into
beer? Are you dead wood bored through by a woodman's
awl? Ferdiad has entwined you like bindweed on a tree trunk.
He has dived upon you like a hawk upon a sparrow. What
are you? An imp? An elf? Go along with you! You are no
more a champion! You have lost all claim to courage and
arms!"

Thus taunted, a third time Cuchulain rose to his feet,
poised a second, and leaped ... He leaped (how shall one
describe him?) as cutting and keen as March wind, as direct
in flight as a swallow swooping through air, as coiled in his
long limbs as a springing dragon, with the power of a tawny
lion crouching and then springing from taut hind legs into the
cloudy sky above him, into air, until he came down lightly
this time also upon the great golden boss in the center of Ferdiad mac Daman's shield.

But Ferdiad caught him, yielded at the knee, and rose
again upright, with such a mighty thrust upward, that Cuchulain bounded back into the water, at the middle of the ford,
returning faster than he had come.

This time Cuchulain surged like a giant. He swelled at the
onset of his battle frenzy. His second wind filled him like a
bellows as he rose before everyone's startled gaze, a great,
taut, swelling arch of sea monster rising from the deep, rip-
pling and rolling out of the river.

So close was their combat that their heads touched over

their shields, and their toes touched below their shields, and their hands touched on either side of the shields.

So close was their combat that their shields buckled, and burst, and split from top to middle, and at the bottom.

So close was their combat that the guardian spirits of the woods and the godkins of the mounds, and the denizens of the forest, and the half-gods of the bogs, and the hobgoblins of the air screamed and shrieked every time metal rasped against metal at top or middle or side or bottom of their shields, at the tips and at the guards of their spears.

So close was their combat that then the river parted, each half frantically seeking a new course and cooler bed, leaving the bottom dry where once it ran, large enough a space for a king's couch or a queen's, perfectly dry except for what ran off the two warriors. Still they grappled and grasped there in the dry riverbed.

So close was their combat that the war horses of the host plunged, reared, and finally broke their hobbles and their halters. They grew mad with approaching death. They were crazed with the smell of blood from the warriors. The horses broke free from their tethers, hobbles, halters, traces, harnesses, and ran. So did the women and children among the host of Erin. All took flight: horses, women, children, dwarfs, the weak, and the insane. From the confines of the camp they fled in panic, out into the open country to the southwest.

The champions were now performing the ritual called "In-fight with sword blades." Swiftly Ferdiad made an unparried thrust into Cuchulain's chest, burying his dagger up to the hilt, and making the blood gush down into his belt. Still Cuchulain showed no sign of flagging but kept striking at Ferdiad's middle, varying long swipes and short strokes with slashes. Suddenly he was comforted by airy presences on either side.

Throughout Cuchulain's life he was often accompanied on either flank by the spirits of his godly ancestors, the Tuatha De Danann. Now they had again left the *sidh* to fight on his either side, as frequently when Cuchulain was a mere boy entrusted to Queen Skatha on the Isle of Skye. Ferdiad too felt the triple attack.

"We are no longer equal, are we, Cuchulain?" he panted.

"Why not?" Cuchulain replied.

"Because the olden gods from the *sidhe* have come, like fairy folk, silently, to assist you."

"I could not lift their veil of concealment," said Cuchulain, "for it falls by their science, or their magic. Do not complain to me, however, for a son of the Gaels like yourself can never see the ancient gods of the Northeast. For your part, you wear a horny skin, which is magical to me: I know not how it is penetrated."

Then in the last moments of this "In-fight," each hero let down his defenses, Cuchulain showing Ferdiad the magical folk from his otherworld ancestry, and Ferdiad teaching Cuchulain the secrets of his horned armor. Thus, Ferdiad too was deeply and gravely wounded. Cuchulain by the same token, however, lost his unseen allies. In any case, the partial divinity of Cuchulain again stood him in good stead for a while.

The tide of battle swung back to Ferdiad, however, as soon as he realized that Cuchulain's elfin allies had been slain. Then he took heart anew and swung his sword with redoubled fury. Cuchulain drew in enough breath to swell himself like an arched rainbow through a rain shower, so brilliant was he among the flying water. Laeg brought him down to earth, however, with a warning of Ferdiad's new power.

Then Cuchulain called for his terrible harpoon, the secret weapon from Queen Skatha, which Ferdiad had never studied. Laeg rushed to the water's edge and set the weapon. It was fired by the foot, and it shot in a upward direction, rising through water and into a man's abdomen. It entered as one spear, but then opened into thirty barbs. Thereafter none of it could be drawn out of the victim's body until the flesh around each barb had been cut away.

Three times Laeg set the white weapon, and three times Ferdiad's charioteer sprung the trap. Finally the *Gae Bulga* (harpoon) was set, released in the water, and then fired by Cuchulain. As soon as Ferdiad saw it finally readied, he lowered his shield to soften its impact, at least. At that moment Cuchulain hurled a short spear, aiming over the rim of Ferdiad's belt and horned skin. The spear shot true into Ferdiad's heart. Automatically, Ferdiad raised his shield, leaving his lower body unprotected.

Cuchulain cast the terrible harpoon with all the power of his right foot, to his left and upward at Ferdiad. The *Gae Bulga* passed directly through the millstone of adamant, which the champion had bound across his abdomen. It passed through his kilt of iron armor, cracking the adamant in three places, and passing through it. It bore a passage into the soft parts of Ferdiad's body, gradually filling every limb and every cavity with its terrible long hooks, as they unfolded.

"Ah," groaned Ferdiad, "that will last me. I have fallen from that weapon. That was a powerful shot from your right foot. I saw it fired, but reacted too fast."

Before Cuchulain could move a muscle, he heard Ferdiad call to him once more. "I have not fought well," he said, "but you have killed me today unfairly, even so. Queen Medb turned my head with her offers. Now I shall feed the hungry crows. Henceforth, I shall live only in the chronicles and songs of Cuchulain. I am your greatest story, O Cu, your supreme triumph."

By that time Cuchulain's head had cleared somewhat, so that he could heave himself over to the dying Ferdiad. Cuchulain took all of him into his arms: Ferdiad, his armor, his weapons, his helmet, and his battle dress. He bore his friend upstream away from the host of Erin, which watched from the west side of the ford. He laid Ferdiad down upon the grass and leaned over him in a daze.

It required much shouting on Laeg's part to revive Cuchulain and draw him from his grief. "Erin will attack you now, O Cucuc," cried Laeg. "Show them no weakness now!"

"See what I have done," moaned Cuchulain. "Why should I rise from his body?"

Laeg attempted to comfort Cuchulain with all the words of wisdom he could offer, but the warrior remained overcome with grief. This was his lament:

"Why, O Ferdiad, did you not listen to those who know my real accomplishments?

"Why, O Ferdiad, could not Laeg make you regret your decision?

"Unhappy man, why could you not have heeded the warning of Fergus?

"Unhappy man, why could you not have heard the counsel of King Conall? These are men not suborned by Queen Medb.

"These leaders know that until the end of time no hero shall be so mighty in deeds, so famous for battle, so victorious in the defense of his homeland as Cuchulain Mac Sualtam."

Cuchulain followed his lament with a hymn of praise for his dead friend:

"Nevermore shall a rosy hero wound hero's flesh like Ferdiad!

"Nevermore shall the raven goddess of war Badb greet such a challenger!

"No contender shall ever rise till the end of life with the beauty and courage of Ferdiad!

"You were deceived. You were misled. You were abandoned, O Ferdiad.

"Never have I met in arms such a warrior, so keen, so skilled, so fearless, so powerful as my lost friend Ferdiad. I make exception for my own son, Connla, who was a brilliant warrior also."

Cuchulain then asked Laeg to strip the garments from Ferdiad's body so that he could see and hold the golden brooch which Queen Medb had given her champion. "Has it been for this pittance alone, Ferdiad, that you have died?" he cried. "Ah, golden brooch, you are not worth it. Truly, the combat was unfair."

Then Cuchulain ordered Laeg to cut the *Gae Bulga* from Ferdiad's body. "Here you lie," he said to the dead warrior, "in your pool of gore, while I stand dripping gore upon you. Who could have thought it?

"Sad is this day in March. Sad is this precursor day of spring. Red and sad the spring sun rises at the horizon. I have pledged Ferdiad in blood. The spring may enter. We two have drunk blood together."

"O Cucuc," Laeg pleaded. "Come away now. We have stayed here too long."

"Yes, let us leave," said Cuchulain. "All combat next to this one was a game. All contests with champions, compared to this contest, was play only."

While Cuchulain was carried by his people to the healing rivers of Murthemney to be cured of his terrible wounds, the funeral games of Ferdiad were solemnly celebrated.

Meanwhile Cuchulain's father Sualtam, even though a head without a body, succeeded in rousing the terrible host of King Conor. They drove out the host of Queen Medb.

8

Russia: Prince Igor

INTRODUCTION

IN THE FIFTH CENTURY B.C., Herodotus in Book IV of his *History* speaks of the Scythians, who inhabited northern Europe and Asia. He tells even then of their "gold-guarding griffins," and that they drank the blood of the first enemy that they conquered in battle, that they did not bathe in water, that they used the bark of the linden tree for prophecies, that they drank from the skulls of their conquered enemies, that they hung the scalps of those they killed on their bridle reins, and that they worshiped a sword fixed in the ground and watered with blood. We have already seen from the myths of the western invaders of Europe some survivals of these traits, particularly among the Goths and Huns, as recollected in the *Nibelungenlied*.

Moving eastward from the Danube realm of Attila, we come to the area north of the Black Sea where the Slavs, another Indo-European people, appear in the pages of history with their own variations of culture and language and their own epic story or poem, older by some fifteen years than the *Nibelungenlied*. It is the *Slovo o polku Igoreve, or The Lay of the Host of Igor*, which belongs to one particular group of Slavic peoples—the Russians. In the ninth century, according to their first historian, a monk named Nestor who lived some 300 years later, they occupied a limited area around the Dnieper and Dniester rivers. They were surrounded by enemies—the Lithuanians on the west, the Finns on the north, and the Turks on the east and south. Their subsequent story is one of colonization and expansion.

In the ninth century Scandinavian conquerors called the Varangians crossed the Baltic and descended through Europe to Constantinople (Tsargard). From their kings and heroes dates the history of the Russian people. Within a hundred years one of their rulers, Olga, had been converted to eastern Christianity, which brought the Greek alphabet to Russia; and around 1000 Vladimir, who like Olga became a saint, had tumbled into the Dnieper at Kiev the statue of the ancient Russian thunder god. Under Vladimir's son Jaroslav (1018?-1054) Russia was united around its splendid capital at Kiev, which possessed like Tsargrad its cathedral of Saint Sophia and its Golden Door.

After the death of Jaroslav occurred a long period of civil wars in which warring princes struggled for supremacy. *Prince Igor* deals with this period. Our unknown author laments the dissension which has laid his land open to invasions from the Polovcians or Qumans (Kumans) who spoke a Turkic language. As a result of these wars and invasions Kiev ceased to be the center of Russia; its focus moved northward toward Novgorod and Moscow.

Our story tells of a particular invasion into Quman territory by a Russian prince named Igor Sviatoslavov from his home city of Novgorod-Severski in 1185. His Turkic-speaking enemies are nomads whose names, Qumans and Polovcians, mean "blond," or "fair-skinned." They may be the same Caucasian peoples whom the Persians in the *Shah Nameh* call the "white demons"; certain terms applied to them in the Russian epic recall similar appellations applied to the central Asiatic khan Afrasiab.

The story of Prince Igor's raid is historical. However, under these actual occurrences lies an invaluable and unique testimony to the pagan beliefs of the Slavic peoples. Here is the prime document which speaks of Horus, the Egyptian sun god; Voloss, guardian of herds and patron of poetry; Stribog, the wind god whose grandsons are the Russians; the thunder god Peroun who did not disappear even though Saint Vladimir destroyed his statue; and the swan-maiden of death. This last symbol was very widespread; it is found from the time of Aeschylus down to Lohengrin via Beowulf and Brunhilde.

One observes also in the *Igor* story an element of mythology that, passing through the folklore of Slavic, Turkish,

Scandinavian, Germanic, Icelandic, and French cultures has left a superstition visible even in America today. Our author stops his narration to tell of a Russian prince named Vseslav who at night changed into a wolf. This is the werewolf myth (Anglo-Saxon *wer*=man) or the *loup-garou* of France. Popular belief through the ages was that a baby born with a caul about its head became bloodthirsty, crafty, lucky, swift of foot, wizardlike—a wolf at night. They thought his skin was as hard as horn and invulnerable, owing to the second skin or caul. After death he became a vampire, thus *Dracula* and *Dr. Jekyll and Dr. Hyde*. According to French tradition the lycanthrope or werewolf could only be killed by that person who wore or carried a four-leaf clover! It would seem as if this widespread superstition had colored the myth of Alexander the Great, whose story was written and rewritten so many times during the Middle Ages, and also that of Sifrit.

The following adaptation of the *Slovo o polku Igoreve* is taken from the book *La Russie Epique* by the French scholar and Academician Alfred Rambaud (1842-1905), although historical elucidation comes from Professor Rambaud's *Historie de la Russie* (1878).

There was only one copy of this work, discovered in a Russian monastery in 1795 and subsequently burned during the Moscow fire of 1812. Professor Rambaud thinks it was written partly in poetry and partly in prose. It has been suggested that the work was composed by a friend of Prince Igor, perhaps by a warrior in his *droujina*, and that it may have been sung at the wedding of Igor's son Prince Vladimir. Many volumes were written in the nineteenth century to dispute its authenticity, which seems today unquestionable. Since Professor Rambaud does not give the whole text, some liberties have been taken with the narrative, as will be indicated.

Among the many histories of Russia that appeared in the nineteenth century, after Napoleon's invasion, is one written by Count Lamartine, who is not only beloved as a romantic poet of France, but respected as a scholar and statesman. In the introductory paragraph to this book he talks about the difficulty of tracing or establishing the history of those peoples whose mythology is the subject of this present book. He says:

An almost impenetrable mystery floats over the cradles of peoples, as there floats over the sources of those rivers which descend from their glaciers to flood a continent ...

a cloud. Whatever may be the struggles or the systems of scholars to retrace after the events, race by race and step by step, those immense and inexplicable migrations of men who according to the learned scholars seeped out of the high plateaus of Tartary, the mind becomes troubled at the hypothetical accounts of these *historians of mystery;* one can only glimpse flashes, one can only discern a confusion, one cannot explain one enigma by another enigma, and if one is then sincere and lucid, of a mind not satisfied with words alone, but wanting to walk toward the true light upon solid ground, one ends by abandoning those poets of darkness who are called erudite, and by uttering humbly the words of the profane, . . . which are also the words of the philosophers: "I do not know!"

THE HOST OF PRINCE IGOR

How shall we begin this story, brothers? In new words or in old? In what fashion shall we sing of the deeds of Prince Igor? Shall we mimic the verses of Boyan[1], the olden bard?

Boyan was a poet who knew how to stir the heart! When he consented to celebrate the deeds of a hero, his words ran as swift and as footless as a field mouse to the top of fancy's tree. Or like a lean, gray wolf he could slink, belly to the ground, across the deep ravines of poetry! Then in our listening ears he transformed himself into the blue and lonely eagle that soars over our heads until it has merged into the blue-gray thunderheads of autumn, that drive northward from the sea. Such was the wizardry of that poet!

Do you not remember the spells of Boyan? As he sat meditating the works of the hero, some great *bogatyr,* Boyan would swiftly release ten falcons upon a flight of white swans

[1] Unidentified.

that arched the southern blue. The first white wounded swan,
pierced by the swift avenger, had first to sing her plaintive
melody, faint as the dying words of the hero. Sad and thin
were the words of Boyan as he charmed our ears: tales of
Jaroslav the Elder, of Mstislav the Brave as he killed Rededya
there before the Cherkess horde, and a pleasant lay about the
fair warrior Roman, son of Sviatoslavov.

Do we not know, my brothers, that the ten fierce hawks,
swift to cut the summer winds with their winged flight, were
the ten slender fingers of Boyan which plucked the living
strings of music. Those were the chords of memory his
magician's fingers played upon. They sang the glory of our
princes. . . .

We could have begun our lay with the life and works of
Vladimir the Old. Let us not do so, brothers. Let our
thoughts and our song drift down the winds of memory until
they halt at the deeds of Prince Igor. He in our lifetimes has
lived nobly. Prince Igor has dipped his soul into the well of
truth and whetted his nerve like a steel blade. Let us likewise
discard the rhapsodies of Boyan, and tell only those true
deeds of Igor; they will more than delight our souls.

Prince Igor set out from Novgorod with his train of warriors and rode due east. Warlike and valiant, the Russians
under Igor spurred their swift chargers far from home, away
from their peaceful fields and tame forest paths, eastward
over the black earth of the steppes. Out of their warm, wind-
sheltered homeland they rode gallantly toward the open
prairies that stretch their rolling backs in grassy undulations
far eastward toward the hordes of invading Qumans.

Then in a twinkling the sun hid its face. The whole earth
grew black. Prince Igor sought in vain the bright sun's glare,
sought in vain in the swift darkness the faces of his host. His
men had reined in their horses and dismounted.

"Brothers and companions," said Igor, "mount up and ride.
Is it not preferable to be hacked into pieces by the Qumans
than to be captured here in this day that has turned to black
night upon our shoulders? As for me, I have set out to strike
my lance against the Quman breastplates! Ride forward,
brothers! Let me leave my head upon these endless prairies,
or let me pierce to where the Don rolls blue into the sea! I
have sworn to drink his waters from my helmet!"

Boyan, you great poet of the bygone days, Boyan, nightingale from our distant past! You, and only you, Boyan, great

poet, should have sung the host of Igor! For only you like
the nightingale could hop upon the high tree of thought and
fly in fancy through the fluffy clouds of summer. Only you
could have chained these circumstances to the olden legends
of Russia. Only you could have sprinted after Igor and
caught him where he stood, brave and unafraid, on the grassy
sea of the steppes.

Above the head of Prince Igor the fierce hawks streak
across the stormy sky! Above the wide plains, high over the
wilderness of grass, masses of jackdaws flee in thick clusters
toward the great Don.

Back in the homeland the call to arms thundered through
Kiev! From Novgorod to the marches the shrill trumpet
blared the alarm! Knights mounted their war horses. Banners were unfurled. The host fell into ranks behind Igor and
set their faces eastward. Prince Igor waited for Vsevolod,
his dear brother.

"Igor, my only brother," Vsevolod had told him, "saddle
your war horse. Raise your battle flag. Are we not brothers?
Are we not both sons of Sviatoslavov? . . . My warriors await
you in Kursk. They are all tried men, battle-proven and
brave. They were born to the call of the trumpet, trained
from childhood under their war helms, fed from a lance point!
They know the roads to the Polovcian lands. They know
every gulch and dry stream bed. Their bows are strung, their
quivers are opened, their sabers are filed to a razor edge.
They lope through the steppes like gray woves in packs, thirsty
for glory for themselves and for us, the princes! Mount up,
dear Igor, and ride!"

Then Igor set his foot in the golden stirrups and rode
swiftly out into the black earth of the plains. Before him
the sun dropped a curtain of darkness. Night blanketed the
land. Igor listened to the voices of darkness. There was a
moaning in the air, so threatening it awakened the birds from
their sleep. Around the host wild beasts roamed through the
high grass and screamed their wild scream as they hunted.
The little soft creatures huddled in fear, their eyes like pin-
points in the gloom. They flattened their bodies against the
earth mother and listened. From a swaying treetop the fierce
Diva shrieked the alarm to the foreign land upon which Igor
had set his feet. "Awaken," cried the Diva, "awaken!" Thus
she alerted the Volga, and also the Great Don, and the shores
of the Black Sea.

By uncharted tracks the Quman hordes began to stream toward the Great Don. In the dark night the heavy wheels of their carts squeaked and squealed on the wooden axles, like the terrified screams of wild swans overhead. Through the darkness they shuddered and wailed their piercing news, "Igor is leading the warriors toward the Don!" Then the earth creatures roamed, smelling the smell of hot blood that will slake their thirst. In deep ravines the wolves howled to the moon. The eagles answered, summoning the toothed animals to the carrion piles. The foxes barked and snarled at the red shields of Igor.

Earth of Russia, where are you? Where are you, land of home? You are far behind the funeral mounds, far distant now for Igor, who has crossed the soil of the steppes! Igor and his host stand alone on enemy earth, in the trackless plains that stretch a long way to the Don.

Black night has changed to gray mists swirling their heavy webs over the host. White shrouds have lifted at dawn. Day has come to the prairie. The nightingales have hushed their cries as the daws croak and quarrel in the swaying grasses.

In a golden line the warriors of Igor have barred the roads to the west. In the white light of day they meet the Quman warriors and trample them into the earth. Like swift arrows the host of Igor pierces the heavy line of the foe and drives them about in panic. Pile after pile of rich fabric, silks and velvets, are torn from the Quman carts and trampled under foot. The foe are so loaded with cloaks, with fur robes, with brocades, with pavilions, that these stuffs under the horses' feet make a bridge through the marshy soil. The Russian horses tread on a causeway of furs and samite. The beautiful girls of the Qumans fall also as the spoils of war. The brave sons of Sviatoslavov take as their booty a red battle standard, a white banner, and a red yak tail on a golden staff.

That night in the lonely fields slept Igor and Vsevolod with the little princes, their sons. Lost, far in the trackless waste, slept the sons of Sviatoslavov. After their victory they had pushed on behind the scattered Qumans and camped for the night. Little did they know that the Khan Gza was on the march, swift and silent as the gray wolf of darkness. Little did they dream that the Khan Koncak of the Polovcians was streaking across the plains behind them to cut off their retreat.

You were not born, Prince Igor, to endure their insults, nor those of the falcon, nor those of the hawk, nor yours either, black crow of a Quman, pagan Polovcian!

At daybreak a red sun, blood-red and fiery, flooded the plain where the Russians slept. The day dawned red under black thunderheads that drifted closer and closer from the sea, that descended slower and slower toward the orange earth. The rain clouds dropped their swaddling mists over the four sons, the four princes of Russia. From their black maw blue streaks of lightning hunted among the host of Igor. Thunder shook the earth and rattled the sabers. The horses rolled apprehensive eyes and pressed closer together for comfort.

Like stinging arrows the rain struck the host full in the faces. Like the sharp clang of steel-tipped arrows the rain, slanting sharply from the east, hammered at the Russian breast plates. From the Don came the driving shower of arrows. Lances shivered. Sabers blunted on the conical helms. By the shores of the River Kayali the princes of Russia were surrounded by fierce Quman warriors. The battle thundered not far from the waters of the Great Don!

O land of home, where are you now? Where are you, earth of Russia? Igor and Vsevolod and the two little princes have left you far behind them. They have crossed the last mounds and plunged into the trackless prairies that lie between the Dnieper and the Great Don.

Fierce winds from the seacoast, those ungovernable sons of Stribog, are whipping Polovcian arrows against you! Full in your faces they rain the steely lances of battle. Under your feet the strange earth moans and disowns you. Beside you the strange river flows uneasily, hesitates turgidly, roiled with unknown blood from heroes it cannot welcome. Damp clouds of storm roll over your desperate arms. Back and forth the battle standards call to each other; they rally their friends in that tumult. The Polovcians pour on the battlefield from all directions, from the Don and from the Black Sea coast. Step by step the Russians retreat; their shields behind their backs, they form a circle facing inward.

And you, brave Vsevolod, impetuous bull, standing fierce at the rear guard, how you rake them with your arrows. How you beat upon their casques with your battle sword of hardened steel! This way and that you leap and plunge like a savage buffalo. Over here and then there your golden helm shines and glints. Under your hooves the earth is strewn with pagan heads. The Caucasian helmets crumple beneath your flashing blows. The nomads lie tangled upon their soil.

See his fury! Like a mad bull Vsevolod has struck from his mind all thoughts of home. In a flash he has forgotten the spendor of his princely life, his home city, the golden throne of his father, and the soft arms of his wife, that gracious daughter of Gleb. Vsevolod has forgotten a lifetime of happiness. What are wounds to him?

Did you hear that clang of metal? We have seen wars before, and battles at Troy. All, all is past like the days of Jaroslav and the days of Oleg. He was a prince who brought disorder to our land so that harmony was broken. Prince fought prince and brother fought brother. In all these wars the grandsons of Dazbog[2] laid down their lives over the fields of Russia, where the carrion crows quarreled over their corpses while the jackdaws grew fat from feasting. Those indeed were great battles, bloody and cruel; but none was so awful as that second day when Igor and Vsevolod fought the Quman hordes.

The black earth of the plains was churned by the furious horses. The very grass had been trampled so that it was stamped into the earth. No grass color showed any more. Bones and dying warriors, wounded and bleeding heroes lay in heaps across the prairie. What a crop of tears was planted in that rich earth!

What are those clinking sounds I hear? Ah, it is Igor's men riding again into the fray! Their armor clashes! Their swords ring against helmet in the heart of the Polovcian land. Igor could not let his brother think that he had been abandoned there at the rear guard! They had both fought hard all the first day. Then the battle had begun afresh in the rain of the second day's dawn. This was Sunday, the third day.

Not until noon of the third day did the torn banner of Igor tremble and fall! After that the brother princes were separated by the banks of the swift-flowing Kayali River.

The bloody red wine has all been spilled. The princes have risen from the feast and departed. The Polovcians are thirsty no more, for they have drunk their fill of blood. The Russians have lain down to die in the Quman fields. They have laid down their lives for their motherland. In sighing waves the long grasses of the plains have bowed their heads

[2] Also a sun god.

in sorrow. A tree, stricken with grief, has bent its head until
its trembling fingers trail on the ground.

Then the goddess of Discord flew over the sleeping warriors. Lo! my brothers, sad in the hour when she glides down
the wind! The wasteland has eaten our beloved friends and
companions. The turf has sucked their blood. They have all
been chewed and swallowed in that expanse of grass. All the
"children of the glorious Sun" sleep now in darkness. Now
over their dreamless bones flies the swan-winged goddess.
See her glide through the blue skies! She has come from the
Don to spread death among our peoples. All one will find
in her path are mounds of bleaching bones!

Oh! how the swan goddess has brought in days of misfortune! How in Kiev the women wail! How the women of
Novgorod weep and lament! Prince Igor's banner has fallen
on the black soil of the prairies How shall we sleep with
the nomads at our doors? When shall we see our loved ones
riding up to the door? When shall we hear the sharp whinny
of his horse? What black night shall we hear in our slumber
the clang of his spurs on the threshold? When shall we feel
his strong arms enfold our trembling shoulders?

What calamities did the warring princes bring upon us!
How they have thrown our gold to the four corners of the
Quman land! Why were they not all with Igor when he and
Vsevolod affronted the hordes alone on the murmuring,
foreign soil? What shall we answer, and where shall we hide
when the fierce conquerors ride through our villages and call
for a pelt at every door? We have made them rich, the fierce
nomads of Quman. Their carts groan from the gold that over-
flows! Their rivers overflow from the golden swords, the
gleaming helms, the gallants' shields that lie under their
currents.

Prince Igor has just exchanged his golden saddle and
harness for a nomad's pony and a length of coarse rope!

In his palace at Kiev the crown prince of Russia dreamed
that night, he who is suzerain lord to all the princes of Russia,
he who is "uncle" of Igor. In his prime this Prince Sviatoslavov sent for swords from the Burgundian Franks. He used
these weapons well. With his Frankish metal he cleaved a
path that Quman chieftains remembered from father to son.
Now in his palace the crown prince dreams.

"Hear my dream," cries Prince Sviatoslavov. "I thought that
early last evening here on the hills near Kiev, they swathed
me in a black shroud as I lay on my high-carved bed. They

poured me wine that was cloudy[3] and mixed with gall. Over my chest they emptied their quivers. The quivers of the heathen nomads were full of pearls![4] Huge, misty pearls rolled over my body. And lo! in my gold-domed palace the roof tree was missing; the mainstay of my house was gone! All through last night the black crows perched under the eaves of my house and croaked, cawed and croaked, in my ears!"

The boyars replied to their prince, "Sorrow has stolen into your heart, and we understand your affliction. Your two young falcons have slipped their leashes and flown away from their father's throne. They have left your golden palace and galloped across the land toward the seacoast. They longed to drink the waters of the Don in their helmets. You have cause for grief, O Prince. Your dream was not false. The heathen Polovcians have snared your swift hawks in their nets. They have clipped their wings and chained them with iron fetters.

"On the third day of battle two princes, radiant like dawns of royal purple hue, were hid by storm clouds and pelting flurries of arrows. Two boy princes, their sons, as slender and graceful as two crescent moons, were shrouded in cloud as they sank into the sea.

"All these disasters have brought abounding joy to the khans of the Qumans, who lope over our fields now like a band of hungry leopards. Black shame has, indeed, shrouded our former glory. Like the thunderbolts that fell upon Prince Igor have bondage and slavery fallen now upon all our people.

"The Diva, terrible goddess, croaks from our own tree-tops. Now that our warriors lie moldering, their bones bleaching beside prairie rivers, will not our defenseless homes invite the plunder of the hordes?

"Now the pretty handmaidens of the Goths, those allies and slaves of the Qumans, sing songs of our defeat all along the seacoast. They jingle our gold in their slender palms and hail the khans. For gold they sing songs of the long-dead chiefs of the Polovcians. For us, for you, Prince Sviatoslavov, there is no more joy!"

Then the crown prince in this golden palace at Kiev let fall his golden thoughts drenched in his tears, "Oh, my nephews, my children, Igor and Vsevolod! Too early, much too early,

---

[3] Sign of long affliction. See *Berta of Hungary*, p. 190, "the river was as cloudy as ale."

[4] Sign of tears.

you rode forth into the rolling prairies of our enemies, thinking to cover yourselves with glory. You have not distinguished yourselves, young Princes! You have only let the
blood of your faithful followers seep into the pagan soil. I
know your hearts were valiant. I know your heads were
high and your swords tempered in baths of courage. But
look at the grief you have brought down upon my white head!

"See the sorrow I now must endure in my old age! Now I
no longer see my valiant brother Jaroslav come riding at the
head of his armed host, he so powerful and so rich, he whose
warriors hastened to his banner from all the neighboring
peoples. How would he have defeated the Qumans, my young
fledglings?

"The host of Jaroslav in the old days had no swords like
yours, of tempered Frankish steel. With only a cutlass stuck
in their boots, they spurred into the nomad hordes, screaming their resounding war cries, raising the honor and renown
of our cities! Jaroslav was the terror of the hordes!"

The old prince's head fell upon his chest. Of whom could
he seek aid? One after another he passed in review the
warring princes, those who had thundered across the plain,
those whose sleds had sped swiftly down the frozen rivers in
winter, whose oars in summer had raised showers of water
drops from the Dnieper, from the Don, and from the Volga
with their blades. It was up to the princes now that Igor
had fallen. Only they together could stop the Quman invasion. If only Igor had not been so impetuous, they might
have destroyed the enemies' winter homes while they were
still in their northern pastures.

It was that Prince Vseslav who first years ago craftily
brought the Qumans as mercenaries into Russian fields. He
was not human, that Vseslav! At night like a wizard he
slipped out of Kiev. He was no longer a man. At night he
was the bloodthirsty werewolf. Through the forests he trotted
from Kiev to Belgorod, all covered in a blue-gray fog. Then
by morning he was thundering his battering rams against the
oak gates of Novgorod. With his extra measure of good luck,
Vseslav crushed the fame of Jaroslav.

Under cover of darkness Vseslav could leap all the way
to the Nemiga in Lithuania, where he drank much blood.
During the day he sat in judgment over whole nations, hand-
ing over cities and villages to his followers. Every night he
changed himself into a wolf and trotted through the moonlit

forests from Kiev to the heathen idol at Tmutarakan[5] before
cockcrow. Thus in the form of a wolf he nightly followed
the route of the sun god Horus. . . . If the princes do not rally
to save Kiev, then we are lost!

What is that sound I hear? One would think at first the
voice of the cuckoo. Do you hear its soft notes? It is not
the weak cry of a bird. It is the lament of Jaroslavna, daughter of Jaroslav. Why does she weep? She weeps for the love
of her beloved husband, who is far away on the lonely
prairies of the east. Jaroslavna weeps, ever so softly, poor
lady, because her beloved husband, Prince Igor, is far from
her arms. In the cuckoo's soft voice at dawn Jaroslavna weeps
on the walls of Putivl'.[6]

Leaning over the walls of her castle, straining her eyes
toward the east, Jaroslavna weeps for her beloved.

"I shall fly like a cuckoo all the length of the Don. I shall
fly to the Kalayi and dip my arms in its water . . . even up to
the beaver cuffs of my sleeves. With my own hands I shall
carry water and gently wash the wounds of my Prince Igor,
all the bloody wounds there are on his powerful body."

Leaning over the walls of her castle, straining her eyes
toward the east, Jaroslavna weeps for her beloved.

"O Wind, terrible Wind! Why, Sir Wind, do you blow so
hard? Why do your light winds bear the arrows of the khan
against my husband's warriors? Is it not satisfying enough to
you to blow up high among the clouds? to rock the vessels
on the blue sea? Why, Sir Wind, must you overthrow all my
joy on the grass of the steppes?"

Leaning over the walls of her castle, straining her eyes
toward the east, Jaroslavna weeps for her beloved.

"O glorious Dnieper! You whose swift current cut a bed
through the stone mountains of the Polovcian land! O Dnieper, you willingly rocked the warships of Sviatoslavov when
he carried his war into the land of the Khan Kobyak! Please,
Sir River, carry my lord home to me. Then I shall no
more have to send him my tears which drop now on your
waters."[7]

Leaning over the walls of her castle, straining her eyes
toward the east, Jaroslavna weeps for her beloved.

[5] Perhaps a reference to a secret alliance between Vseslav and the
Caucasus.

[6] Putivl' is a castle where this lady is besieged.

[7] Sita prays to the Jumna River in the *Ramayana*. See Goodrich,
Ancient Myths, p. 181. See also prayers in the *Rig-Veda*, earliest Hindu
scriptures.

"O, brilliant sun, you thrice brilliant sun! You warm us all with your yellow rays. You shine for us all. Why, Sir Sun, must you shoot your burning rays upon my husband's warriors? Why do you dry up their bows in their hands, in that hot waste without water? Why do you make their quivers so heavy that they cut into the warriors' shoulders? Why, as they ride through that thirsty land?"[8]

Toward midnight great swells mount in the sea. Huge funnels of fog rise from the deep and prowl inland over the coast. Their trailing veils cover the marshlands. They swirl their mysterious mists through the prairie grasses and engulf the camp of the Polovcians where Igor and the princes lie prisoner. God opens a path through fog, a clear path opening out to the west, a plain corridor of light down which a prince could walk between thick, gray blankets of cloud. If Prince Igor were to step boldly into that hallway, were to ride bravely down that unknown, midnight path, it would lead him surely to the golden throne of his fathers!

The evening dawn has finished her work. She has welcomed the horse of the Sun and prepared him for the second half of his daily journey over the heavens. She has lifted her purple robes and sunk to rest down the evening sky. Mist and darkness play at hide-and-seek on the prairie.

In the Polovcian camp the warriors sprawl in sleep, drunk with the sweet wine of victory. Does Prince Igor sleep? Can Prince Igor sleep when he knows that tidings of grief have already been carried back to the anxious cities of Kiev and Novgorod?

No, Prince Igor lies wakeful and watching among the prisoners. His eyes seek the path through the trailing, wet fog. In thought he measures the distance from the Great Don to the little Donets River. He rehearses the lie of the land, its folds and ravines, and counts off the tens of miles on his fingers. The most dangerous part of the journey would be the first day. As soon as the sun rose and dried up the fog, he would be clearly visible to his pursuers. For miles they would see him, one black speck, horse and rider, standing out clearly against the pale grass of the prairie. At night they could only guess the general direction of his flight from

[8] This lament of Jaroslavna opens Scene II, Act I of the Borodin opera *Prince Igor*. It is the beautiful arioso *Da lungo tempo*, or in the English libretto, "How long a time has passed." Borodin died before he had completed this work; the opera was finished by Rimsky-Korsakov and Glazounov.

the distant, faint thunder of hoofbeats, if they laid their ears
to the resonant earth, their earth of the steppes, friendly to
them and hostile to Igor.

Just at the hour of midnight Prince Igor hears a low
whistle. Cautiously he raises himself on his elbow and listens
again. There it comes, a soft, low whistle from the reeds on
the opposite bank of the Kayali. That was the signal he had
arranged with the Polovcian Ovlor, who had agreed to saddle
a horse and lie waiting for Igor on the opposite shore of the
river.⁹

"You have a chance to escape. Fly back to Russia," his
fellow prisoners had urged Igor.

"No man could do it," another argued. "No man alone
with one horse, or even with two, could ride all those days
alone over the prairie."

"No," replied Igor. "I was captured fairly. The Qumans
rely on my word. For that they have allowed me to talk with
my fellow prisoners."

"Fly, Prince Igor. Fly like a bird to the homeland," urged
his attendants.

"No," replied Prince Igor, "and leave my comrades prisoner
in the Quman camp? Perhaps if I were to escape, I might
save my own life. Perhaps I might even arrive unscathed in
our motherland again. No. We set out together to make this
raid. It was on our own initiative, without the knowledge,
the wise plans, or even the consent of Crown Prince Sviatoslavov. We rode together, and we shall die together as one
man."

"Your thoughts run low like foxes, from burrow to burrow.
Your thoughts are sad because your body is weary from
wounds, from battle, and from the heavy shame of defeat.
Be not a fox in your plans, Prince Igor. Let your hopes soar
with the eagle who sees the two dawn goddesses at once. He
flies so high that he looks from his flight of today backward
into yesterday and forward into tomorrow.

"Fly, Prince Igor," urged the members of his *droujina*.
"Remember that there is above us all a greater cause, that of
our country. Kiev needs you now, and Novgorod on the
marches. The Qumans have defeated our armies. Their
horses have trampled the sons of the Sun into the sod of the
prairies. Let us not lose our leader also! Is it not terrible
enough to have seen our warriors perish?

⁹ The following passage, extending to the next space break, is taken
from a Russian chronicle.

"Run the gauntlet of your pursuers, Prince Igor! Ride, leaning double over your horse's neck. Make a dash for freedom! Escape, Prince Igor, and may God go with you!"

Now in the midnight fog, when the campfires are blackened ash and the creeping fog mantles the land, Igor has heard the whistle of Ovlor. "Do not stay here. Prince Igor! Come! Leave the Quman horde! Fly," it seems to say.

Cautiously Prince Igor rises to his feet and steps carefully over the legs of his sleeping companions. Silent and swift he makes his way through the fog to the outskirts of the camp, past the last blanketed forms, past the last tents and heavy carts, past the tethered horses of the enemy. The earth stirs and complains at his measured footfall. The treacherous grasses of that hostile land catch at his boots, swish against his spurs, murmur noisily at his passage. Like giant trees in the gloom two Polovcian sentinels walk toward each other on his right hand. They have left the path clear in front!

Swift as an ermine Prince Igor darts into the reeds that cluster higher than his head along the Kalayi shores. His feet sink into the wet soil which sucks loudly at his boots and tries to betray his passage. Like a teal, so swift in its flight, so rapid to fold its wings and dive headfirst into water, Prince Igor plunges under the Kayali current. With strong strokes he swims like a teal under the surface while over his legs the fog has covered the widening circles on the water. The river does not struggle against the swimmer. Prince Igor passes its water and wades ashore on the opposite bank.

There Ovlor awaits him, holding the bridles of their strong horses. Prince Igor vaults into the saddle and the horse awakens under him. Like the light-footed wolf, used to running through fog and through darkness mile after mile, the mount of Prince Igor leaps over the grasslands. The only other sound is the pounding hoofs of Ovlor behind him. They cut a deep path in their flight, leave the grasses darker where they have passed because of the silver dewdrops that brush off on their horses' legs and on their flanks. Like a fierce hawk Prince Igor feels the wind on his head and senses which way is due west. They ride without stopping for breath, without once slackening speed, until both their horses heave and founder under them.

Then Prince Igor and Ovlor walk mile after mile through

the rolling land on the eastern bank of the Donets. With their
arrows they bring down wild swans and honking geese for
their breakfasts, for noonday and for supper. As soon as
they have eaten and stamped out their fires, they start out
again under the blinding sun of day or wrapped in thick fog
at night. Oftentimes they travel through grasses that are taller
than their heads, where only the eagle could see their tracks,
or the gray rabbit could hear their tread, until they come
finally to the shores of the Donets.

Then that river, rolling its majestic way toward the Don,
speaks clear words to Prince Igor. "Prince Igor," says the
Donets, "as great glory as your escape will bring about your
person, so will it bring equally great derision upon the Quman
khans, Gza and Koncak. You may be sure there will be great
rejoicing throughout your native land."

"O Donets," answered the prince, "nor is there little glory
for thee who has rocked so many princes gently upon blue
waves. Was it not you who through all time spread a carpet
of thick grass, so green and pleasant, along your silvery
shores? Was it not thee who set the white ducks bobbing
along your currents as sleepless sentinels? Was it not you
also, O Donets, who encouraged the sea gulls to patrol your
estuary and the swift teal to span your course. Your tribu-
tary, the sluggish Stugna, was never such a river as thou art!
Scant and grudging are her treacherous waters that watched
defeats by the Polovcians, encouraged them even, by clawing
at our friendly crafts and then ripping out their bottoms on
hidden tree stumps!

"No praises shall I sing for the muddy Stugna's waters.
What treachery did that river use! Surely you remember, wise
Donets! She caught our Prince Rostislav[10] as he fought for
his life in her bosom. She held his dear head down ... down
... thrice down under her waves, until he rose no more to
the sunlight! Now his mother wails and weeps, wakes and
weeps for her son. All along the thin Stugna the wild flowers
bend their heads pensively as they see their faces in her mir-
ror and are reminded of Prince Rostislav. Even the trees
droop and mourn along her shores!"

Did you hear that? One would say a horde of magpies
squabbling over seeds! Over there, beyond the grass! Do
you hear it? One would say two magpies hurling insults at

[10] This prince died in battle in May 1093. He was twenty-three years
old.

each other, coming in our direction! Hark! All of a sudden
the crows have stopped circling and calling! Look! Look
in the air above us! It is suddenly empty! Where are the
jacksaws who swoop and wheel in the sun? The air is too
silent! The earth is too still!

It was no horde of magpies whose chattering had drifted
across the breeze to Prince Igor. That was the furious oaths
of the Quman khans, Gza and Koncak, who fan out across
the steppes and halloo up and down their lines as they hunt
through the grasses for Igor! The crows caw no more. The
magpies have ceased their chatter. Only the woodpeckers,
climbing nimbly over the gnarled willow trunks, announce
by their sharp little cries the line of the river.

Far in the distance the nightingale heralds a new day!

Riding hard, Khan Gza calls to Khan Koncak, "Since the
Russian hawk has fled toward its golden nest, let us pierce
his young fledgling prince with our golden arrows!"

Then Khan Koncak replies, "Since the proud Russian hawk
has fled toward its golden nest, let us entangle his young
fledgling in the meshes of a pretty, young Quman girl!"

Khan Gza replies, "If we let that fledgling get enmeshed
in the charms of a pretty, young girl, we shall be able to keep
neither him nor his lady love! You can see what would
happen after that: in a few years time their young would
fly vengefully at us and again lay waste the Polovcian
fields!"

We must always return to the wise words of Boyan. You
remember what Boyan said: "It is painful for a head to be
without shoulders; and a misfortune for shoulders to be without a head is it also."

So would it have been for the Russian land a calamity
to have been without Prince Igor and his son, Prince Vladimir!

No. Darkness did not fall upon us! Misfortune did not
altogether lament and spread her wings over our land!

A new sun rose with a new dawn!

Prince Igor made his way back into the motherland.
Maidens sang with joy all along the distant Danube. Their
cries were wafted by the wind all the way from Kiev to the
waters of the sea!

Prince Igor rode up the steep ravine of Baritchef, which
led from the shores of the Dnieper to the high hill where
gleamed the golden domes of Kiev! He knelt in prayer at
the Church of the Virgin of the Tower. The motherland re-

joiced. Bells rang in domed churches. Songs were sung in honor of the older princes, and new songs were composed at once for Prince Igor.

Poets sing of the glorious exploits of Igor, son of Sviatoslavov. They sing gladly of the impetuous buffalo, Vsevolod, of young Prince Vladimir the fledgling and son of Prince Igor.

Long life and health to such princes and to their retinue who fight so nobly for the Christian people of Russia, against their pagan foes!

All hail to the Prince, and to his attendants.

A M E N

9

Spain: The Cid

INTRODUCTION

How LONG POETS in Spain had been celebrating the deeds of their medieval hero, Rodrigo Díaz of Vivar, before the Abbot Peter copied it in the manuscript form that will be used here, is very difficult to say. Rodrigo Díaz was born about 1043 (?). He actually did besiege and conquer the beautiful city of Valencia on the eastern coast of Spain; he ruled it for some five years with a clemency and skill that caused him to be remembered and adored as their own hero by the simple people of Spain; he did only leave Valencia in 1099 at the time of his death, leaving the reins of government in the hands of his wife, Doña Ximena; and he was interred at the monastery of San Pedro de Cardeña near Vivar and Burgos, where he was born. It is also true that great nobles, even kings, are supposed to have descended from him. The family of our early Floridian, Ponce de Leon, was one of them.

Rodrigo Díaz was called the Cid not by his fellow Castilians, but strangely enough by his enemies, the Moors he defeated in Valencia and elsewhere. The word Cid (sidi) means "champion" or "hero." Our author calls Rodrigo Díaz endearingly Mío Cid—My Hero; he even has Rodrigo call *himself* Mío Cid! In a medieval Latin chronicle this champion is referred to as *"Ipse ... Mío Cid semper vocatus,"* or "He was always called Mío Cid." The reader will note in the following abridged translation who among the characters in the story do not refer to him by that affectionate nickname.

Our poet may have thought that he was composing in Latin, but he was actually writing Spanish; this poem of the Cid coincides with the birth of the Spanish language. It probably dates from the early twelfth century (1140?) because it is much closer to Latin and to Old French, much cruder in versification and elegance of expression than the language of such poets as Don Gonzalez de Berceo, who we know wrote in the thirteenth century. Señor Juan Cabal in his book *Los Héroes Universales de la Literatura Española,* published in Barcelona in 1942, says that the *Poem of Mío Cid* would be more or less unintelligible to the average reader of Spanish. However that may be, it is true that a large part of our poet's vocabulary does not occur in a modern Spanish dictionary, but does occur in medieval French.

Some scholars in Spain hesitate to admit connections between this poem and French medieval epics, and yet it seems no reflection on the *Mío Cid* poet to remark that aside from the unexpected closeness of words and expressions, it does have traits that tie it to the *Song of Roland,* which is older, and to the *Berta* story, which is much more recent.

As the reader will see, Charlemagne did not have a monopoly on Saint Gabriel, nor on the possession of a magnificent beard. Prince Igor's father, who also dealt with the Franks, had a beard, and so does the Cid. The latter also has a pet lion in a cage, as did the father of King Pepin. This king, by the way, had sent 25,000 men into Spain to fight the Moors in 735.... These traits, it may be argued, do not of necessity have to have been borrowed. Perhaps they only show the similarities between the European cultures. The reader, thinking back to the bleeding lance of the *Peredur* myth, will find its signification fully explained by Mío Cid's wife, Doña Ximena.

The land of Spain was settled and in touch with the other parts of the ancient world by at least 1500 B.C. It was colonized by Phoenicians, by Greeks, by Carthaginians, by Romans, and then early in the Middle Ages by the Goths and the Mohammedan Moors. It remained under Roman rule from about 218 B.C. for six hundred years during which time the Latin language became that of Spain. The Moors or Arabs invaded Spain around A.D. 711 and occupied its southern half for long centuries—the Dominion of the Almohads—until they were finally expelled in 1492.

By the thirteenth century, however, there was such a thing,

despite all these mixtures of cultures, alphabets, and languages, as the Spanish tongue. There were great, *very* great "Spanish" authors living long before the days of our unknown poet who composed *The Poem of Mío Cid;* but they wrote in Latin, and their names are Seneca, Lucan, Quintilian, and Martial. In classical times Spain was known as Hesperia, a beautiful land somewhere in the west. The Romans knew its oranges, the "golden apples of the Hesperides," and its "dancing girls from Cadiz." Hannibal had come from Spain when he crossed the Alps into the Po Valley.

Spain and France were very close during the Middle Ages, as both the *Roland* and the *Cid* show us. In the thirteenth century the regent of France was the Spanish princess Blanche of Castile, one of the most pious and most remarkable women of the Middle Ages. Not only was she the mother of Louis IX of France, he who died in Africa during the last Crusade and was canonized in 1297 as Saint Louis, but she also helped establish the cult of the Virgin and the traditions of courtly love.[1] One notices already in the *Cid* the emphasis upon women that became so strong during the Crusades when they assumed unwonted responsibilities of government and administration during their husbands' absences in the Holy Land.

Just as we have seen in the *Roland,* one good yarn deserves another. Poets therefore gave Charlemagne a childhood, and Roland also. Then they moved backward to give them ancestors whose lives made attractive subjects. The same is true of Rodrigo Díaz. The original poem passed through many hands, into songs, poems, romances, and the glamorized accounts of early historians. From Guillén de Castro, a noted Spanish dramatist, it passed to France where it became *Le Cid* (1636) of Pierre Corneille, as French schoolchildren and students of French know. This masterpiece is to the lover of French classical literature what *Hamlet* or *Macbeth* would be to us. Rodrigo Díaz, no matter how humble his origins, has had a brilliant career in European culture!

The *Cid* is in a way the story of a self-made man. Although the actual life of Rodrigo Díaz was probably one of wandering and incessant quarreling with King Alfonso VI of Castile, our poet has, with almost the novelist's gift for characterization, presented us with the story of a real man's

[1] See Henry Adams, *Mont-Saint-Michel and Chartres,* Mentor edition, New American Library, New York, 1961.

love and devotion to his family, his struggle to rise in the world and to become accepted by his social superiors. One knows the Cid better than one knows any other national hero of the Middle Ages. His words ring true; it is therefore no wonder that he is synonymous with Spanish! That very word "Spain" may convey instantly to the mind Don Quixote and Sancho Panza, or Don Juan, but most probably the first thought one has is Rodrigo, My Cid.

THE CID

Then weeping and distressed Mio Cid said, "Father in heaven, you see what my wicked enemies have done to me!"

Mio Cid and his dear friend Alvar Fañez rode forth from Vivar. There was a black crow on their right; as they entered Burgos, there was a black crow on their left. Even so, Mio Cid shrugged his shoulders and held his head high. "Alvar Fañez," he sighed, *"we have been exiled from Castile!"*

Sixty of his knights, all bearing pennants, fell quietly in behind Mio Cid as he rode through the streets of Burgos, up to his own palace. The city dwellers watched them from their balconies; no one dared greet Mio Cid on pain of the king's displeasure. Mio Cid dismounted before his own door. He knocked loudly on its panels. He knocked loudly and again. There was no answer from his people within the walls. Mio Cid turned away from his own door. Even that was barred against him.

That night Mio Cid camped outside the city, on the banks of the Arlanzon, just as if he were campaigning in the mountains. There Martin Antolinez of Burgos joined him, and supplied food for the company, in defiance of the king's injunction. Mio Cid was able to borrow six hundred marks from Señors Rachel and Vidas. At cockcrow he and his companions, those who had freely chosen an exile's wandering life with him, rode to the monastery of San Pero de Cardeña, where their ladies had taken refuge.

"From this moment," said Mio Cid to those who still

followed him, "since the king of Castile has seen fit to banish me, I am about to depart from this kingdom. I do not know whether I shall ever in my life enter my home again. Queen of glory, sustain me!"

He and his loyal knights arrived in the courtyard of the monastery just before daybreak. Doña Ximena, the wife of Mio Cid, and her two daughters, Doña Elvira and Doña Sol, were kneeling at matins when the word came of the knights' arrival. Joyously they ran into the dark courtyard, where by the flare of candles and torches they recognized Mio Cid. Doña Ximena fell on her knees before her husband. She kissed his hands.

"I see that you are leaving us," she wept, "and that you and I must part, even in our lifetimes."

Weeping also, Mio Cid put his arms about his two young daughters. He pressed them close to him. "Yes, most accomplished Lady, whom I love as I love my soul, I see that we must, indeed, part in our lifetimes. I must leave you here, Lady. May God grant me a few more days of life and happiness in this world. May He grant me to earn dowries for our young daughters. May He grant me life so that I may do you service and homage, most honored Lady, my wife."

During that day heralds rode about the countryside announcing the present departure of Mio Cid from the lands of King Alfonso of Castile, and inviting all men who so desired to rally to his banner. Within six days, 115 men-at-arms had joined Mio Cid. They knew he had no money, for he had left his cash at the monastery for the care of his wife and daughters. Whatever he still possessed, they knew he would share gladly, down to the last coin. Since only three days remained before Mio Cid would be arrested by the king, his whole party prepared to ride at daybreak toward the frontiers of Castile.

Doña Ximena prayed, "Glorious Father, who art in heaven. Thou who appeared in Bethlehem, Thou whom Melchior, Gaspar and Balthazar came to adore, Thou who spent thirty-two years upon this earth, Thou who upon the cross did a wonderful deed! Longinos, who had been blind from birth, pricked Thee with the point of his lance so that Thy blood streamed down the lance's point and dripped on his hands. When Longinos lifted his hands to his eyes, they were *healed* and he saw! I adore Thee and believe in Thee with all my heart. I pray Saint Peter to keep Mio Cid from harm and to make us united again in this lifetime."

After Doña Ximena and her husband had heard mass together, they rose and left the chapel. Mio Cid kissed his wife
tenderly, for she was weeping so hard she did not know what
to do. He entrusted her and his daughters to the abbot,
promising to reward the monastery for their trouble and expense. Then he tore himself from his family painfully, like a
fingernail from the finger, and rode away over the eastern
mountains at the head of his knights.

One night as Mio Cid lay sleeping alone and exiled, near
the Duero River, the Angel Gabriel appeared to him in a
dream. "Ride forward, Cid, good Campeador! Never did
baron ride into the eastern lands with such a promise as I
now make you: as long as you live, Cid, your life will turn
out well for you!"

By the time that Mio Cid had reached the Sierras, he
could count three hundred lances behind him. How could
he feed such a host? . . . He took the town of Casteion, captured its fortress, and received three thousand marks as a
tribute. All this money, herds also, fell to Mio Cid who cared
nothing for wealth. To each of his knights he gave one hundred silver marks and to each footsoldier fifty marks. Then
he restored their freedom to the Moors he had vanquished,
and to their women also, so that people would never speak
badly of Mio Cid. He then set out again, for King Alfonso
of Castile was still close behind him. Mio Cid would never
have raised his lance against his liege lord.

Before the walls of Alcocer, Mio Cid camped for fifteen
weeks. He finally took that city also, by artifice. He left one
tent pitched before the town, folded his other baggage, and
set off down the riverbanks. The people of Alcocer, thinking
that he had run out of bread for his men and barley for his
animals, spurred after him. When he had drawn them far
enough away from the gates, Mio Cid wheeled about, cut
a path through his pursuers, and entered the city ahead of
them. The banner of Mio Cid was raised over the citadel.
He allowed the Moors to re-enter as his subjects.

When the neighboring cities of Teca, Teruel, and Calatayud
heard of this victory, they sent a messenger to King Tanin at
Valencia, asking for aid before they too were seized. Two
Moorish kings set out with three thousand well-armed Moors.
They recruited supporters and came to besiege Mio Cid in
Alcocer. They cut off the water supply to the city and waited.
After three weeks Mio Cid and Alvar Fañez put all the
Moors out of the city one night. Then they armed themselves

for battle. They were six hundred. The honor of carrying their banner was accorded to Pero Bermuez. At daybreak they threw open their gate and plunged without warning into the Moors' encampment. . . . You should have seen the Moors scurry about to arm themselves! At the roll of their drums you would have thought the earth wanted to split!

The men of Mio Cid clutched their shields against their chests. They lowered their lances, from which bright pennants streamed. They did this as one man. They bent their faces over their horses' necks. In stirring tones Mio Cid called to them, "Strike them, Knights, for the love of charity! I am Ruy Díaz, the Cid Campeador of Vivar!"

Trescientas lanzas son, todas tienen pendones.
Sennos Moros mataron, todos de sennos colpes.
A la tornada que facen otros tantos son.
Veriedes tantas lanzas premer è alzar,
Tanta adarga aforadar é pasar,
Tanta loriga falsa desmanchar,
Tantos pendones blancos salir bermeios en sangre,
Tantos buenos cavallos sin sos dueños andar.
Los Moros laman Mafomat: los Christianos Sanctiague.

They are three hundred lances, all bearing pennants.
Each man killed a Moor, each one at one carom.
At the turning, as they wheel, they are still as many.
You should have seen those lances, lowered and raised,
So many bucklers pierced, so many perforated,
So many coats of mail broken and unlaced,
So many white pennants with red blood defaced,
So many fine horses without their riders stray.
The Moors call on Mohammed: the Christians on Saint James.[2]

That day there were the following brave men with Mio Cid: Alvar Fañez, Martin Antolinez, Muño Gustioz, Martin Muñoz, Alvar Salvadoros, Galin Garcia, and Felez Muñoz, who was the Cid's nephew. They fought so valiantly that the Moorish kings fled the field of battle and rode for dear life into Teruel and Calatayud to nurse their wounds. Mio Cid pursued them right to the gates of Calatayud. Then he returned to the battlefield, where the Moors lay dead and

[2] Verse 731.

dying. Sword in hand, he waited for his Castilians to rally around him. "Grace be to God that we have won this pitched battle," said Mio Cid. So much wealth lay in the Moorish camp that it seemed one could not count it.

Mio Cid allowed the Moorish people to return to their city. He also ordered that they should each be given something. Mio Cid's part of the spoils was one-fifth. In his share were one hundred war horses. He said to Alvar Fañez, "Ride back to Castile. Announce to my lord and king the news of this battle. Take him thirty caparisoned horses, each with a fine sword hanging from the pommel. Ask him to receive this gift from me. Take also this purse of gold and pay for the thousand masses I promised at Saint Mary of Burgos. Give what is left to my lady wife and to my daughters. Say to them that if I live, they shall all three become wealthy ladies."

In all Mio Cid's party now there was not a needy man. However, the Campeador could not stay in Alcocer, for the country was too bare and the land too poor to sustain him and his growing forces. When he prepared to ride forth, the Moors and their women sent their prayers along with him. They wept to see Mio Cid go. The Castilians camped on the high hill of Mont Real and sent requests for tribute to Teruel.

Meanwhile Alvar Fañez had arrived in Castile. Kneeling before the king, he begged him to accept Mio Cid's gift. "It is too early," said the king, "to pardon a vassal who has incurred my displeasure. However, I accept his offering, and I am happy for his success. I reinstate you, Alvar Fañez, in your fiefs. As for the Campeador, I have nothing to say except that I hereby declare that any knight who wishes to join him is free to do so. I also ordain that the hill of Mont Real where Mio Cid is encamped be duly and legally called from this day forth the Hill of Mio Cid."[3] Alvar Fañez took two hundred more knights to his lord, who had moved north to Saragossa and put it to ransom. Saragossa paid willingly; it congratulated itself to be acquitted so easily.

The news of Mio Cid's incursions in the north reached the Count of Barcelona,[4] Raymond Bérenger. This Frankish nobleman was highly insulted and deeply offended. "Mio Cid de Vivar," said Count Raymond, who was a rash sort of fellow, "is dashing through lands which are under my pro-

---

[3] El Poyo de Mio Cid.
[4] Don Remont.

tection. I never sent him a challenge. I never acted as the aggressor. Since he has dared to provoke me, I think I shall have to go ask him why."

Large forces of Christians and Moors flocked to the banner of this Frankish count. They caught up with Mio Cid as he was winding his way, heavily loaded with spoils, down a sierra into a valley. To the count's angry message Mio Cid sent this answer: "Tell the Count not to take it so badly. I am carrying away nothing that belongs to him. Tell him to let me go in peace."

Count Raymond replied haughtily. "He shall have to pay me now. This exile must learn that he has dishonored a count!"

Then Mio Cid ordered that the baggage be unloaded. He saw that Count Raymond would not let him escape without a battle. When Mio Cid observed the silken hose and cushioned saddles of the Franks, and compared them to his sturdy wooden saddles and coats of armor, he did not doubt but that three Franks would fall before each Castilian lance. In the ensuing short encounter Mio Cid easily won 1,000 silver marks, and took Count Raymond prisoner. The Frank was escorted to his captor's tent and served a delicious dinner.

As each dish was presented to him, Count Raymond turned up his nose in disdain. "I would not touch a mouthful of your food for all there is in Spain," he said scornfully. "I prefer to leave here both body and soul rather than to confess I was defeated by such a motley band of ... leggings!"

Then Mio Cid told him, "Eat some of this bread, Count, and drink some wine. If you do what I advise, you will escape from your captivity. If not, then you will never see your Christian land again."

Count Raymond answered, "You eat, Don Rodrigo, and enjoy yourself. I prefer to die, for I refuse your food and your drink." For three days, while the Castilians were apportioning the booty, the Frankish count sulked and fasted.

Mio Cid watched him all this time. Again he said, "Eat something, Count, for if you do not eat you will never see Christians again. If you do eat enough to satisfy my honor, I will liberate you and two of your gentlemen as well. You shall be freed."

When he heard that, Count Raymond exulted. "If you really do it, Cid, I shall be marvelously pleased with you as long as I live."

"Then eat, Count, for when you have done so, I shall set

you free with two others. However, know that of all the
spoils I have taken from you, I shall not return a red cent.
The men who follow me would be poverty-stricken if I did
not provide. Therefore I need this plunder for myself and
for them. We have to live by taking what we can find. Not
only that! We have to lead this kind of life as long as it shall
please our Holy Father, since I am a man who has incurred
his sovereign's displeasure, for which I was banished."

Mio Cid was seated in his tent, higher than the count. "If
you do not eat enough of my food to satisfy my honor, Sir,
you and I shall never be free, the one of the other."

"I accept with all my heart," said Count Raymond, "your
gracious hospitality." Mio Cid was pleased when he saw the
Frank call for water, wash his hands, and then plunge his
flashing white fingers into the meats that were set before him.
When both had dined, Count Raymond courteously thanked
Mio Cid. "Since the day I was dubbed, I don't recall such a
delicious meal," he said. 'The pleasure it has afforded me
will not soon be forgotten."

Three palfreys with beautiful saddles were brought, and
heavy cloaks and furs. His Castilian host escorted the three
Franks to the edge of the camp. "Are you leaving me so
soon?" inquired Mio Cid. "And in such a Frankish manner?
Let me thank you again for all the rich gifts you have left
behind you. If it ever occurs to you to wish for revenge, and
if you come looking for me, I am sure that you will find
me. If you do not, on the other hand, send after me, but
leave me alone, I shall see that you receive something from
my wealth or from that of yours which I have."

"Give not a thought to it, Mio Cid," laughed Count Raymond. "You have nothing to fear from me. I have paid
you enough tribute for one year. And as for seeking you
out, I doubt if it will ever cross my mind."

Then the Frankish count dug both spurs into his palfrey's
sides and looked over his shoulder, expecting that Mio Cid
would repent and chase after him. His Highness (*el Caboso*)
would never have committed such a disloyalty for anything
in the world! Mio Cid returned to his camp where he spent
many more days distributing the plunder from this battle.
He and his men were so rich now that they couldn't tell how
much they had.

Aquí s conpieza la gesta de Mio Cid el de Bibar.
Here begins the story of Mio Cid of Vivar.[5]

---

[5] Verse 1094.

MIO CID, LEAVING SARAGOSSA and its lands far behind him, turned toward the sea, toward the east from which rises the sun. The more towns he seized on his passage, the more he came to understand that God was with him. His triumphs weighed heavily upon those in the princely city of Valencia; you may as well know it. Those of Valencia therefore took the initiative. They left their rich city and advanced to besiege the Castilians in Murviedro. Mio Cid was delighted. "Here we are," he said, "in their land, drinking their wine and eating their bread. They have every right to question our presence. If we wish to remain here, we must chastise them thoroughly. Let this night pass. On the morrow we shall advance and then see who among my followers is worth his pay."

Now listen to what Alvar Fañez replied. "Campeador, let us do what pleases you. Give me a hundred knights—I ask for no more. Attack them full in the face, and I know you will not flinch. I will circle round and strike them from the rear." His spirit always pleased Mio Cid.

At the very break of dawn Mio Cid aroused his men. Each one knew where to go and what to do. "Hit them hard," cried Mio Cid. "In the name of our Maker and the Apostle James, strike them, knights, with all your will and heart. For I am Ruy Díaz, Mio Cid of Vivar!"

There you would have seen the Castilians spur between the Moors' tents, slash the ropes, and topple the pegs! As the Moors tried to search for their leaders through the confusion of falling pavilions, Alvar Fañez struck them from behind. They had a choice then—to surrender or to run! Two Moorish kings were killed. Mio Cid pursued those who escaped all the way to Valencia; those who made it to that haven had only the fleetness of their horses to thank. Great was the joy of the Castilians, for they were rich beyond all their hopes. Nor did they stop there. Sleeping during the day and marching at night, Mio Cid spent three years taking one Moorish city after another. He gave them a good lesson in Valencia.

The news of his victories traveled across the sea to Morocco. The people of Valencia complained bitterly as they saw Mio Cid tightening the circle he had drawn around them. They no longer knew what to do, for all the roads were cut. No bread came into the city any more. Father no longer fed son, nor son father. Friend no longer helped friend. They found no crumb of consolation. It is a disastrous state of affairs, sirs, not to have bread and to watch your women and children starve before your eyes. The king of Morocco knew this, and yet he sent them no aid.

When Mio Cid saw no reinforcements disembark, his heart was gladdened. He dispatched heralds throughout Aragon, Navarre, and Castile to proclaim far and wide: "He who wishes to lose all care and arrive at great riches, let him rally to Mio Cid, who desires to take a daring ride! Mio Cid intends to besiege lordly Valencia itself! He wants it to be in Christian hands. He will wait three days by the Canal of Celfa. Let each man who joins him do it of his own free will, and not under duress!"

After knights and footsoldiers had swollen his ranks, Mio Cid led his army to the very ramparts of Valencia. He besieged that great city honorably, without trickery, simply allowing no one to leave and no one to enter. He established and announced the delay he would grant the city: nine months and no more. He thought that their reinforcements, if any, would have ample time to succor the besieged if that was their intent. At the beginning of the tenth month the lordly Valencia fell to Mio Cid. As he rode through its streets, those of his followers who had joined his ranks as simple footsoldiers were mounted and equipped as gallantly as knights. Who could begin to tell you the quantities of gold and silver each had earned? How happy was he as he watched his banner being raised to the top of the Alcazar!

Within a short time thereafter the king of Seville rode forth to challenge Mio Cid's possession of Valencia. Although this king had thirty thousand warriors under his banner, Mio Cid vanquished him. His share from Valencia, which was thirty thousand minted marks, plus this second landfall, surpassed his dreams. Each Castilian took from this battle one hundred silver marks, so you can imagine what Mio Cid's fifth was!

Then Mio Cid vowed that he would never pull a hair from

his ample beard or cut it in any way. This would show his long trials, his great love for his lord Alfonso of Castile, and would be a subject of marvel for Moors and Christians alike. Next he decreed that any man who deserted Valencia without permission, and without having first kissed his hand, should be hanged and his wealth donated to the public coffers. He also appointed Alvar Fañez to have a census made of his followers, their lands and estates, and the amount of wealth they had earned. He found that his forces totaled 3,600. Smiling and satisfied at how his position had improved, he then asked Alvar Fañez to take one hundred horses as a gift to King Alfonso of Castile.

"Beg my king to spare me my lady and my daughters, so that I may now enjoy their gracious presence here in Valencia. Now that I am lord of this proud city, I can begin to do them honor. Therefore urge my suit before the king. ... I can entrust my family's safety to you, dear Alvar Fañez, during the journey where they must be honorably escorted. Let no indignity fall upon them." Mio Cid dispatched one hundred men with Alvar Fañez and a gift of one thousand marks to the monastery which had provided shelter and care to his family.

While these deliberations were being taken, there arrived in Valencia from the Holy Land a distinguished priest and scholar named Don Jerome. Mio Cid was struck by this priest's learning and prudence; he observed also how Jerome[6] sat a horse as skillfully as a knight, and how he bore himself in all situations requiring learning and diplomacy. This erudite Jerome explained to Mio Cid that he was a militant priest, who wished to share their fortunes and their rude trials. He said he expressly forbade any Christian to weep for him if ever he fell under a Moorish sword. Mio Cid studied this Frankish priest, his speech and his actions, and judged him to be honorable and holy. He therefore decided to elevate Jerome to the rank of bishop and to create a diocese for him in the city of Valencia. This decision was also to be announced to King Alfonso of Castile. There was great happiness in the city when the people learned that they now had within their walls their own Lord Bishop.

Alvar Fañez found the king of Castile in the estates of

[6] "*De parte de orient . . . don Hieronymo.*" This priest, so similar to the Archbishop Turpins in the *Roland*, probably came from France instead of from the Orient, or Holy Land. His name was Jerome, and he died around 1126.

Carrion. He fell on his knees and presented Mio Cid's gift in full view of the populace one day as the king came out from mass. King Alfonso smiled as he heard from Alvar Fañez' lips the list of Mio Cid's conquests—Xerica, Onda, Almenar, Murviedro, Cebola, Casteion, Peña Cadiella, *and* Valencia—when he learned of the five pitched battles he had won, and of the wealth he had acquired for himself and his men. With his right hand King Alfonso made the sign of the cross at such good news. "My heart is glad," said the king. "I am pleased at the prowess of the Campeador. He brings me glory. I accept his gift."

Then Garcia Ordoñez, long a bitter enemy of Mio Cid, added his acid comment, "It seems to me, Sire, that the Cid Campeador has not left us a single man alive in the land of the Moors."

"Stop such talk," commanded the king. "He serves me better than you do."

"Mio Cid craves your mercy," continued Alvar Fañez, "if such a request does not displease you. He asks that you permit his lady and daughters to leave their monastery and to journey to Valencia."

"I accede to his request," answered King Alfonso. "I wish also to provide for these noble ladies while they remain within my lands. See that neither insult, nor evil, nor dishonor fall upon them. Let your Mio Cid look to their safety at the frontier of Castile. Think of it, and make your plans accordingly.

"Now hear you all," continued the king, "I wish Mio Cid to be deprived of nothing. I hereby reinstate his vassals in all their lands and privileges and exempt them from my jurisdiction in cases of capital punishment. I do this so that they may be free to serve their feudal lord."

The two young princes, or Infantes, of Carrion were present at this interview. They spoke to each other secretly. "The fortunes of the Cid Campeador are increasing steadily. Perhaps we should marry his daughters.... However, how should we, Infantes of Carrion, propose such a thing to this adventurer, this Mio Cid, who is only from Vivar?"

"Tell your lord," said the crafty Infantes to Alvar Fañez, "that we greet him, that we are at his service as much as princes are able, and that he should think kindly of us. He could not lose thereby."

"I shall transmit your words," replied Alvar Fañez. "There is no trouble in that."

After he had humbled himself before Doña Ximena, and

told her of her coming travels, Alvar Fañez sent three knights toward Valencia to tell Mio Cid that his family would be leaving Castile and that within five days he should have an escort waiting for them at the frontier. Then he spent five hundred marks in Burgos on palfreys for the ladies and their attendants, upon the saddles and accouterments so that they would suffer no indignity from their appearance.

Mio Cid, you may be sure, sent his most courageous and most trusted vassals to escort his precious ladies. He dispatched Muño Gustioz, Pero Bermuez, and Martin Antolinez with one hundred knights armed to the teeth, and he also asked Bishop Jerome to join their party. He instructed them to pass through Molina, which was ruled by the Moor Abengalvon, long a personal friend of Mio Cid. The Moor would surely add another hundred knights to the escort. "Tell my old companion Abengalvon that I count on him to do full honors to my family. I shall remain in Valencia because it is now my hereditary fief," declared Mio Cid. "I spent years to win this realm and will not lose it now."

The Moor Abengalvon, understanding the weight of his responsibility, set out to meet the ladies himself. Not satisfied with one hundred knights, he took two hundred with him. Nor would he accept any money for their maintenance. He ordered stores, lodgings, horses, servants for the entire company plus that of Alvar Fañez, all at his own expense. In this way were the ladies of Mio Cid honored. Their attendants rode the finest horses. Their palfreys were draped with satins and damasks. Silver bells hung from their saddles. Every knight's equipment was elaborate. Each lance bore a silken pannet. Every knight wore his shield hung about his neck. Their polish reflected the sunlight proudly. Alvar Fañez rode up and down the columns. He left nothing to chance. Abengalvon was equally vigilant, and openhanded. He would not let Mio Cid's party pay for even a horseshoe!

When Mio Cid heard that the party was approaching the gates of Valencia, that his family were all well and not too tired from their travels over the Sierras, that they had been greeted everywhere with the greatest ceremony and show of respect, it was the happiest moment in his life! Immediately he dispatched two hundred knights to ride forth from the gates. Mio Cid still remained in the Citadel, watching and standing guard. Then when he was notified that the party was almost at the gate, he chose men to stand guard in his stead. He deputed armed sentinels for every tower of the

Alcazar, for every entrance and every exit, where they could within instants spread the alarm.

Then Mio Cid called for his horse, a new one named Babieca,[7] which he had acquired recently. He did not know whether or not the horse was swift, whether or not it would stand for him. Mio Cid wanted to remain at attention just outside the city's main gate, where with his back to the wall he would be safe enough. Don Jerome arrived first and hastened to the chapel to put on his vestments and take the silver cross so that he could welcome the ladies.

Mio Cid put Babieca through his paces, guided him through intricate figures, and stopped him short at the gate. The new horse performed beautifully before all eyes. Then Mio Cid dismounted and advanced on foot towards the party. Babieca stood as still as stone. From that day forth the honor and reputation of this war horse traveled throughout Spain. What man did not dream of seeing the bearded Mio Cid astride Babieca!

Doña Ximena and her daughters wept so hard they could hardly see Mio Cid. "Thank you, Campeador," cried Doña Ximena, kneeling at her husband's feet. "You were, indeed, born at a marvelous hour! You have rescued me and my daughters from ugly humiliations! Here are your daughters. With God's aid and yours, they are well trained and good."

"Dear and esteemed Lady," said Mio Cid, "and daughters who are my heart and soul, I salute you. Do me the honor of allowing me to escort you into your new heritage, which I won only for you."

The lady and her daughters kissed Mio Cid's hand. They rode into the city, receiving the respect and honors due them. Mio Cid conducted them first to the highest tower of the Alcazar, from which they could look down on Valencia's white streets spread out below them, and also eastward toward the blue Mediterranean. When they saw the beauty of their new home, how surrounded they were with thick groves of perfumed lemon and orange trees, the ladies lifted their hands to God in prayer. Mio Cid and his knights felt their hearts swell with pride. The winter sped by happily, and we come to the month of March.

Now I want to tell you about Morocco across the sea, and about its King Yucef, who lost his royal temper because of Mio Cid, Don Rodrigo. "He has entered my domains by violence," cried King Yucef. "And he only honors Jesus

---

[7] A masculine noun meaning "idiot, fool."

Christ!" The king of Morocco embarked with fifty thousand
warriors to seek Valencia. He pitched his tents on the beach
beside the city. Mio Cid saw him and was not afraid.

"All I have in this world is right before my eyes," mused
Mio Cid. "I conquered Valencia fairly. I shall not abandon it
except when I die. This city is my inheritance. I shall fight
these Moors with my wife and daughters watching me. They
will then see how an outcast gets a home in a strange land,
and with their own eyes learn how an exile earns his bread."

He sent for Doña Ximena and her daughters to come to
the tower of the Alcazar. Then he pointed downward where
the Moorish tents blanketed the earth as far as one could see.
"God save you!" they cried. "What is it, Mio Cid?"

"Why, that, honored wife, is no cause for alarm. That is
more wealth about to drop into our coffers. Since you are
newly arrived, the Moors are bringing you a gift. Since you
have daughters to marry, they are bringing them African
dowries. Watch the battle, if you like, here from the Alcazar.
Have no fear on my account, Lady, I shall win it."

By the end of the second day the Moors were defeated
and their treasure carted within the walls of Valencia. Mio
Cid rode back from the battle, sword in hand. His face was
dark and tired. He reined in Babieca before the ladies
and dismounted. They knelt before him. "While you ladies
kept Valencia for me," smiled Mio Cid, "I fought out in the
orchards. Look at this bloody sword and sweating horse!
With such a steed as Babieca, the Moors defeat themselves!
Pray to God that Babieca lives for several more years. You
may then be sure that many will humbly kneel to kiss your
fingers!"

After they had entered their palace, Mio Cid, seated on his
expensive bench, which had a backrest to it, announced
welcome news. "I should like all in Castile to know that
those ladies who escorted my señora and her daughters in
days of misfortune have been amply rewarded. I hereby
bestow a dowry of one hundred marks on each one of them.
As for your daughters, Lady, that will come later."

Mio Cid was so enriched by this victory that no proper
count of his wealth could be taken. The Moors who dwelled
near Valencia were also bettered, particularly as Mio Cid
let them keep the stray horses. Mio Cid decided to send
King Yucef's pavilion—so large it was upheld by two posts
inlaid in gold—to King Alfonso of Castile. From his fifth
part Mio Cid granted one-tenth to the church. Don Jerome
was delighted, he who had fought side by side with the

Campeador, he who had killed uncounted enemies. The next morning Alvar Fañez set out for Castile, taking the tent and this time two hundred horses as a gift. He found the king in Valladolid.

Don Alfonso was overjoyed at the presents and wondered how he could reward the Mio Cid. Don Garcia, who hated the Campeador, regretted his successes. The young princes of Carrion again took counsel with each other. "The fortune of this Cid is still better," said they. "Sire, consent to ask for the hands of the Cid's daughters. We consent to marry them. It will be an honor for them and an advantage for us."

After an hour's reflection King Alfonso replied, "I exiled this good Campeador. I have done him only harm; he has returned only good for evil. I do not know whether he desires these marriages. Let us broach the subject." Then to Alvar Fañez and Pero Bermuez he said, "I pardon Mio Cid. Let him come to see me. Diego and Ferrando Gonzalez, the Infantes of Carrion, desire to wed his daughters. Tell your lord this union would do him great honor. Tell your lord to meet me at the frontier."

When Mio Cid heard the king's proposal, he thought for an hour. "These princes are haughty and have wide influence at court. I should not have desired these marriages. However, since he who is above us all has counseled it, we will with God's inspiration discuss the matter with him." Then Mio Cid sent a letter saying that he would meet the king at the Tagus River.

In three weeks' time both parties, magnificently attired, met at the river. The Infantes of Carrion rode beside the king in high spirits. They paid for this and that, right and left, on credit, knowing that they would soon have gold enough to last them all their lives. What sturdy mules there were in the two retinues! What prancing palfreys! What handsome coats of mail! What galloping horses! What gorgeous cloaks and satin cloaks and fur cloaks! Young and old, tall and short, wore robes of dazzling colors! Mio Cid rode gaily too, for he had left Valencia well defended, with strict orders that not a person was to enter or leave the city until his return.

When he had come before the king, Mio Cid dismounted with fifteen of his chosen knights. He advanced on foot. He threw himself face down before his lord. He fastened his teeth on a clump of grass and wept bitterly, so happy was he! In this way, thudding his knees and his hands flat on the earth, he made his gesture of submission to Don Alfonso.

The king was pained. "Stand on your feet, Cid Campeador. Kiss my hands. As for my feet, no! Obey me, or you shall not receive my love."

Mio Cid did not rise. "I crave your mercy, my lawful lord. With me prostrate before you, give me back once more your love, so all present may hear you."

"Gladly," said the king, raising his voice. "I hereby pardon you, Mio Cid, and accord you my love. From this day forth receive access to all my domains."

"Thanks, great lord," cried Mio Cid, "I accept. Now surely God will protect me day and night." Rising, he kissed the king's hand. "Be my guest, Don Alfonso, my liege lord."

"That would not be fitting," replied the king. "We have been here since yesterday while you arrived only now. To-morrow we shall do as you please. Today you are my guest."

Then the Infantes of Carrion humbled themselves before Mio Cid. "You were born in a good hour, Cid. As far as we are able, we shall walk toward your welfare."

"God willing," replied Mio Cid.

After two days of entertaining, during which the king feasted his eyes admiringly on the magnificent beard of Mio Cid and could not praise it enough, they heard mass cele-brated by Don Jerome and then settled down to the weighty business at hand.

"Give us your daughters in marriage," said the king. "These princes ask it and I order it."

"I have no daughters to wed," replied Mio Cid. "I en-gendered them, but they are not mine. They are also of a much tender age. These Infantes of Carrion could look for a much more honorable match, owing to their high birth. We are all of us at your mercy, Sire, Doña Elvira and Doña Sol as much as I am. Therefore here are the hands of your daugh-ters, Don Alfonso. Bestow them as *you* please, and I shall be content."

"With these words then," ordained the king, "I bestow Doña Elvira and Doña Sol upon the Infantes of Carrion. Their troths are plighted. Take these sons-in-laws to Valencia with you."

"I thank you, Sire," replied Mio Cid. "It is you who give my daughters in marriage, and not I." There was a celebra-tion then for all present. Mio Cid bestowed gifts on every man who asked. Then leaping on Babieca, Mio Cid cried, "Let all who desire rich presents attend these weddings in Valencia!" It had been decided that Alvar Fañez would act in

proxy for Don Alfonso, since Mio Cid repeated that he would
not give away his daughters at the altar. As he rode back to
Valencia, his party greatly increased and the king's diminished
by those who accepted the cordial wedding invitation. Mio
Cid asked Pero Bermuez and Muño Gustioz to watch the Infantes carefully, to report their personal habits to him, even
after they were lodged in the palace he assigned to them in
Valencia.

The wedding celebration was lavish and festive. Mio Cid
outdid himself in generosity. For fifteen days he entertained
his guests at tournaments and feasts. Everyone was pleased
with the Infantes of Carrion. They remained in Valencia for
two years.

Las coplas deste cantar aqui s van acabando.
The couplets of this song are just ending now.[8]
May the Creator and all his Saints save you and keep you.

DISHONOR AND REVENGE

MIO CID WAS IN Valencia with his vassals, and also with his
sons-in-law, the two princes of Carrion.[9]

One afternoon as Mio Cid lay sleeping on his high-backed
bench, a frightful event occurred. A lion burst from its
cage, broke its chain, and started roaming through the palace. Those brave men of the Campeador threw their capes
over their right arms and retreated cautiously until they had
formed a barrier between the huge cat and their master. The
Infante Ferrando saw no place to hide, no tower stairway
unbolted, no chamber door open. In terror he crawled under
the settee where the Campeador lay resting. The second Infante, Diego, darted out a door and squeezed himself between
a beam and the wall, moaning, "Now I shall never see Carrion again!"

At this moment he-who-was-born-in-that-good-hour awoke.

[8] Verse 2286
[9] Verse 2288.

He saw his barons encircling his couch. "What is it, friends?" asked Mio Cid. "What do you want?"

"It is only, honored Sir, that a lion has escaped."

Mio Cid had his wide cloak about his shoulders. Rising to his feet, he walked deliberately toward the lion. The beast, seeing that man approach so confidently, was cowed. It drooped its head and looked toward the floor. Then Mio Cid grasped it by the mane and succeeded in turning it and forcing it back into the cage. All present were amazed. When they had recovered from their excitement, Mio Cid asked where his sons were. No one knew. Up and down the palace people called them. Neither one nor the other answered. Finally they were discovered hiding. Don Diego had soiled his shirt and his cloak. Both Infantes were as pale as sheets. You never saw such amusement as the looks of them caused at the court. Mio Cid had to forbid conversation on that subject! He saw that the Infantes were sensitive.

Before these jokes had ceased being remembered, a now force of fifty thousand Moors under King Bucar of Morocco—I suppose you have heard of him—came to besiege Valencia. From the Alcazar, Mio Cid saw their tents spread through his orchards, and their sight delighted him. He thanked his Maker that more booty was about to fall into his hands. The Infantes, on the contrary, were panic-stricken! "We'll be expected to leave our palace and advance to battle! What will happen to us then? These Moors could not have come at a better time! Now we shall certainly never see Carrion again!"

Muño Gustioz reported their conversation to his lord. "Your sons-in-law are so brave that they are frightened," he told Mio Cid. "They are so homesick that they can't go to battle! You should go and console them now, and may the Creator help you! Let them sit home and receive no share of the spoils. We will win this engagement also, if our Maker wishes!"

With a pleasant face Mio Cid strode to the Infantes. "Good day, my sons-in-law, Princes of Carrion. Why do you not today hold my daughters, they who are as bright as sunlight, in your arms while I go out to meet the Moors. You know I am for the war, and you are for Carrion. Amuse yourselves today here in Valencia. Do whatever you like for your pleasure. Leave the Moors to me. I am an old hand at this sort of nastiness. I assure you, the Moors shall be vanquished."

[Here the manuscript is torn; at least one page is missing, but the story of this day is told later by Pero Bermuez.]

The Infantes armed themselves for battle. Mio Cid asked his nephew Pero Bermuez to watch over the princes. Alvar Fañez stood ready to ride when Bishop Jerome rode through the press to Mio Cid.

"Today I said mass for you at Holy Trinity. Now you understand that I left France to fight the Moors. I came here to Valencia for that express purpose because here I could best serve my order. I demand the right to strike the first blow on this field. You see that I have raised my own pennant. You see that my arms are of the finest. If you refuse me this right to try my worth against our foes, I shall never serve you again!"

"I am pleased with your words," replied Mio Cid. "There the Moors are, right in front of you, Lord Bishop. By all means, go and test them. We shall watch from here how an abbot wages war."

Then all alone Bishop Jerome spurred into the enemy. He killed two at the first lance thrust and five more with his sword. Blows fell upon him from all sides; his armor was proof against them. He struck about him with heavy, ringing swings of his sword arm. Mio Cid waited until he saw that the bishop was heavily surrounded. Then, followed by his knights, Mio Cid spurred Babieca into the foe. What a battle was that! Heads and helmets fell to the ground and rolled in the grass! Riderless horses, maddened with wounds, plunged through the falling tents.

Mio Cid marked the African King Bucar. He gave chase, calling, "Wait for me, Bucar! You have traveled so far to meet me! Come greet the Cid of the long beard! We should salute each other like true knights! Who knows? We might strike up a friendship!"

"God damn such a friendship!" cried Bucar. "I know what you want to strike! If my mount neither falters nor stumbles, you will find me in the sea!"

"That's a lie, Bucar. I'll overtake you first!" cried Mio Cid. He spured Babieca to great, thundering strides. Little by little he overtook the Moorish king, caught up with him about three lengths from the water. With one stroke of his sword Mio Cid dashed the jewels in the golden helm of Bucar over the sand, split the helm and all that was under it down to the waist. That blow ended the battle quickly, for the Moors hastened to lay down their arms. Mio Cid rode back through the tents. His forehead was wrinkled. Then he met the two Infantes, in full armor, there on the field. The sight of them delighted his heart.

"Come," smiled Mio Cid. "You are both of you now my real sons. Good news and high praise shall travel to Castile. All men shall know that you conquered Bucar, the king of Morocco. We shall all come out of this victory with pleasure and honor." Every good word Mio Cid said the two princes twisted into evil. When they had received their share of the booty, however, they saw that they would never need any more wealth as long as they lived.

"I thank God humbly," said Mio Cid. "I see laid out before me everything I have wished for all my life. My sons fought beside me on the field on honor. Once I was poor, and now I am a rich man. My dear daughters are wedded to princes. I win battles, one after another, thanks to my Creator. Over there in Morocco, where the mosques are, men fear that some dark night I may take it into my head to cross the sea and besiege their cities. They have no basis for their suspicions. I never think of it. I shall never go to seek them. I shall live in Valencia, and allow them to send me tribute instead."

Then the two princes—truly they were brothers—withdrew and whispered to each other. "Let us return to Carrion. We have stayed here long enough. We could never spend all this gold our whole lives long. Let us ask the Cid for our wives. We could tell him that we want to take them to Carrion. We have stayed here long enough. We could tell him we wish to show his daughters our lands and castles. Yes, say we want them to see their inheritance. Only let us escape his vigilance! Once on the road we'll go where we like and do as we please. Let us go before someone mentions that incident of the lion again. We were born princes of Carrion.

"We will transport out of Valencia all the wealth that we now have. Then let us humiliate these daughters of the Campeador. Let us revile them! We are rich enough at present. Let us think of marrying only the heiresses of kings and emperors. We are princely by birth and by taste. Let us abase his daughters before anyone mentions the incident of the lion again!"

At once they put their request, very courteously framed and delivered, to Mio Cid and to his favorites. The Campeador made no difficulty at all about granting their suit. He had no suspicions about their real intentions. "Yes, I shall give you my daughters, and something of mine also," he said proudly. "Let people up and down Castile see how richly my sons are wed. I am pleased that you have settled estates and revenues upon Doña Elvira and Doña Sol, who are the very coverings of my heart. I grant you 3,000 silver marks as an additional dowry. I present you with two fabled swords, which I wrested hardly from my foes. Here they are, Colada and Tizon. Serve my daughters well, for they are yours in holy wedlock. Honor them, and I shall reward you for it."

When Doña Elvira and Doña Sol were ready to take their leave, they knelt before their parents and said, "We beg your favor, father who engendered us, and mother who bore us. Señor and Señora, you are sending us now to the lands of Carrion. We are honored to do your bidding."

"Go, daughters," replied Doña Ximena, "and may the Lord preserve you. You have our favor, mine and your father's. Go now to Carrion where lie your inheritances. I think we have married you nobly."

Mio Cid and his knights escorted the girls out of the sunny city and through its surrounding orange groves with all the panoply of chivalry. Although their father rode joyfully before his knights, his mind was not entirely at ease because he had seen from omens that these marriages would not be without sorrow. However, he could not retract the contracts; both girls had been duly wedded. Because of his deep concern, however, he asked Felez Muñoz to accompany the girls to Carrion and then to bring him back word how they were received and how honored.

It was hard for Mio Cid to break away from his daughters, very painful for him to be obliged to turn his back on them, and return to Valencia. He wept, and so did his two girls. "We commit you to God's care, Doña Elvira and Doña Sol," he said. "Bear yourselves in such a way that we here in Valencia shall be happy."

The princes replied, "God willing."

Still Mio Cid could not depart. The separation was as painful to him as if a nail were being torn from his finger. "Listen, my nephew," he instructed Felez Muñoz, "pass through Molina. Tell my friend, the Moor Abengalvon, that my daughters are entering their estates at Carrion. Ask him to receive them, and to furnish them with anything whatsoever that they may require or desire. Tell him I wish his Moors to escort my children to the frontier. He will do this for love of me. He knows that I repay my debts. He knows what my word is worth."

The Infantes of Carrion, once Mio Cid had turned his back, thought only of covering ground as fast as possible. They soon arrived at Molina, where Abengalvon met them with every sign of joy. God! How he served this company! Early next morning he awaited their departure, and accompanied them with two hundred knights, for they had to cross high and lonely mountains in order to reach Castile. Abengalvon spared no expense. Every rich sword and jeweled helm in his kingdom was paraded in order to honor Doña Elvira and Doña Sol. He escorted them as if they had been born of princely rank, like their husbands.

"Look," whispered the brothers to each other, "since we have decided to leave the Campeador's daughters, we could kill this Moor Abengalvon; all his wealth would then accrue to us. As sure as we stand here, if the sum were added to what we now have, not even the Cid could bring us to a reckoning."

While they were plotting, a certain Moor who was a good Latinist overheard their conversation. Instead of keeping this secret to himself, he naturally hastened to Abengalvon. "Master," he warned, "be on your guard, as you are my liege. I heard the Infantes conspiring your death."

Abengalvon was a man of no uncertain courage. He did not stand on ceremony, even with princes. With his knights in close ranks behind him, and with his own sword drawn, he rode up to the princes, face to face. "Now tell me, Infantes of Carrion, what I have done to incur your wrath. I have gone to some inconvenience to do your service, without guile or malice. And you are planning to murder me! If I were not bound to refrain because of Mio Cid of Vivar, I would whip you now so soundly that the reports would re-echo about the world! I would then escort his daughters back to Mio Cid. And as for you, you wouldn't get to Carrion at all!

"I take leave of you here and now, for I see your rascality and your treachery! By your leave, Doña Elvira and Doña Sol, I shall retire from your company. I care little for the reports that may come from Carrion. May God ordain that Mio Cid have joy from these alliances." Leaving the Infantes highly outraged, Abengalvon like a sensible man returned home to Molina.

After the Moor had disappeared down the road, the Infantes ordered their party forward on the double. Not content with their previous rate of speed, they pushed on day and night until they were high in the Sierras de Miedes. Through these high, white peaks they hastened, forcing their horses

and setting a hard pace. They passed gigantic caverns and
precipices that dropped off into the dark forests below them
until they came one evening to the deep woods where the
trees were of a tremendous height. Their branches seemed
to reach to the clouds. In a clearing they came upon a grove
and a spring of clear water. Wild animals hunted for food
even up to the edge of this encampment.

The Infantes selected a spot for their tent and allowed their
weary wives to dismount. The whole company settled down
for the night. The brothers from Carrion caressed their wives
in their arms that night and gave them evidences of their
love. . . . They will prove it to the poor Doña Elvira and to
the poor Doña Sol when day breaks!

Early in the morning the horses and pack animals were
saddled, the baggage was reloaded, the tents were folded and
packed, and the party set off through the woods. The princes
ordered everyone to leave. They said that not a man or a
woman should remain at the campsite except themselves and
their wives. They wanted to be quite alone with their ladies.
According to their wishes, everyone rode ahead down the
forest trail, leaving the four under the trees. . . . What do you
think the Infantes of Carrion had been hatching?

"You may believe us when we tell you, Doña Sol and Doña
Elvira, that you are now going to be disgraced," said the
princes. "Here in these forbidding mountains you are both
about to be debased. We shall continue on our journey; first
of all, we have an account to settle before we abandon you
here. This is as much portion of the princely domains of
Carrion as you shall ever inherit. We want the news of your
fate to reach the Cid Campeador. We intend to take our
revenge here for that adventure of the lion."

Then before the horrified eyes of the two young ladies, the
Infantes of Carrion took off their fur cloaks, and then their
jackets. That was not all! They next proceeded to strip the
ladies of their rich mantles. They ripped off their cloaks, their
dresses, and left them naked in their thin shirts and tunics.
They buckled on their spurs and unhooked the leather girths
from their horses!

When Doña Sol saw them approaching herself and her
sister with these straps in their hands, she spoke. Doña Sol
said, "In the name of Heaven, Don Diego and Don Ferrando,
do not use straps on us! Hear my plea! You both have swords
that are strong and trenchant. I should know because I have
often seen these blades in my father's hands. They are called
Colada and Tizon. . . . Then use them on us! Cut off our

heads, and give us martyrdom! Moors and Christians alike
will declare that we have earned it. Even though we do not
deserve to die, even though you will not treat us according
to our actions, do not, I pray you, make upon our persons
such a bad example. If you beat us here in the forest, you
will only abase yourselves, not us! ... You will be called to
account for it too, either man to man or at the court of
Castile!"

Doña Sol's prayer did not help either herself or her sister.
Suddenly the Infantes raised the leather straps and began to
rain stinging blows upon their naked shoulders. Leaving the
girths unknotted and at their full length, they whipped the
girls so unmercifully that both fainted. After both had fallen
to the ground, the princes tore their shirts from their backs
with their spurs and bruised the girls' hips and thighs. The
bright red blood flowed over their rags of tunics. The weeping
girls felt each blow all the way to their hearts. What a blessing
it would have been, had the Creator so willed, if the Cid
Campeador had suddenly appeared riding through the trees!

The princes beat those ladies until they lay totally unconscious on the ground, their shirts and their tunics drenched
with blood. They struck them until their arms were tired, for
each one tried to get in the hardest strokes. For a long time
neither Doña Sol nor Doña Elvira had made a sound. Then
the Infantes picked up the girls' robes and cloaks, picked up
their ermine shawls, mounted the palfreys, and rode away,
leaving their wives for dead where they lay. They abandoned
their bloody remains to the birds of the mountain peaks and
to the beasts of prey. They left them for dead, hear, and
not for alive! What a blessing it would have been if the Cid
Campeador had suddenly appeared before them, riding
through the trees! Oh!

The Infantes of Carrión left the poor girls under the trees.
Neither girl could even crawl to help her sister any more.
Down the trails and out into the patches of sunlight the brothers rode laughing and congratulating each other. "Now we
have exacted our revenge for such marriages! We shouldn't
have even welcomed such girls as these for concubines, unless,
of course, their father begged us to do so on bended knee!
They were not our equals. And to think we actually had to
hold them in our arms! Another score too! We have also
avenged ourselves for the lion." So they rode down the mountainside, joking and thumping each other on the back.

Now I am going to tell you about Felez Muñoz, who was
the nephew of Mio Cid the Campeador. He had been ordered

that morning to ride ahead with the others, and he did so, but not of his own accord. As he followed the path, his heart ached and pained him so that he gradually slipped away from the others, down side paths. Then he stole backward along the trail, keeping to the thick underbrush, and making no noise. After a while he not only saw the Infantes riding down the trail; he also was able to overhear snatches of their banter. They neither saw Felez Muñoz nor suspected his presence. You may be sure that if they had, he would not have escaped with his life!

Felez Muñoz waited just long enough to let them get a good distance away. Then he dug his spurs into his horse's flanks and galloped frantically back up the trail. There he saw the pitifully wounded girls lying on the earth.

"Cousins! Cousins!" he cried, leaping from his horse and tying its bridle to a tree. "Cousins! My dear Cousins! Doña Elvira! Doña Sol! Oh, what evil have these princes done! I pray to God and to the holy Saint Mary that they receive as bad a punishment!" As gently as he could, Felez Muñoz turned each girl over on her back. Their eyes were closed. They did not breathe. Not a sound, not even a whimper came from either one. It would have broken your heart. "Cousins, live! Wake up! Awaken while it is daylight, while the forest creatures are in their lairs asleep. Wake up before the wild beasts eat us all!"

Then Felez Muñoz saw that the girls were coming to consciousness. Little by little their eyelids began to quiver. Then they opened their eyes and recognized their cousin leaning over them. "Take courage, Cousins, in the name of the Creator!" he urged them. "As soon as the Infantes of Carrion notice that I am no longer with them, they will send after me. If God does not provide for us, we shall all die here."

Then painfully Doña Sol said, "If our father the Campeador has ever merited your love, Cousin bring us a little water . . . and may God bless you."

With his sombrero, which was a new and clean one he had recently bought in Valencia, Felez Muñoz fetched water and poured it over the deep cuts on the two girls' bodies. He then helped them to sit up. He kept talking to them and encouraging them. He comforted them as best he could, for their bodies were bruised and torn. He pleaded and exhorted them to be brave. The girls with his help finally managed to limp to his horse, where he gently lifted each one to the saddle. Then wrapping them in his wide cloak, telling them all the time how proud he was of their courage, he left the campsite.

Leading his horse by the bridle, he plunged under the trees and away from that bloody soil as fast as he could walk. At the hour between daylight and dusk they came down out of the mountain, up to the banks of the Duero River. He found shelter for the girls, for everyone knew their father, at the first castle on the river. Then he spurred hotly down the dusty road and into the nearest town to seek strong friends.

While Doña Elvira and Doña Sol were recovering from their wounds, surrounded by sympathetic and distressed friends, the news of their humiliation traveled westward to the king and eastward to Mio Cid the Campeador. When their father heard all the details of this premeditated outrage, he raised his hand, enjoining silence upon his court. For an hour he sat, stern and alone, digesting the awful news. Then, gripping his beard, he spoke. "Thanks be to Christ, Lord of the world, that the Infantes of Carrion have done me this signal honor. I shall see that their joy is short-lived. As for my daughters, I vow that they shall never again wed counts, only kings!" Then he dispatched two hundred knights under Alvar Fañez' command to bring home his beloved children.

Tears came to Alvar Fañez' eyes when he next looked upon the ladies Doña Sol and Doña Elvira. They said to him, "We are as happy to see you as if we were looking on the face of our Creator! Give thanks to Him that we are even alive! Please take us home. We will tell you all that happened when we are safely home again."

"Dry your tears, dear Ladies. It is enough for all of us that you are alive and well. Your father and mother send you their love. The day shall come very soon when we in Valencia shall have our revenge!"

There was a holiday in Valencia the day the daughters of Mio Cid rode into their home city again. Mio Cid smiled contentedly to see his dear girls safe in his palace again. Then he drew up a message to King Alfonso of Castile. "Tell the king that I sympathize with his affliction," dictated Mio Cid. "Say that I lament his dishonor, for it was he who gave my daughters in marriage. Ask Don Alfonso to summon these Infantes of Carrion to a tournament or to a plenary session of his court, for I am about to seek retribution for their insults, to say nothing of the wealth they took from me under false pretenses. Rancor lodges deep in the heart of a man like me."

When Don Alfonso heard Mio Cid's messengers, he deliberated and then announced that he would convene his court at Toledo. The king acted promptly. He sent his cards into all of his vast realms—throughout Castile, León, Saint-James, Portugal, and Galicia—summoning his vassals to Toledo in seven weeks' time. He who failed to appear would lose at least his titles and lands.

The Infantes of Carrion, having taken counsel with their family, asked to be excused from attending. They feared having to face Mio Cid. However, King Alfonso replied, "Absolutely not! You will attend my court or else leave my kingdom. You must give satisfaction to Mio Cid, who has complained to me about you." Don Garcia collected his friends, summoned all the great nobles who made up his faction to support the Infantes. Don Garcia, who had always hated Mio Cid, saw in this assembly an opportunity to insult Mio Cid himself.

The assembled court had to wait for five days until Alvar Fañez came to announce Mio Cid's arrival. Don Alfonso rode out of Toledo to meet him. Mio Cid came, escorted by all his chosen companions, all fully dressed in armor, all ready to defend their Campeador with every ounce of the strength and skill they possessed. As soon as he had come in plain sight of the king, Mio Cid dismounted and fell to his knees.

"By Saint Isidore," cried the king, "I will not allow you to humble yourself to me today. Mount up, or you will incur my displeasure. Let us greet each other in all sincerity of heart and soul. Know that my own heart is heavy with the weight that hangs upon you. May God grant that your presence may grace my court, Mio Cid."

"Amen," replied Mio Cid the Campeador. "I prostrate myself before you, Sire, and before these great nobles who accompany you. My wife, Doña Ximena, who is a lady of property, kisses your hand. My two daughters greet you humbly. May what has happened to us weigh heavily upon you."

"I shall attend to your plea," answered Don Alfonso, "and may God oversee us all."

King Alfonso of Castile returned to the city of Toledo, but Mio Cid remained that night by the banks of the Tagus River. He explained that he needed to await his men before crossing the river and entering the city. He also desired to spend the night in vigil in a holy place. "I shall present myself at court before dinner at noon," he promised.

"I consent willingly," answered the king.

All that night Mio Cid remained kneeling and praying in a holy place. He lighted taper after taper, taking counsel with his Lord as to how he should proceed on the following day. He knew that he had the faction of Don Garcia to outwit and intimidate. He realized what powerful friends and allies the Infantes of Carrion claimed among the great nobles. At daybreak Alvar Fañez found Mio Cid still at his devotions. He and his men then worshipped together. The mass was ended at sunrise. Mio Cid then made a handsome donation to the chapel and addressed his followers. He named his dearest, oldest companions as his escort and asked them to bring their number up to one hundred by designating others.

"Wear undergarments that will keep your full armor from chafing," said Mio Cid. "Dress yourselves as for battle in complete suits of armor and coats of mail underneath. Let your breastplates be as radiant as the sun. Then put over all this your ermine and your fur cloaks. Fasten them carefully at throat and waist so that the armor does not show. Under your cloaks be sure that your swords are sharp and ready. Wear them loose today. Thus garbed shall we fare to the court where I may say my say and demand justice; in the case that our princes of Carrion seek a quarrel, I shall have no fear with one hundred warriors like you. We know each other's worth, I think."

They answered to a man, "We shall do it, Señor."

While his knights were dressing, Mio Cid attired himself to go before the court. He drew on tights of fine wool, and a shirt of white linen as dazzling as sunlight. Its tucks were edged with gold and silver. Over his armor he wore a gold-brocaded tunic, bordered with so much gold that you would have said he gleamed like the sun itself. Then over his shoulders he draped a red fur scalloped with gold. On his head he fitted a cap of scarlet linen worked with gold and so cut that it covered all his hair that had not been trimmed. To protect his beard in like fashion he tied it with a scarlet ribbon and tucked it inside his tunic. Over this he fastened a sweeping cloak that fell from his shoulders to the ground in such ample folds that it hid his sword perfectly. He leaped to Babieca's back and rode into the city of Toledo at a sharp clip.

Mio Cid dismounted at the palace door. Surrounded on all sides by his hundred magnificently attired knights, he entered the audience hall. Courteously the king arose, and so did most of his nobles. No so Don Garcia and the Infantes of Carrion.

"Come sit beside me," invited the King Don Alfonso. "You shall take this seat of honor, here upon this bench which has

a backrest. It is the one you so thoughtfully presented me.
Certain people here may be afflicted because of the honor
I do you, but sit down. You will be more comfortable than
all of us."

"Pray keep your seat," answered Mio Cid humbly. "Sit on
your high-backed bench as a king and great liege lord should
do. I shall sit here with my men around me." When Mio
Cid had taken his place, all eyes in the room were free to
inspect his splendid attire. Such elegance had never before
been paraded, except by the king. They noticed how full his
beard was and how he had tied it with a satin cord. They
were impressed by his manner, that of a great baron accustomed to rule. The Infantes alone could not meet his gaze.
When they felt Mio Cid direct his glance in their direction,
they bowed their heads. They were ashamed to meet his
eyes.

"Hear ye, gentlemen of my house, if you wish the Creator
to hear you," began King Alfonso of Castile. "Since my cor-
onation I have held only two plenary sessions of all my vassals, one at Burgos and one at Carrion. I have seen fit to
convoke this third at Toledo out of love for Mio Cid, who
was born in a good hour, in order that he may receive his
right from the Infantes of Carrion. They did him a great
wrong; we know this. Let the Count Don Anrrich and the
Count Don Remond[10] be our judges; they are unaffiliated
with either faction. You will all hear this case, inasmuch
as you are thoughtful and experienced, so that justice may
be done; I shall sanction no injustice. Let the one side be
for this day at peace with the other. I swear by Saint Isidore
that whoever causes commotion in my court today shall be
exiled from my realm. I shall side with the right. Let us hear
the demands of Mio Cid first and then the replies of the
Infantes of Carrion."

Mio Cid rose and kissed the king's hand. "I give you
thanks for having convened this assembly out of love for me.
Here is what I demand: in the case of my daughters that
these princes have left me, I feel no dishonor; for you
married them, Sire, and you will know what to do about
them today. However, when these princes led my daughters
out of lordly Valencia, because I loved them in my heart
and in my soul, I gave them two swords, Colada and Tizon.
I had won these blades like a baron with the intention of
using them for your glory and vassalage, Sire. Now since

[10] Two Burgundian nobles.

these princes have abandoned my daughters in the woods, it is clear that they no longer cared about me. In consequence they have lost my love. I ask that they return the swords to me since they are no longer my sons-in-law."

The judges decreed, "All is reasonable."

Then the Count Don Garcia spoke for his faction. "We must deliberate this point." After he, the Infantes, and their friends had spoken together, and had decreed, Don Garcia counseled them secretly, "This Cid Campeador still shows us his love, since he does not call for a reckoning today concerning his daughters. We shall give Don Alfonso satisfaction on that score. Let us give up the swords since this Cid limits himself to that penalty. After he receives them, the court will be adjourned. The Cid Campeador will have lost his opportunity; he will never extort satisfaction from us then!"

The party of Don Garcia and the Infantes replied in open court, "Thanks, King Don Alfonso. We do not deny that he gave us the swords. Since he calls for them and desires them, we wish to deliver them to him in your presence." They unsheathed the swords and laid them on the king's hands. A murmur of admiration moved the courtiers. The pommels of these blades were so bright that they lighted up the room. When Mio Cid took them, he smiled at their beauty, perhaps at the pleasant memories of his victories.

The swords sparkled in the hands of Mio Cid, who smiled broadly and thought to himself, "By this beard which no man has ever dared pluck, we shall see how Doña Elvira and Doña Sol shall be avenged!" Mio Cid called his nephew by name. Holding out Tizon to him, he said, "Felez Muñoz, take this beauty. You are worthier of her." He then stretched out Colada. "Martin Antolinez, vassal of renown, Colada is for you. I earned her from a gentleman, Count Raymond the Frank of Barcelona. I entrust her to you. Care for her well. If you have occasion to wield her, she will earn you fame and high esteem." Martin Antolinez took Colada reverently, bent low, and kissed Mio Cid's hand.

Mio Cid then rose to his feet again. "Thanks be to God, and to you also, King, that I have been put at rest concerning Colada and Tizon! When they led my daughters out of Valencia, I gave them 3,000 silver marks. While I was thinking of gifts for them, they were planning to execute another project. Let them return my money since they are no longer my sons-in-law." You should have heard the complaints of the Infantes then!

Count Don Remond instructed them, "Answer yes or no."

Then the Infantes replied, "We returned his swords to the Cid Campeador so that he would not ask for anything else. That was all he demanded. May it please the King; that is our answer."

The king intervened, "To this demand of the Cid, you must also give satisfaction. I decree it."

Alvar Feñez then said hotly, "Insist, oh Mio Cid, Campeador. Part of that money was mine. I also demand restitution."

The Infantes took counsel together. It was a staggering sun of silver, which they had already spent. They pleaded with the court, "He is pressing us sorely, this Cid who conquered Valencia. Now he covets our wealth! We shall have to pay him later, out of our lands at Carrion."

"You must pay him here and now, before this court," advised the judges.

"Mio Cid is right," said the king, "and he must be paid. The Infantes of Carrion gave me two hundred marks, which I now return. Since they are to transmit this money, I don't want it."

The Infantes' faction complained, "We don't have the money."

The judges answered, "You mean you have spent it. Then pay its equivalent in kind." When the Infantes understood that there was no other alternative, they began to round up whatever they could. You should have seen their finest charges, mules, palfreys, swords, equipment, furs! Mio Cid accepted it all at the court's evaluation, except for the two hundred marks of King Alfonso. The Infantes paid him the whole sum finally, even though they were obliged to strip themselves and borrow right and left in order to adjust the amount. You may as well know; they came off badly jolted.

"Ah, thanks, Sire, for your love and kindness to me!" said Mio Cid, again rising to his feet. "However, I still cannot forget my wrongs. Let me speak to you now about my greatest source of grievance. Hear me, nobles, and then assess my injury. . . . Without a challenge I cannot dismiss these Infantes of Carrion who have so basely dishonored me. Infantes, tell me how I offended you! Did I do it in banter? Did I do it maliciously? In what way did I do you wrong? Where was my crime? I want to hear it *now*!

"When you led my daughters out of Valencia, why did you tear in such a way the very coverings of my heart? I gave you my daughters. I gave you my wealth without stint-

ing; openhanded I poured my riches and my love upon you!
If you no longer wanted my daughters, treacherous dogs,
why did you take them out of their fief at Valencia? Why
did you strike my daughters with leather straps and with
your spurs? Why did you abandon them in the deep woods
where they were to fall prey to ravening beasts and flesh-eat-
ing birds? All this you did to my daughters, which has by so
much diminished your manhoods! Let this court now sentence you for this crime, and give me satisfaction."

Don Garcia replied to Mio Cid's demands. "Greatest King
of Spain, here is before you this Cid, who has had his entrance proclaimed by heralds, who has let his beard grow so
long that it frightens some and amazes others! Our Infantes
of Carrion are such that they could not accept his daughters
even as concubines! Who would have given them such women
as their wives? In deserting them, these princes were within
their rights. We take no account whatsoever of the Cid's
accusations."

Mio Cid leaped to his feet and stood stroking his beard,
"What insolence is this for you of all people to criticize my
beard? My beard has never been plucked by any man of
woman born, by neither Moor nor Christian! Can you say
as much? Is it not the plain truth that I once pulled your
beard, Don Garcia, the day I stormed your castle?"

Ferrando Gonzalez of Carrion rose to his feet. In a loud
voice he interrupted, "Enough talk, Cid. You have been paid.
There is no more quarrel between us. We were born Infantes;
that is our princely nature. We should rather have been married to the daughters of kings and emperors. Daughters from
your station were not highly born enough for us. In so deserting them we were within our rights. We have grown in
self-esteem because of this action, not sunk!"

"Very well," replied Mio Cid. "We have been polite long
enough. Pero Bermuez the Mute, you may now speak, if you
wish."

"You are a liar, Ferrando of Carrion," cried Pero Bermuez,
"a liar in every word you utter! Had you remained with the
Campeador, and only then, your true natures would have been
concealed! Now let me remind you what sort of man you
are! Think back to the battle we fought at Valencia. You
asked the Campeador to let you fight, and he instructed me
to watch over you. Suddenly, brave Infante, you spied a
Moor. You started toward him! Then what? Then you
wheeled about and ran! That's what! I took your place. I
slew the Moor. I gave you his horse, which you promptly

showed Mio Cid, saying that you had done this brave deed.
I kept your secret. Right until this day I never broke faith,
never spread abroad the tale of your cowardice. I let you
brag how brave you were! People believed you out of love
for Mio Cid. You may be handsome, but you are surely not
manly! You are all tongue, with no hands to act! Say, Ferrando, do I speak the truth about you?

"Let's also gossip about the lion, Ferrando. Where were
you hiding when the lion threatened Mio Cid? Ferrando, I
challenge you to a single combat because you are a liar and
a traitor. I shall fight you here before Don Alfonso of Castile to test my statements. As for the daughters of Mio Cid,
you lie! The both of you have sunk, not risen, because of
that action. They are only women, and you are supposed to
be men! Whichever way you look at it, they are worth more
than you! The day we meet in combat, I shall force you to
admit all this publicly."

Diego of Carrion then addressed the court. "We are by
birth the purest of counts. If only it had not pleased God to
saddle us with such alliances! Imagine, having this Cid,
Don Rodrigo, for a father-in-law! That we deserted his
daughters, we have today no compunction. As long as they
live, let them sigh after us! I am ready to fight the most
valiant man there is to prove that we were right!"

Martin Antolinez jumped up and cried, "Shut your mouth,
you liar, you mouth-without-truth! Don't forget the incident
of the lion, Diego Gonzalez! You squeezed yourself in between the pillar and the wall! You never again could wear
the clothes you had on that day! I shall fight you for it!
I want to know from you why you deserted the daughters of
Mio Cid. Know in any case, they are worth more than you
are! When you leave the field of combat, I shall hear you
admit it too, plus the fact that you are a traitor, and that
you have lied today in every word that you have uttered!"

At that moment appeared in the courtroom Asur Gonzalez. He strolled into the room, dragging his cloak on the
floor behind him. His face was scarlet, for he had just finished eating. In any event, he had no reputation for intelli-
gence. "Well! Well! Barons!" scoffed Asur Gonzalez. "Did
you ever see such a fuss about nobody? Somebody tell me
about this Cid of Vivar. Where is he, out filling up feedbags
with grain? Out at his mill? That's the way he lives, you
know. Whoever put it into his head to aspire to alliances
with Carrion?"

"Shut up, you traitor! Liar! Scoundrel!" shouted Muño

Gustioz. "You've been out stuffing yourself instead of praying, as you should have been doing. Every time you get close enough to a man to open your mouth, you disgust him! You speak the truth neither to friend nor to lord. You are false to all, even to your Creator. I wish to have no share of your friendship. I propose to make you own up to what you are."

"Let all talk stop here," decreed King Alfonso. "Those who have challenged will fight. Otherwise, may God help them!"

He had hardly uttered these words when two handsome young knights entered the courtroom. All eyes turned in their direction, watched them approach the king. It was the two royal Infantes, one named Oiarra and the other Yenego Simenez. One was the heir apparent to the kingdom of Navarre and the other the heir of the kingdom of Aragon. Bending low to kiss the hand of Don Alfonso, the two crown princes asked that he bestow upon them the hands of Doña Elvira and Doña Sol in marriage. The king so ordained. Mio Cid, you may be sure, submitted joyously to the king's will.

Then Alvar Fañez asked permission to say what was on his mind. "My resentment against the Infantes of Carrion," began Alvar Fañez, "is great. It was I who at the request of King Alfonso gave these ladies at the altar. I am glad that they shall now become queens of Spain. Now you Infantes of Carrion will have to kiss their hands and call them Señora. No matter what spite you feel, you will now have to attend upon them. So have we seen, from day to day, the honor of Mio Cid increase. As for you, Infantes, you are none the less liars and traitors! Will no one stand up and fight me for my words?"

"Enough," said the king. "Not another word. Let the three challengers appear at dawn tomorrow. The issue will be settled on the field of combat."

"Please, Sire," then pleaded the Infantes, "give us a delay. Those of the Cid are armed and ready, but we must return to Carrion first!"

"Will you name the place and the time?" King Alfonso asked Mio Cid.

He replied with a smile, "Why, yes. Let them come to Valencia."

"Be reassured," answered the king. "Entrust your knights to me. I will guarantee their safety. I hereby decree that the combats will take place in my presence three weeks from today at Carrion. He who does not present himself accordingly shall forfeit the privilege and be branded a traitor."

Mio Cid then thanked the judges, gave rich gifts to those who loved him, and prepared to take his leave. The king told Mio Cid that he was the finest baron in all his realm. As Mio Cid bade farewell, he made one last gesture to show his love for Don Alfonso. "You ordered me, Sire, to ride Babieca into your enemies, Moors and Christians alike. This horse has not his like in all the world. I give him to you now, Sire. Have him led away to your stables."

"I have no such desire," replied the king. "Such a splendid horse and such a splendid rider belong together. I am not the man to mount your Babieca! If any person else were to ride him, God would surely not come to his aid! It is because of you, Mio Cid, and because of your horse that our realm has been so favored."

Mio Cid then took leave of his vassals, the three challengers. "Stand firm on that field," he told them. "Fight like barons. Let the news that reaches me in Valencia be good."

"Why do you say that, Señor?" asked Martin Antolinez. "We made this contract ourselves, and we shall fulfill it. You may learn that we were killed, but you will never learn that we were defeated!" Mio Cid was pleased at those words. Light at heart, he set out for his fief at Valencia.

In three weeks' time the king and his challengers waited at the field of combat. The Infantes were two days late. Finally they came, escorted by their relatives and friends. If they could have murdered Mio Cid's men, they would have done so. Fortunately, they did not attempt it, so great was their fear of King Alfonso of León. That night was spent in vigil.

By morning a large crowd of knights thronged the field to see these trials and to hear Don Alfonso's verdict as to which party could claim the right on its side. On one end of the field Mio Cid's men were armed. The Infantes prepared themselves on the opposite side. As they were being dressed, Count Garci Ordoñez briefed them. Then the Infantes sent word to Don Alfonso entreating him to debar Colada and Tizon, the two trenchant swords, from the combat. They regretted having returned these wonderfully cutting blades to Mio Cid.

"I did not see you draw these swords when you wore them to my court," the king replied shortly. "If you possess other good swords, they will give you their aid. The same will be true for the Campeador's men. Therefore stand up, Infantes of Carrion, and enter the lists. You are now obliged to combat. Therefore acquit yourselves like noblemen. If you ride victorious from this field, great honor will accrue to you. Be sure that your opponents have overlooked nothing, and that they intend to win. If you are vanquished, don't complain to me about it; for everyone here knows that you brought it all upon yourselves."

When the Infantes heard the reply of King Alfonso, they sorely repented their past deeds. They would not have committed them again, had they to relive that past year, for all their estates at Carrion.

Meanwhile the king in like measure had instructed Mio Cid's knights. They replied, "We kiss your hand, since you are our king and lord. Be our judge today. Protect us with your might and justice against any unfair play. The Infantes are on their home ground, surrounded by their vassals. We don't know whether or not they are plotting against us. Mio Cid entrusted us to you, Señor. Uphold the right in the name of the Creator."

"With heart and soul," pledged the king.

The three knights mounted. They adjusted their shields and checked their stirrups. They raised their lances so that the pennants blew in the breeze. Then, making the sign of the cross over their saddles, they rode, all three side by side, up to the barrier. There they waited silently until the Gonzalez brothers rode to the barrier opposite, and halted while the king appointed judges so that there could be no recourse. The king then harangued the combatants carefully and clearly.

"Listen to what I say, Infantes of Carrion," began Don Alfonso. "You were to have competed this trial at Toledo, but you would hear of no such thing. Remember that I am the sponsor of these three vassals of Mio Cid, and that I conducted them to your estates. Seek only your due. If you overstep the bounds of justice, I shall mishandle you badly from one end of my realm to another."

Then the judges measured off the lists as the crowd stepped back away from the barriers. They called out the rules, saying that any knight who left the lists was adjudged to have forfeited the contest. They ascertained that the spectators were maintaining a safe distance of six lance lengths on all sides. Lots were drawn for positions so that those who were lucky had the sun at their backs instead of in their faces. Then the judges retired from the center of the arena.

The three of Mio Cid faced the three from Carrion. Each

man glared fixedly at his adversary. Each man clutched his shield against his chest, lowered his lance until the pennants hung straight down, bent forward with his body over the pommel of his saddle, dug his spurs into his horse's sides, and shot forward. . . . The spurt was so great that the ground thundered underfoot. Each man aimed at his foe. They joined in a shock of metal. . . . The watchers were sure that all six were dead.

Pero Bermuez, who first had challenged his man, met Ferrando Gonzalez face to face. Each one struck the other's shield, with no decisive result. On the second exchange Ferrando Gonzalez pierced the shield of Pero Bermuez, but his lance came out into air instead of into flesh. In two places he broke the wood of his lance. Pero Bermuez sat firm in the saddle. He was not even jolted. Since he had taken a blow, he gave one in return. His stroke broke the shield strap from Ferrando Gonzalez' neck. The shield fell to one side. Then Pero Bermuez pierced him, for his cover was gone. Then he pierced his chest, for the cover was gone. Ferrando wore three thicknesses of mail, which stood him in good stead. Two were shattered, but the third held well. The lance, however, had driven his shirt and the padded doublet he wore under his armor into his chest, to about the depth of a man's hand. Blood spurted from Ferrando Gonzalez' mouth. His stirrup straps broke; neither one held firm. Pero Bermuez threw him to earth over his horse's haunches. The spectators thought he was wounded to death. Pero Bermuez dropped his lance and grasped his sword. Then Ferrando Gonzalez, looking up at him, recognized Tizon! Instead of awaiting its blow, he cried, "I am vanquished." The judges acknowledged his submission and called Pero Bermuez from the lists.

Meanwhile Martin Antolinez and Diego Gonzalez were dealing each other heavy blows—so hard, in fact, that both their lances were shivered. When Martin Antolinez then unsheathed Colada, the light from this blade, flashing in the sunlight, flooded the field of combat, so clear and white was it! At the first swift stroke he severed the straps of Diego Gonzalez' helmet. Then he knocked it from his head. Next he lifted off his mail hood. He then snipped off the top of his cloth hat. With a swishing sound that was almost a whistle, he lopped off his hair and cut to the scalp. Pieces of flesh fell to the ground. When Diego Gonzalez saw with what precision Colada could be wielded, he realized that he would not escape her alive. He yanked the reins of his horse

away from the blows. Then Martin Antolinez whacked him
with the flat of the blade, not with the point! Although Diego
Gonzalez had his own sword in hand, he made no effort to
use it. "Help me, glorious God! . . . Señor, save me from that
blade!" Turning his horse's head about in a desperate effort,
he bounded out of the lists!

"Come, Pero Bermuez, beside me," called the king. "You
have won decisively." The judges concurred. Two knights
from Valencia had triumphed, and I shall now tell you of
the third.

Muño Gustioz was matched against Asur Gonzalez, who
was agile, strong, and courageous. Both knights dealt telling
blows upon each other's shields. Asur Gonzalez broke the
shield of Muño Gustioz, and also broke his armor. When the
lance pierced the broken shield, however, it passed into
empty air on the other side. Then Muño Gustioz at the next
exchange cracked Asur Gonzalez' shield in the middle. Aiming carefully, he drove his lance as he rushed forward right
through the shield with such a momentum that it passed
through his opponent's body and came out, pennants and
all, on the other side. It came out about two arms' length
on the back of Asur Gonzalez' body. Then Muño Gustioz
toppled him from the saddle and let him slip the length of
the lance to the ground. The lance came out red with blood,
tip, wood, pennants! Muño Gustioz sat over his opponent,
his lance pointed downward until the judges shouted, "In the
name of God, do not strike him! You have won the trial."
Everyone thought Asur Gonzalez was dead.

The good King Alfonso ordered the field to be cleared and
the weapons lost there to be confiscated for himself. The
champions of Mio Cid left the lists amid warm congratula-
tions. The sorrow in Carrion was great.

That very night the king dispatched Mio Cid's three knights
to Valencia so that they might risk no reprisal nor any fear
of such. Like devoted vassals they rode day and night to
make their report. They had proven the Infantes of Carrion
to be evil men, and they had accomplished the duty required
of them by their lord.

Mio Cid the Campeador was satisfied. Then was he satisfied. Great, indeed, was the shame that had fallen publicly
upon the Infantes of Carrion. May a similar punishment, or
a worse one, fall upon any man who so jeers at a fine lady,
and then deserts her!

Now let us leave to themselves the Infantes of Carrion
and concern ourselves rather with him who was born in such

a favorable hour.... The beautiful city of Valencia laughed and rejoiced because of the honor their champions had brought upon every one. Mio Cid stroked his beard contentedly and said, "Thanks to the King of Heaven, my daughters have been avenged. I shall be able without shame to marry them to men of great rank or not, as I wish."

Meanwhile the Princes of Navarre and Aragon pursued their courtships of Doña Elvira and Doña Sol. They had a new interview with King Don Alfonso. They made before him new marriage vows, more solemn than the first. You see how the reputation and honor of Mio Cid had increased!

Now, the daughters of Mio Cid became the queens of Navarre and Aragon! The king of Spain today is one of their descendants. Everything he touched turned to glory for Mio Cid, who was born at such a good hour.

Mio Cid departed from this world at a Pentecost. May Christ have mercy on his soul. May He have mercy on us all, the righteous as well as the sinners.

This is the story of Mio Cid, the Campeador. Here ends the tale.

May God be pleased to grant Paradise also to him who wrote this book. Amen.

The Abbot Per wrote it in the month of May in the year of our Lord MCCXLV.

Index